Marina Fiorato

Marina Fiorato is half-Venetian. She was born in Manchester and raised in the Yorkshire Dales. She is a history graduate of Oxford University and the University of Venice, where she specialized in the study of Shakespeare's plays as an historical source. After university she studied art and since worked as an illustrator, actress and film reviewer.

Marina was married on the Grand Canal and lives in north London with her husband, son and daughter.

Praise for Marina Fiorato

'A great read' *Best*

'Captures the scents, passion and vigour of Italy'
Books Quarterly

'Fiorato creates her own masterpiece' *Booklist*

'Mesmerising' *Waterstones Books Quarterly*

'Recommended' *Good Book Guide*

'A sizzling . . . read, and a must to pack in the suitcase'
Italian Magazine

'The enchanting tale . . . is rich with passion, mystery and intrigue' *Booktime*

D1113945

The Madonna
of the Almonds

Marina Fiorato

JOHN MURRAY

First published in Great Britain in 2009 by Beautiful Books Limited

This paperback edition first published in Great Britain in 2012 by
John Murray (Publishers)
An Hachette UK Company

1

A CIP catalogue record for this title is available from the British Library

ISBN 978-1-84854-796-4
Ebook ISBN 978-1-84854-797-1

Printed and bound by CPI Group (UK) Ltd, Croydon, CR0 4YY

John Murray policy is to use papers that are natural, renewable and
recyclable products and made from wood grown in sustainable forests.
The logging and manufacturing processes are expected to conform to
the environmental regulations of the country of origin.

John Murray (Publishers)
338 Euston Road
London NW1 3BH

www.johnmurray.co.uk

To my father Adelin Fiorato - a true Renaissance man.

CHAPTER 1

The Last Battle

'Tis no use telling you my name, for I am about to die.

Let me tell you hers instead – Simonetta di Saronno. To me it always sounded like a wondrous strain of music, or a line of poetry. It has a pleasing cadence, and the feet of the words as they march have a perfection almost equal to her countenance.

I should probably tell you the date of my death. It is the twenty-fourth day of February, in the year of Our Lord 1525, and I am lying on my back in a field outside Pavia in Lombardy.

I can no longer turn my head, but can move only my eyes. The snow falls on my hot orbs and melts at once – I blink the water away like tears. Through the falling flakes and steaming soldiers I see Gregorio – most excellent squire! – still fighting. He turns to me and I see fear in his eyes – I must be a sorry sight. His mouth forms my name but I hear naught. As the battle rages around me I can hear only the blood thrumming in my ears. I cannot even hear the boom of the evil new weapons giving tongue, for the one that took me deafened me with its voice. Gregorio's opponent claims his attention – there is no time to pity me if he is to save his skin, for all that he has loved me well. He slashes his sword from left to right with more vigour than artistry, and yet he still stands and I, his lord, do not. I wish that he may live to see another dawn – perhaps he will tell my lady that I made a good death. He still wears my colours, save that they are bloodied and almost torn from his back. I look closely at the shield of blue and silver – three ovals of argent on their azure ground. It pleases me to think that my ancestors meant the ovals for almonds when they entered our arms on the rolls. I want them to be the last things I see. When I have counted the three of them I close my eyes forever.

I can still feel, though. Do not think me dead yet. I move my right hand and feel for my father's sword. Still it lies where it fell and I grasp the haft in my hand – well worn from battle, and accustomed to my grip. How was I to know that this sword would be no more use to me than a feather? Everything has changed. This is the last battle. The old ways are as dead as I am. And yet it is still fitting that a soldier should die with his sword in hand.

Now I am ready. But my mind moves from my own hand to hers – her hands are her great beauty, second only to her face. They are long and white, beautiful and strange; for her third and fourth fingers are exactly of a length. They felt cool on my forehead and my memory places them there now. Only a twelvemonth ago they rested there, cooling my brow when I had taken the water fever. She stroked my brow, and kissed it too, her lips cool on my burning flesh; cool as the snow which kisses it now. I open my lips so that I may taste the kiss, and the snow falls in, refreshing my last moments. And then I remember that she had taken a lemon, cut it in twain and squeezed the juice into my mouth, to make me well again. It was bitter but sweetened by the love of her that ministered to me. It tasted of metal, like the steel of my blade when I kissed it just this morning as I led my men to battle. I taste it now. But I know it is not the juice of a lemon. It is blood. My mouth fills with it. Now I am done. Let me say her name one last time.

Simonetta di Saronno.

CHAPTER 2

The Sword and the Gun

Simonetta di Saronno sat at her solar window, the high square frame turning her to an angel of the *rererdos*. The citizens of Saronno oft remarked on it; every day she was there, staring down at the road with eyes of glass.

The Villa Castello, that square and elegant house, sat in solitary majesty a little way from the town – as the saying went: '*una passeggiata lunga, ma una cavalcata corta,*' 'a long walk, but a short ride.' It was set where the land of the Lombard plain began to climb to the mountains; just enough elevation to give the house a superior aspect over the little town, and for the townsfolk to see the house from the square. With plaster that had the sun-blush of a lobster, white elegant porticos and fine large windows, the house was much admired, and might have been the object of envy; but for the fact that the tall gates were always open to comers. The tradesmen and petitioners that trod the long winding path to the door through the lush gardens and parks could always be sure of a hearing from the servants

– a sign, all agreed, of a generous lord and lady. In fact the villa symbolised the di Saronnos themselves; near enough to town and their feudal obligations, but far enough away to be apart.

Simonetta's casement could be seen from the road to Como, where the dirt track wound to the snow-rimed mountains and looking-glass lakes. The victuallers and merchants, the pedlars and water-carriers all saw the lady at her window, day after day, as they went about their business. Before this time they might have made a jest about it, but there was little to laugh at in these times. Too many of their men had gone to the wars and not returned. Wars that seemed little to do with this their state of Lombardy, but of greater concerns and high men with low motives – the pope, the French king, and the greedy emperor. Their own little prosperous saffron town of Saronno, set between the civic glories of Milan and the silver splendour of the mountains, had been bruised and battered by the conflict. Soldiers' boots had scraped the soft pavings of the piazza. Steel stirrups had knocked chunks from the warm stones of the houses' corners as the cavalry of France and the Empire passed through in a whirlwind of misplaced righteousness. So the good burghers of Saronno knew what Simonetta waited for; and for all that she was a great lady, they pitied her for the human feelings that she shared with all the mothers, wives and daughters of the town. They all noted that, even when the day came that she had dreaded, she still sat at the window, day and night, hoping that *he* would come home.

Villa Castello's widow, for such she now was, was much talked of in the town square. The old, gold stones of Saronno, with its star of streets radiating out from the piazza of the Sanctuary church, heard all that its citizens had to say. They talked of the day when Gregorio di Puglia, Lord Lorenzo's squire, had staggered, bloody and beaten, up the road to the villa. The almond trees which lined the path swayed as he passed, their silver leaves whispering that they knew of the heavy news that he carried.

The lady had left her window at last, just once, and appeared again at the doorway on the loggia. Her eyes strained, willing the figure to be the lord and not the squire. When she perceived the gait and build of Gregorio, the tears began to slide from her eyes, and when he came closer and she saw the sword that he carried, she sank lifeless to the ground. All had been seen by Luca son of Luca, the undergardener at the villa, and the boy had enjoyed a couple of days of celebrity in the town as the sole witness of the scene. He spoke, as if a wandering preacher, to a little knot of townsfolk that gathered under the shadow of the church campanile to shelter from the fierce sun and hear the gossip. The crowd shifted with the shadow, and it was fully an hour before the interest and speculation had ceased. They talked for so long of Simonetta that even the church's priest, a kindly soul, felt moved to open the doors and shake his head at Luca from the cool dark. The under-gardener hurried to the end of his tale as the doors closed again for he did not wish to leave out the most fascinating and mysterious aspect of the tragedy: the squire had brought something else with him from the battlefield too. Long and metal; no, not a sword…Luca did not know exactly what it was. He did know that lady and squire had spent a couple of hours in close and grave counsel together once she had recovered her conscious state; then the lady had appeared once again in the window, there to stay, it seemed, until Judgement Day. A day, all prayed, which would unite her again with her lord.

Simonetta di Saronno wondered if there was a God. She shocked herself with this notion, but once she had the thought she could not withdraw it. She sat, dry-eyed, stiff-sinewed, looking down at the almond trees and the road, while the sky bruised into night and the stones beneath her hands grew cold. The town of Saronno lay under the distant mountains, silver in the twilight like a dropped coin. The sense of apartness that she had once treasured was now complete: her isolated house was now her prison. She was a tower-bound maid of old besieged by dragons, or a novitiate sequestered in her cell. Raffaella, her tiring maid, put a soft robe of vair around her shoulders but she hardly felt it, and did not register its warmth. She felt instead only the grief that sat in her chestspoon as if she had swallowed a

7

stone. No – an almond; for when she had first been given one of the fruits of the trees her marriage portion bought, she had swallowed it down whole. She had been a bride of thirteen, and Lorenzo, only fifteen himself, had given her an almond as part of the ceremony that had been held in the very grove she now regarded day and night.

They had married in the Sanctuary church of Santa Maria dei Miracoli in Saronno. The pretty white church with its octagonal baptistry, cool tree-lined cloister and slender new tower reaching into the sky had never before witnessed such pomp. The new ring of bells sounded the tidings across the plain – two great families united as the people cheered and feasted in the piazza under the shadow of the campanile. And after, the more pagan ceremony in the grove, when child bride and child bridegroom wore crowns of silver almond leaves and exchanged one of the nuts. The giving and eating of odd numbers of almonds at a wedding was apparently an age-old tradition; meant for luck, good harvest and fertility. But the ceremony faltered when Simonetta had almost choked in an attempt to swallow the thing whole. Lorenzo had laughed at her, as her mother gave her water and wine to wash the nut down. 'You're supposed to bite it, crush it with your teeth!' he cried fondly. 'Only then do you taste the sweetness.' He was right – for it had only tasted of dry wood in her mouth. Then he kissed her – all the sweetness she wanted, ever.

She remembered that the almond sat lodged in her

throat throughout the whole wedding feast. Her mother, fond of homilies and able to see God's hand in everything, had grimly told her not to complain. 'You must remember this lesson, my daughter. Sometimes things must be broken for us to taste their fruits as they are meant to be tasted. Your life has been one of ease and good fortune, you have been a well-loved child blessed with riches and beauty and a great marriage, but no-one's life runs in such a course forever. You will suffer one day and it is best to remember this. Only then do you feel the full power of your humours and life as God meant you to live; in suffering, but also in enlightenment.'

Simonetta was silent and drank more wine. She was mindful of the obedience and duty due to her mother, but the almond moved to her stomach at last and she felt the warmth of the grape replace it. She slid her eyes right to her bridegroom and felt another warmth: a sick excitement and pleasure that she was married to this young god, that it would soon be their wedding night... She shut her ears to her mother's words. She intended to be perpetually happy with Lorenzo, and knew they would live in all good fortune. Besides, Simonetta thought that she knew the source of her mother's discontent – she looked beyond her to her father. Handsome and florid, her father had always adored his daughter, but she was by no means the only young lady he adored. Simonetta knew that her mother had suffered much at the hands of her father's *amours*; maidservants who were suddenly insolent, wine-selling wenches who came too often to the house. Simonetta knew that such a future was not for her. She clasped Lorenzo's hand and forgot her mother's lecture.

Until now.

How could she have known that her life would be broken in *this* way, that she would be forced at last to feel such pain by the death of the man who had made her so happy for so long? She was convinced that she could have survived anything but *this*. Even if Lorenzo had looked at another woman, which he had never done, she thought now that she could have withstood the trials of infidelity. If only he were still here, still real, still warm, to laugh and sport with her as they had always done. *This* she felt, the tumourous lump in her chest, this grief that she could locate to the very inch in her trunk, would surely kill her too. And it would be a blessing. She laid her white hands on the sword – his sword, which Gregorio had brought home from the battlefield. Then she turned to the other thing that Gregorio had brought her. It was long and menacing, made of a metal pipe and a wooden handle, with a curved metal claw protruding from the side. She could barely lift the thing, even if she had had the strength.

'What is it?' her voice was little more than a whisper. Gregorio stood in front of her, wringing his velvet capuchon in his hand, his eyes awash.

'They call it an arquebus, my Lady. It is one of the new

weapons. 'Tis a little like a canon, but a man can hold it and fire it with a matchlock.' He pointed to charred string on the handle of the thing, and the serpentine S-shaped trigger which waited on its metal pivot.

'Why have you brought it to me?' her throat cracked with the question.

'Because it was one such that took my Lord. I had to bring it to you, to show you that he never had a chance. You know my Lord. He was the best soldier there was. The perfect knight. No man could touch him for swordplay. But the Spanish Marchese di Pescara surprised us with more 'n fifteen hundred gunmen. I saw whole ranks of French cavalry go down beneath the fire of the arquebusiers. The men that did not take shot were thrown as their horses took flight. And the noise! T'were as if the *Diavolo* himself had come amongst us and were singing for his supper.' Gregorio crossed his rotten tabard.

Simonetta swallowed. Her voice could not be trusted now. She nodded at Gregorio in dismissal and took the two weapons, the old and the new, to the window, so she could go on watching.

You fool, she thought, suddenly angry at Lorenzo. She laid a hand on each weapon, where the cold steel of both froze her fingers. The past and the future. You were the perfect knight indeed. But you did not see this coming, did you? What use was your knightly code and your courtly rules of combat in the face of such things? Your ways are gone, and a new world has begun. A world where such rules are as straw. Simonetta was not at all sure that she wished to live in such a world. She wondered, not for the first time, if she could somehow fire the arquebus towards herself and join Lorenzo in paradise. Or perhaps she could hang herself in the groves like another long-dead deserted maid. But this she knew to be the greatest sin of all; the sin of the greatest of transgressors, Judas Iscariot. Simonetta had been brought up by her mother in strict religious observance, and re-membered well the Last Judgement in the baptistry where she went to mass as a child, in Pisa. Every day she would sit as the priest intoned the well-known Latin, watching the black devils consume the suicides, knawing their limbs and licking up pools of blood with lascivious tongues. They were terrifying and exciting and she would fidget in the family seat, feeling her face grow hot as if the flames reached her too, until her mother pinched her sharply on the arm.

No – she could not take her own life. But her life as she knew it had gone from her.

She had not believed that marriage could have been so happy. She and Lorenzo had lived as one in the Villa Castel-lo, feasting, hunting, travelling to courts and festivals, drink-ing from their vines and eating from their almond trees. They had observed mass once a week in Santa Maria dei Miracoli, the church of their marriage, but they lived more earthly lives in the pleasures of bed and board. No children came to them, but they felt no loss in the completeness of their affection for each other. They were young – they had all the time in the world. When the plague of 1523 took both their families they scarcely noticed, but lived and loved in their high castle, safe from the siege of pestilence. They laughed the seasons round – Lorenzo was a jocular boy, and he trained his lady in his humour for life and all things ridiculous in it, until she became as quick as he. In marriage Simonetta's looks blossomed and she lost her girlish roundness. She became a renowned beauty with her angelic countenance, her abundance of red hair and her pearl-pale hands. They had no need for indigence – their combined fortunes brought them every happiness and indulgence. Their walls were covered in rich tapestries, they patronised the finest artists and musicians. Their board groaned with the greatest meats and pastries, and their handsome forms were clothed in costly furs and velvets. Simonetta's yards of copper curls were bound up with ropes of pearls and precious coifs of jewels and silver thread.

And then came the wars – years of turmoil and struggle between state and state, Guelfs and Ghibbellines. Milan, Venice, Genoa, the Papal lands, all became pieces in the game of bones between powers both foreign and domestic. Lorenzo, trained from birth in the arts of war, won glory and was soon given leadership. His commissions took him from home, and more than once his lady held Michealmas or Christmas feasts with his great carved chair standing empty at the head of the board. At these times Simonetta felt her spirits much depressed, but turned to her other pleasures of archery or the lute to pass the time. Sometimes in Lorenzo's absence she had a fancy for his child to be with her when he was gone, to give her some occupation, but the wish passed as soon as he rode home up the road between the almond trees and she ran to meet him. He would crush her against his armour and kiss her hard on the mouth, and though they retired directly to the bedchamber she hoped no more for any fruits of their reunion.

Now, such fruits would never be born. From this last campaign, when he had gone to fight under the command of Maréchal Jacques de Lapalisse, Lorenzo would never return. That great French General was dead, Lorenzo was dead, and now at last she felt keenly what comfort she might have had from his son or daughter. But now she was seventeen, and the best years for childbearing were over. She was utterly alone.

And that is why Simonetta di Saronno wondered if there was a God. For would he have broken her in this way? Would he have wrested apart two such devoted creatures, whose union was blessed in his house as one of the sacraments?

Then she began to be afraid. She had not prayed once since Gregorio had come. If she turned her back on God, she would surely sink into the void and take that other path – the darkest path of all. And once in the eternal damnation of hell, she would never see Lorenzo again. This would be a fate worse than the one she endured now, for only in that hope of a far-off reunion in paradise could she draw her next breath. When she had been happy she had always prayed to the ear of the Virgin, for did not Santa Maria know the love of a man, and the joy of marriage to Saint Joseph? Simonetta was resolved: she would go to the Sanctuary of Santa Maria dei Miracoli tomorrow, the church of the Miracles, and pray to that Blessed Virgin for comfort. For that would be a miracle indeed, and she was in need of nothing less. She took her hands from the sword and the gun and left her window at last. She knelt at the foot of her bed to say the *Pater Noster*, then, wrapping herself in the vair, dropped onto the coverlet of her bed as if felled.

CHAPTER 3

Selvaggio

'Nonna, there's a Wildman in the woods.'

'Amaria Sant'Ambrogio, you have been on this earth for twenty summers, and you still have no more sense than a bean. What nonsense is this?'

'Truly, Nonna, I swear it by Saint Ambrose himself. Silvana and I were at the wells, and we saw him. And besides, they talk of him in the town. They call him *Selvaggio*, the savage!' Amaria's dark eyes were as wide as saucers.

The old lady sat down at their humble table and regarded her granddaughter. The girl looked little better than a savage herself. Her black hair which normally hung straight to her waist was tangled with comfrey flowers and briars till it stood out from her head. Her complexion, normally tanned, had a rose blush to it from her exertions. The girl's olive-black eyes showed the whites all around like the stare of a frighted horse. Her bodice was ripped to show more than was seemly of her bosom, her full breasts straining at the lacings, and the girl's skirts were kirtled round her knees for ease of running, displaying her sturdy legs. Amaria could not be called fat; never that, for the indigence of their household would never allow gluttony. Yet she was a softly rounded, peach of a girl, all womanliness in figure and a glowing, glossily healthful embodiment of life. She made a tempting picture for any passing gentleman, with her rosy, abundant beauty; despite the fact that her rounded features and full-bodied figure were at odds with the fashions of the day. Courtly ladies craved white alabaster skin, even rubbing leaden paste into their faces to achieve the right hue; Amaria was tanned to the colour of warm sand. Noble women were whippet slim; Amaria was all curves and dimples. Great Signoras used all sorts of arts to lighten their hair to red or gold; Amaria's fall of hair had the blue-black sheen of a crow's wing. Though no woman could ever be more beautiful to Nonna than her granddaughter, the old lady despaired of getting Amaria wed; for who wanted a maid of twenty, with plenty of meat on her bones but no sense and no fortune? Even more when she went about Pavia like this – like the whores that hung around the square at dusk.

Nonna sighed and transferred the sage that she always chewed from one papery cheek to the other. She fiercely loved Amaria and wished the best for her, and because the love she held for the girl was so great that it made her afraid, she always spoke to her harsher than she meant. 'I might have known that Silvana had something in the case. She encourages you in all your foolishness. Tidy yourself, child, and say your *Ave Marias*. Look to God instead of your fat friend, and pray instead of chattering like a parrot.'

Amaria smoothed her hair and let down her skirts. She was used to such censure and it did not lessen her affection for the old lady. She found a bobbin and needle on the mantle and sat to sew her bodice. 'But I saw him, Nonna. We were…looking in the water and I saw his reflection before I saw his person. He has red skin, claws and fur, but his eyes are kind. Do you think he is a woodsprite?'

'Red skin? Claws and fur? Woodsprite? Where do you get such pagan notions? More like he is a poor fugitive from this lately ended action – a soldier who has lost his wits. Mayhap a Spaniard, for they are witless enough.' (From Nonna's levity of tone it could never be guessed that the Spanish had destroyed her life.) 'What were you doing at the wells anyway, as if I need to ask? We have water aplenty and more besides, and a perfectly good spring in the town square from what I know of it.'

Amaria dropped her head over her sewing and her cheeks flushed. 'We were…that is…Silvana wanted to… look in the *pozzo dei mariti*.'

Nonna snorted scornfully but her old eyes softened. She knew that local folklore had it that if you gazed into one of the natural wells in the woods beyond Pavia it was said that you would see the face of your future husband. She knew that Amaria longed one day to fall in love and be married, but she also knew that the girl's advanced age and lowly station meant a good match were impossible, and a grandmother's love precluded her from a bad one. Her disappointment for her granddaughter made Nonna even more acerbic than usual. 'Girlish nonsense! Depend upon it. He were some hermit, or mayhap a Frenchman. They say the French king is took by the Spanish at Pavia…knocked clean off his horse by Cesare Hercolani…did he wear a crown, your future husband?'

Amaria smiled. She knew nothing of the politics of the recent battle, just that many men had gone and few returned, lowering her chances of a match still more. But at least she had had no man to keen and cry over, and light candles like the widows in the basilica. She knew that the French king Francis was indeed a prisoner of the victorious Spanish who now held Milan. But she knew little of his citizens save that they had tails and it was said that they could converse with their horses, so curious and snorting was their language. She sighed. 'You're right. He must have been a madman. Or some soldier.'

She sewed in silence looking closely at her work, but the talk of war and the French led her grandmother's eyes to the wall where Filippo's dagger hung above the mantle. Had it really been more than twenty years since Nonna had lost her son, her beloved only son, her shining boy? Had all that time truly passed since the great battle of Garigliano in 1503, when she and all the other mothers had prayed for news of their sons? The fate of the others, left to guess whether their sons lived or died was not to be hers though – the Spanish left her in no doubt of Filippo's fate when they brought hundreds of corpses back to Pavia to display in the square. She and those other mothers had searched the grisly pile as the flies and buzzards circled, till she saw his beloved face, beaten and bloodied. The *Comune* had decreed that the pile was to be burnt to prevent pestilence so she could not even bring him home to wash his body as she had done so often when he was a little boy, and lay him out with prayers as she ought. She had time to do little more than close his eyes and take from his body the dagger that he had placed in his hose – all that the looters had left. She had returned home, thinking she would never forget the stink of human flesh as the pyre burned hot and high and the smoke gave her eyes at last the tears that would not come.

She might have continued so forever, numb with grief and feeling nothing, had God not given her Amaria. For at that very well where the girl had gone this morning she had found her, like Moses among the bulrushes. Babies were often left there, and more so now, with so many war orphans of girls that had been gotten into trouble by absent soldiers. Nonna had gone there for water, as the city's wells were polluted with corpses. As she stooped to the pool she heard a strangled cry and parted the rough grass to find a naked, bloody child, its limbs weaving at the unaccustomed light, dark eyes blinking from the squashed features of a newborn. Nonna had swaddled the babe and taken it home, not knowing if it was a girl or a boy. She wanted only occupation, and a chance to *feel* again now that she had lost the son who had been her life. She sat impassive as the babe cried all night from the redgum, when it bawled all day for its honeyteat, when it protested at the swaddle that she sewed her into, for she knew now it was a girl. Nonna remained numb until the day that the baby fixed her currant eyes on her and smiled her first toothless smile, so guileless, so innocent of the war and all that had gone before it. Nonna held the babe to her broken heart and wept for the first time since she closed Filippo's eyes.

Nonna had saved Amaria and Amaria had saved her. She had a heart so full of love and grief that it would have burst had she not found another human soul to lavish it on. She called the child Amaria after *Amore* and gave her the name of Milan's local Saint: Ambrogio. Orphans were always named thus in these parts in the hope of conferring the Saint's blessing on their blighted lives. She had told the growing girl to call her simply *Nonna* – Grandmother – as she thought herself at forty too old to be known as mother. Amaria had grown into a beautiful, lively girl who would forever be talking, of both sense and nonsense all at once. Her beauty and good nature recommended her to many a young fellow, but her orphan status and poor circumstances always caused them to withdraw their affections. Amaria thanked God that she had Nonna to love her. And Nonna thanked the same God that she had found someone to love.

In helping Amaria she had lived again. Now, twenty years later, it sounded as if someone else needed help, Wildman or not. God had taken Filippo but he had sent her Amaria, and she had been blessed. Was he now asking for something in return? She looked at her beloved granddaughter, and back at the dagger. She took it from the wall and placed it in her hose, at the right ankle exactly at the place on the legshank where she had taken it from her dead son. Amaria looked up surprised as Nonna said: 'Show me.'

They walked for the better part of an hour between Vespers and Compline. The bells of the basilica and the constant chatter of Amaria marked their passage and Nonna, as she always did, averted her eyes from the square as she passed the great cathedral. She could never see the piazza without seeing the pyre and smelling the flesh of her son. In doing this she missed, as Amaria did not, the appeals to God and all his Saints that were pinned to the church door – hundreds upon hundreds of scraps of fluttering paper, supplications for the return of the missing, the feared dead.

As the ground began to rise behind the town, Amaria held out her arm to her grandmother and they continued thus, Nonna breathing so hard that she was forced to spit her sage. They paused and looked back at Pavia, the place they called the city of a hundred towers; the second city of Lombardy only to Milan which lay closeby to the north. Grandmother and granddaughter caught their breath, seated for a moment on the tufted grass, arms flung around each other's shoulders. They watched the sunset rooks rising and wheeling around the tall stones that pierced the bloody sky. The red shoulder of the Duomo hunched against the skyline and the russet houses hugged the steep incline down to the riverside, where their own humble cot huddled in the crowded wharf. The Ponte Coperto, the famous covered bridge, seemed a knobbly red serpent which had flung its coils over the river. The waters of the Ticino were the colour of a blade. Beyond the river to the south lay the great field where thousands had lately died. Quiet and empty now; a dark and sorrowing plain looted of all the fallen arms and pecked clean of wasted flesh. As the sun dipped further, the bricks of the houses and towers glowed red in the evensun, as if they had drawn up blood from the battleground as a flower draws water.

Aware of the latening hour, Nonna bid Amaria help her to her feet, and they went into the darkling woods. At last they reached the place they sought, but in the quiet dusk they saw only the dark blue pool and no Wildman. But a twig snapped, and Nonna drew her knife at once. These hard times had sharpened her wits and she often came into these hills to snare rabbits for the pot. Her old ears were sharper than Amaria's and she led the girl through the undergrowth, to the leafy mouth of a black cave.

He was there. As the old woman and the young inched into the darkness, Amaria called the name that she had heard given to the shuffling shadow. '*Selvaggio!*'

'Simpleton,' hissed her grandmother. 'How can he answer to a name he doesn't know he has?' Nonna called in Milanese dialect: 'Do not be afraid! We are here to help you in the name of Saint Ambrose.' There was an awful pause as both women contemplated what they might have called forth. Nonna remembered Filippo and said, 'We are neither Spanish nor French, but friends.'

They saw his bright eyes as he shuffled to the light, but as he appeared Amaria gasped in horror. The creature was painfully thin, his ribs showing each and every one. His red skin was caked blood. His fur was matted hair and a beard of many months growth. His claws were the nails of toes and fingers that had grown unchecked till they curled around on themselves. He could have been any age between seventeen and seventy. But his eyes were leaf green and, as Amaria had said, had the light of kindness in them. It seemed he could not speak but he could hear – he came forward, almost collapsing at each step into the open. Nonna felt herself close to tears for the first time in twenty years, for so might Filippo have looked had he lived, and come back to her. Here was no savage. He was just a boy. Those that had done this were the savages. She stayed her fleeing granddaughter with one hand and held out the other to him. She hardly knew what she uttered but she knew it was right. 'Come home,' she said.

CHAPTER 4

Artists and Angels

At the moment of Filippo's death on the battlefield of Garigliano, a great artist began his great work. At the very instant that Filippo exhaled his last breath; the master's brush touched the canvas of what was to become his greatest painting. But it is not this artist but his pupil who concerns us – a young man of exactly the unfortunate Filippo's age. A man who would one day be great but not yet, a man who was lazy, dissolute and given to easy pleasure, a man with talent but without morals, a man who had never cared about anything in his life, certainly not enough to lay down his life for it, as Filippo had done. On this same fateful day when God took a soldier from his mother and gave an artist the touch of divinity to imbue his work, this creature of pleasure was probably beneath His notice. This man's name was:

'*Bernardino Luini!*' The shout, almost a bellow, echoed through the *studiolo*. Bernardino recognized the voice instantly. It was the voice he and his lover had both dreaded hearing when, last night in her bedchamber, they had sported together until the dawnlight warmed the roofs of Florence. If Bernardino were honest with himself, he had to admit that the fear of the husband's return had added a certain frisson to their coupling, for certes the dame was no beauty; for all that he had met her while she was modelling for his master. Bernardino was used to the anger of husbands, or what his friends laughingly called the *'mariti arrabbiati'* when Bernardino met them with another black eye or cut lip marring his striking beauty. But there was such venom in this voice that he instantly dropped his brushes and scanned the *studiolo* for a place to hide.

Everywhere there were canvases being oiled or stretched, frames being constructed, or apprentices finishing the work of their master. Unhappily, no ideal hiding place presented itself, until Bernardino's eyes lit on the dais at the end of the long room. There sat his current *amour*, hands crossed virtuously, but her eyes a little shaded from her nighttime exertions. Her hair hung in dusky coils about her face, and her green gown helped her sallow complexion not at all. Had there been more time, Bernardino might have asked himself once again why his Master da Vinci was so intent on painting her – she had not even the bloom of youth, being the mother of two sons. When he, at last, was allowed to paint the entire female form he would choose a lady of passing beauty – an angel to reflect the divinity of his work…but there was no time for such speculation.

Bernardino had found his hiding place – there was a rough screen behind the model's head, a sort of triptych that he himself had constructed. It was a covered wooden frame and Bernardino had painted on the stretched cloth, at his master's instruction, a pastoral whimsy of the Tuscan countryside – trees, hills and a stream. Bernardino had balked at the task, he had thought himself ready to paint the human figure, but Leonardo, for some reason, seemed intent on giving his student the most menial of tasks. Bernardino was barely ever allowed to pick up a brush unless it was to paint hands. Hands, hands and more hands. For some reason Bernardino had a natural aptitude for these the most difficult of subjects, and was asked to paint them again and again. He never got a sniff of the more interesting work, unless it was to sketch out the vast charcoal cartoons that his master then completed with his greater genius. He had hoped that Leonardo would recognize his drawing talent and reward him with a commission. But now he was glad that his talent had been so little recognised, for the screen would do nicely. As he ran towards the dais the sitter widened her eyes in alarm – she too had recognised the voice and feared that confrontation was inevitable. But she need not have feared. Bernardino was a coward. He held his finger swiftly to his lips and slipped behind the screen, seconds before the *studiolo's* double doors crashed open and Francesco di Bartolomeo di Zanobi del Giocondo entered the room.

Bernardino applied his eye to the hinged crack where

one panel joined the next in his makeshift screen. One look to his Master told him that Leonardo had seen all – he always did. But, though his beard hid a great number of the great Master's emotions, nothing concealed the raised brow as he carried on his work.

Da Vinci was not spiritual, and his disregard for religion bordered on the heretical, so it was a matter for ironic comment that, with his flowing white beard and hair, he greatly resembled the image of a God in whom he did not believe. The Master cared not if such jests were cracked upon him; he enjoyed human folly in all its manifestations, and so was particularly indulgent of Bernardino in his amorous adventures. He had favoured the boy from the first, even making him a present of his fabled scrapbook known as the *Libricciolo*; fifty pages of the finest grotesques ever drawn. Its pages displayed a wench with just two holes where her nose should be; a fellow with buboes on his neck so large it seemed he had three heads; and a poor wight with his mouth sealed up by nature so that he could only eat through his nose, with a strawlike contraption that Leonardo himself had invented. Bernardino spent hours pouring over the freak-like images, and the Master nodded his approval. 'Just so you know, Bernardino,' he remarked, 'when you are drawing your limpid Lombard beauties, that not all that nature creates is beautiful.' But if the *Libricciolo* showed ugliness in its natural form, its reader was handsome enough to prompt scurrilous rumour that the boy's beauty pleased the Master in ways that were not merely aesthetic. Why else would Leonardo bring the boy back home to Florence with him, a boy whom he had merely apprenticed in his Milan studio, a boy who had never before left the flat disc of Lombardy, bounded by mountains at one end and lakes at the other?

Now, Bernardino could see Francesco striding down the room, with a flourish of his cloak which overturned more than one canvas. All the students turned to watch the scene, but none were curious as to the cause – all knew that the root would originate with Bernardino. The outlook in this case was not promising, for Francesco was flanked by two of his liveried men, wearing the Giocondo arms, with their swords clanking time with their footsteps. Francesco would have all the assistance of Florentine law afforded to one of its wealthier merchant citizens. The wronged husband halted before Leonardo, and that he moderated his tones only slightly marked his contempt for artists and all their kind.

'Forgive the intrusion, Signor da Vinci,' began Francesco in a manner which assumed the pardon already granted. 'I seek your pupil Bernardino Luini, who has done me a great wrong.' Bernardino saw his eyes slide over to regard his wife, where she sat motionless on her chair. Francesco reminded him of his grandmother's cat – sleek, fat and dangerous.

Signor da Vinci deliberately painted a few more strokes

and then laid his brushes aside. He turned to face Francesco, but before he had composed his features Bernardino caught the twinkle of his eye. The Master meant to enjoy himself. 'I am puzzled, Signor del Giocondo,' he said. 'My pupil is a man of three and twenty, a student in the art of painting. What harm can he have inflicted on a merchant as great as yourself?'

Francesco looked a little put out. Bernardino smiled. He knew, as da Vinci knew, that Francesco would never admit to having been cuckolded by a lowly artisan such as he. He knew also that Leonardo would only take so much interest in the affair so far as it affected his work – if del Giocondo decided to take his wife away, and the portrait could not be finished, then the Master would be seriously displeased. Therefore he would protect his model's reputation, and by association, that of his wayward pupil too.

Francesco shifted his considerable weight and answered the question. ''Tis a private matter. One of…business.'

Da Vinci coughed delicately. 'Well, Signor, I am desolate that I am unable to help you conclude your…*business*,' here the brow arched again, 'but I am afraid that Signor Luini is no longer here. I received a commission from his Eminence the Doge of Venice, and Bernardino has just lately gone to that state to begin the work.'

Francesco's eyes narrowed in disbelief, till da Vinci produced a letter from the sleeve of his gown. 'You know, perhaps, the cognizance of the Doge?'

Francesco took the proffered letter and examined the seal closely. He gruffly acknowledged the arms and made as if to open the missive until Leonardo snatched it back. 'You will forgive me, Signore,' he said dryly, 'but my matters, too, are *private*.'

Francesco could do little more. He attempted to regain countenance by saying, 'Well, as long as he is gone from my sight; for should I see him on the streets of Florence again, I will challenge him and he will die.'

Bernardino rolled his eyes unseen. For the love of Jesu, this was 1503! Three years into the new century and the man spoke as a lover from the antique days of the medieval courts! He fixed his eye on his rival and saw him extend a hand to his wife where she sat on the dais. 'Come, madam.'

Bernardino saw his Master stiffen.

'I pray you, madam, remain still.' Leonardo turned to Francesco. 'Surely, Signore, there can be no cause to remove your wife from this place? Now that the man who has offended you has gone, there can be no evil influence? Your wife has no fault in this *affair*, surely?'

This last Francesco could not publicly deny. He seemed to waver, so da Vinci turned to flattery. 'Consider, Signore, what this portrait will do for your reputation as a patron, a lover of the visual arts?'

In point of fact, Francesco had no love for the visual arts, nor understanding of the same; but he knew that Florence's reputation stood well amid the city states on its art and architecture, and he felt all the importance of being a part of this. But he seemed to resist. ''Tis only a portrait,' he said. 'Not one of your great battles, or a scene from scripture or some such. None shall see it but our family circle, where it hangs in my palazzo.'

'Nay, Signore, you are mistaken.' Leonardo became animated by his passion for his work. 'For this portrait will be different. It will be a showcase for my latest techniques. See how I have blended light and shadow in this wondrous *chiaroscuro*? And here at her mouth, how my brush blurs the corners to make her expression ambiguous, in a manner I call *sfumato*? Believe me, sir, your wife will be admired the world over, and in this service to her you are not only proving yourself a great patron and art lover but the greatest of *husbands* too.'

That did it. For despite his family name, Francesco had no sense of humour but a great deal of pride. How better to heal any rumoured rift with his wife than to immortalize her in this portrait? He let his proffered hand drop to his side, bowed to Leonardo and left.

Bernardino leaned his head against the wooden frame of the canvas with relief. He breathed in the sweet scents of oil and poplar, and below that something else…the sweet smell of sandalwood that his lady wore, and still deeper, the sharp spicy smell of her sex, so well remembered from yestereve. The remembrance sent a frisson to his groin and he was obliged to spend the next few moments counseling himself against such folly – he had just escaped a skinning and must not let his lusts weaken him again. He must leave *la Signora* alone. His Master's voice brought him to his senses. 'You can come out now, Bernardino.'

Bernardino sheepishly emerged, to laughter and scattered applause from his colleagues. He bowed to the collective with a theatrical flourish. Leonardo raised his brow again, as if caught on a fishhook. Bernardino bowed in earnest. 'Thank you, Signore,' he said. 'May I return to work, if it pleases you?'

'You may return to work, Bernardino. But not here.'

'What?'

'You have enjoyed the eavesdropper's fate of overhearing your destiny. I wish you to go to Venice and take this commission, for it was not a device which I invented to dispatch your rival, but a genuine request from the Doge.' He pulled the letter from his sleeve once more and waved it at his pupil. 'I think it best that you are out of the reaches of Signor Giacondo for a while.'

'Venice?'

'Indeed. His Eminence writes that he will pay three hundred ducats for a fresco to be painted in the church of the Frari. A Holy scene. The Virgin, angels, the usual kind of thing. I think, at last, you are ready.'

'Figures? An entire scene? Not hands?'

Leonardo gave a rare smile. 'Figures, yes. But hands they should have certainly, else I don't think the Doge will pay you.'

Bernardino's head was in a whirl. Venice. The Veneto. He knew little of the place save that it floated on water, and for this reason the women were leprous and the men had webbed feet. He was enjoying his time in Florence – it was the first time he had left his native Lombardy and was making the most of it. He had friends and…lovers here. He loved Florence. And yet – it would not be forever. A year or two might meet the case. And he was to be entrusted with full-figure work for the first time, instead of the forest of hands he had painted – interminable digits and knuckles – he hated the sight of them. And the money. He could make his fortune. And there would surely be some handsome women in that state too?

He took the letter from his Master with thanks, and took his leave affectionately. Leonardo took Bernardino's face in his hands and looked him long in the eyes. 'Listen to me well, Bernardino. Do not be overwhelmed by the weight of your own genius, for you have none. You are a good painter and could be a great one, but not until you begin to *feel*. If you have pangs of sorrow at your removal from this lady, if your heart bleeds, so much the better. For your work will reflect the passions that you experience and only *then* will you place those emotions on the canvas. You have my blessing.' Warmly the Master kissed the pupil on both cheeks. Bernardino then turned to the model, whose eyes followed him closely around the room. No, she was not handsome, so there would be little for him to pine for. But, leaning close, he whispered, because he could not help himself: 'I hope to take my leave of you later, lady. When your husband is from home.'

Bernardino walked his beloved streets under the cowl of a cloak – he did not wish to meet his rival before he could safely quit the place. But on the way back to his lodgings he went to the places he loved well. He walked in step with the bawling bells that shivered his ribs with their sweet cacophony. Through the Florence he loved, the square where Savonarola had burned, and the vanities with him. Bernardino had little to do with the looking glass, so he could not know that as he said a tender farewell to the wrestling statuary that adorned the Piazza della Signoria, the carrera marble exactly matched the strange silver hue of his eyes. He leaned on the warm stone balustrades of the Arno and said goodbye to the perfect arches of the Ponte Vecchio. The late evening sun – his favourite light of all – turned their stones from amber to gold in her daily alchemy. But Bernardino knew not that his own skin had the same rosy hue. As he wandered through precincts of Santa Croce and bid *arrivederci* to the monks of the *Misericordia*, he was unaware that those Holy fathers wore cowls as black as his own hair. He was innocent of the fact that the pearly marble of the vast domed basilica was precisely the white of his teeth. Yes, whether he knew it or not, Bernardino was as handsome as the city itself. At the last, he took a drink from the fountain of the golden boar and rubbed the *Porcellino*'s nose to be sure that, one day, he would return. Bernardino was not given to introspection. He would miss the place, to be sure, but his spirits were already bubbling to the surface. As he walked home he looked to the future, singing softly a ditty composed by Lorenzo de' Medici, *Il Magnifico* himself:

> *Quant'è bella giovinezza,*
> *Che si fugge tuttavia!*
> *Chi vuol esser lieto sia:*
> *Di doman non c'e certezza.*

How fine a thing is youth but how short-lived.
Let he who wishes to be merry, be so.
For there's no saying what
Tomorrow will bring.

In the *studiolo*, Leonardo was still for a moment as he thought on Bernardino. It was well he was gone, for the boy was too beautiful to be under his eye every day. He thought of the lustrous black curls, the startling eyes that spoke of a heritage far from Lombardy; the black lashes that looked as if each had been painted individually by the finest sable of no more than three hairs. Bernardino even had all his teeth – and white ones at that. Leonardo sighed in vale-diction and turned back to his model. *She* was no beauty, however he may flatter the husband, but still she had some-thing, if only an exquisite seriousness of countenance. He assumed that her nickname *'La Gioconda'* was given to her with ironic bent – a play on her name, and no indication of her general humour. But wait...something was different... round the corners of her mouth there played – almost, but not quite, a smile? Her gravity had dissolved in an instant to this enigmatic, this wholly inappropriate expression. Leonardo cursed Bernardino roundly. What had he said to her? He took up his brushes and worked over the mouth once more. *Damn* the boy.

When Bernardino swore that any woman he painted would have to be as beautiful as an angel, he did not know that he would have to wait more than twenty years to find her. When he painted his first commission for the Doge, her parents were just lately married. When he began his *Pietà* at Chiaravalle near Rogoredo, she was being born. When he painted one of his greatest works in 1522 – the magnificent 'Coronation of Our Lord', painted for the Confraternity of the Holy Crown in Milan – she was at that time being wed to another and choking on an almond nut at the feast. Bernardino's mastery grew, but he never, in all his models, found a countenance he considered worth painting. Not until he accepted a commission in 1525 did he come to be in the very same room as the object of his aesthetic desires. This was because, at the behest of the Cardinal of Milan, he came to be in the church of Santa Maria dei Miracoli in Saronno on the very morning that Simonetta di Saronno came there to pray for a miracle.

★ ★ ★

'Who is *that*?'

Father Anselmo turned to his visitor. He guessed the artist was much of an age with himself, somewhat in the middle years, but his voice betrayed very different sensibilities. While Anselmo thought of God and things heavenly, this handsome fellow seemed made to seek only earthly pleasures. He liked the man already; for all that they had only been acquainted perhaps the quarter of one hour. But the priest's answer held a warning.

'Signor Luini, that is Signora Simonetta di Saronno.'

'*Really.*' Luini's voice was full of hungry fascination.

Anselmo looked the taller man full in the face. 'Signore. She is a very great lady of these parts.'

'Of any parts, I'll warrant, padre.'

Anselmo tried again. 'She is just lately a *vedova*, widowed by the war.'

'Better and better.'

Now the priest was properly shocked. 'Signore! How can you say such a thing? The war has ravaged the entire of the Lombard plain – not just this poor lady, but many others are suffering the loss of those they loved. Great families and humble ones suffer alike. This battle lately at Pavia took away that poor soul's lord – and he such a man! Full of youth and vigour, and proper devotion.'

'Sounds like you're missing him yourself.'

Anselmo tried to quash such inappropriate attempts at humour. 'These wars, as all wars do, bring nothing but evil.'

Luini, unaccountable fellow, merely shrugged. 'War is not always such a bad thing. Hundreds of years of wars on this peninsula of ours have set the city states so much against each other that all try and outdo their neighbours in respect to the arts. We have the finest artists in the world; architects and men of letters too. How many Swiss artists can you name?'

'Perhaps God loves better a country of peace.'

'Peace! They may have no wars at home to promote their arts, but they are hardly a peace-loving nation. The Swiss boast the best mercenaries in the world,' exclaimed Bernardino, his face lively with argument. 'But at least they kill both sides if they are paid enough. Very even-handed. I'm sure God is very well pleased with them.'

Anselmo did not mind how many points he conceded in the debate so long as they had left the dangerous subject of the lady of Saronno. But Luini's mind could not be distracted for long. 'Lombardy is covered in blood and paint; the blood drains away, but the paint stays forever. Especially with such a subject.' He looked back at the lady. 'She is devout you say?'

'Indeed. She attends mass here every week – I myself married her here. It is the nearest church to her home.'

'Which is where?'

Anselmo shook his tonsured head. 'I will not tell you that. You must leave her be.'

But Luini was already making his way down the nave to the Lady Chapel. He needed a closer look. Anselmo followed him and plucked at his sleeve. 'Signore, you must not approach her now! When we pray, we are talking to God.'

Bernardino shook off the hand. 'She can talk to him later.'

She was kneeling next to a woman whom he supposed to be her maid. The lady was clothed in black and wore a veil, but of such thin stuff that he could see the gleam of her red hair through the net. She prayed not with her head bowed but with her face raised to the votive statue of the Virgin. Her hands, pressed together closely, were long and white; but her face! He had been right – she had the countenance of an angel which far surpassed anything he had ever created even in his finest hours. His heart began to thump. He *must* paint her. Bernardino sat down in the pew in front of her and hissed urgently: '*Signora*!'

He saw the maid jump and cross herself, but the young mistress simply turned her eyes on him. They were as blue as the waters of Lake Maggiore, where the village of his childhood – Luino – was placed. Never had he loved the lake so well as now, when he could compare it with her eyes. Her face had no animation, her expression was numb, but the serenity of her countenance did nothing to dim her beauty. 'Signore?' she said. Her tones were low and musical, but her mein icy. She could not be more than, what, seventeen? But such carriage, such composure! Making no attempt to lower his voice, Bernardino said, 'Signora, I wish you to sit for me. I want to paint you.'

He now had all of her attention. Simonetta had come here for a miracle, and the Virgin had sent her this? A man, perhaps forty years old or more, repellently handsome, and making a request of her that she did not understand. Was this another test? What could the Queen of Heaven mean by it? 'Paint...*me?*'

By this time, Anselmo had caught up to them, for his girth and robes had hampered his progress down the nave. 'I apologise for this man, my Lady. He is an artist,' ('a Great Artist!' put in Bernardino, to be ignored by everyone) 'lately come to paint the walls of this church, and if I understand him rightly his impertinent request is that you should... model – for one of the figures.'

'Not just *one* of the figures,' put in Bernardino. 'The *main* figure. The Virgin herself,' and to give emphasis to his point, he slapped a nearby statue of that sacred Lady with a friendly pat on the rear.

Simonetta di Saronno had heard enough. She swept out of the church followed closely by Raffaella. She did not like the man's tone, or his irreverence to the Virgin, but there was something more. She had made the mortifying discovery that she was, despite her grief, susceptible to his considerable physical charms. No remembrance of how long she had been without Lorenzo in her bed could absolve her of this sin. She felt jolted and guilty and resolved to atone for long hours before her *prie-dieu* at home, where *he* was not. She did not hear the apologies of Father Anselmo, but she did hear the parting shot of her tormentor. He actually stood on the steps of the church and shouted at her retreating back: 'I'll pay you!'

Anselmo dragged Luini back from the doorway. 'Don't be foolish! She is one of the richest ladies in Lombardy! She does not need your money!'

'Everybody needs money,' said Bernardino, his eyes on the retreating figure. 'Speaking of which…' he let the priest lead him back into the interior and explain the terms of the commission.

'For each single figure of the Saints you will receive twenty-two francs per day.'

'Want plenty of Saints, eh?' asked Bernardino, with a cynical curl of his lip. 'Add a bit of drama, don't they? Hearts and eyes and breasts torn from the pious body like so much canonised offal.'

'Indeed,' said the priest, unmoved. 'Yet the faithful identify with their suffering, especially at this time. They pray to them for intercession, name their children after them, even invoke them when they curse. They are woven into the tapestry of our lives. In Lombardy, the Saints walk amongst us everyday.'

'What does that actually *mean*?'

Anselmo sighed and turned away beginning to move down the aisle. 'If you don't know now, someday you will.'

Bernardino followed, his business not concluded. 'How about room and board?'

The priest turned back. 'I am instructed to say that wine and bread is included, and lodging here in the bell tower of the church.' Anselmo's voice warmed with pride. 'You'll be very comfortable. The campanile is fairly new, 'twas built from a benefice given in 1516, and is considered one of the finest in the area.'

Bernardino was not listening. 'Good. For that money I'll do you a free Nativity.'

Anselmo tried not to smile. He decided it would be pointless to show Bernardino his pride and joy, the fragment of the True Cross contained in a great ruby-paned reliquary in the apse. He too disliked Luini's irreverent ways; but could not help liking his person. And the man could paint. Anselmo had seen Luini's 'Christ Crowned with Thorns' while at seminary in Milan – in fact he had first recognised Bernardino, as he entered the church this morning, because the artist had, with customary arrogance, painted Christ's figure in his own image. Bernardino may look Godly, but Anselmo knew him by repute to be a man of little faith and low morals. It was apt that his friends and fellow artists had made a play on Luini's name and birthplace of Luino to nickname him *lupino* – the wolf. Luini even signed himself with the Latin tag '*lovinus*' on occasion. Anselmo sighed inwardly and hoped that Bernardino would not be trouble. He returned to his theme. 'How long will so many frescoes take?'

Luini rubbed his chin. 'I'm a quick worker. I did a 'Christ Crowned with Thorns' for the *Collegio* in thirty-eight days, and that had one hundred and fourteen figures.' He revolved around under the vaulted ceiling, admiring as he did so the architecture of the interior – it was a lovely confection of a church, all white plaster and delicate mouldings. A few attempts had been made by anonymous artists to paint the pilasters and panels with biblical scenes, but these would be nothing to the frescoes that he would now paint. He laid one hand on a cold white pillar. He always liked to think of his churches as living things. This one was definitely female, with its pretty white iced interior, delicate belltower and tree lined cloister. The stone of the pillar warmed under his hand in welcome and he began to strafe his palm up and down, as if stroking the thigh of one of his willing conquests. 'Get ready,' he said beneath his breath, as if to a woman. With a sudden association of ideas he looked to the great empty wall at the narthex of the church. 'At this end,' he declared, 'shall be a great scene of the Adoration of the Magi. The scene shall centre on the Virgin, with Simonetta di Saronno as my model.' He said the name he would never forget.

Anselmo shook his head at Luini's persistence. 'She'll never agree to it.'

Bernardino smiled, white teeth flashing like the wolf of his nickname. 'We'll see.'

CHAPTER 5

The Landscape of Lombardy

Nonna and Amaria worked by candlelight. In this they were fortunate, for the wildman's appearance by daylight would have been hard indeed to look upon. The candlelight was merciful. It turned blood-red to treacle-black. It hid the green tinges of gangrenous skin, and gilded the sickly yellow pallor of the flesh beneath the matted hair. It turned to gold the lice and fleas that crawled in the hair, and hid the veinous mapping of the bloodshot eyes to leave only the kindly gleam of life.

They had laid the wildman, or *Selvaggio* as they had dubbed him, on their humble board, which Amaria padded with straw for his comfort. She built up the fire with the faggots she had brought from the forest, and heated a pail of water on its embers. Then they began.

They were obliged to cut the clothes from his flesh with Nonna's sewing shears. Selvaggio watched them, and never uttered a sound, but at length, as the cloth stuck to his wounds and the skin itself began to pull away, he lost consciousness from the pain. Amaria dampened the clothes with water to ease their parting. She threw the pestilent smottered garments on the fire. But round Selvaggio's trunk was wound a fine dark cloth – by the candlelight it seemed black in colour, but it seemed to be some sort of pennant so Nonna set it by to be cleaned, in case he should want it. The pennant had clearly been used to staunch the blood of the severest wound – a gash so deep that Amaria gasped, and Nonna wondered that it had not killed him. Yet this was the only gash he carried – the other punctures in his flesh were not slashes but holes – a rash of round wounds in his chest and shoulders, as round as arrow holes with the arrows gone, and yet smaller, much smaller. Nonna crossed herself and called on Saint Sebastian, a Saint who knew the pierce of an arrow or two. She looked closer, covering her face with a barm cloth lest she breathe pestilence into the fellow. Peeping from one of the punctures was a round metal pea. She eased it out and it rolled from the flesh, dropping with a neat click on the wooden boards on which the wildman lay. Both women leant close.

'What is it?' breathed Amaria.

'Shot,' replied Nonna, the syllable itself as short and sharp as gunfire. '*Pallottola di Piombo*. We are in a new world indeed.' She held the metal up to the firelight where it gleamed evilly – a beady metal eye. She eyed it back. She had learned much of warfare since she had watched Filippo burn – she kept her eyes and ears open as the mercenaries and soldiers had passed through town. 'Tiny cannon balls shot from cannon that a man can hold. Called a hackbutt, or arquebus. Many, many died this way, this time.'

Nonna took the bowl from Amaria and tipped the water on the rushes. It was not suitable that a maid should touch the flesh of a man, even such a case as he, so this task was hers. She heated the blade of Filippo's dagger in the fire and began to dig.

Amaria gasped. 'What are you doing?'

Nonna did not look up. 'These beans must be taken from his flesh. They are made from an alloy of lead and will poison his organs if left.'

Amaria rolled the first ball in her hand. 'It is perfectly round,' she marvelled. 'How are such things created?'

'They are made everywhere now. Even here in Pavia.'

'Here?'

'Yes. The two red towers near Saint Michele's church, you know the ones?'

Amaria nodded. 'Yes. The Devil's legs. You must run between the two as fast as you can with your eyes shut lest the Devil shit on your head.'

Nonna allowed herself a smile at Amaria's nonsense, even at such a time. 'Yes, the *Gambe del Diavolo*. There. These are made there. The Devil shits bullets now.'

'Truly?' Amaria's eyes were wide.

Nonna kept digging through the tender flesh. Some were near the surface, some deeper in. 'No, child. Like most evils, these are made by men. Hot lead is dropped from the top of the tower to the floor below. When it falls, as water does, the droplets become perfectly round in the air. By the time they reach the floor they are dry, and hard as Christ's nails.' She sighed. 'Most of those that died at Pavia were shot through.' She fell silent as she pulled the metal from the wildman's torn muscle. The wound clustered on the white wastes of his flesh like battle sites littered across Lombardy, across the whole peninsular. As she searched the landscape of his body for more of the insidious shot, Nonna named the battles like a litany. She dropped the bullets into the dish with an attendant click for each. She began with Garigliano, the place where she had lost Filippo. Click. Agnadello. Click. Cerignola. Click. Bicocca, Fornovo, Ravenna. Click, click, click. Marignano, Novara. The Siege of Padua. And last of all, the Battle of Padova. The war had come home from far away to their very doorstep. Click. The bullets dropped into the clay dish like the Virgin's tears and lay there clustered together in a string – the beads of a bloody rosary. Nonna bowed her head for a moment in sorrow for all the battles and all the dead.

Then she took the shears and asked the girl to turn her back as she snipped back dead yellow flesh from the lips of the gash – this was the hacked maw of a sword, for sure. She handed Amaria the shears to clean and her granddaughter then used them to attack Selvaggio's hair. Amaria cut great clumps away until his hair was all of a length. She washed it then with water and lemon to clear the lice away, and as she cut the fruit to squeeze it on his scalp he seemed to revive. His eyelids flickered – perhaps from the sting of the juice for there were sores on his scalp – and she felt moved to whisper an apology as the eyes closed again. Nonna took her bone needle and waxed thread and sewed the cleaned gash as best she could. She had heard of such remedies on the battlefield and they made sense to her. Sewing was part of her lexicon. If something was torn or rent, you sewed it closed. Nonna clung to her homespun sense through these moments of horror – she needed something to make sense in this world gone mad – where a young man was peppered with blades and shot. As she sewed she tried to imagine his skin was the cambric of a cushion cover, and that she sewed to stop the flock escaping, not the viscera of his stomach.

Amaria had an easier task – she whetted Filippo's knife on the hearthstone and cut away the beard that covered the savage's face. As she rubbed olive oil into his skin and began to shave him close, she felt a shock at the warmth of his skin and the roughness of the stubble, for she had never touched a man before. She had had no bearded kiss of a father to remember, or muscular embrace of a brother. It was all new, so new and good that her face heated in the firelight, and her heart sounded in her ears. Her ministrations revealed a face with regular, good features and a refined look that was far away from the savagery of the invalid's name. Nonna glanced up when the beard was gone and saw him to be young. So young. She had imagined him to be another Fil-ippo, but she knew as she worked that the wildman was little more than a boy – more of an age of a grandson than a son to her.

At length Amaria began to cut Selvaggio's claw-like nails. When they were clipped away she washed the hands and rubbed in aloes for their wounds and blisters. She not-ed that the left hand – but for its wounds – was fine and soft, but the right had the calloused palm of an accustomed soldier who carried a sword every day. Nonna dressed the wounds of Selvaggio with a salve she had made of sage in hog fat, and poured wine into the deepest wounds before its application. The two women worked quietly, murmuring to each other occasionally over what was best to be done, revolving around the body as the hours passed. The candles and the laid-out body reminded Nonna of a wake, and she knew that their work may end as such, for his wounds were so heavy, and some infected, that he still may not see dawn.

She felt at least that, even should he die, she had done what she could not do for her son. She had cleaned his wounds and laid him out, and finally she covered the boy in a clean linen coverlet and left him to sleep, the sleep of refreshment and recovery, or of death and despair. But as the grey light lessened the powers of the candles, the eyelids flickered again, and a bloom returned to the thin sallow face that had not been there before. In the daylight, with all wounds hidden, the case did not look as grave as before.

They allowed themselves to hope. He did not rave or fever, his skin was not fiery to the touch, nor his colour hectic. They could now fully see his face; the eyes, as they opened, were the green of basil leaves, and the hair the light straight brown of merlin feathers. As he slept, grandmother and granddaughter embraced as they watched him, and then crept from the room up the stairs of the cot to the dormer they shared, to sleep also. But before they slept both of them shed tears; Nonna for what she had lost, and Amaria for what she had found.

CHAPTER 6

The Notary

Simonetta di Saronno had her head in her hands. Those long white hands, with the middle fingers all of a length, concealed her face completely. She had thought that she had reached the bottom of her well of despair, but had now been plummeted to new depths by the man who sat opposite her, across the massive bare board of her great hall.

She was not weeping though. And the man that sat with her was not Bernardino Luini, whatever appearances might be. In fact she had tried hard to forget that impossible man, and had almost managed to dispel his face from her waking hours. Her dreams, however, he penetrated against her wishes, and her prayers were all the more fervent in the morning.

No, the gentleman was a notary – Oderigo Beccaria, a man of middle years who had tended to the di Saronno fortune in many hours of private counsel once a month, closeted with Lorenzo. Simonetta had not realised the littleness of her own plight to others so it was salutary to her to note that Oderigo turned up on the first of the month, with his quill and his ledger, as if Lorenzo had never died. She had not known that she, a woman who had never had to think about anything beyond the colour of her gown and the dressing of her hair, would now have to become intimately acquainted with her own household accounts.

The household accounts, it seemed, were not in a healthy state. Oderigo told her, in no uncertain terms, that her tradesmen had not been paid, nor the servants, from the provision that remained from Lorenzo; a provision which that lord had left him to transact the accounts in what he was sure would be a short absence. Simonetta, at this stage in the conversation, was not unduly concerned. Smarting from her loss, she tired of this financial chatter and heartily wished Oderigo away so that she might mourn unchecked. She took the three bronze keys from her belt and went downstairs to the almond cellar. As always, she made sure she was not observed as she made her way to the back of the room, feeling the nutshells crack under her feet, and felt in the dark for the three keyholes that would unlock the room which held the di Saronno treasure. She was confident as she turned the keys in their proper order, that she would find what she needed within. Even when the first coffer she unlocked – with the cognizance of the three silver almonds on blue painted on the lid – proved empty, she merely moved to the next. Only when every coffer proved to be empty did she return upstairs, sit down and put her head in her hands.

She did this because she felt that she was being punished. In the worst of her grief, she had cried out to God that there was little point in being rich and having fortune and possessions when the one person she loved was taken from her. Well, God had heard her, and had taken her treasure too. Now what?

Oderigo waited for her to compose herself. He was by no means as surprised as the lady of the house appeared at this discovery. He had heard, among the bankers and lawyers in Saronno and Pavia, that Lorenzo di Saronno had pursued his military ambitions in such a way that he was in danger of ruining his own house. A headstrong hot-headed young soldier with an over-developed sense of honour found it more needful to give his horses the best equipage, and his men the finest liveries, than to exercise the prudent, dull exigencies of a lasting income and pension for his estates. Oderigo tutted to himself. Such imprudence was unbelievable to a man of careful finance like himself.

Oderigo was not villainous, merely indifferent to Simonetta's plight. In his line of work, and in such times as these, he was used to dealing with clients who found themselves in reduced circumstances. He removed the kerchief from his pocket that he carried for these occasions, but when the lady lifted her head he was relieved to see that her eyes were dry. By heaven, she was a fair lady! For the first time in his long career, he felt an alien flicker of sympathy thaw his heart, for never had he seen such an expression of hope-lessness on so fair a face. 'Lady,' he began. 'You must not despair. I can buy you a little time. I will quiet your credi-tors and return in a month. Till then, do everything you can to retrench. Sell whatever you can, reduce the number of your servants; it may yet be possible to remain in this house. But it can be no *little* adjustment: everything in your power must be done – only the essentials should be left alone.'

Simonetta met his eyes for the first time. The house! It had never occurred to her, in the worst of the last few moments, that she would have to leave the Villa Castello. She could not, *would* not submit to leaving all that she and Lorenzo had shared, whatever it cost her. She nodded to the notary, and he took his leave, and as he walked the path between the almond trees he relived the thrill of the mo-ment when Simonetta di Saronno had looked him full in the eye.

What a month had she then! What a reduction, a coming down of circumstances! What a difference would Oderigo see when next he walked the almond grove to Castello! Every man and maid who worked on the place was let go, except for her dear Raffaella whom she needed as a friend more than a servant. Gregorio was kept on the place for three reasons – for charity because of his injuries, for his service and strong attachment to her newly dead lord, and for an affection which she saw growing between the squire and Raffaella. Having been rent from her own love, Simonetta could not so part two lovers.

One man and one maid would have to do. Each day Simonetta walked the villa's rooms with Raffaella, determining what chests, what fine draperies, what paintings could be sold. Together they went through Simonetta's closets. Jewels, furs, gowns from happier times were all to be sold. The great tapestry that covered one whole wall of the dining solar, which depicted in wondrous detail the doomed love of Lancelot and Guinevere, was taken from its poles. Simonetta ran her hands over the exquisite stitching as she folded the cloth for sale. She had loved the scene: the passionate embrace of the guilty queen and her shining knight with the shadowy figure of Arthur looking on, and the white conical towers of Camelot set in the hills behind like a shining crown. Lorenzo's clothes too, untouched since he had worn them, would also go. Simonetta did not allow herself to bury her face in the scent of his linens or remember that she had felt, hard, warm muscle within *this* velvet sleeve as she leant on his arm or the breadth of his back under *that* fur as they danced. Dry eyed, she disposed of all, save for his russet hunting garb, and that she kept for a special purpose.

For now there was no money for meat, Simonetta began to hone her skills with the bow. The sport that she had enjoyed as a diversion, a skill befitting to a great lady, now became as needful to her as to the poorest serf. Hour after hour she spent at her chamber window – not weeping now, but firing arrows with increasing accuracy at the almond trees. As her skill improved she left the trunks alone – by now as barbed as Saint Sebastian – and painted a single nut with red clay to become her target. She painted the almonds hanging further and further away from the house until she was a true proficient. Her skill was sharpened by the fantasy that she was shooting Spanish soldiers, and sometimes, secretly, that artist fellow who she could not forget. *That* for his silver eyes, *that* for his dark curls, *that* for his maddening white grin that haunted her – torturing her with the remembrance that it had warmed her where she had thought she would be cold forever. Sometimes she thought of him as she walked the woods, dressed in Lorenzo's shabby hunting garb, setting snares and dispatching the rabbits she caught. She felt a ruthless enjoyment as she found the creatures struggling as they strangled themselves. She took the skins and the stomachs from them with newly learned skill. As the gouts of warm blood ran over her white hands, she revelled in angry pleasure and her heart hardened within her. Like the pagan soothsayers she read her own fate in the entrails. That that had beat warm and strong was now clotted and cold. She straightened and looked back across the parkland. Glittering frost rimed the almond trees like powdered diamonds, and the low winter sun gave the plaster of the villa a rosy blush. She looked at the elegant, square building with the last remnants of her affection. God had taken her love from her; she would not let him take her house too.

She took to wearing Lorenzo's hunting garb at all times. She kept only one gown – her wedding dress of green ore-fois – and never wore it once. She resembled a boy as she strode through the woods, more so now because of her greatest sacrifice. As she trod the dead, red leaves of autumn she remembered the night when Raffaella had cut off her hair – the shears whispering in her ears that she would never be fair again. She had gathered the red skeins from the floor and wrapped them in tissue to be sold to Florence where red hair was the fashion for wigs and pieces. She cared not. She reacted against the beauty that she had, she was gladdened when her white hands became calloused, glad that her crowning glory had gone. She took a last look in her silver-backed looking glass the day before it was sold, saw the hair that stubbornly insisted on curling prettily above her shoulders and round her face, but rejoiced that *he* would never ask to paint her again.

Her board had little to recommend it now. Nightly meals of rabbit or squirrel, with the few roots she found in the woods, were her comfort. In better days, when the ornamental rose gardens and yew walks of Castello had been planted, it would never have occurred to her or Lorenzo that they might be better served by their acres by planting vegetables. In the evening she sat huddled over the meagre firewood that Gregorio had chopped, and sang unaccompanied the airs she used to play on her lute before it had gone to be sold. When she felt her eyes drop from the exercise of the day she went to her chamber and rolled in the one fur cloak she had kept. She slept directly on the stone floor, for the fine wooden box-frame bed of English oak, the bed where she had spent her wedding night, was gone. The autumn winds whistled through the windows unchecked, for the Venetian glass roundels which they had fitted there were gone too. Most nights she slept from sheer exhaustion, but on the last day of the month she was wakeful, for she knew she had not enough money to give to Oderigo on the morrow.

Shocked by the change in the villa and its lady, Oderigo was obliged to seat himself on a log by the hearth for both board and bench had gone. Simonetta was not alone today, but flanked by Raffaella and Gregorio, ready to plead for their lady or protect her if Oderigo became angry. He counted the coins she gave him in silence. He did not need to tell her that there were not enough. He indulged himself with a look at her face. She was thinner, harder, but no less beautiful. The change in her demeanour was great, greater than the change that the loss of her hair and the change in her garb had wrought. If he thought her fine when he left her last time, his reflections would be no less great today. She spoke first.

'Signore,' she said with her new confidence, 'I will not leave this place. What can I do more? Tell me, where am I to seek help? What am I to do? I am ready.'

Oderigo opened his mouth but then thought better of it. He knew of one who would help her, but was reluctant, as a Christian, to send her in his path. He shook his head to himself, but she saw it all.

'What? Who?' she questioned with urgency. She came to the notary and took his arm. 'I know you can help me. Tell me where I can find succour, for the love of God!'

He sighed. 'Lady, I do know of one who can help you. But he will not do it through the love of your God, or mine, or any that we know. His name is Manodorata.'

Simonetta heard Raffaella gasp, and saw her maid sink to the floor and throw her apron over her head. She turned to Gregorio, who rapidly crossed his breast as his lips muttered a prayer. Puzzled, not understanding, Simonetta turned back to Oderigo.

'Manodorata? Who is he? Can he help me?'

'He can help you, Lady.'

'Then why do you all shrink? What manner of man is he? Am I to petition the Devil himself?'

Oderigo would not meet her eyes this time. 'Very like, my Lady. He is a Jew.'

CHAPTER 7

Manodorata

There was a star cut into the door. A curious star with six points, designed as if two triangles had been offset, rotated to leave their points exposed. Simonetta had never seen such a thing, and for a moment her fears left her to be replaced by curiosity as her fingers traced the deep grooves in the heavy oaken door. She might have felt much at this moment, for since her interview with Oderigo Beccaria that very morning she had been given much to think about. She had had to endure the voices of her maid and squire, combined in chorus to condemn the man who lived in this house, and all his race.

Simonetta had ever been a religious girl – she had been devout until this last month when she had stayed away from Santa Maria dei Miracoli. She told herself that she had been absent from the church because she grieved too greatly for Lorenzo, that she was too occupied with the economies of her household, even that she hated God for taking her husband. She never admitted, even to herself, that she was afraid of seeing *him* again.

Simonetta had no intention of turning her back on God forever. It was only that she could not think of him, not praise him, just now. She felt she had little to give thanks for, and much to pray for, but she felt that the Lord had done with listening to her. But according to her servants, she now stood in danger of losing her Christian soul forever, just by consorting with a Jew.

Never had she heard such condemnation, such censure. Never had she heard such bitter words fall from the lips of her beloved maid, and her mild-mannered squire. For the Jews were apparently demons. The men were warlocks, the women witches. They were hideously deformed, as a punishment for the death of Christ, for which they were directly responsible. The genitals for both men and women were the same – they could not mate as God intended, nor give birth in the natural way; but spat their babes from their mouths in bloody sacs. They drank blood and feasted on the flesh of Christian babes. They could not feel the warmth of the sun and walked in darkness but never in daylight. They were skilled in the dark arts and could bewitch and curse good Christians until they sickened and died. They used their arts to accrue great wealth, which they bled from good God fearing folk.

This then, was what Simonetta was to expect. But there was more. The man she was to visit, to plead for money, was the worst of the lot. He was a creature of darkness indeed.

He had the face of a Devil and the body of a bear. He spoke in an evil tongue and took the livelihoods of good hardworking men and women. And he literally wore his wealth on his sleeve, for he had a golden hand ('solid gold!' said Raffaella) which had the power to kill at a touch. This member had given him the name by which he was known: '*Manodorata*' or 'golden hand'. Better to quit the house altogether than to feed Castello with his bloody gold. Even if he helped them the place would be ruined in a matter of months anyway, because of the usurious practices of the Jews that were strictly banned in the Bible. The interest would be crippling.

So said Raffaella and Gregorio as they pleaded with their mistress not to put herself in the clutches of the Jew. And yet she knew she had to go. She would not know how to leave Castello, to start again. Where could she go? What could she do? The plague had taken her family, and Lorenzo's too. And besides, as she made her way to Jews' Street in Saronno she began to feel strongly that, unfortunate as her circumstances were, the fight was what was keeping her going. This survival instinct, that she had not known she had, was the only opposition to her other temptation, which was to end it all by falling on Lorenzo's sword. If the Jew wanted to eat her alive, let him. If her Christian God could not help her, very well. Let the other side try.

She took her fingers from the star and knocked at the door – hard enough to graze her knuckles. She hoped, and then feared, that there was no one within. But at length, the ornamental grille set into the door above the star slid open and a pair of eyes appeared. Simonetta cleared her throat and said what she had been instructed. 'My name is Simonetta di Saronno, and I am here on the business of Oderigo Beccaria.'

The grille slid shut and she was about to despair of entry when the door creaked open. She was met by the owner of the eyes, a lady wearing a purple robe and golden jewellery more costly than the ones she herself had sold. Simonetta took her for the lady of the house until the woman ushered her within. Simonetta marvelled as she followed the maid through cool courtyards where fountains played, through ornamental arches and between tall slim pillars. Everything was coloured and patterned with strange but regular shapes, but to a tasteful, not gaudy, effect. It was warm in the house, for all that it was so great, and a spicy incense hung in the air. It was all so alien and opulent and very seductive. She had headed into something rich and strange indeed.

Simonetta began to fear again, as the stories of her servants returned, and she felt that she was walking into the lion's mouth. But she saw a sight to revive her spirits – through an archway to her left she spied two small blonde boys playing with their nursemaid. The lady wore three long dark plaits and a scarlet robe, and was rolling a silver ball between the little boys. The ball held a bell within, and the laughter of the boys echoed its tinkling sound. Simonetta smiled at the scene. The laughter of children, and the tender look on the nursemaid's face, gave her courage. It seemed the Jews loved their children too.

The fear returned as she was led deeper into the house and she perceived a figure seated at a *tavola* writing with a quill. Simonetta's notion that she had truly entered another world was only compounded when her nervous brain registered that the figure was writing in a ledger from right to left, not from left to right in the Christian manner. Nor were the black characters like any that she had been taught by the good sisters of the Pisan convent that directed her education. The fellow's bulk seemed massive as he leant over his work, and he wore a *berretto all'antica* in the Milanese style, the velvet of the hat obscuring his face. Was this, then, the Devil she had come to dance with? Yes, for the maidservant ushered her into a chair of gold filigree opposite the figure. He continued to direct the quill with a hand that looked the same as most men's – and his bulk was an illusion in that he wore a heavy fur cloak indoors, but Simonetta began to dread what she would see when he looked up. At length Manodorata laid his pen aside and raised his head to his visitor. He had not, after all, the face of the Devil, but yet there was something to fear. His eyes were a cold grey that flickered with fearsome intelligence. His lips were unusually full, but were set in a dangerous line. At a time when the fashion was for a clean-shaven face he wore a beard that was oiled and cut into a point as sharp as a knife. His hair and beard were dark but his face looked old – he could have been fifty or more. When he spoke it was in fluent Milanese, but in accents which betrayed that his tongue was accustomed to another language altogether.

'You have business to transact for my friend Beccaria? But I may not call him a friend; nor yet a foe. He may as likely spit at me as ask me for money. He has not yet decided where he stands with me. Like most Christians he thinks that business is a dirty word. So I suspect you have come on your own account.'

Simonetta was disconcerted at being seen through so soon. She could see there was little point in trifling with the Jew. 'I have come to ask for help,' she said simply.

'Then you have wasted your time. And mine.' Manodorata took up his quill again, and motioned for his maidservant to show his visitor out. Simonetta stood up and, as the quill began to scratch, spoke urgently. 'Please. I may lose my house.'

'I can see you are not accustomed to pleading. The trick is to appeal to something that I actually care about. Try again.'

'I lost my husband.'

'Better, but not good enough.'

Simonetta hung her head and exhaled a deep breath as if it were her last. She spoke in a low tone, almost to herself. 'Then it is decided. I am done for. The Spanish may as well have killed me too.'

The quill stopped. 'The Spanish?'

'Yes. At Pavia.'

'The Spanish took your husband?'

'Yes.'

Manodorata pointed the quill at the chair. 'Sit down.'

Simonetta sat, her heart thudding with hope.

'You see, Signora di Saronno, you have caught the trick of it. *Your* plight does not touch me but you have said something to pique *my* interest. You see, we have something in common. I too hate the Spanish. And I like to think that I am qualified to speak on the matter – that my opinion does not arise from hearsay or conjecture.' He looked at her with his light grey eyes and she had the uncomfortable feeling that he divined exactly what she had been told about him.

She found her voice. 'You know that nation well?'

'I should. You see, *I* am a Spaniard.'

Simonetta's head span. 'In truth?'

'Yes. I was not always known as Manodorata. I was born Zaccheus Abravanel, in Castile. But despite this, I still hate them. For they took something from me too that I loved. In my case, my hand.'

He held aloft the hand that had been hidden under the desk, and Simonetta could not but stare. It was indeed a golden hand. It gleamed in the light from the ornamental windows. She looked at it curiously. Seeing her interest he held it out to her. It was solid, the fingers defined by ingenious moulding. There were even nails to the fingers and lines crossing the palm as he turned his hand. On the palm too, in the very centre where one might press a coin, was the same star that she had seen on the door.

'What do you think of it?'

''Tis wonderfully well wrought.'

'It is. Perhaps more so than your own, for I see that you have three fingers all of a length, a mistake a craftsman would not make. *This* hand was made not by God but by some of my Florentine brethren. It has served me well. And it is the only story they tell of me that is true.'

Simonetta felt a blush spread over her cheek.

'What else did they say? That I devour babes?'

She looked down.

'The rest is easily explained to the rational mind. I may resemble a bear, because I wear a fur at all times as I am used to warmer climes. I have no taste for human flesh. I have a wife and two sons whom I love dearly. You may have noticed them playing.'

'Your wife?'

'Rebecca. And my sons Evangelista and Giovan Pietro. You are surprised?'

'Only at them playing so together. In great…Christian families, nursemaids tend the children at all times. I barely knew my mother.' She surprised herself with such an admission.

'Then perhaps such families are not so great. I hear that even the Christian king Francis, who was taken prisoner

at Pavia, has offered his two sons as hostages in his stead.'
A fastidious sniff was enough to deprecate the conduct of
a king. 'As for my wealth, I have amassed it through fair
means, merely by being able to understand the principles
of banking and the precepts of Arabic mathematics. Which
brings me back to your troubles.'

Simonetta was encouraged by such openness and explained her plight. Manodorata smoothed his beard with his
gold hand as he listened, as if he could feel its fibres with
his false fingertips. When she had done he was silent for a
period, and Simonetta wondered what he would say. He
surprised her.

'I think that I must visit your property. For one thing,
you must offer it to me as security in case you are unable to
pay me.' He held up his hand to silence her protests. 'Such
practice is normal. But for another, I may be able to think
of a way to make the place pay. You see in order to keep it
you may have to make the land work for you, and I must
see if there is a way to do this. I will visit you in a sevennight, but there is a condition. Before that time you must
have made some money for yourself. For it is also common
practice to offer me a sum, or principal, for my help. I can
see you are noble, and unused to work, but you must work
if I am to help you.'

'But how? What you ask is impossible! If I could get
money I would not be here.'

'Think hard. Is there no possible way, has no opportunity

been presented you? Use your wits, for I only help those who help themselves.'

Of course she remembered. The parting shot that *he* had assailed her with, that had at that time been so disgusting to her; that mention of payment so offensive to a great lady, could now be her saviour. 'There was…a man, who wanted to paint me. For the church, here in Saronno. But it was some little time ago. I have…changed. He may not want to paint me now.' She thought she saw a flicker of amusement in the Jew's eyes, for all that his mouth remained impassive.

'I am not given to gallantry, Signora, but let me assure you that any man who has seen you would wish to paint you, if only he could.' He stood abruptly, the interview over. 'I will leave it to your best offices to decide. Come to me in a sevennight, with the money for your principal or not at all.' He held out his golden hand, and saw her hesitate before she took it.

It was surprisingly warm to the touch – clearly its metals had been heated by the limb to which it was attached. Simonetta met his eyes and saw at once that in that moment of hesitation he had divined what she had been told. For the first time in their discourse he actually smiled and his face was transformed. 'Don't worry Signora,' said the man they called Manodorata, 'it won't kill you.'

CHAPTER 8

Amaria Wakes

When Selvaggio opened his eyes at last, he could see nothing but wood.

At first he could not move his eyes. The wood was an inch from the end of his nose. Smooth, worn, polished with age. He could look neither left nor right for some moments so stared straight ahead, blinking. He must be in his coffin. He must be dead.

He did not expect death to feel like this. If he was dead, then why could he still feel? Why did his chest and stomach sting with raw pain? He tried to move; could not. Better to stay still, and look at his casket. Rest. He followed the grain of the wood with his eyes, flowing, beautiful lines, like a landscape in microcosm. Gentle inclines and long plains of a peaceful, fruitful land. Or the waves of a calm sea, rising and falling in unison, now and again punctuated with dark fishes that were the knots. He felt the grain draw him in, embrace him. He became one with the landscape. Dust to dust. Wood was *beautiful*, why had he not seen it before?

Why could he only see it now, now that he was in his coffin, perhaps interred in the earth?

No, he could not be below ground, for there was light coming from somewhere, light that hurt his eyes. And somewhere too, over the landscape or across the sea, somewhere an angry fly buzzed and bounced at a casement, trying to get out, trapped too.

With a Herculean effort Selvaggio moved his eyes from left to right as his head beat time. Despite the pounding, searing headache he could now find his bearings: he was lying on a long table, padded with straw. The straw tickled his nose – here his bedding was golden, here it was black with blood. His blood. He was lying on his side, with his face inches from the wall; the wood he had first seen was the mainstay of the wattle, criss-crossed around the plaster panels of the daub. He tried to call out, to bring someone to aid him, but no sound came from his desert-dry mouth. The sweat of panic rimed his upper lip and chilled his forehead. He could not remember anything, not one thing; not how he came here or what had happened to him, nor where he was from or anything about his life. There was nothing in his memory before the wood that he saw as he woke – he was like a schoolboy's slate wiped clean; a babe newborn. He knew his impression of the coffin was an error; the wood was a beginning for him, not an end. In the beginning was the wood. And yet, there must have been something before this; just as the wood that made the wall had once been a tree that stood in a forest, in another life and another place. How could he know of seas and fishes and coffins and such, if he did not know his own name? How did he know the words for everything that he saw and felt, but could not speak one single syllable? He knew everything, yet he knew nothing. He saw all, but could say naught. The vessel of his conciousness, swelling at every moment like new-blown glass, was already brim-full with questions. How came he here? Why was he lying down? Why was he on his side? Selvaggio rolled onto his back and learned the reason; he was immediately pierced through with a million blades as if he had rolled onto a waiting bed of nails. He rolled again, in agony, away from the pain like a speared fish, and crashed to the floor. The sound brought Amaria running.

When Amaria laid her hand on Selvaggio's forehead, she knew he was out of danger. For a day and a night he had slept on their board on his bedding of straw; they had shoved the table against the wall to lessen the chance that he would roll off if he woke. And he did not wake; for as long as the bells of the Duomo chimed their nine times round. He did not feel his dressings being changed or the sting of the bitter salve that Nonna rubbed into his wounds. He did not hear Amaria make the *polenta* on the fire, no, not even when she dropped the pot. But when she placed her fingers on his head, there on the floor where he lay, she knew he would live.

Amaria told herself she wished to check for his fever. But in truth she wanted to feel his warm skin again. When his eyes looked into hers she started guiltily, then smiled. His mouth did not smile back, but his eyes did. She ran to fetch Nonna.

Nonna was in the yard shooing the chickens with her stick. She grunted at the news that the wildman was awake, but secretly her heart unfurled within her. Since that first brief waking when they had brought him home, she had not allowed herself to feel, in case he should sink and be taken from them. She had kept herself still and close. But now she could hardly feign her indifference as she hastened inside behind her chattering granddaughter. She found the young man already raised on one elbow and the two women heaved an arm each to help him back on to his makeshift bed. Amaria rolled a sheepskin behind his shoulders for support, and lifted the polenta from the hearth, talking all the time.

'Nonna, hold his head. Can you hold your head still? Can you open your mouth? Take a little of this. 'Twill do you good. Nonna, wipe his chin. 'Tis only polenta, but I made it thin with a little goats milk and olive oil and good parmesan. We have a little block of *reggiano* wrapped in canvas in the pantry, just for special occasions like *Pasqua* and Yule, and Saint Ambrose's day. He's our Saint you know – I mean Lombardy's Saint; Milan's Saint. And *my* special Saint, because I share his name. But the parmesan – I thought it might do you good. After all, when something tastes so good, it must be good *for* you, mustn't it? Tonight I think we will kill a chicken. Nonna, we may, mayn't we? I think it would benefit you, for our chickens are the best in Pavia, are they not, Nonna?'

'Nothing like.'

'Anyway, I think a good chicken broth will have you on your feet. And perhaps tomorrow I will find some roots in the forest, perhaps some rosemary for the polenta. Rosemary is a great healing herb, and I know a little of such things. Nonna always says I am quite the *medico*, she has so great an opinion of my physick.'

'I never said anything of the sort.'

'Or you ask Silvana. She's my friend, you know. She had the gripes so terrible last spring that we thought she would die from them – yet my sage water saved her from certain doom. 'Tis true that her skin was something of the yellow hue for a sevennight, and her tongue sweled up somewhat, but afterward she felt better than new.'

''Tis only a pity that her tongue was not disabled forever. That would have been a cure indeed, for she talks only second to you, Amaria.'

'By all the Saints, I forgot to tell you my name! We have not become properly acquainted. I am Amaria Sant'Ambrogio, and this is my Nonna. We found you in the woods. You were terrible bad, but we looked after you and now you look a great deal better. Don't you think him improved, Nonna?'

'There's some danger yet, I'll be bound.'

'Can you tell us your name? Are you Milanese?'

Nonna had heard enough. 'Blessed Saint Ambrose, child! How can the fellow speak with a spoon of polenta in his mouth and your tattle in his ears? Give him some pause – space and silence will do more than all of your prompting.'

Both women looked eagerly at their patient. He had taken a little food, and watched them closely throughout their exchange. His eyes looked amused. It seemed he understood, and he opened his lips a little to speak, but not a sound came. He looked distressed to be mute, and began to exert himself, but Nonna said, 'Do not trouble. 'Tis full early to think of such things. When you are fed and recovered we will see what comes forth.'

Amaria was unable to remain quiet for long. She looked him in the eyes, and spoke more slowly. 'But you are able to understand us?' she asked. 'You speak Milanese? Can you nod?'

Selvaggio nodded weakly, and seemed to fall back a little on the sheepskin. Nonna saw it all. 'Leave him, child. Go strangle one of the birds – the red hen will do. This boy may rest awhile and we will make a broth for later.'

When Amaria had gone Nonna smoothed the wildman's coverlet as he slept again. She too would do everything in her power to heal him but now she knew he would live she was in no hurry. For as he grew well, and spoke, there must be questions, and answers, and plans and schemes; and he must, at last, go home to wherever he belonged. Nonna listened for Amaria's receding footsteps then reached for Selvaggio's hand. She folded his calloused swordhand in her knarled old fingers and held it tight as she had held Filippo's before he left for battle. Nonna knew little of the wildman but she did know this – that she did not want him to go.

Amaria was happy to leave – her heart was full, and she was determined to make her Selvaggio better. She began to chase the red hen around the yard, holding her skirts high, whooping and hollering like a child. Then she stopped suddenly. She should not shout: she might disturb Selvaggio's rest. She dropped her skirts to a seemly level and slowed her steps. She smoothed her hair and tucked stray strands behind her ears. She had a job to do; a responsibility, and she must be equal to it. Amaria had never had anyone to look after before; she had been Nonna's project, her dearest granddaughter, and had been tended and nurtured like a young flower. Despite their poverty Nonna had seen that Amaria never wanted for the things that she needed; always giving her the best cuts of the little meat they had, or the heel of the bread, or the last of the wine. Nonna had even tried to give up her own bed for Amaria when the girl grew too big for her truckle; their one upstairs room was a little dorter up a winding stair, warmed by the fire below – but this Amaria had refused, respecting her grandmother's age and need for the comfort of the bed, and she curled up in a sheepskin on the floor.

Amaria had grown, an only child, without ever having to concede to a demanding sibling, or shift for herself in any way. She had never been responsible for tending anything more worthy than these chickens that now pecked and scratched at her feet. She had made children of them, they had been her dolls in a house too poor for toys. She had always turned her back when Nonna strangled one for the pot. And now the red hen, her particular pet, must go; and *she* must dispatch it. Without fuss, she cornered the witless, unsuspecting bird and caught it in her skirts. Nonna had never asked her to kill one of the birds before, but today was different; there was someone else in need, and Nonna needed Amaria to rise to the occasion. And she would. She took the red hen in her two hands and cracked its neck.

On the way back into the house with the warm bird dangling from her hands, she held her head a little higher. In those short moments in the yard she had grown up. Nonna had looked after her. Well she, Amaria Sant'Ambrogio, would look after Selvaggio.

CHAPTER 9

The Miracles of the Faithless

When Father Anselmo watched Bernardino work he felt he was witnessing a miracle. His duties in these troubled times were often heartbreaking and onerous, so when he was not offering alms to the poor, comforting the bereaved or taking funeral masses for the dead soldiers, he refreshed his spirits by watching Bernardino attack the white walls of his church and bring them to life.

The priest watched as Luini cleaned the walls down with water and vinegar as assiduously as any washerwoman. Anselmo was there when Bernardino strode around with a rope and a stick, making measurements which he marked directly on the walls. He was there when Bernardino mixed his base plaster with chalk and tempera of egg. He was there when the first of the miracles began – the drawing of the cartoons with broad strokes of charcoal – from the black sweeping lines sprung wondrous monochrome depiction of Saints and sinners, angels and demons, apostles and her-etics. And at length, as the colours began to be added, what marvels did Anselmo behold then! He watched as Bernardino first laid down his shadows with pure colour laid on thick. Such strong reds, such blues, such greens and golds that Anselmo had not known existed in God's spectrum! Bernardino made his paints himself as da Vinci had taught him, using the fruits of nature, but surely nature had never seen colours this vivid? Even the brightest flower or the gaudiest parrot would fade beneath the work of Bernardino! And after, for the definition, the lights of the same colour were thinly used and mixed with a little white. Then, what tender, muted tones of pure pastel appeared: mild blues of a summer sky, the faint blush of a rose and the lambent yellow of an egg yolk. Never had Anselmo seen such scenes, so carefully finished, so warm in colour. Such wonders Bernardino painted, as he balanced precariously on a rickety scaffold of planks and ropes, his brushes and palettes hanging about him on an ingenious system of belts and straps. Bernardino worked in just a shirt and hose, the shirt soon becoming as multi-coloured as stained glass as Bernardino wiped his fingers impatiently on its fabric. On warm days he would yank the shirt impatiently from his body when he grew hot from his work. At such times his very flesh assumed these tribal markings, his muscles giving them animation as if he wore the feathers of a bird of paradise.

When mass was taken each day Bernardino fidgeted impatiently at the back of the church while the congregation gawped at the half-finished works that were appearing. Luini never took part in such observances, never uttered a response or knelt in prayer; he was merely anxious for the ritual to be over so that he could carry on. It was a source of great wonder to Anselmo that Luini could depict these scenes of such holiness, and give his figures faces of such sweetness with such an intense fervour of devotion, without having any belief himself. In fact his notions were, to be charitable, classical; and to be harsh, pagan.

Anselmo sat with Luini so often as he worked, and they conversed so much that the priest began to believe that he might be able to bring some small influence to bear upon his new friend. He felt drawn to the man – so talented yet so lost, a creature of God yet a stranger to Him. He wanted, in short, to save Bernardino's soul, and to give Bernardino, through his teachings, some understanding of the divinity of man and his work. In this he was destined to be completely disappointed.

'Bernardino, Saint Jerome held it that the painterly arts are the most divine of all, in that they draw the eyes of the faithful up towards God.'

Bernardino smiled and carried on painting. He knew the game well by now, and knew how he must answer. Anselmo would try to guide Luini, and Luini would attempt to shock Anselmo, and both would fail utterly. 'In ancient Rome, Caesar's painters used to capture the essence of the orgy for his friezes by having slaves copulate in front of them.'

Anselmo tried again. 'In the Vatican, there is a painting of the Virgin which is imbued with such divinity that she weeps real tears for the sins of man. This is just one example of how a talent such as yours can transform the lives of the faithful, if such works are painted with a Godly heart.'

'The ancient Mayan peoples used to wall up live virgins in the foundations of their temples. Plenty of tears shed that day.'

'In Constantinople there is a depiction of the Marriage at Cana which flows with real wine. It was painted by a monk who attributes the miracle to his own scourging and penitent prayers.'

Bernardino turned around on his plank which wobbled precariously. He stuck his brush behind his ear and drank from a skin of water at his waist. He looked down fondly at the rotund priest who had kept him company these many days and hours. 'Are you saying, *padre*, that if I were to become devout, my painting would be better?'

Anselmo sat on the chancel steps, and his tonsured circle disappeared as he raised his head to his friend where he hung suspended above. 'Truly, my son, you are prodigiously talented. But it is your own soul I fear for. And perhaps there may be *some* improvement even in *your* work, for only God creates perfection.'

'Rubbish. My work is already perfect. You're wasting your time,' countered Bernardino shortly. 'Painting is closer to science than religion. A painter without perspective is a Doctor without grammar. I see in measurements and equations; I need no spiritual crutch. I find comfort in a good wine and heaven in the arms of a bad woman.' He smacked his lips with relish. 'Is that the purpose of these catechisms? To convert me?'

Anselmo smiled. 'Why else would I come? 'Tis not for your company, that is sure.'

Bernardino turned back to the figure of Saint Agatha. 'I assume that you were here to stare at the female form, as is the manner of the scurrilous priest. But you will be cheated – tomorrow Saint Agatha will be robed and there will be no more meat for your licentiousness.'

Anselmo shook his head. He could never confide in Bernardino that, in his opinion, the male form held a great deal more charm than the female. But for him, such comparisons were merely aesthetic, barred as he was by his orders from any pleasures of the flesh. He was happy in his celibate state, but he knew Bernardino was not. Such musings put him in mind of Simonetta di Saronno, and her troubling absence from mass. He hoped it was nothing to do with Bernardino's impropriety on her last visit. Perhaps he should travel to the Villa Castello, and hear her confession at home if she chose to give it.

Bernardino noted the silence. 'What, no more scripture for today? Am I released from the schoolroom?'

Anselmo had no wish to reawaken Luini's interest in

the widow by admitting where his thoughts tended, so he cast around for something to say. 'I was merely admiring the work,' he said. Then his eye was caught by a vast space in the presbytery of the *Cappella Maggiore* – virgin white and untouched by charcoal. Not a mark was there – not the nails and strings that Bernardino placed in the wall for guidance, not the charcoal cartoons. Nothing. 'What is that space meant for, Bernardino? Have you run out of materials? For I am instructed by the Cardinal to advance you monies should you need them.'

Bernardino jumped down from his perch, wiping his fingers on his chest, turning the hairs that grew there vermilion. He stared at the void beside the priest. 'No, that's the space for the Adoration of the Magi.'

'And you have no wish to begin it yet?'

'The Virgin is central to the piece. At the birth of her son, she is at her most glorious and most beautiful. So I'm waiting for Simonetta.' Bernardino stared at the wall, as if he could already see the greatness that would one day be there.

Anselmo sighed, and when he spoke it was in measured tones as if to a child. '*Signora* di Saronno will not model for you. She has not been near this place since you insulted her last.'

'That's because she's in love with me.'

The priest snorted with derision. 'You certainly take a good deal upon yourself. You inflate your own charms and insult that lady and the memory of her husband. I advise you to put her out of your mind.'

Bernardino began to clean his hands on a rag. He favoured Anselmo with his wolf's grin. 'She could certainly inflate my charms. She'll be back. And she'll model for me. You'll see.'

At that very moment the great doors at the head of the nave swung open and the lady herself entered. She was wearing a man's weeds and her hair curled above her shoulders. She was sorely changed but her beauty was undimmed. She resembled an avenging angel as she strode toward them.

Simonetta's hauteur was an illusion. She held her chin high to give her courage. She kept her eyes on the two widely different men who awaited her. One, portly, and diminutive with a kindly face that held a great deal of surprise. And the other, slim, saturnine, wearing – Saints preserve us – no shirt, painted like a savage and showing no surprise at all on the face she could not forget. She addressed the latter with a simple, rehearsed question. 'How much?'

CHAPTER 10

Five Senses and Two Dimensions

Simonetta sat as still as she could. She was practiced in the art, for all of those days and nights she had spent at her window grieving for Lorenzo. Well, now she may think of him at her leisure for hours at a time, with the comfort of being paid for the privilege. But she did not think of Lorenzo, much as she wished to. Now, against her will, she thought of another.

It seemed that her past had done with her. Her life had carried on, much as she might wish it had not. She was living and breathing in a world of four elements. She had the use of her five senses, and she employed all of them in her time at the church of the miracles. She felt the cold of the church as the blue cloth wrapped around her offered little comfort against the winter. She could smell the oil of the paints and the woodsmoke of the brazier that the kindly priest had placed near. She could feel the stone beneath her feet and legs, leeching the warmth from her flesh to its freezing blocks. She could taste the familiar bitter tang of perpetual hunger on her tongue. But what she saw over-whelmed all, and her other senses retreated.

How incredible was his work, this loutish, insolent man? How divine his talent, how angelic, how Godlike? How could a man, any man, not just one such as he, create such things? Lambent Saints with their sufferings writ large, angels with wings that seemed to fully support their weight, so tenderly was each filament of each feather described. Simonetta could not believe that she too was to be transformed, transcended into such an expression, turned from three dimensions into two, immortalized in such colour and form. An apotheosis indeed.

And yet, it was the human, not the Holy that assailed her sight. Despite the marvels that surrounded her, why did her eye return to their creator? Why, with all that there was to occupy her sight, could she not turn her eyes from his face? He worked with a passion, quickly and accurately, scrutinising her face and form with eyes that seemed not to truly see her. What calculations and comparisons took place in that quick brain, what mathematical equations, that he might hold out his brush to her nose, mark off a distance with his thumb, and then have it appear on the white wall? And yet it was no science that he practiced, but an art of the highest form. She could not but admire the work, as much as she hated the man. As he painted her form, she scrutinised his. Tall, but somewhat shorter than Lorenzo, his height was disquietingly similar to her own, so that when they were facing, their eyes were at a level. Those eyes, strange silver like a wolf's, raised the hairs on her neck with a prickle of danger. They were alive, intelligent and rapacious. His gaze was never still, it rested nowhere. It looked for ever but never saw. He calculated, and set down. He thought but he did not feel. So believed Simonetta. But she was wrong.

Bernardino looked at Simonetta and knew he had been born to paint her. There were no false starts, no hesitations or erasures. He could not take his eyes from her. Her figure, the moulding of her shoulders, the soft muscling of the arms, the peerless face. The length of the leg and the arched feet, and the soft swelling of her breasts beneath the blue cloak, all bewitched him. Even her hair had retained its beauty – the shortness of it now curled and framed her face as her long braids had never done. She was perfection. But yet not so: for the Creator had given her those hands, those hands of such pleasing asymmetry. *Those hands*: wrong but yet right, freakish yet more beautiful than any other woman's. For the artist, this joke of the Creator, this token imperfection, meant that when the fingers were parted like callipers to cartograph a map they appeared still the same length. Such faults did the Arabs weave into their rugs or their Moorish patterns for the very reasons that, as Anselmo had said, only God should create perfection. But if God, or Allah, could create perfection he had decided to leave Simonetta flawed, and the faithless Bernardino gave thanks for it. He could not think of her as the Queen of Heaven; she was flesh and blood to him. Despite her ethereal manner. For the first time he looked at a woman and truly *saw* her, not as an empirical model of beauty but as a living breathing woman. Her husband was dead but she *lived*. And now Bernardino did too.

'What do you mean, how much?' Bernardino had taken the offensive, even though he knew full well why Simonetta had come, and had expected her long.

'I mean I'll do it. You said you'd pay. Well now I need money. So how much?'

Bernardino circled her, his eyes lively. She excited him, and he was determined to bait her in order to see the fire in her eyes. 'Well, the price may have reduced somewhat. You are wearing – how would I describe it? – a man's hunting outfit. And you look deliciously dirty. And *God* knows what you've done to your hair.'

Simonetta held her tongue, hating him. Anselmo eventually found the use of his mouth, hanging as it was in an 'O' of surprise. 'Signora di Saronno! I rejoice to see you here! I have been troubled by your absence. But is all well with you? These weeds! Your hair? Some…private penance perhaps?'

Simonetta shook her head, her hair flying about her neck, newly short in the way she could not get used to. 'Not penance father, for what have I to atone for?' she pushed the thought of Bernardino from her mind. 'Just necessity, the same necessity that brings me here. I do not look for sympathy, merely for work, for which I need to be paid.'

Bernardino stroked his chin. 'Hmmm.' Then he looked up with decision. 'Four months, three hours a week, two francs an hour.'

'*What*?' Simonetta had been accustomed to spend *three* francs on a ribbon for her shoe. And another three for the other foot.

'Take it or leave it. The Cardinal is not paying for models, be they ever so noble, so it's all coming from my own pocket.'

'Signor Luini…' put in Anselmo. 'You cannot ask this of the Signora. She must be treated according to her rank.'

'Padre, padre.' Bernardino was enjoying himself. 'Let me transact this business the only way I know. She is no longer a lady if she works for me, she is a model and I am her employer. I am her superior. And as such I may set such rates, which are more than fair. But, that said, I am not a monster; the Signora may increase her wages if she agrees to…undertake services over and above her modelling.'

Simonetta closed her eyes, and the mild Anselmo erupted. 'Signor Luini! You will respect this lady as is her due, or leave this church. Signora di Saronno is a noblewoman, she is a widow and above all, this is the house of God.'

'Oh, alright. Three francs, then.'

'That is not the point. Signora,' Anselmo approached Simonetta. 'You do not have to do this. Times are terribly hard, but perhaps I could offer you alms…'

She shook her head. 'No father. I have a house, I am clothed, and I have enough to eat. There are those that are more needful than I; save your alms for them. I can do this work, and however this man treats me I must bear it as best I can. God tests us in many ways. It seemes that these past months and these future ones, are to be my test.'

Bernardino scratched his head. A devout one. This was going to be harder than he thought. He turned down the nave walking quickly, and motioned for her to follow him. Anselmo, feeling that a chaperone was needed, followed behind. When they reached the apse Bernardino tossed her a voluminous blue cape. 'Get your clothes off,' he commanded without ceremony. 'Wrap yourself in that. Bare feet too if you please.'

Simonetta held the cape as if it burned her. 'But it's not seemly. And I'll freeze.'

'Stop bellyaching. I need to see the form of your flesh underneath the folds, how the material falls and drapes. I need to see the colours that the hue brings out of your skin. And I need you to stop complaining. This is *my* time now. Sit here, beneath this great space.'

'Now?'

'No time like the present.'

Anselmo sighed. 'I will bring a brazier.' He pointed his finger at Bernardino. 'One hour to begin with. No more.

And be respectful.'

Bernardino made no answer but waited for the priest go. He began to mix his palette, but watched under his lashes as Simonetta wriggled out of her clothes beneath the cover of the robe. She was perfection, and the blue colour made her eyes sing and brought out the rainbow in her skin; he could see every colour in her flesh like the inside of an oyster. She looked at him defiantly. He came closer till they were eye to eye.

'Now, Simonetta,' he said, 'I'm just going to arrange the cloak over you. But don't worry. We will not be fornicating today. Such things can come later.'

Simonetta made to slap his cheek, but he caught her wrist maddeningly and grinned. 'It's Signora di Saronno, you ape,' she spat. 'And if you touch me again, I'll kill you.'

Bernardino tutted as if to a child. 'Now, now, Simonetta. Don't be like that.' He pulled her close and she thought he would kiss her. He leant in till she could feel the warmth of his breath, but he merely said: 'You need the money, I need a model. Let's begin.'

The first session had passed in stony silence on Simonetta's part. Bernardino spoke only to correct the turn of her head or the placement of a hand. She made the adjustments accurately and without a word. She was the best model he had ever had. When the bells had rung for nones she dressed, took her money and walked out of the doors without a word. When she had gone Bernardino climbed wearily to the bell tower. He felt wrung out and spent in the way he only usually felt after he had been with a woman. He lit his candle and threw himself down on the straw pallet, pulling his fur over his head. He broke his bread and poured his wine, but put them aside. He leafed through the *Libricciolo* but even Leonardo's book of grotesques could not distract him tonight. In a moment he was up and at the window, watching Simonetta ride away. She vaulted onto her horse like a man, riding bareback – he suspected she had sold her saddle. What disaster, what desperation had made her seek him out again, despite what he knew she felt? He watched her kick the animal with her heels – she rode as if to escape, as if trying to outrun the Devil. He watched until she was out of sight, then pressed his head against the cool church wall and closed his eyes. What was the matter with him?

CHAPTER 11

Simonetta Crosses a Threshhold

The green almonds were ripening. The drupes dangled, their hard husks mature, beginning to split to reveal the nutmeat. They hung, waiting, on their boughs. The verdant leaves, lance shaped and serrated, shifted in the autumn breeze. A hand passed through the fruits, feeling their weight, disturbing their leaves, letting them go again to fall and swing on their branches like a ring of bells. The hand caught the light of the low sun, and glowed gold.

Manodorata turned to Simonetta. 'And this is all? No olives, no vines? No livestock?'

Simonetta shook her head. Only now did she realise how profligate Lorenzo and she had been with their wealth. They had thought only of ornament, not practicality – of what was beautiful, not useful. The trees themselves were here by happy accident – one tree had been brought home from the Holy Land by a long dead di Saronno returning from Jerusalem, and had fathered many more to supply the groaning groves where they now stood.

Manodorata dropped his golden hand to his side and shook his head. He made an incongruous picture here among the trees – for he seemed an urban creature, more at home in the filigree cloisters of his home or the black and gold of his temple. In the rural setting he became the bear warlock that all feared – his huge furs brushing the fallen leaves as he moved. The almond walks were empty, for there were no servants to tend these paths. Raffaella and Gregorio, when they heard the Jew was to visit, took themselves off to the market. They could not stay while the Devil was abroad.

Manodorata walked on for a little and then turned to face Simonetta. '*Shakad*,' he said, and before she could enquire, 'almonds.' His disparaging tone dismissed the grove with the single word.

'You know these fruits?' Simonetta registered surprise. Then cursed herself. Why should such a man be ignorant of this simple crop?

'Of course. I had not thought they would grow here in the frozen north.'

''Tis an accident of topography. Lorenzo's…my ancestors brought them back from Crusade, and this warm plain in the lee of the mountains seems to suit the bitter variety very well.'

He nodded, and she could not be sure if he had heard her or no.

'In Hebrew we call them *shakad*. The name is very expressive: it means 'to watch for', hence 'to make haste'; a fitting homily for your situation, don't you find? You have been watching for long enough. Now, it is time to make haste.'

She would not answer, discomfited by his prickly humour. So he, too, had seen her at her window; watching day after day.

He went on in softer tones, almost to himself: 'In Palestine the blossoms appear in January, herald the wakening up of Creation. Beautiful blossoms, of white and rose.'

She could see that her strange saviour had left her side and was far away in the East.

'The rod of Aaron was an Almond twig, and the fruit of the Almond decorates the golden candlestick employed in the tabernacle. The Jews still carry rods of Almond blossom to the synagogues on great festivals.'

Simonetta could think of nothing to say, desperate as she was not to betray her utter ignorance of such rites. Almost every word was strange to her; such observances incomprehensible. But Manodorata moved on, into a more business-like mode.

'And do you harvest these *almonds*? Are they of any use?'

Simonetta shrugged. 'The men and maids used to pick them each autumn and store them in the cellar where we kept our treasure,' she smiled. 'There's an old story that, years ago, two servants from this very house fell in love during the almond harvest. Orsolina and Giuseppe were their names. They picked the nuts and made some sweet biscuits, called *amaretti*, as a gift to honour the Cardinal of Milan, and gave them to him in the sanctuary church in Saronno, in order that he might bless their union.' Her smile faded as she thought of her wedding in that very place – a joyful union now turned to dust. She looked up at Manodorata to see if he had read her thoughts, but he wore a faraway expression and a wry smile.

'Yes, well, no-one is likely to make sweetmeats for the *current* Cardinal, that's certain.'

'What do you mean?'

Manodorata recollected himself. 'Nothing. I spoke out of turn. Please continue with your instruction.'

She turned her thoughts strictly back to the matter in hand. 'Almonds can be pickled, or used to flavour meat and pastries. The English make a delicacy called Marchpane. Or they can even be eaten alone.'

'And are they nourishing? Do they have a goodly taste or medicinal properties?'

Simonetta reached up and plucked one of the almonds. Expertly she pulled the green casing back with her hunting knife and proffered it to Manodorata. 'Try for yourself, Signore.'

Manodorata looked on the nut for some heartbeats before he reached for it with his fleshy hand. He placed it in his mouth and chewed on it for a while, then, as his face changed, he drew out a silken kerchief and delicately spat the nut into it. 'Jacob's bones! It tastes of wood.'

Simonetta smiled. 'So I thought too when I tasted one at first. But they have a sweetness and texture which can be quite pleasing.' Manodorata drew on his glove with his teeth. He sniffed fastidiously, as if doubting the charms of this delicacy. 'Take me to the house,' he said in commanding tones. 'I wish to look at your accounts and maps.'

Simonetta looked down. She had promised Raffaella that she would meet the Jew in the gardens and not let him cross the threshold lest the house become accursed. She had made the assurance to keep the peace rather than to give credence to her maid's superstitions, but was in the habit of keeping her word. She attempted to change the subject rather than anger her guest. 'Are these trees and their fruits truly useless then?'

'It would seem so,' replied Manodorata, 'but there is good acreage here. If we clear this land and plant olives there may be money to be made. Grapes will take too long to answer, for there needs to be many years of growth before a return can be expected. This timber seems sound though – it can be sold for firewood, or for the machines of the war, which seems to have abated for now, but will return soon like the turn of a coin.'

Simonetta looked sadly at the doomed trees. She reached out her long fingers and caressed the bark of the nearest one. It shivered a little under her touch and wept tears of dew onto her hand. She would be sorry to see them fall under the axe, as they were so woven into Castello's heritage. They seemed a part of the di Saronno name – even the family arms featured three almonds. And then she remembered. Such a pennant would Lorenzo had worn when he died. The pain made her grasp the trunk till the bark hurt her fingertips. *Lorenzo*. What would you say if you knew what was proposed?

When she spoke it was with a lightness of tone to belie what she felt. 'My husband once told me a tale of the Greek princess Phyllis, who fell in love with a soldier called Demophon. She was left waiting at the altar on her wedding day by her intended and Phyllis waited for years for him to return from the wars, but finally hanged herself from an almond tree.' Simonetta remembered when she too had thought that the wood of suicides might be for her also. 'In sympathy, the gods transformed Phyllis into the very bough from which she hung. When the remorseful Demophon returned, he found Phyllis as a leafless, flowerless tree. He embraced the tree and all at once it burst into bloom, demonstrating that love and faith could not be conquered by death. Even now, in the land of Greece the almond tree is a symbol of hope.'

Manodorata looked at her closely and his strange grey eyes softened. 'I perceive both a lie and a truth in this tale. Your husband will never return, but love and faith cannot be conquered by death. My people know this more than most.' He seemed lost in thought, then turned up the almond walk towards the house. 'Come, walk with me. In return for your tale I will tell you another.'

Simonetta kept pace with him, side by side as he talked.

'Far away and long ago there was a place called Masada. It was built by a King called Herod – the one who in your scriptures, sought the death of the man you call Jesus. Masada was a fortress of great strength, but also great beauty, as it was set on a mountain overlooking a land-locked ocean they call the Dead Sea. It was, for many years, a Roman garrison until it was captured by a people known as the Zealots.'

'Jews?' questioned Simonetta.

'Jews. When their city of Jerusalem fell into Roman hands, the Zealots took refuge in Masada. The Romans responded by besieging the fortress. The Zealots fought bravely but could do nothing against the might of Rome. They realized that their defeat was near. Their leader, Eleazar Ben Yair, ordered that all Zealots were to be killed. Ten men were appointed to kill the others, then one of the remaining ten was to kill the other nine and then commit suicide.'

Simonetta stopped in her tracks, shocked beyond belief. But Manodorata paced onwards and continued.

'With the fall of Masada, the state of Israel – the land we had been promised – came to an end. And ever since we have been scattered all over the world, hated and derided, yet still existing. Our death, and the deaths of our brethren through the ages, have been a testament to the enduring nature of our love and faith. For it did not end with Masada. In York, Jews were penned into Clifford's tower and burnt, every one. In Mainz, after the first crusade, our community there were driven into the city square and each Jew beheaded. In Spain, even more recently, I myself...' he stopped as if he recollected something, and changed tack. 'Well, you know what they say of my kind even here in this fair and *civilized* town.' He smiled at her wryly and she looked away, thinking of Raffaella and Gregorio.

'But *why* do they hate you so?'

Manodorata shrugged. 'Some Christians blame the Jews for the death of Christ. One such was Saint Agostino of Hippo, whose bones lie in Peter's church in Pavia.'

Simonetta nodded slowly. 'I have seen his tomb there. He is venerated as a great teacher.'

Manodorata raised his dark brows. 'Yes. He is commonly depicted with a flaming, arrow-pierced heart in his hand, symbolizing the intensity of his piety. And yet, to *my* people, he is a purveyor of great ignorance, for Christ himself was a *Jew*, and was killed by the *Romans* under Pilate, as your scripture clearly records. You might say that *your* ancestors were more culpable than *mine*. Yet the accusation has dogged us through the centuries. Here in this town I am hated for a similar charge of murder.'

Simonetta chilled, and suddenly regretted her isolation.

'Murder?' It was little more than a croak.

'I killed a man's wife.'

Simonetta spun round, searching Manodorata's face for the signs of a black jest. They were there, for the thin lips lifted again.

'My offence was nothing more than crossing the square on the same eve as her, walking widdershins, on a night when the moon was fat and full. The dame took the milk fever, sickened and died. Her husband now throws stones at my children in the street.' Simonetta tried to speak, but he went on. 'I do not seek sympathy. The burden of my tale is this: some of the earliest of my peoples – the Zealots – were besieged by the earliest of yours – the Romans. And yet, here we are. We live, we breathe. You have had a husband, and I,' the eyes softened again, 'I have a wife. And, forgive me, but you are young. It may still be that you will love again.'

'That will never be,' said Simonetta shortly, and marched a little ahead.

Manodorata smiled a little for he saw more than he said. He followed her and took her arm and turned her round to him. 'Tell me, Signora, do you pray?'

'Pray?'

'You are a Christian. Do you pray, and attend mass?'

'Yes...that is, I used to.'

'Yet now you look to classical legends for your comfort? Perhaps it would be better to look to your God?'

'*You* can say that? You who have been so persecuted by Christians through the ages? And are persecuted still?'

Manodorata shook his head. 'The offences done to me were done by man, not God. Your faith will help you if you return to it. I hold no hatred for your Christ, only for those who do ill in his name.'

Simonetta was amazed. She had never known such for-giveness, and knew well that Gregorio, Raffaella and the Jew-hating citizens of Saronno would never show such compassion or understanding of another religion. She felt that she wanted to atone for the wrongs done to this man and his people, but what could she do? He turned his gaze upon her, his grey eyes penetrating her thoughts.

'You can do much by doing little. If you treat me with civility, invite me into your house, such small steps will change worlds.' He offered her his arm as if challenging her to show her goodwill. She took it gladly as they walked to the house. Raffaella and Gregorio may have returned by now and could be watching from the windows but she cared not. As she walked through the loggia and led Man-odorata over her threshold, she felt an inner thankfulness. In a heart that felt by turns either the killing cold of the loss of Lorenzo, or the burning heat of Bernardino's gaze as he painted her, she now felt new warmth; that she had found a friend.

CHAPTER 12

Selvaggio Speaks and Amaria Sees

Amaria remembered always the first sound that Selvaggio made. He had been with them for some weeks, and had, as his health improved, appointed himself some small tasks around the house and yard that might help those that had helped him. He never uttered, but his actions spoke for a good heart as he chopped wood, tended the chickens or fed the pig. He fitted into the lives of the two women in a way so unobtrusive, yet so fitting, that they would scarcely have been able to tell of the change, yet they would miss him immeasurably if he was absent. The two of them felt it acutely if he went for water, or off to market, and left them even for a brace of hours. They watched him constantly; Nonna to see her son again, and Amaria through a fascination she could not define. They clothed him in Filippo's ancient garb, fed him and tended to his needs like a child, yet he began to look after them as they had looked after him. It seemed he could no more write than he could speak, for they had tried him with a slice of wood and a charred twig.

His only sound was that of his breathing, and sometimes as they sat by the fireside Amaria listened for the air drawing in and out of his body, like the tides of the ocean she had never seen. Always at these times he had in his damaged hands a piece of wood and Filippo's knife. He seemed fascinated by the turn of the grain, the feel of the material in his hands. He clung to the sticks and logs that he carved as if he held on to something that was fundamental, elemental; he worked with the wood so obsessively that Nonna and Amaria privily agreed that he must have had something to do with carpentry in his former life. (They did not know, then, that wood had nothing to do with his old life but had merely been his first sight in this new world of his.) He would carve awkward lumpen shapes at first, which he cast into the fire. But as the days wore on he began to develop his skills, and fashion little mannikins to delight Amaria. At the end of each evening she would hide what he had made in her skirts and keep every one; secretly populating her closet with an ever-growing wooden throng. She could watch Selvaggio for hours, and did so. She talked to him almost ceaselessly, and when he laughed, as he began to do, he was a strange sight; for his face and body convulsed as most men's do in mirth, yet no sound came.

But sound came at last. Selvaggio had taken it upon himself to stop the hole in the door where a knot had fallen out and the wind whistled through. As he hammered a new plank in place, he struck his hand and gave a cry. Amaria rushed to his side as he dropped the hammer and took the wounded hand; they looked at each other incredulously and laughed – hers musical and his silent as ever. Amaria led him to the hearthside by his wounded hand, and sat him down as she fetched the salve to stop the blood. 'Try again!' she said excitedly, 'it may be that you are able to speak to us. Try again!'

He seemed to forget the pain of his hand as he contorted his mouth and tried to replicate the cry. After a few attempts he began to make a sound, a flat, guttural 'o' like the call of a woodchuck. Amaria laughed and clapped her hands. Selvaggio rose from the chair, unable to sit still in his excitement, and danced round the room waving his hands, the untied bandage flying from one of them. Amaria whirled like a top, skirts flying, also chanting 'o o o' and it was thus that Nonna found them when she returned. When she heard the sound that Selvaggio made she was almost moved to join in, but her age and dignity prevented her – that and the small voice in her heart that whispered that it was the beginning of his going away.

Amaria Sant'Ambrogio now embarked on the task of a lifetime – that of teaching a savage to speak. All her warmth and effusion and the happy nature of her character, was given full reign and she entered into the task with patience and pleasure. Forever a talker herself, she delighted in hearing his syllables painfully and slowly develop. From 'o' it was but a short step to 'i', from thence to 'e' until all the vowels were in place. The chatterer now listened patiently for his rejoinder, she that made noise was silent while he struggled; the speaker became the listener. Nonna watched Amaria school Selvaggio, noting the girl's new maturity; she had grown indeed in the labour she had set herself; no longer the breathless, chattering adolescent, she was displaying a new quality; an almost maternal, nurturing care and attention that complemented her womanly beauty. Nonna could see how well Amaria's new poise suited her, even with the critical, fond eye of a grandmother. So Heaven only knew what havoc this new Amaria could wreak on the heart of a lost young man, a man without name or family. In Amaria he could find, at once, a mother and a lover, a passionate heart and a pair of comforting arms. She was all life and health and warmth, where he had known cold death. Nonna watched her granddaughter school Selvaggio with joy and foreboding.

Still, the old lady could not but rejoice when Selvaggio spoke his first words. She had returned from gathering wood to find the two young people bursting with suppressed excitement. They had rehearsed something for her and she sat at the hearth to watch them perform, as one who sits down to enjoy a *Commedia*. They knelt facing each other, as if about to plight their troths, and Amaria pointed to her hand.

'*Mano*,' said Selvaggio. Nonna made as if to rise from her

chair at the miracle but there was more. Amaria pointed to her heart.

'*Cuore*,' said the wildman.

Lastly, but quite distinctly, he said '*bocca*,' as Amaria pointed to her mouth. Nonna embraced them both, thanked God, and kept her counsel.

From that moment Amaria patiently taught him the names of all the parts of the body and all the things in the house, and had him repeat them over until he could perfectly express the word for olive, or cauldron, or fire. Then they went further afield. She took him to Pavia and had him name each one of the town's hundred towers. They went within the incensed gloom of the great red Duomo, and named all the Saints that glowed in the cathedral candlelight, their faithful faces shuttered and their right hands raised to heaven. There among them all was her own personal patron Saint Ambrose, who looked particularly benevolent that day, as his daughter introduced her wildman to him. They walked together down the Via Cavallotti, dodging the geese and oxen going to market, and went into the church of San Michele. Here Amaria's knowledge was defeated, for even she could not put a name to the strange half-beasts and dragon-fishes that swarmed and curled on the friezes and capitals, doing battle with humans for their souls. They crossed the *Ponte Coperto* and paused to peep into the workshops or watch the traffic of the water. As they watched the exotic, laden spiceships traverse the waters of the Ticino, Amaria wondered which of the four points of the compass Selvaggio was from. Then Amaria took Selvaggio to the woods to name the birds and the flowers and the trees and the herbs. Once they went to the place where she had found him first, the *pozzo dei mariti*, and smiled at the single girls loitering there, ostensibly to draw water. They laughed together like children as they caught young green frogs in a bottle for Nonna's famous Pavian speciality, *risotto con le rane*. Amaria felt great joy as Selvaggio spoke to her, as he began to fix his sentences together like a babe, then a child, then a young man. His tones were low and his voice had a crack to it as if his throat had been hurt by whatever had befallen him. But it was a pleasing rasp, and his accents became pure Milanese, though a hesitance and stammer remained, never to be gone.

Selvaggio would sit by the hearth talking to Amaria as she cooked their simple fare, and all three spoke together in the evenings when they shared a stew and a cup of wine by the fire. He remembered nothing of his name or his fate, or from whence he had come. Nonna questioned him closely, but try as he might he could not recall how he had received his wounds or the horrors he must have seen. Selvaggio returned, when questioned, to his metaphor of the wood that had been his first thought in his conscious state.

'Does a piece of wood know that it has once been a tree?' he asked, picking a rough hewn log from the wood-pile and turning it in his hand. 'No, it does not remember where it stood, in plain or forest, nor the winds that rocked it, the rains that soaked it; nor yet the sun that warmed it. It does not remember that it shed leaves in the winter and grew them again with the spring, many many seasons round, as the rings grew in its belly. And yet *we* know that it did live this life, and yet here, now, it is just a log. I am here, too, and once I was somewhere else, but where that was I know not. I do not even know how many summers I have seen, nor where in the world I stood when I was alive.'

Nonna nodded and began to feel safe, that Selvaggio was truly theirs and would not leave.

Amaria, in her sunny acceptance of him, had never doubted he would stay and certainly wished him to never leave her side. As he began to converse with her she found him exactly after her own heart; his tastes and preferences were hers. He loved the woods and the wells far more than the wonders of the town; he took more pleasure in the silver turn of a fish in the river than the fantastical frescoed sea-creatures of San Michele. He loved nature and cared not for art; he loved the simple act of carving wood, or the simple taste of rough wine. He gained enormous satisfaction from squeezing the fine fat vegetables in the market, choosing the best for the pot with the small coin than they had; admiring the purple sheen of a *melanzana*, blood-bright tomatoes or the pebble-green olives. These vegetables, grown from the earth which his blood had nourished, were more beauti-ful to him than the finest stained glass which pierced the gloom of the cathedral. Nothing of the higher arts could touch him – music hardly penetrated his ears; yet he loved the song of the wind on the river. The awesome bulk of the Duomo did not impress him; yet he craned his head back till his neck ached to admire the tallest trees in the forest. And Selvaggio turned his head from the female icons of San Pietro, to sneak a lingering glance at Amaria's rapt face. The Saints wore closed expressions, their eyes and their bones were dead, yet Amaria lived, and glowed more with mature beauty with each passing day. Selvaggio's heart now beat to the rhythms of the earth, no courtly measure.

The pair walked about town, more sedately now, conversing on all subjects, always in each other's company. Silvana, Amaria's intimate friend, was quite put out; her erstwhile companion and the savage were together so much that Selvaggio's tongue was not the only one which learned to wag. But the pair knew nothing of it, and were all ease and friendliness, until the day that the sister began to see the brother in a new way.

She saw him in the yard one morning, without his shirt, as he dipped to the stoup and scooped the freezing water onto his face and body. He wet his hair and she saw the shapes of the muscle under the skin, the scars newly healed, and the mapping of the veins standing on his arms like the vessels of a leaf. As if he felt her eyes upon him he lifted his dripping head and shot her through with a look, at once warm and quizzical. The winter sun turned to spring in his eyes, which were grass-green as new shoots. She stepped back into the welcoming embrace of the black shadow of the doorway, and bit her lip. Her face heated, her heart thudded in her throat, and she felt she could hardly stand.

CHAPTER 13

Elijah Abravanel Captures a Dove

'Perhaps we could speak a little, Signora, for we have passed many such sessions now in silence.'

Bernardino spoke the truth. Simonetta had been as silent as a clam for three sittings now, and he found her gaze, as beautiful and cold as that of a hawk, rather unsettling. He was past the frenetic drawing stage, and the passionate dash of the block colouring for which he required total silence – now he was adding lowlights and highlights and subtleties and it was his way with his models to talk at this stage. Now was the time to have conversations and discourse that he would never have countenanced before. Of course, when he went on to complete the face (last of all) she must be silent. He could never capture such lips or such eyes if the face was animated. But for now, a little light chat while he painted her robe would ease his hours considerably. Yet at the suggestion Simonetta turned her gaze on him, unable to hide her contempt.

Bernardino sighed and threw down his brush. He had his

answer but he would not be so easily defeated. He stretched and yawned, showing his pink tongue and white teeth.

Like a cur, she thought.

'Well, I'll go to the tavern for a spell then. If you will not speak with me, I'll seek those who will. Don't move, will you, while I'm gone?' He began to move down the nave, jingling the coins in his purse. *Her* coins. She almost rose, startled, and broke her silence.

'What do you mean – what of the sitting?'

He turned as he walked, but did not stop. He moved backwards as he talked. (Would that he would trip and brain himself, thought she.) 'I will be back later when I have had a little society. You must expect these sessions to take longer if you persist in keeping mum. Don't worry – we'll have you home by midnight.'

He had reached the doors. 'Wait!' cried Simonetta. Inwardly she fumed, but by no means would she have her torture prolonged in this way. 'We'll converse if you like,' she muttered in a low tone.

Bernadino cocked his hand behind his ear. 'What?' he bawled down the nave.

She sighed gustily and raised her voice. 'I said we'll converse if you like.'

Bernardino came back and sat down, taking up his brushes. 'Excellent.' He looked at her and raised a brow, waiting.

'What would you talk about?' said Simonetta in measured tones.

He rested his chin on his hand. 'Hmmm. 'Tis a tricky issue – for conversation must needs be stilted between such as ourselves.'

'Meaning?'

'Those who have such strong feelings for each other.'

'What can you mean?'

'I mean hatred of course. For you hate me do you not? What else could I mean?'

She had scarcely hated him more than at that moment but her manners made her desist from honesty.

He smiled. 'Perhaps we will proceed thus. You ask me a question – but it has to be interesting, mark you! – and then I will ask you one likewise. Each party must answer truthfully.'

'You are mad.'

'Am I to go to the tavern?'

'No, no. Who shall begin this peculiar catechism?'

'You may. Ladies take precedence, even mere artists' models.'

She refused to rise, and searched her brain. Her brain failed her. 'Where were you born?'

'Oh, Simonetta. So boring. I said the question must be interesting. But since you ask, in Luino on Lake Maggiore. And now, my turn. Why do you need money so?'

Simonetta looked at her hands. 'Because, my…we… have been impoverished by the wars.'

'Why do you need money so?'

'I have just told you.'

'Not so. I may keep asking till my question is answered. Why do you need money so?

Simonetta sighed with impatience. 'We had much expenditure – servants, many improvements to our holdings – entertainments befitting our rank.'

'Why do you need money so?'

This was too much. Simonetta raised her voice. 'Why does anyone need money? Because their expenditure exceeds their income, and…'

'Why do you need money so?'

'Because Lorenzo spent all of our money on the wars!' burst out Simonetta, angered to respond by his relentless probing. 'He lavished it on his destriers and his men, his liveries and weapons, and when I went to the treasure cellar to find money for our auditor it had gone. Are you satisfied?'

He saw tears in her eyes and was sorry. He had pushed her thus far because he guessed that her husband had failed her. Something in him needed to know that Lorenzo was unworthy, but he had not needed to aggrandize himself by insulting the memory of that poor dead bastard. Lorenzo di Saronno had lost his life and Simonetta too. Now Bernardino regretted the unworthy impulse that had upset her so – she had been forced to realise that the perfection death confers is an illusion, and he was sorry for it. He did not say as much, but softened his tone.

'Yes. Your turn now. And make it interesting – something that I would not expect.'

Very well. 'Have you heard of Masada?' Simonetta's head was full of the tale she had heard yesterday, and such a question he could never expect.

Luini was too suave to express surprise, damn him. 'No,' he said simply. 'My turn.' He thought hard, but she had intrigued him, and he was curious.

'Go on then. What is Masada?'

'*Where*, not what.' She enjoyed her small triumph, but her spirits sank again as she told the tale she could not put from her mind. He painted on, seemingly unmoved, as she spoke and as she finished he shrugged.

'Don't you care?' Simonetta asked incredulously.

'Is that your question? No, not really. Here's mine for you – why should I?'

'Because they were *people*. They lived and breathed and felt.'

'Too much fighting is done in the name of religion. That is why I care naught for any of it. It matters not to me.'

'What does matter to you?'

'It is not your turn. My question is: who told you such things?'

'A…Jew that I know. He is…helping me, where many Christians would not.'

Bernardino stopped painting and looked her in the eyes. 'I would not consort with Jews if I were you. They are bad people, and naught but trouble.'

'I care not for your opinion.'

He shrugged again. 'Your turn.'

'Alright, what *does* matter to you?'

'That I be left alone and allowed to paint. Nothing else is important to me.'

Simonetta snorted with angry contempt, and as the bells rang Sext, gathered her clothes and stalked away. Luini the Jew hater. Just one more reason to detest him.

Bernardino watched her go. He had deviated from the rules of the game for he had said much that was not true in their discourse. Especially his last statement. It was a downright lie. It used to be true, but no longer.

In a spirit of angry righteousness, Simonetta returned to Castello and told Manodorata what had passed. He was poring over her inventories in the denuded great hall. But he set down his quill as she talked. When she had done, she expected anger, and a few homilies on the ignorance of Christian men, but he actually smiled.

'How can such a man amuse you?' she asked, incredulous.

'Because he speaks against his heart. Let me tell you about something that happened to my son.'

★ ★ ★

'Elijah Abravanel, what have you got in your hand?' Rebecca Abravanel noted the sheepish demeanour of her oldest son. He gave a vagabond smile which softened her heart.

'I thought my name is to be Evangelista, since I was lately *christened.*'

Rebecca smiled back, though the history of that event was not pleasing to her. 'You are right – but that is the Christian name we use for you outside these walls. Inside this house you are still my Elijah. Now, show me your hand.' Rebecca went to her oldest son and made him unfurl his palm. She could not explain what she found there. A white dove; beautifully painted on the flesh, wonderfully expressed and quite finished. The dove was in full flight, but she carried in her beak an olive branch. The work was so beautiful that the feathers seemed to stir in the wind, and the silvery grey of the olive leaves seemed to catch the sun. The bird's plumage was snowy, but a close look revealed that there was a rainbow of colours making up the feathers to express the whitest of whites. And the whole was so small as to perfectly fit in a child's hand.

Rebecca knelt. She knew this was not the work of her son, nor yet Sarah the maid. Jovaphet was too little to do such work and even the boy's father, talented as he was in many respects, had no skill with the brush. 'Who did this, Elijah?'

Elijah knew he was on his last chance since breaking curfew and opted for truth. 'The painting man. The one who colours-in the church.'

* * *

Elijah knew he should not leave the house without his mother or Sarah, but he had heard the cry of the peddler and knew that if he wanted to buy the round black marble he had seen on the day of *Yom Rishon* he must go now. It was a fabled thing, this marble, made from the inky glass spewed forth by volcanoes, those fiery mountains his father told him of. Elijah took his only ducat from a secret place between the floorboards – not even his little brother Jovaphet knew where it was – and set out of the starred door.

He followed the peddler's ululating cry through the crowds, dodging the curs and the puddles of piss. At last he saw the motley of the peddler's cloak, bellied like a sail in the wind, and followed the bright fabric till it disappeared round a corner with the snap of a raggedy flag. Elijah followed eagerly into a side street. But here he met not the peddler, but much worse.

There was a crowd of Christian children, little older than he, and much more numerous. They were playing jacks on the street, and looked up at his approach. He knew that his gown and the fashion of his hair marked him out, and he began to back away almost before he knew why. But his instincts were correct. They came for him, and he started to run.

Through the streets he ran for the comfort of the door with the star, but they had thought of this and his way was blocked. He doubled back and ran till his lungs burst. The tears filling his eyes almost blinded him to their twisted features but not quite. The thudding of his heart in his ears almost deafened him to what they said of him and his father and his beloved mother, but not quite. He knew not where he went until the church loomed ahead. He knew he was not supposed to enter such places, but the gaping dark maw offered salvation and he shot through it, straight into the arms of Bernardino Luini.

Bernardino held the boy at arms length. 'What the..?'

'Please Signore,' gasped the boy, his breath burning. 'They're coming. I must hide.'

Bernardino did not hesitate, but threw Simonetta's voluminous blue cloak over the lad and settled him still on the chancel steps, to resemble a heap of cloth. No sooner was this done than the gang appeared. Even they had the respect to slow their steps and moderate their tones in the house of their God. But they were greeted not by God but by Bernardino Luini, hands on hips.

Luini fixed them with an awful eye. 'What are you doing in here? Interrupting my work, that's what. Now clear out.'

'But Signore,' said the ringleader with more bravery than he knew he had, 'we seek the Devil child. A Jew boy – he ran in here.'

Luini shook his head. 'Not here. I would have seen.'

'But he is a demon; he may have used his black arts to hide.'

'Really. I know nothing of that. But I'll tell you what I do know. I am known as the wolf, and when darkness comes I turn into a beast of the night, ravening and knawing the limbs of bad children. See…' he pointed at the darkening sky. 'Evening comes. Now *vaffanculo*.'

That did it. The ringleader's courage defeated him, and he and his cohorts ran off into the night.

Bernardino heaved the heavy doors closed and stepped softly to the chancel steps. The blue cloak was weeping. He lifted its folds and met a terrified boy, sobbing and snotty from fear and relief. His words were a jumble – something of a peddler and a round black marble and Sarah and Jovaphet and a ducat…

Bernardino took the boy in his arms without knowing what he did. 'Hush, hush.' The boy continued to sob, and Bernardino, above his head, cast about for some distraction. He had it.

'Come,' he drew the boy to his paints. 'I'll show you some magic. Hold out your hand.'

Elijah held out his hand, the palm still imprinted with the ducat he had clutched and lost as he ran. Luini smoothed the reddened place, dipped his brush and began to paint.

Elijah started to smile. 'Tickly,' he said.

Bernardino smiled too and the boy's eyes became wider

as the perfect dove appeared on his palm. 'See, she does tricks,' said Bernardino. 'If you open and close your hand, thus,' he demonstrated, 'she will fly.'

The boy manipulated his hand and beamed in pleasure as the dove seemed to flap her wings.

'Let her dry a while,' said Bernardino, 'we will be sure they are gone. What is your name?'

'Elijah. I mean…Evangelista.' Bernardino heard the difference in the names, and divined which had come first.

'And where are you from, Elijah?'

Elijah realised that his identity was known, and decided to reveal his origins. 'I live in Jews' Street. The door with the star.'

Bernardino saw it all. 'Then you better go home to your mother, Elijah.'

Elijah looked doubtfully at the sky, now a purple-black as a melanzana. 'I am not permitted to be out at night. None of us are. There is a curfew for Jews.'

Bernardino sighed. He picked up Simonetta's cloak and put it around his shoulders. It smelled of almond blossom – her scent. But now was not the time for such reflections. He picked up the boy and drew the blue cloak over them both. 'It's alright,' he said. 'I'll take you.'

They walked through the darkening streets unseen. Elijah held monkey-tight to Bernardino's neck, whispering directions. At length they reached the starred door, and Elijah said, 'Just here, Signore.'

Bernardino set him down, and knelt to hold the boy's shoulders in farewell. 'I will watch to see that you get inside. Goodbye, Elijah.'

'Goodbye, Signore. And thank you for my dove.'

''Tis nothing. But you may do something for me in return.'

'Yes, Signore?'

'You know that…phrase I used to those children?'

Elijah smiled, his small white teeth catching the moon. 'You mean *vaffanculo*, Signore.'

'The same. There is no need to tell your mother that you know such words. They are not very wholesome for children.'

'Yes, Signore.'

'Farewell then.' Bernardino knocked on the door and saw the grille slide back. He waited till he saw the boy admitted, and enfolded in the glad and angry embrace of his mother, then took his warm heart home to his cold bed.

★ ★ ★

'So you see, I smile because he speaks against his heart,' finished Manodorata. 'He is not the man that he presents to the world. He dissembles. 'Tis an art I know much about.'

'He did such?' Simonetta was incredulous.

'Yes, all this and more. There is an end to the tale – but no scorpion's sting; an ending of great sweetness.'

★   ★   ★

Elijah was playing in the courtyard of his house, for his im-
prisonment was to be total for a sevennight, in punishment.
He mourned the loss of the black marble, made of volcanic
glass, for the peddler must have moved on by now. He must
be content with his own uninteresting marbles of Venetian
glass. And he tried hard to be, as he was a good child. He
thought at first that he imagined the soft knocking at the
starred door. He fetched a stool and stood on it to slide back
the peephole, and as he did so a tiny bag plopped through
the grille. He jumped to the floor and unravelled the bag
– it was in fact an old piece of canvas tied with a leather
thong – and inside, round perfect and black as night, lay
the glass marble he had coveted. Elijah gave a yelp and was
about to cast the canvas away when writing caught his eye.
He knew Christian characters well, for he was thoroughly
schooled by his mother, so he spelled out incredulously: 'for
Elijah'. He did not need his skills to read the one rune that
was left, for it was a tiny drawing of a dove.

CHAPTER 14

Noli Me Tangere

'When will you finish?'

Bernardino did not look up from the fresco at Simonetta's question. 'Soon. I have a commission at the Certosa di Pavia. The silent monks of the Charterhouse will suit me very well after your incessant chatter.'

She smiled now where before she would have censured. She was getting used to his ways. Then she nodded, suddenly sorry at the thought of his leaving. She felt that at last they had reached a truce, and were taking some small steps towards friendship. Ever since she had learned what he had done for Manodorata's son, she had regarded him with new eyes. She saw him now as something of a boy himself, although he was much older than she. She saw through his swagger and posture – the persona he presented that was not his own, the words he spoke which he did not mean. He was as much of a presentation to the world as his work was; to Simonetta, who truly believed, she saw that the way he presented the human condition was not real. It was theatre. Mary, that great Lady she represented, had suffered the pangs of love and the pains of childbirth and the loss of a son. She could not possibly have looked, in life, as serene as she was to be painted. The Saints too, who suffered and died, did not, she was sure, do so with such poise, such acceptance, however strong their faith. Like her own faith, theirs had been tested by tribulation, and pain, and torture of the soul. Then she gave a small smile at her own arrogance — she should not compare her own small sufferings to those of the Saints. She suffered in her grief, but had not undergone the physical tortures of a Saint Lucy with her eyes torn from her head, or a Saint Agatha with her breasts cleaved from her chest.

Bernadino saw only her smile and not the macabre thoughts. He had just made the delightful discovery that Simonetta's nose wrinkled at the bridge when she smiled. It made her suddenly earthly and approachable; less limpid and moon-distant. He suddenly felt ridiculously happy and returned her smile with one equally brilliant. 'Don't tell me you wish to quit the place?' he teased. 'Don't tell me you are not enjoying your sittings here?' His voice was heavy with irony.

'Of course, it is a great honour to be painted as the Virgin…' she began.

'Don't tell me you believe in all this,' Bernardino interrupted. His dismissive wave took in the whole series of emerging frescoes — the Marriage of the Virgin, the Adoration of the Magi, Christ's Presentation in the Temple; epi-sodes in a life in which he did not believe.

Her gaze was straight. 'Of course I do. It is *lapalissiano*.' The word escaped her before she could catch herself, and her heart sank that she should have used it. For *lapalissiano* meaning 'obviously true', was a new word in the Lombard language, and it took its letters from the name of Maréchal Lapalisse, Lorenzo's General. He was honourable and true – and dead like Lorenzo. She spoke rapidly to cover herself, 'Don't you?'

'No. Not one single syllable or scripture.'

'Why not?' she challenged.

He turned his back and began to paint with furious con-centration the diaphanous, heavenly glow of her blue cloak. Amid the tempest of his brushstrokes, the cerulean blue reminded him, and took him back, all the way back. 'When I was little I lived on the lakeshore of Lake Maggiore. My father was a fisherman, and went out with the boats every day. It's a big lake. Very blue and stretches as far as the eye can see. To a small boy it seemed enormous. I thought it was the sea. I used to go down there on summer days and sit on the shore.' Bernardino let his brush hand fall to his side as he thought of his young self. 'I used to think of all the lands that lay beyond this great ocean – all the sights there were to see in the world, all the alien beasts and for-eign landscapes. I could feel the pebbles hard under my legs, but I didn't mind – I used to get lost in the blue. When I squinted against the sun the lake became the sky and the sky became the lake – they met at the horizon and were the very same blue. That blue – I've never been able to paint it.' He turned then and looked at her eyes – the same blue was there, regarding him, but he did not say as much. He went on: 'I used to watch the water lapping at my feet. In and out, as it washed over the pebbles. I asked my mother that night, why the water behaved like that.' He drew in a lungful of breath against the pain. And released it as he spoke. 'My mother had little time for me. She was always preoccupied with my uncles – I had so many uncles – they used to come over every afternoon when my father was out for the afternoon catch. My mother always told me not to mention to my father that they had been to the house. Said there'd been a family quarrel.' Bernardino looked up briefly and his mouth twisted into a smile that was not a smile. 'So many uncles, and none of them looked like my father.' He turned abruptly back to his work, and carried on his tale in a tumble of words, before Simonetta could interject. 'My mother told me that angels sat on the shore and breathed in and out, in and out, and their breath drew the waters in and caused the tides. I asked her why *we* couldn't see the angels, and she said that it was because we were sinful. One of my uncles was there and he laughed when she said that; he said she was quite right and he kissed her shoulder. I didn't like the way he laughed so I went down to the lake again to wait for my father.' Bernardino unconsciously clenched his brush. 'All afternoon I tried to be a good boy and think good thoughts so I could see the angels. I was still there when my father came off the boats. He asked me what I was doing and I told him I was trying to see the angels that caused the tides with their breath. He sighed and sat beside me. "Bernardino," he said, "there are no angels on the shore." I was hot by now, and tired, and my head ached from the sun and concentrating all afternoon to try and see the angels. What he said made me want to cry so I began to shout. "There *are* angels, there *are*!" I yelled. "Who told you such things?" asked my father. I lost my head, and forgot what my mother had told me. "Mother!" I yelled. "And my uncle." My father's face froze. "Which uncle?" he asked quietly. All of a sudden I remembered the family quarrel, but I had gone too far to turn back. "I don't know which one," I said. "Lots of them come to the house. It was the one that was there today." After that my father stood up and looked at the water for a long time as the tide lapped the shore. He turned round and his eyes were wet. "Bernardino," he said, "your mother is a liar. She always has been." He dipped his hand in the water, and came towards me. He pushed his finger into my mouth, quite hard. "Taste," he commanded. "The water is sweet, not salt," he said. "This is not the sea, Bernardino. There are no tides here, and no angels. And I have no brothers." He took his finger out of my mouth and touched my shoulder, once, tenderly, before he walked away. "It's just a lake, Bernardino," he said. "Just a lake."'

Simonetta waited, hardly breathing. Bernardino passed a hand over his eyes, leaving a blue streak on his brow. 'That was the last thing my father said to me. When I got back to the house, he had gone. My mother blamed me. Her drinking got worse, and my 'uncles' stopped coming to begin with, but soon they were back. I began to draw with the charcoal I made on the beach, on bits of driftwood, old sails, anything. I decided that since angels didn't exist I would invent them. Once, when I was fifteen, I drew over the whole of our wooden house with a huge charcoal fresco. Angels upon angels, cherubim, seraphim; the whole company of Heaven. My mother was furious. She yelled and cried and the 'uncle' that was there that day beat me with his belt. I waited till they were in bed then I stole his horse. I'd heard that the great master Leonardo da Vinci was in Milan working for Duke Ludovico Sforza, and I took my drawings and rode all night. I waited for a week outside da Vinci's *studiolo*, making sure he all but tripped over me every day, until he agreed to an audience. He barely glanced at my drawings, but gave me some charcoal and made me draw a hand.' Bernardino looked up at Simonetta's splayed fingers and smiled at the memory. 'He made me his apprentice that same day.'

Bernardino looked down at his own hand. He had clutched the brush so tight there were four red half moons where his nails had bitten his palm. As he watched the moons suffused with red. He looked back to the angels, his angels, that circled above his head, and blew trumpets from the pilasters. 'Leonardo didn't believe either,' Bernardino addressed the ceiling. 'He said it was perfectly possible to inspire the faith of others without feeling it ourselves. He only revered the Magdalene, as I had only revered my mother, another fallen woman. What my mother had begun, my Master finished. My faith was gone. He set a greater store by human feelings, not religious devotion.'

Simonetta found her voice at last. 'What feelings?' she asked, gently now.

Love, thought Bernardino. He remembered Leonardo's parting advice to him, that when he began to feel again he would be the better painter. And it was true. In his easy conquests, his tumbling of women and girls, virgins and matrons, he had never once emerged from the numbness of the loss of his mother. The day she had lied to him, and his father had left, he had lost his innocence – his picture of her as the ideal of all women. He had placed her on a pedestal as surely as if she had been a statue of the Madonna. But she had lied, and cried, and driven him from her house into the arms of the empty conquests he had sought but never enjoyed. All in the pursuit of that one thing, the Holy Grail of Love. He opened his mouth to say the simple syllable, the syllable that meant everything to him, and nothing, to the woman who meant more to him than she would ever know. But he found that he could not speak. His voice caught in his throat and tears threatened his eyes. Tears! He had not cried since the night he rode from the lakeshore to Milan, the tears streaming backwards and away into the night as he galloped, his face dried by the hot night wind as soon as it was wet. Now, as then, he had the same instinct. He must go, now, at once.

He put down his brushes abruptly, most uncharacteristically leaving them to dry on his palette. The Virgin's face was still a blank oval, but he could do no more today; he almost fell from his perch. As he passed Simonetta, without knowing what she did, reached out her hand to him. He turned his head away, and she heard him mumble – '*Noli me Tangere.*'

So for the second time in his life Bernardino ran from a woman he loved. He climbed the stair to his lonely tower in a terrible hurry without looking back, and it was just as well, for he would have seen a sight that would have confounded and crushed him, the very sight he had been desperate to avoid. Simonetta's lake blue eyes looked after him with an expression of unmistakeable pity.

It was not until much later in the evening that Simonetta realised what he had said to her, in that unhappy moment when she had reached out to him. *Noli me Tangere.* Of course. She reached for the family Bible that rested before her *prie-dieu* on the night table, and turned the yellowing pages till she found what she sought. '*Dicit ei Iesus: Noli me tangere, nondum enim ascendi ad Patrem meum: vade autem ad fratres meos, et dic eis: Ascendo ad Patrem meum et Patrem vestrum, Deum meum et Deum vestrum.*' There it was: the Risen

Christ's exhortation to the Magdalene, the woman he had once loved and who loved him, the first person he chose to witness his resurrection. 'Jesus saith to her: Touch me not: for I am not yet ascended to my Father. But go to my brethren and say to them: I ascend to my Father and to your Father, to my God and to your God.'

Touch me Not.

CHAPTER 15

Saint Peter of the Golden Sky

Amaria looked up at her Saint. She felt no awe or fear of this one, as she did of the others – the punctured Saint Sebastian, or Saint Bartholomew with his terrible coat of flayed flesh. No, this Saint was *her* Saint – Sant'Ambrogio, Saint Ambrose, her keeper, her father, her patron and friend. In the candlelight his eyes were dark, bovine and kind. She liked him, and she liked his image in this church of San Pietro in Ciel d'Oro.

Saint Peter of the Golden Sky.

She would repeat the name to herself, like a poem, so beautiful were the words. She thought of Saint Peter with his jangling keys living in the golden sky, and Saint Ambrose living there with him. Here too, in a stone casket with carved reliefs of his life, lay the bones of Saint Agostino of Hippo. The scenes of the tomb showed the casket being carried from Carthage by Luitprand the Longobard King, and Amaria ran her fingers over the little stone pallbearers. Their plight seemed so far away and Saint Agostino, with his pierced, flaming heart did not really interest her. He was not part of her family as Ambrose was, he did not bear her name. Agostino's bones, that had walked over the arid plains of Carthage and supported muscle, blood and organs, were less real to her than the two dimensional icon of Sant'Ambrogio. She knew little of her Saint's provenance – just that he had been a great Christian in Roman times, who spread the word of God among the pagans. It was enough to know he had once been a man just like any other. She could smile at him without being disrespectful and she did so until she thought her cheeks would crack. For this year her heart was full with thanks. She lit a candle at the foot of the Saint's image. 'Happy name day, Sant'Ambrogio,' she whispered. 'And thank you for Selvaggio.'

Amaria walked out into the square pulling her hood over her hair. She had plaited and bound it in a new way today. Gone were her loose, tangled braids which had been used to gather moss and leaves as she romped through the woods. Selvaggio had made her a wooden comb at her request and she had used it every night, smoothing her tangled mane until it shone like ebony. For her name day she had plaited and bound her locks in the Milanese fashion, placing a red ribbon round her brow and tiny rosebuds in the heavy black coils gathered at the nape of her neck. She had worn her best russet gown, and rubbed red clay paste into her already rosy lips. She had wanted to look her best for her Saint, but as she prayed in the church her conscience whispered soft as shrift that she had done all these things for Selvaggio. For it was he who had once picked a winter rose for her hair and told her how it suited her; he who had admired her russet gown when she had worn it at Michelmas, saying how he loved the colours of the earth; it was he who had said that her hair was best becoming to her worn away from her face, for then he could best admire her countenance. Despite the bitter cold Amaria felt a blush warm her cheek.

She watched her dragon's breath swirl in to the frigid air, there to meet the snowflakes coming down. It was sunset, and late to be abroad – she would go to the well with the pail she had brought for the purpose, and go home to her Nonna and…him.

It was so cold she had to break the ice of the fountain. She filled the pail and turned away, to meet her distorted image in a shiny breastplate. Her face seemed cleaved in two by the seam of the soldering. She looked up and saw the heavy features of a Swiss.

She knew the look by now – the whole town knew it. The sparkling armour, the strange twisted language that sounded like a cough, and the insolence that came with the knowledge of being the best mercenaries in the world. They were not beautiful, these men from Swisserland – they were scarred; they were young, but had faces so weathered by war that they looked old. And they were a nuisance – there had been many complaints to the *Comune* that these soldiers had molested the women of Pavia and fought with the men. They had all the frustrations of soldiers without employment, those who were trained for war but whose efforts had led to peace. They needed a battle to fight. They hated inaction, and looked for quarrels wherever they could, until they were commanded to their next frontline. They styled themselves the saviours of Pavia, for their service in the recent battle, and stayed on, bored and restless. Amaria had been bothered by them before – she knew not what they said to her, but could guess. They always performed the same pantomime with their hands to demonstrate their crude admiration for her curves. She had always had Silvana with her before...but Silvana had been dropped for Selvaggio, and Selvaggio she had not brought today. Why? Because she had wanted to thank her Saint for him, something he could never know. So today she was alone. And today there were three of the Swiss.

She looked about her – there were few citizens abroad in the cobbled square as the temperature froze and the sun was dropping. The soldiers surrounded her, talking, prodding and laughing. They knocked the pail from her hand and the water soaked her feet, turning them to ice. Before she knew what they did, she was forced to the ground, and she saw, in that instant, the snowflakes disappearing into the water she had spilled, as if by magic. From the corner of her eye she could see the few citizens that she had noted, disappear too. They would not oppose such men who wished to take the maidenhead of one poor girl. It was not worth the trouble. Amaria felt hands on the back of her head as she struggled and cried out for help that did not come. Her cheek was pushed onto the freezing cobbles and she tasted blood. Then she heard a sword being drawn – was she to be beheaded? No, worse, for the sword dropped to the ground inches from her sight and she heard the soldier undo his belt. The other two held her arms – she was powerless. She stared at the silver blade of her assailant's sword on the ground as the snow gathered there. The soldier fumbled with her skirts. Then she thought that she had turned mad with horror when she saw a familiar roughened leather shoe shove beneath the blade and kick it high in the air. She was released and raised her head, along with the three mercenaries, united in wonder as they watched the blade sing high above the tower of San Pietro into the snowy sky, and fall perfectly into the hand of Selvaggio himself. Taller than before, unbowed and with a fire in his eyes, he looked less like her dear Selvaggio than an avenging angel. Amaria watched as with one fluid stroke he slashed the throat of her assailant till the blood spewed and steamed on the cobbles. With the next thrust he forced the blade through the second man's gut, expertly finding the gap between breastplate and baldrick. With the backswing he passed the blade under his own arm and buried it into the third man, without even looking at what he did. It was all done in the blink of an eye, with silence and dispatch, and the three lay dead around Amaria. The red winter rosebuds had fallen from her hair and wreathed the scene like funereal flora. The snow fell on it all, white and red, cold and heat as the bright lifeblood ran away. Amaria stared at the butchery, and then at Selvaggio, who looked at her and then the sword, which hung now limply from his hand as if he had never held one before.

Amaria found her voice, for a moment as mute as he had been. But what came were no thanks. 'You were a soldier, then,' she said.

He was still looking at the sword as if dazed. 'For the past I cannot tell,' he said in his new, halting voice. 'But today, I am a soldier.' He looked at her directly then, with the gaze she had seen in the yard as he washed. She never knew whether the trio of deaths or eyes of her avenger caused it, but she lost consciousness and she did not know that Selvaggio caught her just as she fell to the ground.

He tipped his head back to the heavens as he held the girl in his arms, so beautiful in her name-day finery; and without knowing why he opened his mouth to let the snowflakes in. Selvaggio carried Amaria all the way home, rejoicing under the golden sky.

CHAPTER 16

The Breath of Angels

'They are miraculous.'

Father Anselmo was genuinely staggered by the frescoes. He revolved under the roof, marvelling at what he saw. There in the little transept was the Marriage of the Virgin, with the Virgin and Saint Joseph in the same brilliant lake blue – Saint Joseph placing a wedding ring on the strange right hand of Simonetta di Saronno, as her face in profile gazed at her new husband. Anselmo wondered what it must have cost her to pose for this, in the very place where she had wed her dead lord. (Uncannily, Saint Joseph, though only a humble carpenter, had something of the noble looks of Lorenzo di Saronno.) Opposite this masterpiece was another, Christ among the Doctors. Here, with characteristic arrogance, Luini had painted himself as the adult Christ, disputing with his hands spread and his face lively with argument as Anselmo had often seen him; so lifelike that it was disconcerting to stand below with his twin. There too stood Simonetta, presented as an older woman, and by some trick of perspective, larger than her son; dressed in the same vivid blue, she reached out to him with one hand while the other rested on her heart. Anselmo felt a sudden disquiet. Luini had never confided in him about his family but the perspicacious priest suddenly had a glimpse of all that Simonetta might mean to Bernardino – not just a momentary lust that could be easily slaked, but a true and deep love in which he cast her as mother, lover and wife to him. He had painted her without ornament or artifice – there were none of the time-honoured symbols of the Virgin to be seen here. She clasped no gilded lily, nor overblown rose. She was unadorned by almond blossom, the flower which denoted Mary's purity, and would have had an added layer of meaning to Luini's model. Luini must have known of all these tropes, all these symbolisms, yet he had dismissed them all in favour of a more mortal depiction. A worldy worship, in interaction with her human family. Anselmo thought suddenly of Bernardino's own name-Saint, Bernard of Clairvaux, who had revered the Virgin above all, and worshipped her with a burning passion. Discomfited, Anselmo walked thoughtfully to the presbytery of the *Cappella Maggiore*, with Luini following like a shadow. There was the Presentation of the Infant Jesus in the Temple, and there again stood Simonetta in the same cerulean blue, looking on in maternal fondness with long white hands pressed together in prayer for her beloved son. In the hills beyond the scene lay another miracle; his

own church of Santa Maria dei Miracoli had been trans-
ported from Saronno to the hills of Bethlehem, and stood,
white and delicate, amid the alien corn. And here opposite,
brightest and best of all, the Adoration of the Magi. Here
Simonetta, in that peerless blue, held in her arms the Babe
that was the morning star, as Kings came to the brightness
of his rising. All was complete and wonderful; the stable so
perfectly rendered in perspective that it seemed to arch out
of the wall, the Kings and their retinue shining with jewels
as bright as their blackamoor skin was dark, and the camels and destriers striding loftily behind the scene. And yet,
despite all this wonder, the eyes were drawn to that serene
figure in blue.

Bernardino, next to him, was still and silent; his hand
clamped to his cheek. Anselmo turned to his friend. 'Even
to one such as me, who has seen the work at every stage, it
is still a miracle.'

'Hmm.'

Anselmo glanced sideways at his friend. Silence was not
typical of Bernardino – he was usually very happy to sing
his own praises. 'Bernardino? Are you well?'

Bernardino was not sure. He certainly felt like he had
some affliction. He would have visited the apothecary if
he believed in medicine. But he had always been such a
healthy animal, so immune to illnesses and so unsympathet-
ic to those who sported them that he did not trust in the
cures of such men, any more than he believed in the power

of prayer – the cure of a higher power. But it was true he did not feel normal. Wine and food had no savour for him. And women even less. God knows there were enough pretty girls in Saronno; he saw many such looking at him while he prowled the back of the nave waiting impatiently for mass to finish so he could be at his brushes again. Any one of them would be his; he knew how his talents conferred an attractiveness on him that his looks already assured. Yet he had not sampled any of them – he had not had a woman since he came here. But Anselmo must be answered.

'I am quite well, I thank you. Who could not be, when he has produced such work?'

That was better. Anselmo, relieved, felt encouraged to ask a further question, something that had puzzled him as he peered closer. Something missing. 'Is it finished?'

'Yes, Anselmo, I thought I'd leave the Madonna without a face. A trifle modern for some tastes perhaps, but I am prepared to argue my aesthetic corner.'

Anselmo was now satisfied that his friend felt better – his ironic turn of speech had returned. The priest walked closer to the fresco and scrutinised the painting; sure enough a blank oval sat where Mary's face should be. He did not know why he had not seen it before, so forcibly did the person of the Virgin draw the eye from the scene around her. The blue of the cloak and the fall of the material, and the light which seemed to emanate from that Holy Mother, drew all toward the face, which was not there. It made a strange incongruous space – the Lady wore, it seemed, a mask such as the Venetians did, but one where there were no apertures for mouth or nose. It was vaguely unsettling.

Bernardino shuffled behind with an uncharacteristic hangdog gait. 'She will be finished today. One more session with the *Grande Signora*, the Queen of Castello, and all will be done.'

'She comes *today*?' said Anselmo, unable to mask his surprise.

'Yes.' Bernardino's eyes narrowed with enquiry. 'Why? It is…what, the twenty-fourth day of February? Is there some obscure Christian festival which I know not of? The first time baby Jesu shit in a pot?'

Anselmo looked stern at such irreverence. 'Nothing. No matter. And it is well that you have nearly done, for someone important this way comes. The Cardinal himself, on a progress to Pavia, halts his journey here tomorrow and will say mass. He wished to see the work that he commissioned. It is a great honour.'

'The Cardinal of Milan? Tomorrow?'

'Yes. I have his missive here, which his rider brought even now.' He waved the scrolled letter at Luini. 'You know His Eminence?'

'Only by repute.'

Anselmo nodded. 'He is said to be an…exacting man. Yet I think him not to be truly harsh nor cruel as it is said, but merely he is hard on himself in the service of God, and this makes him hard on others. Devotion takes us in many different ways.'

Bernardino smiled, galvanised once again. 'As long as his devotion takes the form of giving me further commissions, I care not for his methods.' He clapped his hands together and rubbed them against the cold. He suddenly had the notion that his salvation lay away from Saronno, and was suddenly impatient to be done, and to be gone. He felt, uneasily, that his malaise was somehow connected with Simonetta di Saronno. Perhaps she had bewitched him, cursed him, or some such. ''Tis settled then. I will paint her one more day. And then it will be over.' And it was not the fresco that he meant.

The truth was that he had dallied, and avoided the end of his work. And the reason was that, for the first time, he was not sure that he was equal to the task he had set himself. He was really unsure whether he could satisfactorily capture her, full-face on the wall. His other frescoes showed the Virgin in profile, oblique, with her great eyes turned from the observer. He had not attempted, yet, to translate the full force of Simonetta's incredible beauty gazing directly forward, out of the wall. And it was not because she hated him. Of late, she had become kinder towards him, and he felt himself in danger. He hardened his heart and was more caustic than ever, but he had the feeling that she was not convinced by his posturing – that she saw through him with those eyes of hers. They battled still, but he was the hard one now, and she the softer. Since he had told her of his childhood – damnable weakness! – he had more than once seen a wholly unwanted sympathy in her great eyes. Once or twice she had even laughed as she teased him, and the sound had affected him greatly. Her face descended from the heavenly to the earthly, and the humours in his body boiled as his blood in his veins rejoiced at the sound. He would be tougher today. No quarter for her charms.

He did not turn as she entered. He knew it was she, for the music of her steps walked through his dreams. He ignored the thrill he felt at her coming and threw her the robe without looking at her. 'Make yourself ready,' he snapped. 'We have much to do, for the Cardinal of Milan himself visits tomorrow, and the last face must be done.'

She did not move and he turned to her at last. She was still and looked pale, her eyes shadowed. She looked at him with defeat, not with her hawk's stare. Something was different. For some reason she was weak. He triumphed. 'Why are you standing there? I have no time to dawdle.'

'Signor Luini' – different indeed, for she had never called him this before – 'I cannot sit for you today.'

'Why not?'

'I am…indisposed.'

'Indisposed? What is that to me? I care not if you are cursed by your women's bleedings, or whether some whelp has got you with child. We speak of higher things here. This is Art. Now get ready.'

She gasped at his harshness but did not bite him back as she was used to do. Bernardino was puzzled by this new Simonetta. He did not know where he was. He had thought that he had the measure of her, but she showed him another face today. He was lost, floundering, and it made him harder still. 'Well?' He could hardly hear her reply.

'It is none of these things. Just that...it is a year to the day that my husband was lost to me.'

Bernardino clenched his fists to stem the tides of sympathy that rose within him. If he let them rise they would engulf him, and he would drown in the sorrow of her plight. He was sorry, so sorry that he had caused her pain. He would not have hurt her for the world. He turned for his brushes – he could not relent, not let her see how horrified he was by his own cruelty. If he did this he felt he would be lost – he feared the strength of what he felt. 'Sit down,' he commanded harshly, and she sat, as if vanquished once and for all.

In truth, Simonetta felt, if possible, even more sorrow this year than she did last. While Lorenzo died in battle she had been living at Castello in hope. She lived through the winter not knowing he was already dead – thinking he would come again with the spring. But the spring brought only Gregorio di Puglia to tell her that Lorenzo had been killed in February when the snow fell to lie on his body.

She found it inconceivable that he had died while she had
lived – she had even danced and supped with the serfs at
Candlemas living on her hope, while he rotted. She remembered the feastday well; she and a bevy of noble ladies
had played the game of the golden cushion, in which a
gilded pillow had been thrown and caught, for a cup of
priceless hippocras held captive by the Lord of Misrule. Simonetta had won the game, and taken the pillow prisoner,
and as she drained the cup proffered by the jester, *then*, right
then, Lorenzo's hot life-blood must have poured from him
into the frozen Lombard ground. She felt a strange irrational guilt that she had not, in some way, *known* the instant he
died. A husband was the flesh of your flesh, joined to you by
the most Holy of sacraments; surely a good and Godly wife
should know the instant that her spouse ceases to breathe?
But no, she had not. Her guilt would not relent. She must
have been a bad wife then – but here her memory would
not trick her. She saw no lapse of faith, no peccadilloes in
their past. They had been not passionate but deeply loving.
They had been unified and in one mind in all things. As a
wife she had had been obedient, dutiful, chaste. Why then
must she carry the burden of this guilt, not just the guilt that
she did not feel for Lorenzo's passing, but the nameless guilt
she had felt every day since she had looked on Bernardino
Luini's face and body and found him, despite herself, the
most pleasing male form that she had ever seen, including
her own Lorenzo. The devilish temptation of him made her

own dear Lorenzo more kind, more temperate, Godlier in her eyes. She yearned for him, and missed him every instant. This year, after the first wild storms of her grief, and the following months of emptiness, she had found a new anger and resolve engendered by her poverty. Matters of money led her to encounters with two very different men – Manodorata had become her friend, and Bernardino her enemy. Both had sustained her in different ways. Manodorata had given her succour and Bernardino had given her anger, and she was clear-sighted enough to know that she owed her life to them both in equal measure. Now, with Lorenzo one year gone, it had begun to occur that there was no end to her loss, that if he was still gone one year on, and that he would be gone the next year, and the next, till the end of her life. She could not even be angry with Luini today, no matter what he said of her. She felt stale and flat, and the wastes of the future stretched out till doomsday. She sat on the chancel steps, in her blue robe, and tears welled and spilled from her peerless eyes.

Bernardino saw it at once for he had not taken his eyes from her face. This was what he had feared. Her tears. He knew he could not resist her tears. Diamonds formed and dropped from her eyes – the eyes that drew him into a muddle of his emotions. The colour of the sky above the beloved lake of his home, Lake Maggiore; the lake and the sky, the sky and the lake; they became a blue oneness when he narrowed his eyes. The angels breathing in and out, in and out, lapping the tide which was not there. The last touch of his father's hand on his shoulder as he left Bernardino forever. His love for his mother, the last woman that had made him truly happy. He could bear it no more and went to Simonetta then. He was on the lakeshore wading through the tide of her tears, kneeling as if in supplication, taking her in his arms and kissing her hard on the mouth, feeling her arms around him and her lips opening under his. He tasted her tears – salt, not sweet – and tasted his cure. He knew at once, at last, what had ailed him; and all was made right in an instant. He had found the grail. He loved Simonetta di Saronno, and knew in that incredible moment that she loved him too.

CHAPTER 17

Gregorio Changes Simonetta's Life
Once Again

Gregorio di Puglia had been drinking again. Since the winter had begun to bite, he had abandoned his outdoor tasks and spent much of his days sitting in the kitchens of the Villa Castello watching Raffaella work. The kitchens were the only warm place in the house as the great fire burned there all day. The huge brick ovens that once roared for hours to prepare the sumptuous feasts of the house were now blackened and empty; the homes to kites and cranes that nested there, riming the blackened bricks with their frost-white leavings.

So Gregorio sat at the board while Raffaella scattered flour on the table to knead the meagre dough for the bread. Snow, it fell like snow – the snow he did not wish to remember. Gregorio drank again, deeply, from his ashen cup. There was still little to eat in the villa but Gregorio managed to make his own *grappa* using grape seeds and a primitive still he had constructed in the treasure cellar. The resulting brew was clear white, evil smelling and burned the throat, but Gregorio used it to numb his days.

Raffaella helped too – she was a handsome girl and had comforted him well this year. But today not even the sight of her breasts juddering as she kneaded the dough could comfort him. He knew why of course. It was a year ago today that he had fought side by side with his lord, and his lord had died and he had lived.

Had he but known it, Gregorio shared much with Simonetta, the mistress he knew little of. He too had felt a crushing guilt for the past year, and he too had doubted his own fidelity to Lorenzo. For could he not, by some different stance, a new action or displaced turn of the sword, have saved the man that he loved like a brother? Could he not have thrown himself in front of the salvo of lead that felled Lorenzo? In his cups he felt that he had done all he could by his lord, and became sentimental as he remembered that it was an arquebus that had taken him. But in the light of day, as his head ached in the grey dawn, his conscience pricked him, and he knew that by the rules of chivalry he should have laid down his life before Lorenzo expired. They had fought together so often, and joked together on the road many a time as their horses kept pace. They had shared their sups from the same bowl and even shared a bed in the field, rolling their mats together for warmth. There had been nothing of the great lord about Lorenzo – the two boys were the same age and they had grown together as brothers. Gregorio's father had been the squire to Lorenzo's father, and Gregorio had known Lorenzo longer than his young wife had known him. Lorenzo would admit no difference between them, and had taught Gregorio to read and write as he himself had been taught. His lady, on the other hand, had always had more of the aristocrat about her. When Lorenzo had married and brought Simonetta to Castello, Gregorio had been put out. In the rules of courtly love he knew that the love of squire and a lord was a bond that could never be broken, yet Lorenzo's devotion to the beautiful willowy maid had ruptured their partnership for a time, replacing their knightly ideal with the sweets of earthly, marital love. And yet Lorenzo had come back; soon they were at war again, and back on the road, traversing Lombardy and beyond in the name of the cause, any cause, for Lorenzo's love of warfare grew with the wealth his marriage brought. Soon the two young men were together as they always had been.

Gregorio knew Simonetta only a little. She had seemed shy and distant, but in the wake of Lorenzo's death he had found warmth in her, they had united in grief and anger and he respected her and began to like her as never before. With the object of their devotion gone, they came together, and Raffaella's love for her mistress, which had blossomed in the absence of the men, had only served to improve his thoughts of her. Simonetta had shown herself to be brave and courageous in their new circumstances, and although Gregorio could not approve her new alliance with the Jew, she did seem to have some scheme afoot to save Castello and the family name – Lorenzo's name. So today he thought well of the dame, and knew she suffered too.

In his maudlin state, to block out the snow and the blood of his memory, he made a clumsy grab for Raffaella's breasts and the comfort she knew well how to give. Raffaella, dividing the bread, slapped him away leaving a floury mark to frost his swordhand. 'Leave me be. This must be done before my Mistress returns, or else there'll be naught for the wake tonight.'

For Simonetta had planned a vigil for the evening, for the three of them to sit up with candles and pray for Lorenzo. The bread, to be made in the shape of the cross, was to remember his passing and pray for his resurrection. Gregorio grumbled. He felt the need for bedsport to warm his bones and his heart. 'Where has she gone, on such a day?'

'Where?' Raffaella wiped her hand across her brow and blew a strand of dark hair from her eyes. It settled across her forehead like a cut. Memory pricked Gregorio again – one such *he* had taken there, a cut to pucker his noble brow. 'Where do ye think she has gone? To the church, you piss-pot, to pray for her dead lord. Mayhap you should do the same.' Raffaella had no time for Gregorio today. He was testing her patience with his hangdog looks, and she tired of him. She loved him well enough but today she wished him out from under her feet.

Gregorio rose unsteadily. 'Very well,' he said. 'I'll go there too, and pray for the best man I ever knew.'

Raffaella was sorry at once. For she knew he had loved his lord indeed. 'Aye, go,' she said more softly, 'and bring our lady home safe, for it freezes outside.'

So, once again, Gregorio took the Castello path. A year had brought its differences though. Last year he had headed towards the house, and this year he headed away from it. Last year he had known full well that he was about to change Simonetta's life forever. This time he did not know. This year Gregorio di Puglia went to the church where he had stood up with Lorenzo to see him wed, to say masses for his beloved master's soul. Again he found his Lady di Saronno, not to see her weeping at a window, but on the chancel steps of her marriage church, in the passionate embrace of another man.

CHAPTER 18

The Favourite Painting of the Cardinal of Milan

Gabriel Solis de Gonzales, Bishop of Toledo and self-styled Cardinal of Milan, was a lover of art, when the casual cruelties of his calling allowed him the leisure to study it. He appreciated the composition of Fernando Gallego, the brush work of Luis Dalmau and the perspective skills of Pedro Berruguete in the cities of his homeland. And, since his arrival on the Italian peninsular, he had developed a particular fondness for the work of Paolo Uccello. But since Uccello had had the bad manners to die before the Cardinal himself was in a position to commission religious art, he had to bring to preferment the likes of Bernardino Luini. In execution Luini perhaps surpassed Uccello, even if he was less enlightened as regarded subject matter. Still, his style was certainly superior. The Cardinal amused himself with a self-important dissection of Luini's influences; the lunar tints of Bergognone's neo-Gothicism contrasted pleasingly with the full-bodied luminous realism of Foppa, with perhaps a hint of the archealogical Classicism of Bramantino?

Yes, Luini had certainly been the author of some impressive works, notably at the Abbazia in Chiaravalle, where his skills had first been brought to the Cardinal's notice. His work there made him just the man for a job that the Cardinal had in mind. It was no small task – that of bringing the faith back to a region that had sickened with *accidia*, the sin of idleness in religion.

After the expulsion of the Jews from the kingdoms of Spain, given the choice of conversion or exile, it had been natural for them to settle here, in the newly Spanish province of Milan. This second invasion troubled the Cardinal and was part of the reason why he had wanted a fresco here in the heart of it all, to promote the devotion of the Lombards. Lombardy was a melting pot, and had been ever since the 1230s when the Lombards had given sanctuary to the Cathars and the place had become a stronghold of heresy. Now, centuries later, there was a crisis in faith because of the war – after human tragedy the ignorant always questioned God – but more of a concern to the Cardinal was this influx of undesirables. An ill wind had blown them from Spain along with the army. The Cardinal covered his mouth with his ringed hands at the thought, as if to keep the miasma out. They had come here on the winds like a pestilence; they had been carried on the ships like a plague. And the Church had not stopped them. Canon law allowed them here on condition that they would lend money to Christians. The Cardinal knew not whether Bernardino

Luini was truly devout, but in point of fact the character of the artist mattered little so long as his work *inspired* devotion. His Master Leonardo was known in the court of the Sforzas, equally reputed as a visionary and a lunatick.

So, on the way to the Inaugural mass of the frescoes of the Sanctuary church of Santa Maria dei Miracoli in Saronno, the Cardinal let his mind wander to another church in Urbino, where one climbed the hill to the great doors, and entered the incensed dark. In the spicy warmth one walked the nave to the altar, stopping to genuflect before the altar. And above the altar, a wonder of wonders. The Miracle of the Profaned Host, the Cardinal's favourite painting. Uccello's depiction, with its scene of Jews burning at the stake, was so striking, so elaborately painted in its presentation of the Host's desecration that one could feel the heat of the fire and smell the scorching flesh of the Infidel. There as a young man and a foreigner, lately given preferment to the Vatican, he had gone to Urbino to look on this new masterpiece. As the colours and golds of the painting shone out of the dark, the young Cardinal Solis de Gonzales had had a truly religious experience. For in a barren, scorched landscape, under a black sky and a tree that grew stars, a Jew in a red hat and tunic and blue hose looked down in agony as the flames licked his feet. Lower in the flames, almost consumed, burned two golden-haired children dressed in black. Ten men and four horses stood and watched the conflagration with expressions as detached as that of the young

Cardinal that looked on them now, straining his neck as he raised his head to see better, get closer. He tipped his head as if drinking it in, as if swallowing the blood, the very Transubstantiated blood that the Jews sullied. If he could have mounted a ladder, a black ladder like the one in the painting, the one that led to the tree and the angel that flew above to bear witness, he would have climbed it and pressed his face against the paint in an orgy of religious and sadistic ecstasy. (Later, analysing the moment as was his way, the Cardinal wondered if in the depiction of the *auto da fe* he had been reminded of home.) Depicted above the scene of burning Jews, Duke Federigo da Montefeltro and his entourage appear in the background of the altarpiece's upper panel. The Cardinal approved of the Duke and his sense of the proper proportion of the relative challenges to the Christian way of life on the peninsular. For he placed external threats, specifically, the invasion of Ottoman Turks, below the concerns of internal adversary, the local Jews. A city purged of those elements would, in the Cardinal's view, be a Utopia indeed. This pictorialized purgation should, in his view be reflected in reality in every city and town of the peninsula, just as it was in the old country. What was symbolic should become real, and the blasphemous act of the desecration of the Host should be revenged.

He had seen the painting as a young man, and had never forgotten it. His hair and beard had silvered, his eyes grown weaker, but he could still see the predella in his mind's eye. His younger acolytes revered him as he came to resemble a painter's depiction of God, but in truth he had no goodness in him. Hatred of the Jews had consumed him, and painted his heart a darker hue. The Cardinal was no advocate of Martin Luther – the fellow had done as much harm as good in this so-called Reformation of his. But on one point at least Luther had been right – in a letter to the Cardinal's friend Reverend Spalatin of Genoa he had written:

'I have come to the conclusion that the Jews will always curse and blaspheme God and his King Christ, as all the prophets have predicted....'

But he could not bring himself to agree with the continuing sentiments;

'For they are thus given over by the wrath of God to reprobation, that they may become incorrigible, as Ecclesiastes says, for every one who is incorrigible is rendered worse rather than better by correction.'

Cardinal Solis de Gonzales believed in the correction of the incorrigible, and he meant to see it done.

As it had been done in Spain.

Such were his pleasing reflections as he entered Saronno in his litter, accompanied by his guards in their scarlet livery. He could expect no such invective in the frescoes here, but it still pleased him to see his faith reflected in fine painting, and he felt as satisfied with the work he had commissioned as if he had painted it himself. He waved his jewelled ring from the window of his litter in a limpid gesture at the citizens that lined the streets to see the spectacle it pleased him to create. Some cheered in a desultory fashion. He scanned the crowds negligently with pity and contempt. They could not resist a procession, 'twas an awesome sight in these times of penury; an almond to a parrot. He knew the Jews had settled here, but was satisfied there would be none on the streets today, as he had had it proclaimed that he wished to impose a curfew, that all Infidels were to stay indoors as he passed.

One *was* there to witness his coming, though. He stood at the back of the crowd, silent as others cheered, under the disguise of a cowl. His light grey eyes, the grey of the cold sea he had crossed to come here, looked on the litter and at the face of its occupant. He knew the Cardinal, and the Cardinal knew him. Had the Cardinal examined the watchers with real scrutiny, instead of being lost in the imagined images of his favourite painting, he might have seen the cloaked figure turn away as he passed, and the cloak parted by the wind to display a glint of gold.

CHAPTER 19

The Faceless Virgin

Simonetta's senses failed her.

She could hear the words of the mass being intoned but she barely heard what was said. She barely saw the Cardinal and his entourage as they made their jewel-encrusted progress up the nave. She could not smell the incense nor taste the moon-white Host as it was pressed to her tongue. She could not raise her eyes from the cup as she tasted the blood of Christ at the altar. She could still feel though, oh yes. She was not spared those sensations. The imprint of Bernardino's hot mouth on hers lay on her lips like the bruise of red wine. She raised her long fingers to her mouth to wipe him away, to erase the stain of treachery. She was bowed under by shame.

She had come here to pray, for her sins were great. How could she have let him kiss her – on the very steps where she had pledged her troth to Lorenzo? The remembrance that he had kissed her first was no comfort – she could not forget that her lips had opened under his, that their tongues had touched, that she had sunk into his embrace. She had held him hard and gratefully, feeling happiness that she had forgotten. Not even that – happiness which, if she was honest with herself, she knew she had never had. This realisation had made her break away at last. She had run from him then, sobbing, and would not go back. She had pushed past a figure in the doorway, but had not seen the worshipper's face, blinded as she was by tears of mortification. Bernardino had followed her but she had ridden fast, heedless of the icy paths that threatened the legs of her horse. The snow flew in her face but could not cool the burning blush of her cheeks.

Simonetta spent a long sleepless night of tears and regret, but reached a decision as dawn greyed the skies. She knew he would seek her out, and that she would not have the strength to send him away. So she must go to the church again, in the safety of numbers, to brave him one last time, and tell him that they could not be together. The notions of seeing him again and never seeing him again were equally painful. And to sit here, now, in the world of colour and holiness that he had created for the church, was torture indeed. To bear witness to his miraculous talent, and to know such a man wanted her, was almost more than she could bear. A huge reliquary had been placed before the figure of the Madonna – her figure – by the tactful Anselmo, who knew not of the incident but just that the Virgin was not finished. Behind the monstrance which held a fragment of the True Cross, sat the Queen of Heaven without a face. Anselmo thought that only three people would know of this fact, but in fact there were four. Simonetta shivered. She knew that Bernardino was at the back of the church, prowling like a cur. She could feel his eyes on her, and tears burned her throat.

He moved from one side of the apse to the other switching back and back on himself as a wolf weaves in a figure of eight. He was more than usually anxious for the mass to end. He *must* speak to her. He was consumed by impatience but also joy and anticipation. She *must* know, as he now knew, that she loved him. The kiss had told him, it had told both of them. *Now* he had found the centre of his life. His ills were healed. The discordant note that had sounded in his heart had found its true cadence and sounded a sweet chord in his soul. His head was full of poetry; his body was full of heat. He could not wait to possess her – all must give way before their love. Not for Bernardino the trouba-dour's notion of courtly love; all sighings and moanings in vain for a distant lady-love who could never be truly pos-sessed. Simonetta's distress, her scruples, her husband and her God could be nothing to them. They would live as in the old days in the old ways, when the pagans could not hear the songs of Holy choirs but only the thrumming of their blood. There was no heaven to hope for, no afterlife. Heaven was here, and when they died their bones would be dust to lie together in the earth for eternity.

He could see her now – he would know her anywhere. She sat in the crowd next to that maid of hers, her head bowed under a hood. But he recognised so well how fabric fell across her body and the angle of her head, that he knew her at once. She would not look at him, but if he could but speak to her, and hold her again, he knew all would be well.

Raffaella looked at her mistress. She did not know what ailed her, but perhaps it was the same malaise that beset Gregorio. She knew they had both felt deeply for the day of Lorenzo's death, but she had seen such fresh outpourings of grief that it were as if the event had just occurred. All of last night her lady had wept over the candles of her lord's wake, but Gregorio's response was stranger still, for he had not attended the wake at all. He had come in at dawn, stinking from the alehouse, his eyes red with tears and wine. He had given no apology to their lady, but a look of such venom that she could not have failed to see it. He had ever been a respectful squire, and Raffaella was perplexed, but she had been forced to stay her enquiries as he had fallen into a deep slumber, and she and a silent mistress had had to ready themselves for church. Raffaella supposed that the mystery would be solved after mass. She followed her lady back to their seats after the taking of the sacrament, and scanned the faithful for a shamefaced Gregorio. But he had not come. She supposed that he was still sleeping off the wine, and would not appear at mass. But she was wrong.

While all were silent in prayer in thanks for the Host, the doors opened and heads turned to see Gregorio himself staggering into the church. He weaved his way up the nave as all turned to gaze at him. Bernardino stopped in his tracks with a dreadful foreboding, for he saw here the man that had come into church last night. The man that both he and Simonetta had passed at the door, her to flee and he to chase her.

The Cardinal, straining to read his texts, continued to intone the *Ave Maria* with his eyes on the Book of Books. But as he named the Holy Virgin Gregorio began to laugh, a manic horrible sound, and the Cardinal himself stopped. He fixed the intruder with a freezing gaze and motioned to his hidden guards. They moved as one from behind the twin pillars of the rood screen and advanced to take the intruder. They took an arm apiece and pulled him to the door as Raffaella gasped in anguish. But the nave was long, and Gregorio had plenty of time to say what he wanted to say.

'The Queen of Heaven indeed. But did you know, your Eminence, that the model for the *Virgin*,' he spat the word, 'is not Mary Mother of God,' he crossed himself clumsily, 'but Mary Magdalene, the first among *whores*.' Bernardino moved then, quick as a cat. He did not know whether to strike the squire down or attempt to silence with him, but was stopped in his tracks. 'And here is her seducer,' crowed

Gregorio. 'Your genius, the great Bernardino Luini.' Gregorio had learned all that he had to of Luini in the tavern last night, and despised what he heard. His drunken invective came back to him and flowed long. 'How can a man live like this, painting pretty pictures, seducing the wives of good soldiers; a man that has never seen a battlefield or felt neither the handle of a sword nor the point as it enters his flesh. And here they hide, kissing and cooing like doves in the house of *God*. I spit on you both.' He suited the action to the words, but his thick phlegm dribbled down his contorted face, to be joined by tears. 'How could you, my Lady?' he appealed directly to Simonetta, his voice thick with sorrow and drink. She met his eyes, but looked away at once, appalled by the pain she saw there. 'You were wed here! Wed! And to a man worth a thousand of him. A man that fought and died for us all. Like Christ! Yes, like Christ himself!' Gregorio's voice grew loud again as his confused thoughts took shape, and the parallels burst in upon him like a lightning strike. 'Christ who died on the cross, and his cross now hides their shame.' With a new zeal he broke free and leapt for the reliquary. Before he could be stopped he knocked it to the ground to reveal the faceless Virgin at the heart of the Adoration of the Magi. The monstrance rolled away, the ruby panes held the fragment of wood safe within, but the crash sounded into the silence. Gregorio was quickly recaptured but shouted above the melee. 'Aye, there she sits. But she is not finished, no; for they were too busy in their bodily pleasures to think of Heaven.'

The crowd looked on, shocked by such iconoclasm. They stared at the unfinished Madonna and back at the lady of Saronno. Bernardino had stopped in his tracks, and Simonetta stood, stony and still as a pillar. Gregorio's maudlin appeal to her, his tears, had affected her more than his anger; more than the falling of the reliquary, more than the revealing of the incomplete fresco. She could not fault him; he was right, and far more loyal than she.

The squire had done at last; he slumped and sobbed, docile now as the guards recaptured him and bundled him outside. Simonetta and Bernardino were suddenly the only two standing in the church. They gazed at each other over desert wastes, parted forever now. She lowered her eyes and sank to her seat, dry eyed and utterly defeated as the hubbub around her grew. The eyes were arrowshafts, the words were barbs to her flesh and she knew she deserved every one. Bernardino stood now alone, filled with horror that the new and tender shoots of their love had suffered the killing frosts of scandal before they had had chance to grow. The world's eyes were upon them, judging them, weighing their worth with grubby fingers and finding them wanting.

The Cardinal in his ceremonial chair gazed on them both, his eyes limpid, pale and dangerous. He could not countenance what he had heard and seen; he knew only that disrespect, the heresy and licentiousness had entered God's house, and besmirched the frescoes that he had planned and paid for. Now the miraculous paintings were darkened in his eyes. He did not see the Saints or angels, just the ugly expressions of sin writ large on their faces. He looked at the pair before him and saw the same sins written there. The moment was broken as the guards re-entered, and the Cardinal spoke these words; the first that he had uttered without Latin, in Milanese so all could understand.

'Arrest him.'

CHAPTER 20

Saint Maurice and Saint Ambrose do Battle

'Will they arrest him?' Amaria's firelit face was lively with concern.

'Who? The *Comune* of Pavia arrest Selvaggio?' asked Nonna. 'Never. The Swiss have no friends here, no one will miss them. No one loves a mercenary. Their families are far away in Swisserland. The bodies will have gone, never to be found. The citizens of Pavia may be cowardly, but they are quick to clean up their affairs after the fact. All will be dispatched, swift and secret. There has been discontent brewing about the ways of the Swiss for long enow. This will serve them well.'

Selvaggio was silent as he sat before the fire, rubbing his sword hand where it had rung like a bell with the blows. Three blows, three dead, and three days had passed. Days which Selvaggio and Amaria had spent shuttered in the house, abandoning their customary walks, much to Nonna's surprise. Finally they had confided in the old lady, in an attempt to end Amaria's constant agony that each moment would bring the constables to their wooden door. The Swiss sword, witness to all, had come home with them. Selvaggio, in a gesture he did not know for his own, had sheathed it in his belt, to guard against further challenges on the road home. He would bury it later, but for now it stood in the corner of the hearth. Set into the handle, winking reproachfully in the firelight was the charm of Saint Maurice, the martyr of the Theban legion. The Swiss kept his medals close and trusted in his protection. But that day, Saint Ambrose had prevailed. In Selvaggio's head the Saints had fought and Saint Maurice had lost. Saint Ambrose had protected his own on his day, that shining girl who shared his name. Selvaggio looked at Amaria where she sat in the only chair, warming herself by the fire. Nonna had wrapped a sheepskin round her shivering granddaughter and given her a cup of broth. She was shocked beyond measure at what she had been told, but Selvaggio's rescue of Amaria warmed her so completely that she had no need of the fire. Yet Amaria's teeth still chattered like a monkey and her hands still shook till the wooden bowl clacked against her teeth. Selvaggio took both her hands in his, warming them round the bowl.

''Tis done,' he stammered. 'They are gone, and cannot hurt you.'

Amaria did not say what she feared. For though she had thrilled at his action and strength to save her, she feared that Selvaggio, her dear kind Selvaggio that would not hurt a flea, had gone too.

CHAPTER 21

The Bells of Santa Maria dei Miracoli

As Gregorio had rightly said, Bernardino was no soldier. He ran. Had he had time to reflect, he might have been amused by the ironic twist of his fate, for here he was, twenty years on, running once again from a brace of liveried guards in the cause of the virtue of a woman. But he had never felt less like laughing in his life; he had, it seemed, lost his love – he wasn't about to lose his liberty too.

His way to the church door was guarded, and so, with no clear idea why, he headed for the side door into the bell tower – his bell tower – and swarmed up the stair and the rope ladder like a ship's monkey. He knew the way well, through the darkness and the ropes and the menacing sweet whisper of the bells. He climbed at last to his chamber where he had slept these long months. He could not hear them following. They were heavier men than he, and armed, but they would find him eventually. He was a rat in a trap. Then he understood. They were not coming. The Cardinal had a much more effective way of getting him down.

Bernardino watched in soundless horror as he saw the bell ropes pull tight and the massive bells creak upwards, mocking him with their open black mouths. He covered his ears just before their great tongues fell, but still the sound hit his body like a blow fit to stop his heart. He screamed then, but could not hear himself. Desperately, as the twin giants bawled again and again he looked from the four arched windows and faced the four winds which forced him back inside with freezing gusts. He could see nothing of what lay below as the winter's breath and the unbearable song of the bells brought tears to his eyes. His ears and nose wept blood in sympathy. He knew he must get away before he ran mad, but could not climb back down into the lion's jaws. In the end he headed for the north window – for north was where Lake Maggiore lay – and plunged out and down into the night as the stars fell away.

Landed with a crunch, laid winded, but the branches of a friendly tree lay under his back and told him that his fall had been broken. He could not rise alone, but he had help. A dark figure loomed, stooped. Bernardino took the proffered hand and was hauled to his feet.

'Can you walk?' was the urgent whisper.

'Yes.'

'Run?'

'I think so.'

'Then do it. Follow me.'

Along narrowed streets and through close alleys he followed the bearlike figure. Bernardino's muscles cracked and his ribs pained him. The snow stung the leaf cuts of his face, and he could taste the blood the bells had drawn from his nose. Perhaps he ran straight into the jaws of a trap, but he cared not – anything would be better than the thugs of a merciless Cardinal.

At length they arrived at a door, a knock was given and his saviour turned to go. Bernardino's memory struck a familiar note. Once, at a different door, he had done as much for a small boy who needed him. The thought made him hold the other's arm as he made to vanish into the night. His rescuer turned back and silver eyes flashed from beneath the cowl.

'Where are we?' Bernardino mumbled through the blood.

'At the house of the priest. He is your friend I think?'

'Why do you do this?'

'Because if you help me and mine, you too shall be helped.'

With this enigmatic answer Bernardino's rescuer was gone. The door opened, and Bernardino fell through it, into the arms of Father Anselmo's tiring woman. The motherly soul clucked over him, for Bernardino was known to her through his friendship with her Master. Bernardino, dazed by events, could not answer her questions. Perhaps the fall had addled his head, for he could have sworn that the hand that had hauled him to his feet was made of gold.

CHAPTER 22

Alessandro Bentivoglio and the Monastery in Milan

Bernardino wandered round the well-appointed house, fit-fully fiddling with objects and putting them back. When he had time to think about anything but the loss of Simonetta, he wondered that Anselmo, who had ever seemed a humble and Godly man, had been granted a benefice so large that he could afford a house like this, with servants and rich furnishings. He had plenty of time to acquaint himself with the house, for Anselmo had told him that the Cardinal's men were still seeking him and it was too dangerous to venture out. The Cardinal was not a man to forget a slight, and his anger boiled vengeful and black.

It was the third day since Bernardino had escaped from the church, and his body had healed but his heart had not. For he had learned that Simonetta had exiled herself – she was shuttered in her house like a maiden that lived in the dragon-days.

He had not written her a letter, for his fist was awkward and he was no orthographer. He had painted instead, using all his skill, on a small piece of vellum which he prepared himself from lamb's skin. He had concentrated hard, for never had a picture seemed more important. He had sent Anselmo as his emissary. The priest, with his inexhaustible goodwill, had agreed to deliver the vellum while strongly deprecating the whole affair. Only when Luini had sworn that the encounter overseen by Gregorio was chaste and prompted by the truest love, did Anselmo agree to carry the missive. Bernardino waited impatiently for his return from the Villa Castello, and when the door opened he was upon the priest at once.

'Did you see her?'

'Yes.'

'And?'

Anselmo shook his head. 'She will not see you. She bids you leave her be.'

'Did you give her the picture? Surely now she must understand!'

'Bernardino. I gave her the picture. But she wishes to put an end to this, and you must respect that.'

'I must go to her myself.'

And he did. But his reward was only to see at last the great house, with its crennelations, an uncanny echo to the one he had imagined. He had seen, too, with his farsighted eyes, a figure at the window; a figure with shoulder-length red-gold hair, wearing a man's russet hunting tunic. She was there, holding a parchment in her hand. She saw him and turned away with such anguish that he was struck, as if by an arrow. He knew then, but did not wish to admit, that he was torturing her. He came away, back to the priest's house, to think on what to do next – how to reach her. He was angry and reckless in his return, and entered the town with little disguise. The place was hedged about with the Cardinal's guards, on their third day in steadfast pursuit of his person, and he felt an uncanny sense that he had been seen and denounced. The circle was closing in. Against all his expectations he reached the house safely. He challenged Anselmo by candlelight, and had the bitter fate of a candid friend – to hear what he already knew.

'You are endangering yourself by being here.'

'I care not.'

'And you are hurting the lady you claim to love by your very presence. Now say that you care not.'

Bernardino was silent. He had no wish to hurt where he loved, but he could not give her up. He felt his innards bleeding out of him like sand from an hourglass, and if he did not stem the tide he would be lost. Yet what more could be done here? He could not lay siege to her, for she was resolute, and he would be starved and broken. He could not storm her castle; could not break in and take her in his arms, much as he wished to. Anselmo detected a weakening and pushed forth, for he had a scheme to save his erstwhile friend. 'There is a great man by the name of Alessandro

Bentivoglio. He is a great patron of art, and has in his gift the decoration of a great monastery in Milan of which he is the patron. His eldest daughter has taken orders there. The foundation is in the honour of Saint Maurice.'

'Saint Maurice?'

'Saint Maurice was a martyr of the Theban legion.'

Bernardino had no patience today. 'You know I have little theology.'

Anselmo's face was lively with the expansion of the subject he loved. 'Eucherius, bishop of Lyons, specifically names his immediate source as Isaac, bishop of Geneva, who had himself learned of the story from another bishop, Theodore, identifiable as Theodore of Octodurum...'

'Quicker...'

'In essentials Saint Maurice was a Christian martyr,' Anselmo opted for brevity rather than lose his audience, 'an officer massacred along with his legion when they refused to participate in pagan sacrifices prior to battle.'

Bernardino gave a bitter humourless laugh. 'I, who have been publicly derided for *not* being a soldier, am now to glorify a military martyr. Your God has quite a sense of humour, Anselmo.'

'Still, the work would satisfy you. Think of it – an entire monastery and its attendant church. And once there, you could think on your situation with more clarity.'

'But Milan? The See of the very man who seeks my ruin? Why would I enter the lion's den?'

'Because the lion never seeks his prey at the heart of his territory. You may hide from His Eminence by concealing yourself right under his nose, in his own city.'

'Would he not visit the foundation?'

'It is not permitted, for the monastery is for women only. Though all may worship in the convent church, only the sisters may enter the cloister itself. Behind the clerestory you will be safe. The frescoes could be attributed to 'a painter of the Lombard school' until it is safe for your authorship to be revealed. You know this is oftentimes done.'

Bernardino was silent. He was being offered sanctuary. And his hand itched to be at the brush – he had never in his memory gone for so long without painting. A full day and a night had passed since he had drawn his message to Simonetta.

Anselmo, encouraged, went on. 'And Bernardino; I know of your reputation as a wolf to the fairer sex. But in San Maurizio you would be among Holy women. You must behave with propriety. This is your last refuge from justice; I cannot help you more.'

Bernardino exhaled sharply. 'Believe me, Anselmo, the sisters have never been safer from me. My heart belongs in that castle on the hill. No Holy moppet in a habit can tempt me when one such as *she* walks the earth.'

Anselmo smiled gently. 'I thought as much. Not for worlds would I have recommended you *before* this had come to pass. But *now* I feel that you will be as harmless as a monk – nay,' he said with a wry smile, 'more so, for not all monks are blameless. Let us say a eunuch then.' He waited in vain for his friend to smile in the old way at the jest, then tried to sweeten the draught. 'It need not be forever. But at present, it is better that you are far from here.'

Again Bernardino was visited with the far-off memory of his exile from Florence.

'And your patron is a fine man,' Anselmo pushed forth, 'a soldier and courtier, who loves the arts.'

'How do you know this?'

The priest hesitated. 'He is my uncle.'

Bernardino's eyes narrowed. He had lived in the world long enough to know what this meant. 'You mean he is your *father*.'

'Yes,' admitted Anselmo. 'He is my father. My natural father. He is a good man, but like every good man he is not without sin.' Anselmo looked down at his ringed hands as he spoke. 'He has been good to me, for although I carry the stain of bastardy he has given me preferment.' He waved his hand in a way that encompassed the fine house and all things in it. 'I have come far. It may be that I will go further. But scandal or infamy touching my name will hold me back,' he looked Bernardino full in the eye, that his friend might feel the full weight of his meaning.

Now Bernardino looked down. 'I understand you. I am endangering myself? Very well. I am threatening her happiness that holds my heart? Even in spite of this, I would not leave. But I will not endanger *you*, you who have been my dearest friend. Commend me to your uncle. I will go.' The embrace that followed was one of true brotherhood.

Just hours later, as the bells rang for Compline, Anselmo watched him go under the cover of night and reflected with sadness on their discourse. When he said that good men were not without sin, he had meant it. If he himself were to stand at the gates of Heaven, and were weighed by Saint Peter and writ in the ledger on the side of good, he would still have to account for the fact that, while Bernardino Luini had lost his own heart, he had in his keeping the heart of another – Father Anselmo Bentivoglio.

CHAPTER 23

Three Visitors Come to Castello

Simonetta watched from the window once more. She saw the priest come and admitted him to her house and heard him in silence. But Anselmo saw that she had turned her back on God and was sorry for it. He expressed a hope that he would see her at mass, but knew she would not come while she was so derided. As the almond trees waved him goodbye he thought that, while her likeness lived forever in his church, he may never see her there again.

Simonetta watched from the window once more. Then *he* came as she knew he would. She saw him from the window, and had his vellum in her white hand. She met his eyes over the distance and saw him caged behind the winter branches of the rose hedge, caught in a blackthorn web. She turned away deliberately before he could see her tears, crushing the missive in her palm. When she turned back he was gone, and she was pleased and destroyed at once.

She may have shunned God but she still could not go to Bernardino. She could not come by happiness so cheaply.

She loved him, but she could not give herself to him; there could be no good end to such a beginning as they had had. She could forget God, but not Lorenzo, and the public shame she had brought upon herself.

Now she was totally alone. Raffaella had come to her in tears, and told her that Gregorio had told her to leave Castello with him or never see him more. Simonetta released her beloved maid, for although she was horrified at Gregorio's denouncement of her, she could not say he was wrong. As one who had been divided twice from the men that she loved, and could not visit such pain on another soul; she told Raffaella to go.

Simonetta had thought that there was no greater pain than the death of a husband. She was to learn she was wrong. To lose Bernardino before their love could even begin was infinitely worse, and such recollections only added to her guilt and pain. She knew that if she saw him close just once and let him speak to her she would run to him, and live their lives in secret passionate ruin. But the loss of her religion could not free her from her moral code. She still knew right from wrong and wished that she did not. In the cold empty fortress she had the useless comfort of a warm full heart, and the guilty remembrance of his kiss to heat her when the fire burned low. She shivered equally with the cold and the remembrance of his touch. She wandered the frozen almond groves and watched the leaves fall from the trees she had reprieved from the axe. She knew now it was a matter of time until she must leave this place. Her income from the paintings had come to an abrupt end, and Manodorata had not been near her since the incident in the church. She could not hope for the help of a respectable man, even one from another church and faith than the one she had sullied. She feared the jeers of the citizens of Saronno and so kept to herself. She dared not venture to town and approach the Jew in his house with the star on the door.

But she had underestimated him. She had not known that one who had lived with jeers and ridicule could turn the other cheek. She had not seen that those who are derided make up their own minds before they themselves deride. She had not realised that the censure of Christians only recommended her to him.

Simonetta watched from the window once more. And when Manodorata came up the path to Castello and she saw his bearlike furs she was so grateful, and so warmed by the approach of a friend, that she ran down to the loggia, and held out her arms in welcome. She did not know that her gesture mimicked the stark almond branches that held their dark fingers towards him too.

CHAPTER 24

Saint Maurice and the Sixty-Six Hundred

When Bernardino Luini first set foot in the chapel of San Maurizio in Milan, he felt like he was entering a prison.

The impression had begun to form when he had entered the city that morning at dawn, dressed as a friar and riding a humble mule. He had been waved through the great Roman gate of Porta Ticinese with no inquiry from the sentry, and had even felt cocky enough to sketch a cursory cross of beneficence over the guards' heads. But when the pikes had crossed behind him again he began to feel trapped. Milan was a closed place, ringed with a rosary of walls and gates. The streets were designed to show the glory and importance of the ideal city to the world – long, wide roads with massy silver-stone buildings; it was not easy to be anonymous here as one might have been in a warren of cramped medieval streets in the old cities. A civic utopia, Lombardy's capital was a dwelling place for courtiers, not plague-ridden peasants. Bernardino passed the elegant Roman pillars of the colonnade of San Lorenzo, under the cold shadow of the massive bulk of that same Saint's huge, squat Basilica. Bernardino pondered that for all its shining new buildings and broad throroughfares Milan was still an antique city at heart; the Roman origins lay all around, the new marched side by side with the old, and past and present shared the same modus: grandeur and civilization beyond their time. He shivered and pulled his robe closer – the weak dawn sun had not yet penetrated the streets and the city's vast architectural marvels looked stark and bleak. Even the miraculous high-gothic Duomo, with its forest of silver spires, seemed a bed of nails set to impale him. Bernardino knew the city well; had spent many happy years here in Leonardo's *studiolo* before his master had taken him to Florence and their acquaintance ended with his Venetian exile. But now he felt no affection for his former home. Perhaps it was the fact that Leonardo had died some years ago and was no longer here to welcome his favourite pupil. Or was it that no place save Saronno could feel like a home to him now? Simonetta was his harbour, his mooring was wherever she was; and he was now cut loose, drifting, and had been caught in a net that closed behind him. He was a lobster in a pot. The grandeur of the pot was of no consequence to him – he was still trapped.

Yet not *all* that was here was so grand. That evening, as Bernardino kicked his tired mule up the Corso Magenta where the monastery was to be found, he entered the humble doorways in the blunt stone façade sure he had mistook Anselmo's directions. The chamber he entered was square and he was struck by the cold, and the darkness. He soon realised, as his eyes penetrated the gloom, that he was standing in the lay hall of the convent church, and the illusion of a cube was given by a dividing wall that reached up into the dark and just stopped short of the curved ribs of the ceiling. A yawning gap above told of another space beyond. High in the walls a series of small round windows in the Lombard style so loved by Ludovico Il Moro provided the only illumination. Bernardino walked forward with his footsteps echoing and examined the wall. Disguised among the panels sat two small grilles and shuttered doors, the only connection, it seemed, to anything on the other side. As he looked, the oaken doors through which he had entered slammed shut with a trick of the wind. The illusion of prison was complete. As one imprisoned might do, Bernardino fumbled about for an exit, and at last found an open door, through the side of one of the dark chapels that ringed the room. Here was another hall, but more rectangular in aspect – larger certainly. He walked to the middle of the great vaulted space and revolved under the crossbeams. The pilasters rose away into the dark void overhead. A painter that had gone before him – one with more enthusiasm than skill, had painted gold stars in a dark blue heaven and these stars now wheeled over his head. He was no longer in prison, but he was not yet free. This piece of decoration, and the cold, merely made him feel like he was outside.

In truth he had not felt warm since he had left the circle of Simonetta's arms. He sat down hard on the nearest pew and put his head in his hands, appalled by the task ahead. Why had he agreed to this? How could he, who felt so dead, make the place live – the two main halls and the numerous chapels? Would the brush answer in his hand or had he lost his passion along with his love? And where the hell was everybody? He was cold and a terrible tiredness settled on him. He wanted to lie down on the cold floor and sleep.

But he could not. His first task, if he was to warrant the money he had been paid, was to portray his patrons. It was ever thus. In each place he had painted, be it ever so Holy, his patrons had insisted that their images take precedence, over the Virgin and the Saints and Christ Jesus himself. To-day he had come with his sticks and chalks, his charcoals and scaffolds and ropes, and was to embark upon the image of Alessandro Bentivoglio, the greatest lord in Milan, and the father to his dearest friend.

He had met Signor Bentivoglio this very morning, when he had first entered the city; fully aware that he must pay his respects to his lay patron before making his obesience to God at the monastery. He had walked the marbled halls of Signor Bentivoglio's great palace in the Borgo della Porta Comense, and been received by a man who surprised him with his quiet nobility. He was a good subject to be sure – a man of later years but of strong features, with a beard and hair as black as a moor's. Bernardino had expected more of a dandy, a profligate – one who wasted words and wealth, and scattered Lombardy with bastard children such as Anselmo. But as he made sketches of Bentivoglio, the reason for this seriousness became clear, as Alessandro began to speak of the second patron Luini must paint: his wife. Alessandro's great love, Ippolita Sforza Bentivoglio, was the patroness of the Benedictine order of San Maurizio, and was to be portrayed in a fresco as great as his own.

The noble voice warmed so much when it spoke of the lady that Bernardino looked up from his broad sweeps of charcoal. He was attracted suddenly by fellow feeling – for here was a man whose love recalled his own. He vowed to do the lady justice, and said so. 'If I may have the honour of sketching the lady, I will answer for it that my portrait will do her no dishonour.'

The sad, stone grey eyes met his. 'That you may not do. I wish it were possible.'

Bernardino hesitated. 'Signore, I cleave to your wishes of course, but I must tell you that a portrait is always better if it is taken from the life.'

Now the pebble eyes seemed suddenly awash, as if the tide covered them. 'My lady has been dead these five years past. You may only paint from what others captured of her, when she lived.'

This, then, was to be the start of his commission in San Maurizio. A patron and a ghost. Bernardino could not face the painting of the lady yet. He had been appalled at Bentivoglio's story and had almost wept with his model as the sitting finished in silence. He felt the nobleman regarding him closely, and the warmth with which he took his leave of Bernardino gave the artist the impression that he was being given credit for an empathy that he did not feel. He was sorry for his new lord, to be sure. But the tears he shed were selfish ones. Only his own loss could move him so. The loss of Simonetta.

So when he hauled himself up on his ladders and platforms, he began to draw Alessandro first. There was no-one here to greet him, the huge lay hall stood empty. Beyond the partition on which he began his drawings, the great division where the public could not trespass, he at last heard the Holy sisters moving around, making their devotions. Through the gap above the wall he could hear the prayers and praisings from the sequestered nuns, without looking upon them. He was glad of his solitude. He wished to be alone when he began, to see if the gift was still with him.

As he drew, the charcoal answered him and he transferred his sketches efficiently to the tempera he had laid. Alessandro began to come to light and as Bernardino drew he heard masses being sung through the wall as the hours passed. The plainsong that the sisters sang was so beautiful and sweet that the sound threatened his composure. He felt that he was drowning, that the tide would flood his eyes too, and he would be lost. He drew his brows together and shook his head, the song stopped, and only then did he realise he was observed.

A lady stood there, tall and still. She had the carriage of a noblewoman, but her face was as scrubbed and homely as any village maid. Her skin was tanned and rosy, her thin lips dry, her eyes small and dark and friendly. She could have been any age between twenty and thirty, for she had eschewed all the unguents and artifices with which ladies of her birth improved their faces. She was unplucked, un-painted, and clearly used to the outdoors. Despite this she seemed to be an aristocrat, in all but the fact that she wore the habit of a nun. She was no beauty, but had a calm about her, and when she smiled in greeting, her face lit from within with a goodness that Bernardino wished he could paint. He felt soothed by her before she had even uttered. She was a balm to his wounded feelings. He felt he had met her before, that he knew her already. After the smile words soon came. 'You must be Signor Luini. It grieves me that there was no one here to greet you, but you happened to come at a time when my sisters and I walk the cloister in silent contemplation. No,' she held up her hand as Luini made to scramble down from his platform, 'do not descend, for it seems a perilous business.' She smiled her sweet smile again. 'I am Sister Bianca, Abbess of this house.'

Bernardino stared. She held up the ring of her office and

he reached down to kiss it. He looked closely at the ring she wore as his lips drew nearer. It was a red cross of Bohemian garnets. It was the colour of warm blood but as cold as stone against his mouth. He thought only older matrons sought to wear such a ring.

With uncanny perception she said, 'You are thinking that I am full young to hold such an office.'

Luini dropped his eyes. 'Forgive me. I just...that is I thought...that a lady such as yourself...there is much to see and do in the world...' he blustered, 'I thought that ladies entered Holy offices as widows or...' he tailed off.

The Abbess smiled again. 'But when God calls you, Signore, he can do so at any age. I entered this place a full four years ago, at the same time that our Lord Duke Francesco II Sforza did reconquer the city. The rhythms of life that apply for other ladies – the age of marriage, the age to bear children – do not call to me. I dance my measure to the canonical hours, and my year passes according to God's calendar.'

Luini smiled too. 'Sister Bianca. Do you mind if I continue my work? I must take the moment when it presents itself and I have a following wind today, it seems.'

The Abbess stepped closer. 'Yes, it goes well. It is very like him.'

Luini drew on, and felt, rather than saw, that the Abbess stayed to watch. He was reminded of Anselmo in the Sanctuary of Saronno and smiled.

The Abbess asked, 'You do not mind being observed?'

'Usually, yes. But in this case you put me in mind of another that watched me in this way. He too was a person of Holy orders.'

'Perhaps he was captivated by the gift that God has given you. It is no small thing to make a man appear on a wall as if he were here in this room. Nor is it every day that we in Holy orders get to see a miracle take place before our eyes; for all that we read and study the miracles of the Saints every day. Perhaps we thought the age of miracles has past. It is heartening to know that it has not.'

Bernardino was robbed of his usual arrogance today. Under the Abbess's gaze he felt unworthy of the compliment, and cast about for a diversion. His eye fell on his work, and the man that he drew. 'Your patron. What manner of man is he? He seemed a person of great nobility.'

'He is a soldier and a poet and many things besides,' came the answer. 'He also has a great faith, which is why he wished to be painted as you portray him here, kneeling in prayer. He feels that our community can transmit the fervour of our faith much to the laity of Milan. See,' her graceful wave indicated the delimiting wall. 'This partition divides the Hall of the Nuns from the Hall of the Believers where we are now.' Bernardino's lip curled at the irony of the name, and his presence in this room, but the Abbess continued. 'Ingress and egress can only take place through secret doors in the side chapels, and it is forbidden for the sisters to pass to this side, or the laity to enter our Convent hall. You and I remain the only exceptions to this rule; for you must pass into my world as I must come into yours. And yet we all worship together. Observe,' she pointed heavenwards. 'The wall does not reach the ceiling, so the laity can hear our song. And here,' she indicated the two small grilles hidden in the wall's panels, 'these grilles allow us to participate in the most Holy parts of the Mass; through this little door on the Gospel side we can watch the elevation of the Host, and through this grille on the Eucharist side we may adore the Holy Father.' She smiled her illuminating smile. 'For this great faith, and the sharing of it, our patron supports our sisterhood and this foundation of Saint Maurice.'

Again Luini was reminded of Anselmo's story of that Saint. He missed his friend abruptly. 'Why does Signor Bentivoglio honour Saint Maurice in particular?'

'Because Signor Bentivoglio served as a *condottiere* with the Swiss in the battle of Novara. Saint Maurice is greatly revered in Swisserland, and his church stands there in Agaunum. Do you know the tale?' Bernardino was about to answer in the affirmative, but because he missed Anselmo, and the Abbess recalled him to mind, he said something quite different.

'Why don't you tell me, if you have leisure?'

'During the reign of the co-emperors Diocletian, Maximian, Constantius and Galerius, there was, according to the legend, a Roman legion raised in Upper Egypt, known as the Theban Legion,' she began. 'It numbered sixty-six hundred men, all of whom were Christians and command-ed by an officer named Maurice.' Her voice was musical, and she made the story live. Bernardino had never known such a gift before, the gift of making the listener see what was described. He could understand how such a gift must assist her in her calling, for anyone who heard her tell a parable or read a chapter from the scriptures must believe every word at once. Bernardino turned to look at her, and then raised his eyes above her head. In front of his eyes the blank wall, that vast grey space began to warm into colour and take form as she spoke. Bernardino blinked his eyes as the Roman legion marched over Sister Bianca's head. 'In the year of our lord 286 the legion was part of a force led by Maximian to quell an uprising among Christians in Gaul. After the revolt was put down, Maximian issued an order that the whole army should attend the offering of sacrifices – including the killing of Christians for the Roman gods – for the success of their mission.' Bernar-dino held his temples as he smelled the blood and heard the screams of death. 'Only the Theban Legion dared to refuse the order to join the rite. The legion withdrew and encamped near Agaunum. Maximian was enraged by the insubordination of Maurice and the legion and ordered it to be decimated.'

'Decimated?' questioned Bernardino.

'Every tenth man was to be executed.'

'So Maurice and his men stood firm, even though one in every ten of his soldiers were to die? Who would do such a thing? Who would have such strength, or such folly?'

'A man who truly believed that what he was doing was right. The penalty was carried out, but still the legion refused to comply. Maximian was enraged and another decimation was made. When Maurice and his legion persisted, Maximian ordered that the remaining men should be executed. The men offered no resistance, but went to their deaths convinced that they would become martyrs.'

'So they all died? *All* of them? Sixty six hundred men?'

'Every man was put to the sword, including Maurice and his fellow officers. Those elements of the legion that weren't at Agaunum were hunted down and executed.'

Bernardino shook his head. Now the scene in front of him ran red with blood, the legion of martyrs lying dead on the field of battle. 'What a waste.'

'Why a waste?' asked Sister Bianca gently. 'They believed in something enough to die for it. You may think you believe in nothing,' she looked him full in the eye. 'But everyone believes in something. Don't you, Signore, believe in something, or someone, enough to die for it?'

Bernardino was silenced for a moment, for there was one to whom he would give his life in a heartbeat. Yet he persisted. 'What good has come from such a sacrifice?'

The Abbess waved her ringed hand. 'This foundation is

built in his name and will give succour to many of the poor and needy in Milan. And not just this foundation, but many are built to honour the Saint. Our patron feels as I do, that it is a story of hope. Hope and faith do not die, and nor does love. A church was built on Maurice's grave. Here, Signor Bentivoglio is doing the same.'

'You seem to know his mind very well.'

'I should. For when I lived in the world, before God named me Sister Bianca, my name was Alessandra Sforza Bentivoglio. Our Patron is my father.'

Bernardino turned away in shock and confusion. Little wonder the Abbess reminded him of Anselmo – she was the priest's natural sister! Did she know that such a brother existed? Had her father told this unworldly woman of his sins?

Sister Bianca saw him turn, and made her own interpretation. 'You wish to work. I'll leave you now.'

Bernardino turned back, to reassure her that he did not wish her gone, but she had disappeared back to the nuns' side of the monastery. He climbed down from his perch and looked at the wall where he had witnessed the scenes that she and her brother described. The blood was gone, the dead legionaries gone. 'Love does not die,' he said to himself. 'No indeed, Simonetta.' (He did not know that a good man of a different faith, had spoken the same words to Simonetta; not in a chapel, but in a grove of almonds.) As he watched, the green grass grew and a city was built before his eyes. Saint Maurice, young strong and alive again, founded his church on the bones of the sixty-six hundred. Hope sprung from the ground. Furiously, before the image faded, Bernardino began to draw.

CHAPTER 25

The Still

'What will you do now?'

Simonetta and Manodorata sat on the floor of the treasure cellar. It was not a comfortable place; cold, with remnants of almond shells scattering the floor, but Manodorata had seemed to wish for privacy. He had sat down first, cross-legged like a moor, and she, clad again in Lorenzo's clothes had copied him, and found the posture surprisingly comfortable. Simonetta sighed. 'I do not know.'

Manodorata looked down. 'This artist man. Luini. He has gone.' It was a statement, not a question.

Simonetta spoke forcefully, to keep her voice from cracking. 'Yes. He has gone.'

Manodorata nodded sagely. She felt no need to explain herself to him, nor to ask how he knew what had passed in a church that was not his own. She knew he would not judge her. He had said she would fall in love again and he had been right. He had not said it would hurt more than the first time. His grey eyes, so like another's and yet not so, held a world of sympathy and understanding. He began to speak. 'It is well he has gone. The Cardinal is a vengeful man. His thirst for revenge knows no bounds. He hates and he waits.'

Simonetta drew her cape about her, feeling the threat like a draught. 'You know of this man?'

Manodorata let out a breath in defeat, like the wind's end when the sail drops. 'I do. For it was he that took my hand from me.' Her eyes widened. 'Yes,' he went on, 'there is a time to tell every tale and the time for this one is now. You shall know how it went with me.' He picked a rotten almond from the floor and peeled it, one handed, as he spoke. 'In Toledo, three years past, Gabriel Solis de Gonzales was a Cardinal in the employ of a new institution called the Holy Office.'

Simonetta looked blank.

'It has another name. The Inquisition.'

Did she imagine it, or did Manodorata lower his voice as he uttered the word of terror? 'Toledo was my home. I was a banker, a moneylender of good repute. I had lately married Rebecca and Elijah and Jovaphet were babies.' He smiled at the memory, but the smile soon faded. 'We loved each other greatly, but the world began to hate us. We were forced to live in a *Juderia*, a place the Venetians would call a *ghetto*.'

Like Jews' Street in Saronno, thought Simonetta.

'But this was not enough. Under the new influence of

the Inquisition I was forced to convert to Christianity, or leave the country.'

Simonetta gasped – she could not imagine what he had suffered to be brought to such a pass. Manodorata reacted defensively to her exclamation. 'Yes, it is not something of which I am proud. It was for show only, and at home we carried on our religious observances in secret. But I wanted to protect my family and my home.'

Simonetta reached out in the gloom and laid a hand upon his arm. 'You mistake me,' she said. 'I do not judge you, only those that forced you to do such a thing.'

He nodded, and went on. 'They made us give the boys Christian names and we chose Evangelista for Elijah and Giovan Pietro for Jovaphet, as they at least sounded close to the boys' own. We attempted to live as Christians for the outside world, yet we were still derided. They called us *Marranos*. Pigs.' He shook his head. 'Still, the Inquisition were not satisfied. I was arrested and questioned by the very man that seeks your love, Gabriel Solis de Gonzales himself, who had found good odour with the Holy Office by holding the hardest line he could against my people.'

Now it was Simonetta's turn to shake her head. What evil chance had brought the Cardinal here, right into the path of one he had already damaged so much? She had little time to contemplate on the littleness of the globe, as Manodorata's exotic accents came again, like the tide bringing ill news.

'I was asked to denounce others of my race, other *Conversos* who had accepted the Christian faith as a mask for their Judaism. And here, I reached the end of the road. I had given away much of my own person, and my own dignity for the sake of my family. I had abrogated my faith and my place in Abraham's bosom. But all this I did on my own account. It was not my right to make that decision for others. I looked him in his pale Devil's eyes and told him: this, I would not do.' He paused before delivering the blow; lopping off each word abruptly. 'They took my hand from me.'

Simonetta did not breathe.

'I remember the stench of my own hand burning as Gonzales's eyes shone brighter than the flames that took it. They let me go when they knew I would not tell them. One night my friend Abiathar came to me and warned me that the Cardinal sought my life. He had only released me so that I may lead him to other prominent Jews. The next day we sailed for Genoa. When we came to these shores I had the Florentines make me a hand of gold as an act of defiance. We settled here, in this quiet place, for here we hoped we might find tolerance. And we did.'

Simonetta was astonished. 'You call what you experience *here* tolerance? And what I myself…' her voice tailed away.

Manodorata smiled a thin smile. 'Words? Insults? The spittle of ignorant men? Such things do not really hurt. For my kind, tolerance is a day without a broken bone. A day when you come home and your house is not aflame. A day when your property is not stolen, and your children and womenfolk left to walk in peace, undefiled. These are the days we have lived in Saronno. Until this day, when ill wind blew this Cardinal into my path again.'

Simonetta drew her brows together. 'What do you mean? Is he still here?'

Manodorata laughed shortly. 'Not he. He will return to his palace in Milan, to his comforts and luxury, but he has left his miasma behind him. In his search for your friend he has found our houses and our businesses, and seen the Jew living and working in his See. He will not let us lie here long.'

Simonetta was silent. They were both outcasts now, for as she had run blindly from the church last week the citizens had jeered her and one or two had spat in her path. She had never fully understood before what Manodorata endured every day, until now.

Manodorata broke into her reverie. 'So, I have come to say this. If you decide to stay here, we must move swiftly to secure your fate. For I may not be able to help you for long.'

'Do you…you don't mean Gonzales will seek to harm you?'

Manodorata meant exactly that, but sought to reassure Simonetta. 'Of course not. He does not know that *I* live here. I meant only that he may seek the property of my kind, or prevent us from trading. So,' his voice took on a businesslike bent. 'Our conversation has sailed full circle. Will you stay here?'

Simonetta stared, as if mesmerised, at the almond in Manodorata's hand. It represented Lorenzo's family and her own, and all that was here at Villa Castello. 'Yes,' she said, and in an echo of what she had told him a year ago. 'I have nowhere else to go. You of all people know the lengths to which a person will go to secure their home.'

He nodded, understanding. 'Very well. I will engage a gang of Jewish labourers on the morrow. They will bring axes and we will fell your groves and till the soil for farm land. I know of some good Arabic practices whereby, by rotating your crops from field to field, the soil stays rich from one year to the next.'

She nodded, and he pitched the nut from his hand into the dark and made to get up.

The nut landed with a chink of glass in the dark. The two looked at each other and Simonetta scrambled to her feet. She moved gingerly into the dark corner and emerged holding a strange arrangement of bottles connected by tubes. Manodorata followed her and found a brazier and a copper dish in the gloomy corner.

Simonetta set the thing down with wonder. 'What can it be?'

Manodorata laughed. 'It's a still. Someone has been brewing liquor here.' He sniffed one of the bottles. '*Grappa*. And here,' he took a cork from the neck of a clay amphora and moved his head swiftly away as if struck; 'Brandy.'

'How does it work?' Simonetta examined the odd machinery, cold and sticky in her hands.

'It's a very ancient art, and one unfamiliar to me. But I think the principles are that you place your fermented juices here.'

'Juices from what?'

'You can make liquor from anything. *Grappa*, that evil brew, is made from grape seeds. You heat them from below, till they condense…become liquid again, here, and pass through this filter here…'

'How did it come to be here…not Lorenzo…he only had taste for wine.'

Manodorata smiled wryly. 'I would have asked your squire. He always looked well jug-bitten.'

Simonetta would have smiled too, but the events of last week, and Gregorio's cruel exposure of her sins was too raw. She took the amphora and made to throw it away. Manodorata held her wrist. 'I am no medic, Simonetta, but if I were you, I would take this bottle to bed and get yourself a night's sleep. For you have not slept since mass, if I am not mistook.'

Indeed she had not. She could not rest while she thought of Bernardino, and the manner of his leavetaking. Manodorata took his own leave before she could demur. Alone, she looked at the amphora, shrugged and made to carry it to

her chamber. As she turned, the naked almond that Manodorata had peeled and cast away glowed from the dark like
a star...she stopped, kneeled and put down the amphora.
Then she went into the dark to find the almond, and more
of its fellows. For the first time since Sunday Simonetta
forgot her aching heart.

She had had an idea.

CHAPTER 26

A Way with the Wood

Nonna sat in her new fireside chair, rocking on the curved runners, marvelling at comfort that she had never known. The man whom she considered kin to her regarded her with one arm across his waist and the other elbow propped on it, hand to mouth. He had a rough polishing cloth tied round his waist, just as the blue banner had been when they found him. He was regarding his handiwork through narrowed eyes. 'It goes well?' he asked.

'It is wondrous,' she said and smiled with as many gaps as teeth. It was wondrous indeed. And so were the new beams that he had placed in the low roof, white cedar glowing in the firelight and oozing sticky amber gum. Her doors were new and solid, her casements mended with the draughts banished. He had even built a new loggia in the tiny courtyard where the hens scratched. He was always to be found collecting wood, chopping, planning and shaping, and miracles sprang from his hands with a new found skill which would not have shamed Saint Joseph himself, father to Our

Lord and the first of all carpenters. He smiled at last, enjoying the moment with her. She nodded in time with the chair. He was a gift from God.

And now she had to admit what she had never known before. She had always compared him to Filippo, and seen in Selvaggio her son born again. But now she had to acknowledge that he was a far far better man than the son she had lost. Memory now prompted her that when Filippo was at home he either had his boots at the fire, or went gaming with the Romanys that collected under the arches of the Ponte Coperto bridge when the sun went down. He would rather spend time with the gipsies, before their bonfires that the *Comune* had banned. They had their dice and their sweet wine, their dusky girls and violins, and Filippo would be found there rather than at his mother's fireside. Her evenings now were a joy to her. She and the two young people would sit before the fire, enjoying the warmth and the company of their close circle.

There was much else now to enjoy, for at some time in these last weeks Selvaggio had learned that he was able to write. On one of those firelit nights with Amaria he had taken a charred stick from the fire and written on the hearth, characters that were clear and schooled and spoke of an education. He now delighted in being able to teach Amaria to write, to reciprocate the gift of speech she had given him, but he felt a distant disquiet. As the girl formed the very characters that she had taught him to say, questions crowded his mind. How did he know this skill? Had he been a scribe or notary? Or a schoolmaster?

For with the writing came his partner skill of reading; Nonna, when she saw this new development, had brought down the family Bible from her dorter. The old lady could not read the Latin texts herself, but Selvaggio let the ancient pages fall open at random and read at once. His tones were still rasping, but he spoke fluidly, and his brain leapt ahead of his lately-schooled tongue.

'Blessed is everyone who fears the Lord, who walks in his ways. For you will eat the labour of your hands. You will be happy, and it will be well with you. Your wife will be as a fruitful vine, in the innermost parts of your house; your children like olive plants, around your table. Behold, thus is the man blessed who fears the Lord. May the Lord bless you out of Zion, and may you see the good of Jerusalem all the days of your life. May you see your children's children. Peace be upon Israel.'

Selvaggio shut the book, much pleased with the lesson. God did not belong in a cathedral; he was not to be found seated among the snowy clouds of a priceless fresco, or in the exquisite counterpoint of a choir. God was in the simple things: the fruit of the vine, food, family, children. He looked about him, at the homely, firelit faces of the two women who tended him. Here was where true beauty and goodness lay.

So now, in the evening time, Selvaggio set aside his carving to read parables or scriptures; Nonna listened, nodding over some mending or some lace tatting, and Amaria would practice her letters. The Bible texts were familiar to Selvaggio, but not just because he read them now; he knew he had heard them before somewhere, heard the intonation of a priest's voice in a far-off church. And he knew that the cadences of his reading, the rise and fall of the words that he read, were not his own; but were prompted by this other, shadowy preacher he had once known.

Soon, too, Selvaggio began to teach Amaria to read; they bent their heads together over the good Book, one dark and one light, and Nonna realised she had been wrong about Selvaggio. He had not needed only a mother to nurture and care for him; he had needed a child too. He that had nothing, that had been given so much charity, had also wanted to feel needed; to give something back. In Amaria he had found all the family that he lacked. Nonna could see him revelling in his role as tutor to the one who had so lately tutored him. And he gained great pleasure from being able, now, to make their humble home a better place with the furniture he made. He was becoming so skilled that he even sold a little of his wares about the town, and they could now afford better meat and vegetables, and finer wine. Nonna saw Selvaggio's face glow with pleasure as he brought his booty home – bought from the labour of his hands – and knew him for a truly good man. She would watch him through her steepled hands as they all prayed at mass every Sunday, at the church of St Peter of the Golden Sky. Nonna could see him praying with fervour, and true belief, and knew that in his reading of the Bible he had come home to a faith that must have lived in him once before. She could see in him a moral strength, and a determination to live the new life he had been given by the law of God, to do right by all. At such times she would feel a misgiving, that his own family, who had lost such a son or brother, must be missing him indeed. But then her heart told her of what she had gained and she quelled the thought. After mass they would return to their little house by the river and share their supper of risotto or polenta, then sometimes Nonna would go to the dorter early to give the two some private moments together which she thought they now needed. Now, as she rocked back and forth in her new chair, she smiled at the way of things, and Selvaggio smiled too, thinking that she still dwelt upon her gift.

''Tis a design from Flanders,' he began, then stopped abruptly as his brows drew together. 'I do not know how I know that.'

Nonna stopped rocking. 'Do you begin to remember, then, Selvaggio?' she asked, with a sudden jag of fear.

He rubbed the back of his neck as his head shook. 'Recollections come to me from time to time; they light for an instant like stars pricking through the night. But when I reach for them, they melt away, as if the day has come. All my senses have remembrances; tastes, smells, even the feel of things.' Nonna began to rock again, gently, relieved.

'Sights too,' Selvaggio went on. 'For instance, I recall a dovecot — a little wooden house for doves — but I know not from whence.' He shook his head and said, 'No matter. Perhaps I shall make one such for Amaria, and leaven my memory that way.' Was it Nonna's imagination or did he redden and look down a little when he mentioned her granddaughter's name?

'Ah, Amaria,' she said and smiled again, 'she is tending the chickens, if you're wondering.' He caught her teasing tones and threw his polishing cloth at her. She caught it easily, and as he left through the new back door of the cot she mused that even if his head remembered what it had to, his heart might yet keep him here.

CHAPTER 27

Taste

Taste, taste, taste.

Simonetta shut her eyes and stopped her ears. For that one night she was inured to the pains of her heart. She would not strain to hear Bernardino's voice whispering through the doomed almond groves as she walked them one last time in the darkening night. She would not seek his face in the form of an evening cloud, dark above and fiery below as the sun dropped. She went back into the house and sat down at the scrubbed board. She lit a rush dip candle and surveyed the apparatus before her. Her tongue would be her guide this night – her taste buds would lead her.

She had brought the still up from the treasure cellar, piece by piece, dismembering the copper skeleton to rec-reate it in her kitchen. She carried each dusty limbic or copper pipe singly, cradled in her arms like children. She set the thing together again and cleaned it carefully with a soft leather cloth dipped in vinegar water, admiring as she did so the warm copper of the bowl and the green craquelure of the glass. At last, she poured *grappa* and water into the copper, adding at the last some ancient brandy. Then she took her taper and lit the brazier. As the fire died in the hearth the brazier burned merrily, making the liquid bubble and heating there instead with its flame and the heady scent of the brew. Only now did she add a handful of almonds, peeled to the white quick, as luminous and firm as bone. As the steam rose and settled into diamond drops, she tasted the water-clear juices that fell into the end vessel. They tasted of *grappa* and brandy, no more. She stood and fetched a mortar and pestle and this time ground the almonds down fine in a square of clean linen. She added virgin oil to the pounded ivory until the paste was thick and smooth. She then pushed the mixture through the cloth into the copper and poured in water to make a milk-white emulsion. Now after the boiling there was a definite hint of almonds.

Simonetta did not heed the bells of the sanctuary, brought on the breeze to tell her that it was now Vespers, now Compline. She could not hear or see, her taste told her that more paste was needed, so she added more, and yet more. Her pace became frantic – she felt that she raced the dawn. She pulled the great accounts ledger to her, and cut and split a new quill with her peeling knife. She dipped and wrote down all that she did, her carefully schooled hand becoming more and more erratic as the bells tolled the hours.

She stood and wandered the kitchen, opening Raffaella's jars and adding a spice here, a herb there. In an inlaid box she found a brown rock of sugar, a delicacy that a wealthy guest had brought as a gift. She dropped it in too and watched the stone turn to golden gum, then honey, then suffuse the clear liquor with a beautiful amber brown. This bubbling smelled sweet and heady, and the resulting brew was sweet and bitter at once.

But still not right.

Simonetta had a fine palate, and had tasted the finest of wines since she was given her honey teat dipped in Venetian marsala as a babe. Then as a married lady, Lorenzo had expanded her experience as she tasted beers and brandies, *grappa* and *limoncello*. Their board had groaned with the best wine of Lombardy and beyond: the Sassella and Grumello of Valtellina, the Valcalepio reds and Oltrepò Pavese whites; San Colombano from Lodi and Chiaretto from the western shores of Lake Garda. She knew what pleased the tongue, and worked towards it now. All night she worked, invoking the Holy fathers of Chartreuse, who distilled their green brew in the name of God. She was sister that night to the Arab nomads that worked in the desert to distill their strong sweet Arrack. Again and again she tasted, until her head span and at last her senses began to creep back. Her eyes could not focus, and her thoughts, like homing doves, came back to Bernardino. In her befuddled state she thought that the brew she made was for him. She put all that lived in her heart into the brew. She went out into the night and picked apricots from the espaliers in the fragrant dark, their flesh still warm from the sun, their skin like a mouse's child. Apricots for sweetness, the drowning sweetness that she had felt when he had kissed her that one burning time. But then she added too cloves from a Chinese jar, black as his hair, and as bitter when crushed as the memory of his leaving, of the last time when he turned away from her and headed away into the hills. The curling peel of the greenest apple which slipped over her hands like eve's serpent as she peeled, reminded her of the fortunate fall that had led her into his arms. But the yellow zest of a golden lemon stung the cuts in her knuckles, punishing the fingers that had clutched the warm hair of his head as she had pulled his face to hers. Only then, when she let the remembrance of him help her, when she combined the bitter and the sweet, the very essence of their entire encounter, did she know she was done. She drank deeply of the finished draught, while she wrote rapidly with her quill the exact proportions and ingredients she had used. Her head nodded over her ink black fingers and as her brow touched the creamy pages of the ledger she thought of sharing a cup with him, laughing, somewhere where the sun warmed their skin as they drank in a way she knew could never be.

She woke, cold and stiff, with the scrape of a boot. She raised her head and her brains pounded within. Her mouth was ashes, and her eyes, fat with sleep, burned in her head. She lifted weighted lids to greet the sight of Manodorata, an amused smile lifting his patrician mouth. Her head was suddenly too heavy and she placed it in her hands. Someone was groaning – it was she. Manodorata cast his eye over the still. But did not comment. Instead he said: 'The woodcutters are here. Shall I tell them to begin felling?'

His voice was different. Fuzzy. She barely knew what he said but nodded. He went to the door and barked a command to his men – far too loudly for Simonetta. He came back and sat before her. 'You have been experimenting?' No reply. 'May I?' He pointed to the willow cup. She knew it was not possible to nod so she merely shut her eyes which he took as assent. He raised the cup to his eyes. '*Shalom*,' he said, and drank. Only his long silence could at last pull her heavy eyes to his face, and she found astonishment there.

'Alchemy!' he said.

'In truth?' she choked gruffly.

He raised his false hand. 'As surely as those Florentine Jews turned flesh into gold, so have you done. What in the name of Jehovah is in here?'

'Mostly almonds.'

Bloodshot eyes met steel grey, consternation grew as their thoughts chimed as one. 'The axes!'

He rose at once. 'Get you to bed. I'll stop them.'

As she mounted the stair, which seemed today as spiral as

a castle tower's, she heard him run into the grove. 'Spare the trees!' he shouted. She had never known Manodorata to run before; never heard him shout. He had looked like a crazed bear as he ran from the kitchen. As she fell on her bed and closed her eyes against the spinning room, Simonetta allowed herself to smile.

CHAPTER 28

The Circus Tower

Bernardino began to feel that the monastery was his home. His cell held nothing but a bed, a cross and the Book of Books, but he had no need of more. He lay Leonardo's *Libricciolo* sketchbook – his constant companion – next to the Bible; a partnership that made him smile: strange bedfellows indeed. His dress, while he lived here, was the simple habit of a lay brother: brown, rough, very soon covered in paint, but comfortable to his needs. His feet, clad only in sandals, were permanently cold, but soon he forgot to notice. His room, set at the southern end of the little cloister, looked onto a peaceful square of green grass butted by the fragrant herb garden. At the corner of the cloister was a round red tower which held the herbarium on the lower floor and the well-stocked library above the stair. His notion that he was in a prison had not entirely abated, for it had been made clear to him by Sister Bianca that to avoid his pursuer it was better that he did not go out into the city. The Cardinal had the reputation of a vengeful man, so Bernardino hardly ventured into the city in which he lived, but he cared not for sightseeing anyway. He had spent many years in Milan in his youth, when his Master had been summoned here by the dusky-skinned Duke Ludovico Il Moro, whom Leonardo had charmed with a vision of the ideal city with automated bridges, elevated walkways, and other fantasies of machinery. Bernardino had studied under Leonardo at the inception of the Master's greatest piece; the '*Cenacolo*' or 'Last Supper'. The fresco was produced over three tortuous years in the nearby monastery of Santa Maria delle Grazie, trying the patience of the good brothers and the Duke alike. Then, Bernardino had compensated for his monastic days with hot sweet nights with the goodwives and badwives of Milan. Now, his world was here in San Maurizio, his work was between the Hall of the Believers and the Hall of the Nuns, and he had no desire to breech the walls after curfew. His prison, if such it was, pleased him. He had already come to know and like his jailer, and he came to learn that the other inmates were all women of such good breeding and character that he marvelled – it was like being at court or summering in a great house. Several Sforzas, a brace of Borgias and an Este graced these cloisters. The chambress that laundered his habit was a Medici. The nuns were by no means uniformly ugly, nor crabbed by age. There were some lovely faces among them, faces that would have tempted him not so long ago, or at least make him mourn their calling. But his heart was done with women, all save one, and if she could not be his he wanted no other. He needed only friendship, and here at San Maurizio he found it in abundance. He gradually came to know the nuns. Sister Ugolin ran the herbarium and brewed him sage tea when his head ached from hours of painting by candlelight. Sister Petrus brought food and ale to his cell each morning and night, for it was not seemly for him to eat in the refectory with the sisters. The old lady would sit and talk while he ate his simple meal of pasta or meat – tales of the outside world which she gleaned from the beggars who came to the gate for alms. Sister Petrus had a great taste for the macabre, and Bernardino chewed as the elderly nun waxed lyrical on the latest civic atrocity: a known plague-spreader had been burned alive in the Piazza Vetra behind the basilica of San Lorenzo. 'San Lorenzo!' she cackled, her toothless mouth opening wide as she good naturedly prodded Bernardino in the ribs. 'Do you not see God's humour at work? For was not Saint Lorenzo cooked to death on a grid-iron, and bade the Romans turn him over, as he was done on one side? I wonder if the foul spreader of the pestilence offered up a prayer to the Saint as he burned in brotherhood?'

Bernardino tasted the news and the food together. He smiled and nodded as the nun shuffled off, but the fate of the hapless plague-spreader seemed very far away.

More real to him were the stories he heard from Sister Conceptione, the librarian. Tall, androgynous and frighteningly intelligent, the kindly sister allowed Bernardino to climb to the top of the red tower and, in her presence, look through the illuminated lives of the Saints. One book in particular he found invaluable: the 'Golden Legend' by Jacobus de Voragine. There, in that fabled book, there, in the airy Scriptorium with the silence broken only by the sound of the nuns' industriously scratching quills, there in the perfect black letters and the jewel-like colours of the marginalia, he found inspiration for his work. Bending over the volume in the morning light, using the reading skills that Leonardo had taught him, he learned much of the ways of sanctity. As he read, he remembered what his old Master had said: 'You must learn to read Latin, Bernardino. For it is the language of all the world's secrets; sacred and otherwise.' It was in this volume, the Lives of the Saints, that he learned the story of Saint Lucy. As he read of the unfortunate virgin's descent into prostitution he thought of his mother. His own eyes stung as he read of Lucy's eyes being plucked out of her head, and yet he snorted cynically when he read that God damped the faggots of her death-fire so that they would not light, and she had to be put to the sword.

'May I ask,' said Sister Conceptione's dry voice from over his shoulder, 'what you can possibly have read in *that* volume which prompted that peculiar noise?' But she smiled, and he returned it, unsure what he could say without being insulting.

'I wondered…that is…do you take these readings to be

the literal truth? Do you believe that God put out the fire under Lucy's feet? Or did it just rain that day?'

'Ah yes. The Martyr of Syracuse,' Conceptione's voice was as dry as the leaves of the vellum. 'She was saved by the weather, but does not Our Heavenly Father make the weather, and decide on its moods?'

Bernardino shrugged. 'Then why could God not save Lucy from the sword at the last? Why could he not save her eyes?'

'Sometimes a soul is given in martyrdom so that we can learn from their suffering. Our Lord may have saved Lucy from one fate so that she may come to another, but Saint Apollonia,' she leaned in and turned the page for him, 'willingly leapt into her death fire rather than blaspheme the name of Christ.'

'She did so?' Bernardino was aghast. 'Of her own free will? She was not forced?'

Conceptione shook her head till her black wimple crackled. 'She suffered much at the hands of Decius and his soldiers – all her teeth were broken and she is often portrayed with the pliers that pulled them from her head. But she leapt into the fire of her own accord. And when you paint Apollonia with her broken teeth, or Lucy with her eyeballs in the chapel here, their suffering will lead others to God.'

Bernardino shook his head. 'And Agatha?' he said, turning the page as the gold leaf flashed briefly in the sun from the casement. 'Her breasts were cut from her chest! Why did not God save her from such a fate, the loss of the very essence of her womanhood?'

'Signor Luini,' the tall nun began. '*God* did not visit this suffering on any of these Holy women. These tortures were laid upon them by man. Come with me.' Haltingly, with steps that betrayed a great age that no one would guess, the librarian led Bernardino down the stair and out into the cloister, and he turned back to look where she pointed, at the red round tower.

'This tower was not built for this foundation. It is much older. It is the tower of the old circus, the Roman circus, which was built when the Emperor made Milan the capital of the Western Roman Empire. Here, where we now stand, and where we sisters read and worship, and grow our healing herbs, was an arena of bloody sport and death. The playground of the Godless Romans. Lucy suffered under the purges of Diocletian, Agatha during the Decian persecution. The sufferings that were visited upon them were done to them by mortal men and pagans, mighty men in their time, kings and emperors. This very tower was a prison for the earliest of Christian martyrs: Gervase, Protase, Nabor and Felix. Here in this circus, the chariots circled and the gladiators fought for the pleasure of Emperor Maximian.'

'Maximian?' Bernardino's memory jolted him.

Sister Conceptione turned her rheumy eyes on him. 'Yes. You have heard of the Emperor?'

'Yes,' said Bernardino, wonderingly, remembering the Abbess's story. 'He martyred Saint Maurice. He murdered the sixty-six hundred.'

Sister Conceptione bent her toothless smile upon him. 'Exactly so,' she said, and started to shuffle off to the tower again. 'You are learning, Signor Luini,' she said as she went, without turning back. 'You are learning.'

He was learning. He revolved in the cloister like a top. Spinning with wonder at the connection. The stories of Saint Maurice, which had come alive for him on the chancel wall as the Abbess told the tale, were now given credence by the existence of the living, breathing, monster of an Emperor who had taken his macabre pleasures here in this spot. This very place which was now to be hallowed in the name of the man he had murdered. Bernardino lay down, dizzy, on the grass as the fat clouds scudded overhead. A change had come in him. He was learning.

He was beginning, despite himself, to believe.

CHAPTER 29

Amaretto

'Amante?'

'Amare?'

'Amarezza?'

Simonetta and Manodorata faced each other across the table. Each had a willow cup of the sweet new amber elixir, and each tasted periodically as they tried to fix upon a name to christen Simonetta's liquid alchemy.

'Well,' began Simonetta. 'Let's get back to the start. *Mandorla* is the word for almond…'

'A name very close to my own.'

'Indeed. Then perhaps we could call it Manodorata, if you agree. 'Twould not have been made without you.'

Manodorata shook his dark head, and the velvet tail of his cap swung behind his shoulders. 'That would never do. I am known in these parts, and association with a Jew would do your sales no favours. Let us canvas your other suggestions.'

'Well…the old Latin for almond is *amygdalus*…'

'Meaning…'

'Tonsil plum, I think.'

Manodorata gave a snort of laughter. ''Tis hardly an attractive root for a name. What else?'

Simonetta tasted the brew again. She felt too raw to reveal the epiphany that she had had while making the drink, that she had distilled the pleasure and pain of her feelings for Bernardino. 'It struck me that the drink is both sweet and bitter at once. And the words for love – *amare* – and bitterness – *amarezza*, are very close.'

Manodorata nodded. 'In fact one might say that love lies within bitterness – the word *amare* is found at the beginning of *amare-zza*.'

Simonetta smiled wryly. 'So love *ends* in bitterness? Not a very encouraging homily.'

'But a true one.'

'Not for you. You have your Rebecca, and your sons.'

'Even those who love the most, rarely die on the same day. Everyone is alone eventually, but love lives for ever, as we once discussed.'

Simonetta shivered, as she thought of Bernardino. Had he remembered her, or did he even now lie in the embrace of another, wherever he was? A bitter thought indeed. 'Let us say *Amarett-o* then. For our drink is only a *little* bitter. And we must hope that its taste can at least give cheer, for the time that we are on the earth.'

From the day that Amaretto was given its name, Manodorata and Simonetta moved fast in their joint venture. Manodorata brought a gang of Jewish workers to harvest the almonds and cut back the trees correctly for the next growth. Simonetta oversaw this process – she told the axe-men what she herself had once been told by Lorenzo: 'the branches must be spaced so that a swallow may fly between the groves without flapping his wings.' When it was done, and the trees were elegantly spaced, Simonetta looked back from the arches of the loggia and actually saw one of the small birds dip and turn through the pleached grove. Just as he had said, the swallow did need to fold its wings. She felt a shiver of foreboding, for had not the Romans foreseen ill auguries in the flight of a swallow? She shook off the feeling and went inside to the kitchens, where the womenfolk that Manodorata had employed had created a buzzing hive of industry as they set to to make the almond milk.

Manodorata had thought of everything. He laid out money to bring brown rock sugar from Constantinople, lemons from Cyprus and apples from England. Cloves and spices came from the trade ships of the Black Sea, and were brought by runners from Genoa. The still worked day and night, and the industrious Jews made the house live again, filling it with their chatter and strange beautiful song. Sweet melodies and guttural words floated through the rooms.

From Venice came the most precious cargo, clear bottles of *cristallo* glass, swaddled in silk like babes. When Simonetta opened the first parcel she gasped – for the bottle was a thing of beauty, mirror-bright, water-clear and with the elegant shape of a Roman amphora, with a flat bottom so the bottle might stand. The whole was finished with an almond shaped stopper, tied in place with a riband the same blue of the Castello arms.

Simonetta did not know nor ask how many ducats Manodorata poured into their enterprise. But as the bottles were filled, tied and crated, she was to learn that Manodorata had not yet completed his investment. He climbed the stair to her chamber and knocked and entered. In his arms, a festoon of red and gold almost hid him from sight.

Simonetta turned from her window and laid down her bow, for she had been shooting pigeons for the pot. She wore Lorenzo's ancient garb. Her hair was longer now, and matted, one cheek red from the twang of the bowstring, her fingers raw and chapped from plucking her quarry. Manodorata sighed and threw his bundle on the bed.

'What is that?' queried Simonetta, leaving her perch.

'Time was you would not have asked that question. It is a dress. Have you forgot that such things exist?'

Simonetta was drawn to the material, which seemed to glow from within. She rubbed her hand on her breeches before she dared touch the cloth, which was soft and cold as snow. The ruby red was fretted with gold thread and where the thread crossed, seed pearls sat like stars. She had a sudden urge to feel the dress against her skin. 'For me?' she asked, incredulously.

'I don't think it would suit me.' Manodorata sat down on the bed. 'Simonetta. I cannot sell your liquor. You must do it yourself. Whatever may have…come to pass in recent weeks you are still a lady of good name, and unless I have forgotten everything I ever knew about trade, you will shortly be a very successful merchant.'

'I?' said Simonetta aghast. 'I was not…that is, I cannot.'

'What is the matter?' asked Manodorata, testily, as if he already knew her answer.

She sighed. 'I was not born to trade. I was born nobly, into the *Signori*. I do not have the way of…*business*. My father and mother – Lorenzo, they would say it shamed my name, and theirs. God knows,' she turned her great eyes on her friend, 'that I have lately shamed that name enough.'

Manodorata sat down on the coverlet. 'There are many things about your people that are a mystery to me. Principal among them is the Christian view that the word 'trade' is tantamount to the vilest curse ever uttered by a tinker. Things change, Simonetta. The old world is gone. Your name alone will not put meat on your table, it is true, nor lay faggots in your hearth. Yet coupled with this liquor your name can do much.' He took her chin in his hand. 'You will be the *face* of this drink – the ship's figurehead, and as such you cannot dress like a poorly paid groom.'

Simonetta released herself and looked down ruefully at her garb. She secretly longed to wear women's weeds again, but till now had felt that she was paying a penance to Lorenzo.

'Put it on,' urged her friend, 'and here,' he produced more bounty. 'A looking glass, also from Venice. A comb. Rose ointment for your hands. A small vial fell on the bed. 'And lastly,' he held high a glittering constellation that blossomed in his fingers. It was a coif or *cuffia* for her hair made from the same gold net and pearls. 'Do something about that nest, 'tis fit for sparrows,' he said, and disappeared.

Simonetta shut the casement and flung off her clothes. She washed from head to foot with water from the rain stoup, and the cold made the bumps rise on her skin like the pigeons she had plucked. Her teeth chattered from cold and excitement and her eyes burned blue. She stepped into the dress and laced herself in as tight as may be, the silk soon warming against her skin. Then she combed her knotted hair till it fell in ripples past her shoulders. It was long enough to go up now, and she began to bind it into a *coazzone* plait, her unaccustomed fingers remembering the old ways, the way she did her hair when she was a wife and a lady. She fixed the *cuffia* in place, patting the wayward copper tendrils into the precious net. Lastly she bit her nails till they were even and rubbed the cream of roses into her hands. She pinched her cheeks and bit her lips to make the blood come, and only then did she lift the Venetian glass. What she saw there made her skip with excitement. Her eyes were enormous and brilliant, her skin pearl white. Her lips were rosy pink and her eyes as blue as the Amaretto ribbons. She looked thinner than she remembered and her eyes were more shadowed, but her hair was still the same burnished red and it shone with her ministrations in a way that rivalled the pearls and gold that adorned it. She moved the glass down to see the dress reflected, and saw that her arms were more willowy and subtle muscles had formed from hard work; her waist now greyhound slim. As she descended the kitchen stair her workers stopped their tasks to goggle, and even Manodorata lost his composure for an instant. Her eyes suddenly stung as she felt their admiration, and she wished that Bernardino could have seen her thus. She turned to Manodorata, dismissing the thought with a grateful smile to her benefactor. When he didn't speak she prompted him. 'Well?' she asked, 'will I do?'

He slowly began to nod and smile. 'Yes,' said he, 'you'll do very well.'

It was the day of the spring fair of Pavia, the first fair of the year and the greatest of the region. Simonetta donned her red dress and went down to the loggia. Her new white palfrey, whom she had named Raffaella in remembrance of her maid, was saddled and her mane beribboned with holiday red and gold. Waiting too was a pack mule, loaded with crates of Amaretto bottles and jingling like a Russian's sleigh. As Simonetta pulled on her riding gloves, Manodorata, who had come to bid her farewell, drew forward a dark young lady from his shadow. She was tall and capable looking, with sad black eyes and a beauty that spoke of the south. 'This is Veronica of Taormina,' he said. 'She will help you today. She will not invite comment, as she is a Christian, not a Jew.' Simonetta nodded, understanding his tact. 'Greetings Veronica,' she said.

Manodorata went on. 'Veronica will assist you at the market, and she will protect you on the road. You permit?' This last to the girl who nodded as he opened her cloak to reveal a neat rank of daggers, each in the shape of the Maltese cross. 'She will defend your person and your earnings. Where she is from brigands are more plentiful than hognuts.'

Simonetta was curious and addressed the girl. 'Perhaps you will tell me of such places along the road.'

The girl's sad eyes met hers as she shook her head. Manodorata put in, 'I regret there will be no traveller's tales from this lady.'

Simonetta looked from one to the other. 'Does she not speak our dialect?'

Manodorata looked at the pavings. 'She did once. Veronica is known to me because she married one of our kind – Joce of Leon. She was a Christian marrying a Jew, and her kind took her tongue, and her husband's life.'

Simonetta was stunned, and clasped the girls' hand warmly. She marvelled at the misery that love wrought, and that the world held such great obstacles to men's happiness.

In this case, needless obstacles set against those that loved in the name of God. She had little time for her God now – here was just one more reason why.

The two women set out for Pavia, each thinking of those they had lost, but there was much to lift the spirits along the road. Simonetta found the green hedgerows and the warm sun charming, and when she hummed an air of the May Veronica hummed along too. She found that she could converse well enough with her companion; their discourse continued with questions on the one side and nods and smiles on the other.

As the women drew into Pavia the press of people became almost oppressive; curs barked and livestock jostled. Here a fool in motley juggled fire and there a chicken seller spread the wings of his goods like fans. As they rode across the famous covered bridge of Pavia they were obliged to dismount and lead their mounts; Veronica led the way and her strange silent authority somehow cleared the path for her mistress. They climbed ever uphill as the throng intensified, and at length they reached the square at the rear of the squat red Duomo where the cacophony reached its peak. Minstrels coaxed folk tunes from their wheezing instruments, while vendors called out their wares. The delicious aromas of pies and pasties fought with the spicy rank odours of sheeps'urine and goat dung. The two women found a Marshal in a quartered tabard who showed them to their pitch with a pained and busy air. Simonetta noted with a jolt of pleasure that the pitch that they were assigned was placed in the exact centre of a six-pointed star, marked out by white cobbles set into the grey. She decided to see this as a sign – she found it pleasing that in mere decoration, a Jewish symbol had unknowingly been placed in the shadow of a Christian building, and hoped it would bring luck to their enterprise. Simonetta unloaded the bottles while Veronica pulled their trestle from the mule and set the table together. Hundreds of other pitches competed for room and Simonetta began to doubt that they would even sell one bottle of their precious elixir. But she draped the trestle with blue velvet and ranked the crystal bottles on the cloth, making the wares look as tempting as she could. At Manodorata's initiative she had opened one of the bottles, and brought a cup on a chain which Veronica affixed to the table leg, so that the liquor might be tasted by perspective buyers at the price of a *centesimo*. They stood back and waited as the sun climbed and the people milled around their table. As Manodorata had suspected, many folk gathered to stare at the lady in the red dress, but some stayed to taste, and then to buy. Simonetta became bolder with each sale, losing her shyness and chatting with the crowd, charming noble customers with her breeding but using a lower kitchen wit for the tradesmen and servants. Veronica was a solid welcome presence at her back, her fingers dourly counting the money while her dark eyes saw everything. She shooed the bold brave urchins that crept below the table to catch the falling drops from the pewter cup and chain in their mouths. Twice she clasped the wrist of a pickpocket in her iron grip, and once she saw, as Simonetta did not, that a friendly noblewoman who fingered the stuff of Simonetta's gown was plucking the pearls from the golden net. A flash of the Maltese knives was enough to send the dame back into the crowd. By the time the bells of the Duomo struck Nones they had sold every last bottle, and the town buzzed with the news of the miraculous new drink. As the two women packed away, the townsfolk became so clamorous with their advance orders that Simonetta caused Veronica to borrow quill and vellum from a notary, so that she could write them down. By noon they were gone, with promises to return. Both sang in earnest now, and a fat bag of ducats jingled and bounced against the neckbone of Veronica's mule.

Amaria Sant'Ambrogio, in the market to buy figs, saw the wonder of the lady in the red dress and tasted from the cup on the chain. She felt – as she always did when she experienced anything to delight her – that she must fetch Selvaggio to share in it too. Once she would have hoisted her skirts and run all the way home, but mindful of her new-found decorum she merely hurried home as fast as she could with no unseemly displays of her flesh. She found Selvaggio in the lean-to workshop he had built in their yard, and she took his arm to come at once, even in the carpenter's apron he wore. They hastened back to the cathedral square to see the fabled beauty and taste the wonderful liquor of almonds. But by the time they reached the Duomo the sun was high and the pitch was empty. Amaria identified a passing Marshal by his quartered tabard and was told they had just missed the lady by a matter of moments. Only the accounts of the townsfolk remained; the good burghers of Pavia seemed dazed by the May madness as they enthused about the noblewoman in red and her incredible brew. Even Amaria, whose discourse had become more measured of late, talked all the way home of the lady, whom she claimed was as beautiful as the Queen of Heaven herself. But Selvaggio kept his peace. For his own taste, the only true beauty in womanhood belonged to she who told him the tale.

CHAPTER 30

Pogrom

Manodorata, swaddled in his bear furs, walked through Saronno's square. If any of the good citizens spat in his path, or crossed themselves as he passed, he did not notice today. His mind was preoccupied by a growing unease that had loomed larger over him since he had broken his fast with Rebecca and the boys. The day was cold and bright, and nothing seemed away from the ordinary, yet he was not comfortable in his chair, or his gardens. He could not sit or stand easily, and he thought to walk off his fears, but the foreboding followed him like a shadow. He was not wearing a ruff today, but his neck prickled uncomfortably. He ran his finger around his collar, but found no relief. He felt like a man on the block, throat exposed and cold, waiting for the axe to fall.

As he passed the Sanctuary a flutter of white caught his eye. As he approached the church doors his dread grew stronger, and there he found the source of his fears. The feelings that had stung him in the morning, like single wasps, had led him here; gathering more and more until there was a black swarm, emanating from this: the wasps' nest. It was a placard, written in precise Latin, elegantly calligraphed, and bearing the Cardinal's seal. What he read there made him turn for home at once.

Once inside his starred doorway he dropped his furs and called for Rebecca. For the second time in their marriage he told her that they must leave their home and fly for their lives. For the Cardinal had decreed that the right of Jews to own property or conduct business in the region had been revoked, and any that sought to contravene this edict would be put to the fire. Rebecca put her arms about him and he felt soothed, assuring her there would be time to pack and leave in the morning.

This was his fatal mistake.

For the sake of their sons they kept their eventide the same: they ate together and prayed together as the boys went to bed. Elijah held two white candles in his hands as he said the *hashkiveinu* evening prayer, flushed with this rare privilege. 'Lay us down to sleep, *Adonai*, our God, in peace; raise us erect, our King, to life, and spread over us the shelter of your peace.' His young voice chimed like a bell, the creamy candles were almost as tall as he, and the tallow light kissed his gold curls and turned him to an angel. His face though, held an earthly expression of half pride, half cheek. His parents smiled on him and Manodorata's heart ached. He had never loved the boy more than this night. Elijah, bright eyed and intelligent, knew that Sarah was packing their trunks, but trusted his parents to tell him what he needed to know when the time was right.

Soon both boys were asleep and Rebecca came again to her husband. 'Shall I lie with you tonight?' she said, with a smile and an arch of her dark brow.

He smelled the frankincense on her skin and could feel her shivering with fear despite her playful nature. He smiled and shook his head. 'My jewel,' he said. 'No. We must rest well, for tomorrow we must travel far.' He pulled her close for a kiss by hauling gently on her black ropes of hair, just as he had done when they were first married.

When she had gone to her chamber, he had a visitor. Isaac, son of Abiathar; a great friend, wearing his distinctive black and white robes of the Jewish scholar. He sat, as bidden, by the fire and took a cup of wine, but was soon up again, his ugly face lively and agitated. 'Zaccheus, you have heard what is decreed against us. Where will you go?'

Manodorata sighed. 'Genoa. We will find a ship and travel east, perhaps to the Ottoman Empire. It depends where I may buy passage.'

Isaac scratched his chin. 'Genoa.' He weighed the word. 'Jew-hating and plague ridden. 'Tis a bleak place.'

'It is. Yet it is the nearest major port, and it is hard to know in these times who *will* welcome our people.'

Isaac nodded sagely. 'Why do you tarry? If you leave tonight, you could reach Genoa by the Sabbath.'

Manodarata smiled thinly, his eyes shadowed by the fire. 'Isaac, my friend, you know not what it is to have a wife and children. I must not alarm my sons. A few more hours will not matter.'

Isaac drained his cup. 'I hope you are right. I head for Pavia this very night.' He held out his hand. 'I will not see you again. But you have been my good friend, and I wish you well. *Shalom.*'

'*Shalom,*' Manodorata replied. 'Once again I am indebted to your family for the good offices of friendship; for it was your own father Abiathar who warned me to quit Toledo, may he rest in peace.'

The scholar nodded. 'Yet it was your gift of monies without interest to my father that saved us from penury and enabled us to escape here too. So let us not speak of debts.'

In answer Manodorata held out his hand of flesh and pulled Isaac close for an embrace. When his friend had gone he sat for perhaps an hour, watching the embers die but seeing nothing. When he felt cold he went at last to his chamber and laid, fully dressed, on his fur coverlet. He was suddenly too tired to disrobe.

Manodorata's dreams were strange and threatening. He dreamed that he was dressed in a red velvet doublet and hat with blue hose and was tied to a tree. By his side was a black ladder climbing to the stars. His sons Elijah and Jovaphet were tied at his feet, both wearing black, one lashed to each of his legs. When he looked down he could see their blonde heads shine. They were crying. Surrounding him were ten men and four horses, the colours of the horsemen of the Apocalypse, watching his fate with blank expressions, unmoved. The black sky arced over his head, with white stars hanging like blossoms. In the tree above him, the same blossoms waved in the breeze. Under his foot he felt the bump of a round stone. Then he felt the heat as they put the fire to the ropes at his chest and he began to burn and choke. Heard the boys' screams as the flames threatened them. His golden hand grew hot and his wrist scalded with the fire.

Then he woke.

His bed was aflame, the curtains and poles consumed and the flames licking the coverlet. His gold hand had lain in the fire and he had not felt it. He leapt from his bed and ran to Rebecca's room, but the fire beat him back. There was a furnace within. He backed away and ran to his sons' chamber. He almost wept with relief when he saw that they still slept, untouched. He gathered them up, blankets and all, and ran down the stair. At the starred door he could hear the ugly chanting of a mob. He doubled back through the courtyard, hushing Elijah's questions and Jovaphet's cries. He kicked open the gate to the herb garden and crashed through the fence. Holding the boys high he waded through nightearth, through the wastepits of his house and those of the whole street till they emerged on the outskirts of

Saronno. Without once turning back, he began to follow the well-known path to the Villa Castello.

Simonetta saw them come. Ever at her window, up at dawn for the almond harvest that was to take place this day, she saw them stagger up the path, through the almond groves. She ran down and could see at once that something was very wrong. The usually immaculate Manodorata was stinking and besmottered, the boys and he were black with smoke and the older child – Elijah? – had white stripes on his face where his tears had run through the grime. Manodorata shook his head as she began to question him.

'Ask no questions. For your mercy give the boys a bed. I must go back,' his face contorted in anguish. 'Rebecca…'

She understood and took the boys in her arms at once. Her friend turned and fled down the path as Elijah screamed 'Father!'

She gentled him. 'He will come back,' she said, hoping it was true.

The boy's blue eyes stared out from his blackened face. 'And mother too?'

She knew not what to say. 'He has gone to find her. Come, we will clean you and find you a warm place to sleep.'

Elijah submitted then to her ministrations, and Jovaphet ceased his bawling and plugged his mouth with his thumb. The smaller boy played with her hair as she took them up

to the kitchen. She was at sea – she had never had anything to do with children. Women of her class always had
nursemaids and she had known no younger siblings or small
cousins. She laid Jovaphet on a fur before the fire and cast
her eye around for something to amuse him. The Chinese
clove jar answered the task and he played happily, amused
by the bright colours and tiny wreathed dragons while she
took a cloth to Elijah's face. She ran to Jovaphet just as he
was about to roll into the hearth, but was too late to prevent
him from adding to the soot that already rimed his clothes.
He had opened the clove jar and was about to put one of
the spicy black nails in his mouth just before she rescued it,
and had to sweep up the rest. As she swept up the precious
cloves, Elijah kicked over the bowl of water and soaked his
already freezing feet. She knew not whether to laugh or
cry at her own hoplessness, but Elijah's face decided her.
The boy was shivering, and said not a word as his little
mouth was set in a line. His eyes were glassy with unshed
tears in the firelight. She chattered in a way that was alien
to her as she wiped him clean, then let him help wash the
face and hands of his little brother. Then she carried them
both up the stair and laid them on her own bed, pulling
the coverlet of vair over them both. She knew she must get
down to the harvesters, to direct their work, so was relieved
that Jovaphet was asleep almost at once, his thumb firmly
in place. But as she laid Elijah down, the tears spilled at
last from his eyes and into his ears. He held tightly to her

hand and turned his eyes upon her, and suddenly she knew what to do. Her awkwardness and her ineptitude disappeared. She shrugged her cloak off while he still held her hand, and climbed in beside him. She held him close and kissed his white blonde head, closing her eyes and breathing in the sweet bitterness of woodsmoke. She marvelled at the blondeness of these Jewish children and then cursed her ignorance – why should they not be blonde, why must they have black hair and swarthy eastern features?

As her lips touched Elijah's head and she tasted his tears she felt an overwhelming desire to protect him and his brother. In that moment she loved him like her own son. She held him close until he slept, and then reluctantly disentangled her fingers from his, kissed his sleeping lids and went down to the men. She turned at the door and murmured to the sleeping pair that all would be well, even though she knew that it would not.

In the grey dawn Manodorata walked back to Saronno. He had no need for fading stars to guide him, for a black pall of smoke rose in a black column from Jews' Street. As he got nearer his house he saw it was nought but charred snaggle teeth, open and roofless to the sky. The blackened stairs climbed to nowhere. He prayed every prayer he knew that Rebecca might have escaped the flames before they claimed her. He covered his face and joined the looting mob that trampled his home, like jackdaws pecking at carrion. He witnessed one man, the baker with the wall eye, spit on his mother's filigree box and rub it on his sleeve till the silver shone through the soot, before putting it in his pocket. Manodorata wanted to kill him.

He searched through the wreckage till he saw what he dreaded. A blackened spider of a hand reached heavenward from beneath a charred beam. It wore a gold ring with the Star of David, the ring he had given her in Toledo on their betrothal day. He knelt then, for his legs would not support him. He touched her warm ashes once, then took the ring from the dark bones. The baker clapped him on the shoulder, almost sending him into the ashes. 'You lucky knave! That's a rare prize indeed, too good for a Jew's whore. Would that I had seen it first,' then he continued in his search, lumbering through the things that the family had loved. Manodorata's eyes darkened and he forgot to breathe as the rage boiled within him. He would have struck the man down had he not remembered his sons – Rebecca's sons – and he slipped the ring on his smallest finger and walked away quickly, head bowed, back to Villa Castello.

He headed up the path through the almond grove. The trees wept blossom for him and he remembered his dream. He found the largest sturdiest tree with the most beautiful aspect and crouched at its foot. He made a small hole in the groin of two large roots and buried the ring in the cold earth. He said the *tehillim*, the wind whipping the Hebrew words from his mouth and scattering them in the hills.

Then, as was the custom, he took a round stone and placed it on Rebecca's grave.

He walked to the house then. Two of the Jewish harvesters raised their hands in greeting but choked back their *shaloms* when they saw his face. His eyes were flint and tearless but his heart was black, as black as his charred house, as black as Rebecca's bones, as black as the earth where her ring lay, with hatred for the Cardinal of Milan.

CHAPTER 31

Candle Angel

Bernardino had dreamed of Elijah, the boy with the dove in
his hand. He did not know why the memory troubled him
now. All his dreams were of his time in Saronno, but mostly
he slept in the slim circle of Simonetta's arms. He did not
dream of the paintings he had done, or the friendships he
had made. Only of her. After his troubled and early awaken-
ing he left his cell at dawn and walked through the cloister,
thinking of the boy as he had clung to him when he carried
him from harm. He had never felt a connection to a child
in his life before, yet this one had struck him to the heart.
Though it was yet daybreak he could hear the sisters' song
from the Hall of the Nuns and marvelled at the steadfast-
ness of their devotions. Then he smiled at himself, for was
not he rising early to follow his own religion?

He walked straight into the Hall of the Believers and
took up his brushes. As he mixed his pigments he remembered again, as the dream faded, the sweet face of Elijah. The
tow head and the smiling eyes when he caught Bernardino

uttering an oath he should not have spoken. Bernardino shivered as he drew the face from memory. He hoped the boy were not dead, for he knew well that the dead visited in dreams. Dead or in danger. If so, this would be his memorial. The charcoal lines grew into an angel, wings sprouted from the shoulders and a loveable *putto* formed – not a lofty cherub with a heavenly countenance to sit in the fabled ranks of the seraphim, but a human child with a human expression. Bernardino worked till noon, laying shadow and colour. He placed two long white ceremonial candles in the child's hands where they weighed like the scales of justice. Lastly the same tallow-white provided highlights to burnish the gold curls. Bernardino stood back and rested his chin on his aching hand. He remembered when he had met Elijah, that the boy had instinctively trusted Bernardino and told him his true name before correcting himself with the Christian version 'Evangelista'. This gave Bernardino pause. The boy was a Jew. Did he have a right to depict the child here, among the Christian Saints, watched over by a God that was not his own? Without knowing precisely why, he mixed a thick blood-scarlet and adorned the wing feathers till they were a rich red. Should posterity question, the red wings marked him out – an angel apart.

CHAPTER 32

Hand, Heart and Mouth

Amaria and Selvaggio went into the woods. As soon as they were under the cover of the trees, they clasped hands, as was their custom when none of the townsfolk could see. Today she felt the pull of his hand as he led the way. 'Where are we going?' she asked.

He slid his leaf-green eyes sideways and smiled. 'You'll see.'

She asked no more. She was happy, holding his hand, going wherever he would. Now and again she looked at him – his beloved serious face dappled by the leaves under the sun, now light, now dark.

Selvaggio looked back at her, and rejoiced in her beauty. On this shining day she seemed all of a piece with the coming of spring – she could be the goddess *Primavera* herself. Her skin glowed with health, her hair shone in its carefully dressed loops and coils about her ears and neck, studded today in reverence for the spring with white and yellow days-eyes. Her gown was the same green as the sward, cut from a bale of cloth that he had bought her with his earnings, made up before the fire by Nonna. Her dark eyes sparkled with animation and promise. She was so *alive*, so fecund. Selvaggio could see her lying above and beneath him, laughing, her abundant hair spread on a pillow. He could imagine her carrying his child, his children – the curves of her body growing in amplitude with the passing months. Sun-spots danced in his eyes and desire beat in his chest so hard that he thought he might lose conciousness. He wanted her *so* much, wanted her not just as his lover, but as the root of his family. She had brought him back from death and made him live again. She was as a fruitful vine, and he wanted to live to see their children's children.

They walked through the glades and the clearings, following the crystal brook till they came to the *pozzo dei mariti*. As Amaria saw the wells and heard the splashing of the falls she gasped in delight. ''Tis where we first met!' she said.

Selvaggio smiled, and led her to the nearest pool, where a fish leaped and dropped with a sudden flash of silver. When the surface had settled again, mirror bright, they looked into the pool together, his hands on her shoulders. 'Do you know what they say of this place?'

Amaria blushed. 'They say that…if you look into the pool, you can see the face of…your husband.' She spoke falteringly, as if in a dream.

'And is it true?'

She looked closely at him, mindful of his teasing. But his face was serious, and she suddenly saw that he was not playing a game. 'You tell me.'

'I think it is.' He turned her to face him, and her heart leapt too, like the fish they had seen jump. 'I love you, Amaria Sant'Ambrogio.' He said the words she had first taught him; '*mano*,' as he took her hand, '*cuore*,' as he placed her hand on his heart, '*bocca*,' as he kissed her, tenderly, on the mouth.

When at last they broke apart her eyes were filled with tears. She was beautiful as she laughed with pure joy. 'Come home,' she said, 'we must tell Nonna.' They hurried back through the woods and across the river, and this time Amaria held Selvaggio's hand all the way through the town so that all may see, as if she would never let it go.

CHAPTER 33

Saint Ursula and the Arrows

Bernardino suffered a troubled night. He twisted on his pallet of straw, and opened his eyes to horrible visions that marched across the roof of his cell. Fire, screams and Simonetta in danger. He slept at last, but the visions lived then behind his eyes, and he awoke to the grey day with his cheeks wet, in a panic of consternation that he could no longer remember Simonetta's face. He headed for the lay hall to begin his work, and as he heard the nuns finish the songs of Terce he waited for Sister Bianca's footsteps. He knew she would come, as she always did before she began the day's offices. She took his instruction seriously, and he welcomed her company, more than ever today when he was afraid to be alone with his own forebodings.

Presently he knew she was there, though she had entered on silent feet; and he felt rather than heard her seated behind him, knew he would turn to see her with her hands piously crossed, watching with wonder as a heathen painted a Holy scene as if he believed every story and symbol. He felt the comfort of her presence, not as a mother figure nor yet a sister, but as something apart from every woman he had ever known. He had never felt such indifference to the female person, and yet such a warmth of friendship, without the difficulties and challenges that normally beset men and women in their discourse. His mother, frequently jug-bitten or absent with this lover or that, had had little time for him. Simonetta he had loved with his whole heart and she had sent him away in the name of her God. But Sister Bianca asked nothing from him, yet gave her time and her knowledge, her comfort and solace.

'Today's subject?' her gentle tones reached him.

'Saint Ursula.'

'Ah, Saint Ursula.'

'Tell me. I know only that she is depicted with arrows. I should like to know why.'

She told him then, speaking as a mother who tells a tale to her children, as his mother had never done. As in the best tales there was happiness but also sorrow, and there was evil as well as good. She spared him nothing. 'Once, in the land of Brittany, there lived a good king whose name was Theonotus. He had one daughter who was the sun in his sky. He taught her well, and she soon knew all there was to know about the lands of the earth, the elements that it held, she could name each flower and bird, each heavenly body, and which countries lay in the breath of the four winds. The princess grew to be as beautiful as she was wise, and she was soon sought in marriage by Conan, son of the king of England across the sea, which was at that time a heathen country which had not accepted the Christian faith.'

As before, when the Abbess spoke, Bernardino saw the scenes she described to him appear on the blank panel he was to paint. He did not understand what had happened to him to make him see in this way, that he was now brother to those seers, or scryers or soothsayers of the pagan world, or even the religious visionaries of the Holy one. He knew only that what came to him was real. He saw now the golden princess, growing in beauty and learning, kneeling to kiss the papery cheek of her greybeard father.

'The king was saddened that his daughter may leave him,' the Abbess went on, 'but the girl agreed to the match on three conditions.'

Bernardino watched the scene as Ursula drew herself up to address the English emissaries, tall and straight as a willow wand. '"I would have the prince send to me ten of the noblest ladies of your land to be my companions and friends; and for each of these ladies and myself, a thousand handmaidens to wait upon us," said Ursula. "Secondly, he must give me three years before the date of my marriage so that I and these maidens may have time to affirm our faith by visiting the shrines of the Saints in distant lands. And thirdly, I ask that the prince Conan shall accept the true faith and be baptized a Christian. For I cannot wed even so great and perfect a prince, if he be not as perfect a Christian."'

Bernardino smiled to himself at the resolute nature of the young woman he now watched. He lowered his voice as if Ursula were actually there. 'So she witheld her person so that he should convert.'

'In truth she believed that her conditions would be too much for Conan and she would remain free,' replied Sister Bianca. 'But Ursula was fairer than any lady that walked the earth – her skin was pearl; her hair was gold, and her eyes were as blue as the Virgin's robe.'

Bernardino swallowed as he thought of Simonetta, for she had eyes that could be described so. Again he struggled to see her as clearly as the Saint before him. Of her he needed no such description, as he could clearly see the princess on the wall before him; he began to draw Ursula's face as Bianca spoke with quick and accurate strokes. 'The English sent letters to all points of the compass, to Ireland, Scotland and Wales, bidding all knights and nobles to send their daughters to court with their attendant maidens, the fairest and noblest of the land. Ursula gathered the eleven thousand maidens about her, and in a green meadow with a silver stream she baptized all those that had not yet accepted God. They set out for Rome to visit the shrine of the Saints, and their journey through the icy mountains was so hard that our Lord God sent six angels to help the eleven thousand on their way. Presently they descended into Italy and journeyed past the great lakes of our own dear Lombardy where the white mountains gaze at their twins in the looking-glass water. At last they reached the Holy City and there Conan followed, to be reunited with his lady at the end of the three years and be blessed by the Pope himself. Great was the rejoicing of the pair at their reunion, for despite her initial reluctance Ursula had come to love her betrothed. He had received instruction in the Christian faith and caused himself to be baptised, and as he had bent himself to her will and fulfilled her conditions, she accepted him with her whole heart in the sight of God.'

Once again Bernardino's sight was filled with a vision and the wall came to life. As he watched the transfigured scene he knew that such happiness invited doom, the doom he had seen in his dream. All sweetness faded to death and despair, as his own love for Simonetta had done. He knew Conan and Ursula would not remain united, and as he watched the happy pair kneel at the fabled shrines, he felt a shiver of pity.

'They worshipped at the shrines of Peter and Paul then set out for Cologne to continue their pilgrimage. But the barbarian huns that laid seige to that city were troubled by their coming. They knew that such a company of fair pilgrims would likely settle in the city and in a short time would marry and convert their husbands – and so the whole region – to Christianity. So the huns fell on the defenceless pilgrims and turned their deadly bows upon them. Prince Conan was the first to fall, pierced by an arrow, at the feet of his princess. Then the savage soldiers fell upon the gentle maidens like a pack of wolves, and these eleven hundred white lambs were slain, every one.'

Once again, Bernardino saw the carnage carried to him by the nun's sweet voice. He looked among the fallen for Ursula. He knew she must be there, but needed to know her fate. 'Ursula stood brave and steadfast through it all, with courage and fortitude. Her beauty and courage shone forth so brightly that she was spared by the barbarians. And when she stood alone over the dead they took her to their king. He was so taken with her beauty and courage that he offered her marriage. She refused with such scorn and censure that he bent the bow that was in his hand, shot three arrows through the heart of Princess Ursula and killed her instantly. But Ursula and her eleven thousand virgins defeated death; for they became famous in their martyrdom, and Ursula, in losing her earthly crown, attained the crown of heaven. She is still the Saint of intercession for all those who die by the arrow; a plentiful company I'm afraid, in these times.' The nun fell silent at this, no doubt in the hope that Bernardino would reflect on her words.

Bernardino clenched his fists. He fought to resist the piety of the tale, the pat conclusion of inevitable martyrdom. How foolish had he been to hope, to think that Ursula could survive, as her end was painted on every chapel in Christendom. But then he thought of Simonetta, of her courage; not in battle but in everyday life, the way she had come to him, chin high, for the money to save her house, her fortitude when the townsfolk censured her in the church, the way she had faced him and sent him away when everything but God's law cried out for them to be together. He thought of the times she had told him of her daily hunts with her bow, the way she had honed her aim from day to day, thinking of the Spaniards that had shot her husband. Did she know this tale? Did she pray to the patron Saint of arrows? He now gave Ursula a robe of gold and white, and a cloak of purple and red. Her hair was twisted back but red-gold curls still framed the lovely face. He worked long after Sister Bianca had gone, till Ursula held a sheaf of arrows in one hand and a palm leaf in the other. The brush in his hand led the Saint's eyes down to the red winged angel on the panel below, and he completed the depiction with a cruel death barb protruding from the Ursula's bosom. The eyes, serene with hooded Lombard lids, remained unmoved despite the sticking arrow; bent on the child Elijah, as if the dying woman could see the future in children. Finally Bernardino mixed his whites and golds and placed a crown of heaven on her head, a crown of gossamer light filigree, with fleur de lys and circlets of silver and gilt. He wondered if Simonetta too would show such courage in the face of a true life or death conflict. He could not shake his sense of impending darkness, as if night was falling around him as it did outside. He climbed down from his platform and, in an awkward genuflection, knelt on the cold stone. He began to pray for the first time in years. His language was halting, his tones unnacustomed. He did not address anyone, not a Saint or Deity, not Father, Son or Holy Ghost. He just fervently asked that the day that would ask so much of Simonetta and her arrows would never come.

CHAPTER 34

Rebecca's Tree

Manodorata and his two sons stayed at Castello at Simonetta's insistence. She made it a home for them, using her newfound wealth to furnish their rooms with Castilian artefacts that she found in Pavia and at Como and Lodi, the other markets she attended with her Amaretto brew. Manodorata never once spoke of Rebecca, and Simonetta never asked of her, but she knew that the second time he came to her house that fateful day, she was gone. Jovaphet, too young to understand, asked for her daily but was easily soothed with a comfit or an embrace. Elijah, silent and taciturn, soaked his bed nightly and awoke fevered and screaming. Simonetta saw that Manodorata was too damaged to comfort his boys, so she took the task upon herself. She began to lie with them, so that Elijah could find her hand with his in the night, and drift back to sleep never knowing, in his dreamlike state, that she was not Rebecca.

With the spring, Elijah began to thaw; his smiles came again and she heard him laugh as he chased Jovaphet around the groves. She was glad of it but concerned for her friend. Manodorata seemed to concentrate only on the selling and production of the Amaretto, and never looked in his own heart once. Night after night, in the light evenings of the dog days, they sat in fireside amity drinking the almond draught and speaking of their new venture. At these moments Simonetta thought that he may speak to her of what he had lost. But he did not, nor did she speak of Bernardino, so they sat on, both hobbled by love; turtle doves with their wings clipped, doomed to flightlessness.

The next time Simonetta and Veronica went to market in Pavia they were approached by a man in black and white robes. He greeted Veronica in Hebrew and asked Simonetta if Manodorata was well. Fearing a trap Simonetta looked to Veronica, on whose sound judgement she had come to rely. The mute nodded, and so Simonetta told the man all she could of her friend and his sons. The Jew asked a few courteous questions, then bowed and said: 'Please tell him that Isaac, son of Abiathar of Toledo, wishes him well. I once was lucky enough to call him my friend.'

Simonetta looked to Veronica again and said, 'Why don't you tell him yourself? You're welcome, Signore, to come back to my house, where he now resides.'

Isaac rode back with them, telling Simonetta along the way what a debt he and his late father owed to Manodorata, and as Simonetta listened to the complicated tale of usury and rescue from bankruptcy she once again marvelled at the solidarity of the Jewish people. When she had been in need no Christian would lend her a hand; only a Jew had given her succour, and friendship.

She knew her instincts were sound when the two friends embraced each other on the loggia of her house. She retired early and let the men talk. She hoped that Manodorata could find solace in an older friend; and perhaps speak, at last, of Rebecca.

Isaac never left Castello. Simonetta noted his scholarly status and engaged him as a tutor to the boys, deeming it fitting that they should have a good education and a thorough knowledge of the Jewish Holy texts. Her own knowledge grew with theirs as Elijah began to share tales and fables with her. She marvelled again at how different, yet how similar the religions were. As summer blushed into autumn her family warmed too. Manodorata seemed happier and mellowed with the seasons. She watched with joy as a friendship began to blossom between Isaac and Veronica, with a promise of more. Then came the unforgettable day when Elijah ran into the kitchen to show her a red lizard from the garden. The creature lay still and hot in his hand, tongue flickering like a tiny dragon, and Elijah called Simonetta 'mother' in his excitement. She made no comment, and admonished him for the mud on his boots, but her heart thrilled as she hugged him close and fiercely. He soon fell into the use of the name, and Jevophat followed suit.

Simonetta looked anxiously at Manodorata when the boys called her so; his eyes remained inscrutable but he uttered no reproach, nor did he correct his sons. She was delighted at this new love that had come to her. She had not known that children could mean so much to her, that her love for the boys could use the limitless resources of a wasted heart. She had always thought to fill these walls with a family that she loved and who loved her in return. She had just always thought that they would be flesh of her own flesh. She was learning that family meant more than bloodlines, much more.

All was well until the baker from Saronno brought bread and pastries to the house. A sign of their new prosperity, Simonetta had ordered treats for the boys to celebrate the second almond harvest. It was a full year since they had come to the house, and she wished for them to find happiness on a day that might bring bad memories. Manodorata, working in the groves, knew the wall-eye and bulbous nose of the baker at once, and stared for a fraction too long. As he had last seen the knave spitting on Rebecca's ashes, he could not resist a freezing glance at the man's face. Later he cursed himself as the baker turned his mule to go. Manodorata was without his furs or velvets; he wore the red hat and tunic with blue hose like all the harvesters, and his gold hand was gloved, but he knew he had been seen.

The next day, they came.

Night was falling and the stars began to prick out the sky. Manodorata was at the great almond tree, which he privily called 'Rebecca's Tree', plucking the last of the harvest nuts from the branches. The boys were at his feet playing 'hot cockles'; they wore black tunics for their mother which contrasted strongly with their father's red and blue harvester's garb, but they seemed happy enough. They took turns to don a makeshift blindfold while the other poked his brother with a switch. Laughing and giddy, the blinded one tried to capture his assailant who stood, tantalising, out of reach, crowing 'hot cockles!' Manodorata was jolted by the image, thinking suddenly of Synagoga, the female symbolic personification of Judaism. The Jewess was always presented in religious art wearing a blindfold to indicate her ignorant practices, and worse still, holding the head of a goat to symbolise the Devil. Manodorata had seen such an image once, Synagoga's sorrowing blindfolded head drooping as she stood, petrified in statuary, high in a niche on the cathedral in Strasbourg. That day he had turned away, sickened, thinking that such ignorant iconography had little to do with him. But today he remembered and knew that such prejudice had everything to do with him. It had taken his hand and his wife, and once again Manodorata smelled the evil scent of premonition. As the sun dropped it grew cold, and Jovaphet's little eyes began to close under the blindfold, and Manodorata knew he should get them within.

He turned to break the news when a new sunrise caught his eye – a light warming the path, then another, then another.

Torches.

Fire had only ever meant trouble for him and his. He clasped the boys to him and hurried up the path to the loggia, but there, his ugly face and wall-eye illumined, stood the baker.

They took Manodorata then, and tied him to Rebecca's tree; with ropes that bound his chest about and about till he could scarcely breathe. He shouted at the boys to run, but they were stunned to stillness and were taken too. As he saw that they could not escape he choked to his sons that it was just a game, but nothing could stop their screams as they were tied to him, one to each leg, and black faggots laid at their feet. Now they struggled and keened like rabbits caught in a snare and called out to him, tears dripping onto their mourning clothes. He could feel their little hands scrabbling to touch his legs, their shoulders turning against his thighs. He could do nothing. They were in the hands of God; and God, it seemed, had turned his face away. He searched the ugly faces for one sympathetic countenance, someone who hung back, unsure of what he did; someone to reason with. If Manodorata could just find that one wavering man in the crowd he would not plead for his own life, but would beg till his last breath that the boys could go free. But every face was shuttered, every eye evil, and every mouth spat forth the ugly epithets he had spent his life trying to keep from the ears of Elijah and Jovaphet. Manodorata raised his eyes to the fat stars hanging in the black sky, and the black ladder the mob had brought to gather kindling, and he understood at once. There was to be no escape. This hour was written in his fate; he knew that his dream had come to claim him. He was there, in the tableau of his nightmares. Tied to a stake, with his children tied to him, a trinity of martyrs awaiting the death-fire. There were ten men surrounding them, six jeering in an ugly knot of a crowd around the baker, and four mounted. Just like his dream, they rode the pale horse, white horse, black horse and saffron horse of the riders of the apocalypse. The sky was as black as the world's end, and he knew he was finished. He looked down at the blonde heads of his children, and twisted his hands till the ropes cut; he knew he could not pull free but he wanted to place his hands on their golden hair one last time. So warm, so soft. 'I *love* you,' he whispered. He had never told them before, and never would again.

The baker stepped forth with his torch and spat foul phlegm at Manodorata's face. Manodorata would not flinch, nor turn his cheek as the Testament said, but his gaze bored into the baker's ugly eyes and damned him for what he did. The baker dropped his head, discomfited, and vengefully thrust his torch into the woodpile at the boys' feet. He cursed and spat as the faggots refused to light. Manodorata stamped impotently at the falling sparks with his bound feet but there was no need, the fire would not take. Suddenly he felt Rebecca's memorial stone, the stone he had placed there a year ago, lying round and hard under his foot. At that moment he knew that she was with him. A small flame of hope leapt in Manodorata's heart but was soon doused as the baker soaked the ropes of his chest with oil of olives, and set them aflame with a burning brand. As the fire scorched his flesh he knew *he* was done for, but the blaze rose upwards above the ropes, clear of the boys' heads. Perhaps God was watching and *would* save them, if asked. Manodorata closed his ears to the jeers of the crowd and the tears of his sons. He lifted his eyes to Heaven and began to speak in Hebrew. His hectic brain, confused and boiling with the unbelievable pain, could not find the right prayers of supplication. It could only fix upon the words that Elijah had spoken, for their last evening prayer before Rebecca died. 'Lay us down to sleep, *Adonai*, our God, in peace; raise us erect, our King, to life, and spread over us the shelter of your peace.' Before he reached the *Amen*, the fire claimed his throat.

Simonetta was brought to her window by the conflagration, and thought at first that a forest fire had come to claim her trees. But her horrified eyes soon registered the tied figure in the ring of torchlight, and the men and horses gathered round the great almond tree. She did not hesitate over the weapons of old and new – she knew little of the arquebus, not how to either hold or fire it, and could see that the children were bound close to their father. There was no time. She took up her hunting bow at once and in a second had set an arrow on the string. She narrowed her arrow-eye at once upon the baker, who seemed to be leading the mob, but her friend's face above the fire gave her pause. She forced herself to look at Manodorata – he showed no pain as his chest burned but looked at her directly, steel eyes bright in the charred face, she saw him fix his eyes on her, then give a slow nod and close them forever. She knew he was lost. She knew what must be done, and as a ruff of flame began to light his beard she shot him once, precisely, in the chestspoon where the ropes bound him. She knew that she had pierced his heart, for his head dropped at once. All was done in an instant. Shaking, she ran down the stairs, pulling Isaac back from the doorway as he ran to help. Veronica was mutely readying her Maltese knives for revenge but her mistress shook her head. 'Stay inside,' she hissed, 'there are too many; they'll take you too!'

As Simonetta walked outside, she blinked back her brimming tears and forced her chin high. She clasped her bow tight in one hand and a sheaf of arrows in the other, to stop the shaking. She wore a new golden gown trimmed with white vair. She was Saint Ursula to the life. She knew the test was yet to come. It felt as if the world had ended and indeed the stars began to fall as she strode to the mob. Her fevered brain could hardly register but as the cold blossoms touched her face she knew them to be snowflakes. In September. The Book of Revelation had come to pass and the skies wept for it.

She faced the baker as the fire burned her friend's body with the hideous stench of charred alien meat. Burning oil dropped on the heads of the crying boys and she feared that their hair would catch but she forced herself to look away from them, and face the mob with a cruel smile.

'A goodly shot, my lady,' said the baker, with deference borne of surprise. He had heard it said that the whore of Saronno harboured Jews here and let them work for her. Apparently not.

'As is my right to dispatch such Infidel filth that trespass on my land.' Simonetta forced herself to say the words.

There was a murmur of approbation.

'Would you had fired the Jew's brats too,' she said. 'But I see the snow has damped your kindling.' Which, miraculously, it had.

'Aye,' replied the baker, clearly the ringleader. 'We had to soak the ropes instead. The oil of olives caught a treat, and he suffered more for his heart burned first.'

Simonetta blocked her ears to the science of her truest friend's end and walked to the tree through the falling snow. She took Elijah's face and forced his chin high, till his eyes met hers. *'Trust me,'* she mouthed, her face turned from the crowd. She turned back with decision. 'Good people,' she said. 'Of your kindness leave these heathen whelps with me.'

She forced Elijah to splay his fingers. 'They have little hands and can be my labourers. You have my word that they will be raised as Christians. They are too young to have caught the full contagion of the Hebrew. God will smile upon us all for claiming two lost sheep.'

The mob murmured again, and Simonetta dare not breathe.

''Tis true,' said a pardoner at last. 'So it says in the scripture.'

'Aye,' said the tavern keeper. 'I've two young lads myself. 'Tis best that they be spared. Their sire has paid for his sins.'

Simonetta could not look at the charred body of her friend. But she took her hunting knife and cut the boys down, her skin prickling with fear that the mob might stop her. She longed to cradle her boys, but such things could wait – she held each harshly by the wrist as they keened and cried.

The crowd began to melt away, but the baker lingered, his eyes magpie-bright at the thought of the golden hand that the fire had not touched.

'Let the crows peck at him,' she said dismissively, but he lingered still. She forced him to ask.

'And the hand?'

Simonetta thought fast. 'I will give it to Father Anselmo. Meet it is that the Infidel's gold shall be put to Godly use.'

'She's right,' said the pardoner, her greatest advocate. 'Why should you have it? If it goes to the church it will benefit all, not just your greedy purse.' He dragged his friend away, but both made a sketchy reverence to the lady before they left, a mark of their new-found respect. Simonetta, sickened by the admiration of such men, flashed a gracious smile. Lest she was watched, she pulled the boys into the house, and as she crossed the threshold her legs gave way, and she collapsed, at the feet of Isaac and Veronica. She clutched Isaac's arm. 'Now you may help him,' she said. 'Wait for a moment, to be sure they are gone. But then cut him down and lay him out and do such rites as your faith demands. He deserved a better death, but all shall be done right now he is gone. I must put the boys to bed.'

She let Veronica help her bathe and settle the white and silent boys. She thought of the time she had held them after their mother had died, and knew it would take time to quiet them. But the shock of the night's events had taken their toll. She kissed their closing eyes and this time, she made no assurances that all would be well. This time she made a promise that she knew she could keep. 'I'll look after you.'

Simonetta went down to join Isaac by the great tree. He had already dug a trench for the body, black in the white earth. She shook with cold and emotion, her mind struggling to countenance what had happened. How could her greatest friend be here and gone in the blink of an evil eye? And by her own hand? Manodorata now lay under Isaac's magpie cloak, waiting for internment. From the lie of the fabric Simonetta could tell that the arrow she had shot had been pulled from his chest. She was glad that Isaac had taken this office upon himself; that she would not have to see the protruding shaft of her handiwork. She damned herself for cowardice, and watched while the falling snow turned the pied cloak to pure white.

'It is fitting,' said Isaac.

Simonetta blinked away the snow. 'What is?' For nothing seemed to fit this night: the world had turned upside down. The snow gave the illusion of stars dropping from the sky and she felt that she was falling into infinite space. 'What is fitting?'

Isaac pointed to his friend's body. 'The shroud is now white. The correct colour for a *tachrihim*, the funeral wrappings of our people. God is at work.'

Wordlessly Simonetta di Saronno rolled back her golden sleeves and took the second shovel. She was moved that Isaac could think of God at such a time, when He seemed to have deserted his faithful servant, and taken him from his innocent children. Suddenly she saw in her mind's eye the image that Manodorata had described to her when first they truly talked, here under these trees. The flaming, pierced heart that Saint Agostino held in his hand, the Saint that had blamed the Jews for the death of Christ. The image seemed, now, to have enormous impact, and import, but Simonetta's spinning mind could not make sense of it. She knew only that when she saw such images again, she would know the burning heart, pierced by her own arrow, that beat in the Saint's hand. She would know it for the heart of her friend. She kept her peace and they worked in silence, joined, soon, by Veronica. Together they dug as the snow fell. Something metal sang on Simonetta's spade and the earth turned up a golden ring. She rubbed it on her gown and it showed clearly in the moon white night, a star with six points.

'Rebecca's,' said Isaac. As Simonetta nodded she felt a sob squeeze her throat like a cold hand. At length they were done and they laid Manodorata in the cold earth. Isaac intoned the last words and the *tehillim* psalms, as Manodorata had once done here for his dead wife. Simonetta did not uncover the body, but before they began to fill in the earth she knelt and felt beneath the shroud for the golden hand. She slipped Rebecca's ring onto the cold metal and felt it warm under her touch at once, almost as if he were still alive. Hot tears began to slide from her eyes. For although flesh would perish in time, the two golden symbols of the husband and the wife would lie in the earth forever. She vowed, here and now, that this grave, under this tree, was the nearest that the hand would ever come to Anselmo's coffers, and Simonetta knew the priest would approve.

They filled the grave and the black mound turned to white in an instant as the snow fell relentlessly. Veronica took Simonetta's arm to lead her inside, gesturing that they should leave Isaac be. The tutor nodded to his mistress briefly, and touched her shuddering shoulder once. 'Get you inside, lady,' he said. 'In the absence of his family I must be the *shomrim*, guardian of the dead. I will bide here a while and keep watch, and pray.'

Simonetta nodded. She was suddenly deathly tired, but not sure she would ever sleep again after what she had seen. She walked to the house arm in arm with her maid – her friend – and climbed the stair to rest with the boys lest they should need her in the night.

She was physically and mentally shattered by what she had done. Her hands shook and her teeth chattered despite the warm of the chamber. Her knees trembled at each step, her stomach churned and her throat threatened vomit. Had she been called upon to set an arrow on her bowstring now, she could not have done it. And yet in a moment of cold dispatch one short hour ago, an instant of rapid thought and speedy execution, she had killed someone. She had shot her bolt through a flaming heart and the fact that that heart was dying seemed to mitigate her actions not at all. Was this really what Lorenzo had done, on a daily basis, when he was away from her side on his lengthy campaigns? She had taken a life in mercy but he had done it for glory, and victory, and political gain; all much much more flimsy motivations than her own. In an action that surprised herself she pressed her shaking hands together, bent her weakling knees and moved her chattering teeth in prayer. She had been a stranger to God for some months now, and had, after the shocking, sickening events of this evening, admired Isaac's steadfast faith without understanding it. She had not prayed since Bernardino had gone. She knew she need not ask pardon for the taking of a life, for she had done it to end Manodorata's pain and save his children. So she did not pray for forgiveness, nor even for the soul of her friend. That could all come later. No, Simonetta suddenly felt she had thanks to give for a miracle; for the freak fall of snow that had damped the kindling that was to make the death-fire for the boys. The teachings of scripture came back to her and she remembered Saint Lucy had been saved from the fire as the faggots would not light. She remembered, too, Saint Apollonia, who willingly submitted to the fire, just as her friend had done. The tales were suddenly at her fingertips, as if they had been waiting – just out of her memory's reach – to be welcomed back and beckoned into her chambers like long-lost friends. She looked out of her window at the moon and stars and spoke, hands clasped, to those Saints; one who lived in Paradise without eyes and the other without teeth. 'Thank you,' she said.

CHAPTER 35

The Countess of Challant

Bernardino became well used to the rhythms of the Canonical hours. Matins, Lauds, Prime, Terce, Sext, Nones, Vespers, Compline. They sounded like footsteps; the steady tread of the single syllable – Lauds, Prime, Terce, Sext, Nones – breaking into a trot of double ones –Vespers, Compline – at the close of the Holy day. Race the sun as it falls, rush to cram in our devotions before the night's end and prayers begin the new day with the dawn. And yet there was never any rushing here, no hurrying, no urgency. Bernardino knew how long he was taking on each piece only by the prayers sung by the sisters. He became used to the quiet of the place; the thoughtful nuns walking in the gardens, or digging the herbs, or reading aloud from scripture. He inhabited a world where there were no harsh words, no awkward passions. Here there was no utterance louder than a prayer, no sound above the whisper of a long habit on the pavings, no assault to his ears beyond the modes and cadences of the plainsong. He felt the balm of his friendship with Bianca as a natural progression, a natural continuation of his friendship with her brother, a benign sequel to a sinister birth. He smiled a secret smile when he thought of how the two bars of the lineage resembled one another, of how the legitimate and the illegitimate both shared much from their father.

Bernardino set forth for another day of decorating this quiet world, another day when the osmosis of the religiosity that surrounded him would seep into his skin. Since he had prayed the other night he had begun, tentatively, to talk to God when Bianca was absent. So as he looked for his friend on this day, the day he was to begin the panel depicting Saint Catherine, he felt imbued with a sense of peace. And quietude. He was surprised, therefore, to find the Abbess pacing and agitated. She broke the egg of his calm, and took him at once to that other world, a world of violence, passion and death.

'What is it?'

'I need your help. Will you come?' Bianca's tone held an urgency and direction he had not known.

'What is the matter?' Bernardino was perplexed.

'There is little time,' said the Abbess. 'A friend is in grave danger. It is well you wear the robes of our lay brothers. Dressed thus, you will be safe in the crowd.'

'What crowd?' Bernardino was grateful for the disguise – he had set foot in the city a very few times in the last months – needful excursions only to meet his patron and buy pigments, for he was conscious that the Cardinal might still seek him. As if echoing his thought the Abbess said, 'I know that you risk your life if you leave these walls. I would not ask it of you lightly. Will you come or no?'

Bernardino only thought for a moment. He had a certain amount of natural courage, but a great deal of natural curiosity, and was suddenly galvanised with a desire to see what had come to pass in Milan. 'Of course,' he said.

Without further explanation Sister Bianca led him through the herbarium and out of the gatehouse in the old circus tower. They made their way slowly down the Corso Magenta for the street was crowded, and the people that milled around had the uneasy buzz of a thousand bees. Bernardino was suddenly moved to look back at the frontage of the monastery, with its Ornavasso stone façade and marble mouldings, as a child might yearn for his home as he crept, snail-like, to school. He felt an odd sense of foreboding and vulnerability now that he was outside of the safe haven of the convent walls. The sun had barely risen behind a lid of sickly yellow grey cloud and shone like the dim orange lozenge of a comet that presages contagion or war. Bernardino drew his hood about him and turned from the ugly faces that seemed to leer after the calm and Godly countenances of the sisters. He plucked the sleeve of the Abbess.

'What is this coil? Where are they all going? Where are *we* going?'

'To see an execution. Come, we may be too late.'

'Tell me as we walk then. Who is to be dispatched?' Bianca seemed visibly distressed, and Bernardino bit his lip at the flippant choice of words.

'The Countess of Challant, a great friend of mine and of my family.'

'Of your father? Then surely he may intercede?'

'It may have gone too far for that. Her death is demanded by the people.'

'By the people? Why?'

'They have taken a moral stance against a woman known to be a libertine. A woman whose sin is to love more than one man; in truth, more than two.'

A knell sounded in Bernardino's chest. Here then, was proof of the censure that awaited women that loved freely. His own rival for Simonetta's heart was dead, and yet Lorenzo's ghost had been enough to divide them forever. Simonetta was derided by the people of Saronno, and here in Milan a lady's passions could buy her death. 'How did this come to pass?'

Bianca unfolded the tale, as they walked through the streets, guided like leaves in the current as the mob streamed past the Duomo. 'The Contessa di Challant was the only child of a rich usurer who lived at Casal Monferrato. Her mother was a Greek; and she was a girl of such exquisite beauty that, in spite of her low origin, she became the wife of the noble Ermes Visconti in her sixteenth year.'

Bernardino had heard of such matches. 'How old was the husband?'

Bianca smiled, and the furrows of her brow cleared, shortly to return. 'Old enough to be her grandsire. He took her to live with him at Milan, where she frequented the house of my father but none other. She played with me as I grew with great kindness and gaiety but was kept from other society. Her ancient husband told my friend Matteo Bandello that he knew her temper better than to let her visit with the freedom of the Milanese ladies. Upon Ermes' death, while she was little more than twenty, she retired to Casale and led a gay life among many lovers. One of these, the Count of Challant in the Val d'Aosta, became her second husband. He was captivated by her extraordinary loveliness, but they could not agree together. She left him, and established herself at Pavia. Rich with the wealth of her father and first husband, and still beautiful in her middle years, she now abandoned herself to a life of profligacy. She took numerous lovers.'

Bernardino, jostled by the crowd, thought that the Countess had found herself the ideal life, but sensed a sting in the tale. He had to hold the sleeve of the Abbess's habit in order that they might not be separated, that he might hear the rest.

'Two of her lovers must be named. Ardizzino Valperga, Count of Masino; and the Sicilian Don Pietro di Cardona. She tired of the Count of Masino, but Don Pietro loved her with the insane passion of a very young man. What she desired, he promised to do blindly; and she bade him murder his predecessor in her favour.'

Bernardino was shocked that the libertine had turned murderess. He was unsure of the Abbess's intentions but had to shout to voice his queries. 'But Sister Bianca, it seems that this lady did indeed have an evil influence. Can you, a servant of God, defend such a woman? Can you hope to intercede for her?'

'We are all sinners, Bernardino. But no man has the right to take life, only God. If she is now killed, then the Duke Sforza is no better than Don Pietro the murderer.'

'So the murder was carried out? What came to pass?'

'At this time she was living here in Milan. Don Pietro waylaid the Count of Masino, as he was late one night from supper. The Count was killed: but Don Pietro was caught. He revealed the atrocity of his mistress; and she was sent to prison. She is now held in the Porta Giova fortress, the castle of the Sforzas, and awaits execution this very morn.'

'Then what can you do?'

'I hope to buy her freedom. For, although she acted wrongly, I believe she has atoned and it grieves me that she may pay for the actions of another. Though I wear a habit I am still a woman and it burns my heart that a woman may be killed for what a man has done, however strong her influence. I hope to appeal to her to become one of the sisters, to live her life in repentance in the circle of our cloister.' The mob stopped for a moment, and the Abbess faced him. 'You see, Bernardino, when I think of the Countess I don't see a libertine, nor yet a murderess. I see the gentle lady that played and laughed with a lonely child in my father's house.'

The crowd slowed at the Duomo where vendors sought to sell to the unwary. There were images of the Countess, a reputed beauty with yellow hair and a comely face. Bernardino and the Abbess lowered their heads to push through the press of people. Peddlers sold Holy water to bless the body and the more enterprising thrust fistfuls of yellow horsehair in their cowls, purporting to be hair from the Countess's head. On a wooden thrust stage, players wearing grotesque masks reenacted the tale of lust and murder, with the two lovers sporting huge phalli of papier-mâché at their groins. An actor with a long yellow wig stroked them lasciviously, before the dusky Sicilian killed the Neapolitan, who flung rolls of red ribbon into the crowd to mimic blood. At the finish, a huge silver axe fell on the Countess's white neck as more gore ensued.

The crowd reached a pitch of excitement that was at once disgusting and disorienting to Bernardino after his months of peace. He knew well why the Abbess had wanted protection on such a day, for couples openly pressed themselves on each other in a libidinous expression of their excitement, and he saw a lone maid fight off a circle of men that cat-called and pulled at her clothes. He raised his

eyes skyward and saw the Saints standing atop the gothic
pinnacles of the Duomo, sorrowing as they looked down,
themselves players against the sickly saffron backdrop of the
sky. He too began to feel disquiet that a high-born lady
was to be murdered for the sins of her lovers and pressed
forward urgently.

They neared the ramparts of the great red Porta Giova
fortress, its battlements like the wards of a thousand keys
that served to keep the Sforzas in and the city out. But not
today. Today the great gates of the Torre del Filarete clock
tower were open, and the crowd streamed though, beneath
the baleful eye of the coiled Sforza serpent that adorned the
castle arms. Poised to strike, thought Bernardino; poised to
kill. Today the *paghe vive* guards, salaried soldiers employed
to guard the castle, uncrossed their pikes to let the multi-
tude through. Inside the great parade ground of the Piazza
d'Armi was crammed with citizens, all jostling for position.
Sister Bianca took Bernardino's arm, and pulled him to the
outer reaches of the crowd, leading him up a flight of stone
steps at the Ghirlanda curtain wall. Here a figure in bright
blue silk loitered, waiting. The figure knelt at the sight of
the Abbess and kissed the garnet ring.

'Greetings Matteo,' said the Abbess, 'were it not such a
dark day this would be a meeting of minds indeed. Matteo
Bandello, a great writer, meets Bernardino Luini, a great
artist.' Both men bowed and eyed each other curiously. One
who was a stranger to Holiness wore the habit of a brother,

but was more handsome than any monk had a right to be. The other, ugly and ill-favoured, was in fact a monk but wore the finest clothes that ever complimented a courtier. The writer's eyes fairly shone with lively intelligence.

'I hope we may have an opportunity to speak later, for I have admired such of your work as I have seen, Signore,' said Bandello.

Bernardino, never a great reader, could not respond with glowing reviews of Bandello's novellae. But the fellow had already moved on; his quick mind working, his hands gesturing, as he resumed the urgency of the day. 'Have you got it all?' he questioned the Abbess.

'Yes,' replied Sister Bianca. '15,000 crowns.'

'From the *Monastero*?'

Even at such a time she smiled. 'Hardly. From one who knows the Countess and wishes her well.'

Bandello nodded. 'Alessandro Bentivoglio. Your father was ever the true noblemen, such largesse is typical of his generosity.'

Sister Bianca smiled her strange half smile, and whispered back rapidly. 'And the diplomat; he knows that I must act for him in this matter – that it would not do for him to be seen as partisan. The Countess has offended the people greatly, and my father cannot afford to so do. Nor can the Duke: is he here?'

Bandello shook his head. 'Not he. Francesco Sforza will not risk his neck among the crowd, for all his wartime campaigns. Yet you may be sure he watches, from the safety of the Rocchetta.' In explanation he nodded to the safe, windowed portion of the castle. 'The Rocchetta can be reached only by drawbridge, which as you see, is drawn up. Let us hope that the name of the moat it crosses is not prophetic.'

'The name?' Bernardino questioned.

'*Fossato Morto*. The moat of the dead.' Bandello gave a ghoulish grin and took the heavy leather bag from the Abbess. 'Well, let us try what may be done with this purse. Wait here. I will come again.' They watched as the blue figure climbed the ramparts and disappeared into the great round tower named for Bona of Savoy, the long dead chatelaine. Below the Ghirlanda wall the crowd grew restive and chants began to relay around the courtyard – hymns fought with filthy tavern songs as the crowd awaited the bloodletting they had been promised. Bianca closed her eyes on the scene and her lips moved in prayer. Bernardino felt unsettled enough to interrupt her devotions. 'Could not an escape have been attempted?' he whispered.

The Abbess did not open her eyes. 'It has been tried. There are many passages that lead from this castle to safety – one out into the Barco hunting reserve and thence to the country, and the other leads to the Monastery of Santa Maria della Grazie.'

'Santa Maria delle Grazie?'

The Abbess opened her eyes. 'You know it?'

'Yes. My Master's great work, the *Cenacolo*, hangs there.'

She nodded. 'The Last Supper. I have never seen it. Yet there is a secret covered causeway that connects this fortress to that place – it was built by Ludovico Il Moro himself, as he made nightly trips to visit the body of his dead wife in the chapel there.' Tis said that you can still hear the old Duke's sobs in the passage at night.' The Abbess crossed herself. 'A sevennight ago the Countess attempted to make her escape to the monastery by that route, but she was betrayed. The purse is our only hope now.' She closed her eyes once again and began to finger the beads of the rosary at her waist.

Bernardino was silent. His eyes searched the crowd, collecting the ugly expressions, and his memory registered the details of the mocking faces. He thought of the book that sat in his cell next to the Bible, the *Libricciolo* that Leonardo had made of the grotesques that interested him, but Bernardino's head was a library for such characters. There were many in the crowd that day that would find themselves immortalized on the walls of San Maurizio, when Bernardino would paint the Mocking of Christ.

A friar in the magpie robes of the Dominicans mounted the square block that crowned the ramparts and began, in a nasal whine, a Latin diatribe on the evils of women beginning with Eve and persisting through the ages to the present day. His sentiments drew roars of approbation from the crowd – the learned who knew Latin and agreed with the sentiments expounded, and the ignorant who merely found vent for their feelings in their raucous 'Ayes'. The friar was a good few moments into his speech before Bernardino realised the purpose of the block that the friar stood upon, and he grew cold despite the wool of his habit.

Presently Bandello returned. He carried the bag and shook his head as he descended. 'No one would take it,' he said. 'Even in this age of corruption they dare not cheat the crowd of their moment. She is doomed.'

Bianca nodded her head in solemn acceptance and the three of them watched the scene unfold. From the Torre di Bona di Savoia emerged two Sergeants-at-Arms followed by a figure with brass-bright hair. As the trio walked between the battlements Bernardino could divine that the Countess was an ample figure clad in a golden gown chased with silver gilt. The crowd mocked and hissed, as the sorry procession emerged from the shadow of the great tower, and flung such vegetation and ordure as they had brought from their cots. Cries of 'Whore!' were taken up and echoed round the square. Bernardino admired the Countess's quiet composure in the face of such censure but was privily amazed that such a woman had caused two hearts to beat so strong that their thoughts had turned to murder. Her best years were well behind her, her figure had spread at the waist and her skin was tanned as a peasant's. Bernardino noted that nature had little to do with the bright gilt of the hair, but that she obviously used such arts and unguents that Venetian ladies used to lighten their tresses. Then she turned to the weeping handmaiden that carried her train, kissed her on the cheek and favoured her with a dimpled smile, and Bernardino saw the face lifted into the promise of beauty and bedsport. The lady unhooked her ruff and laid her head on the black block as the hooded executioner stepped forward. As her head went down Bernardino saw from their privileged position, a vast spectrum of emotions writ upon her face. Gladness of a life well lived, a memory of what it was to love and be loved, regret for what was to be left, and bowel-opening terror. And over this all, like the finest actor, pride and dignity, and a will to leave the world with the nobility she was born to. Bernardino felt tears prick his eyes as he registered the reality of what she felt: here was no plaster Saint, but a real woman under the shadow of the axe. All was so rapid that Bernardino could not believe what was happening until it was done. The axe fell with a scything sweep and the sickly sun kissed the blade in valediction as it fell. Ribbons of blood flew into the crowd and the deed was done. The Countess's head was held high, eyes rolled back to the whites; her dimples would dip no more.

Bernardino knew that Sister Bianca suffered at that moment, and threw an arm about her shoulders.

Bandello took the Abbess's hand and said, 'It counts for little at such a time, but I will write a history of the Countess, so that her passing shall not be forgot. But now I must go, before I am missed by my Masters.' With a further kiss of the ring and a nod to Bernardino, he melted into the throng.

The minstrels struck up and the crowd danced in a weaving dragon, fat with blood and sated, back to the Duomo square to carouse for the rest of the day.

'Stay here,' said Sister Bianca suddenly. 'I must see the Sergeant-at-Arms. There is one more thing that I may do for her.'

Bernardino waited as the sun climbed higher and the castle fell silent. The red stones warmed and the blood clotted in the walls, steeped in the memory of this and other killings, but protesting its innocence as the light showed the fineness of its architecture; the thrust of the walls, the turn of a stair, the reach of the round towers into the orange sky.

Sister Bianca returned with the leather bag, no longer jingling but full and rounded and dark at the base. With a lurch of his stomach Bernardino knew what was within, and that 15,000 crowns, which had not been enough to buy a life, had been enough to buy this. 'Come,' said Bianca, 'we will see the rites done at least.'

Only Bernardino and the Abbess knew that the Countess of Challant's head lay in the herb garden of the monastery of San Maurizio. Despite her sins she was admitted to the consecrated cloister, and came among the sisters indeed; though not in the way the Abbess had intended. Sister Bianca placed her under the white spreading flowers of the

Valerian plant, the herb known as 'heal all', which guards against evil and induces peace and calm. As the bells rang for Nones the shadow of the circus tower fell over the plot like a gnomon, and Bernardino now felt the significance of this garden that had once been the arid sand centre of the arena of death. This playground of the Emperor Maximius had seen much. More than one head, or limb, would have lain here – still did perhaps – and blood would have daily darkened the sand beneath this turf. The blood beat in Bernardino's head as he heard the crowd's roar from the cavea, saw the bloodthirsty Emperor waving from the meta. 'The peoples' joy,' Ausonius had said, *populique voluptas*. By God, Bernardino had seen that today. The baying mob and the blood lust. He knew then the peace of the cloister that he had felt only this morning was an illusion. Round that still centre, the world still turned, as bloody and violent as it had ever been. When they entered the Hall of the Believers at last it was only noon, though Bernardino felt as if a year had passed since he had crossed the cloister in the quiet and contemplation of the morning. Bernardino took his brushes, but could not think of anything other than the scenes of the morning. As he sketched the blessed Catherine, he could not help drawing the homely face of the Countess, imbuing her not with the hot passions of her life but the quiet and dignified manner of her death. He drew the gold gown embroidered with silver gilt, and her noble head bowed before the sword of her assassin.

'Saint Catherine,' he said to Bianca. 'What happened to her?'

Once again the Abbess told him of the life of a Saint, but this time her voice was shaking, her tone full of sorrow, and her tale halting; imbued with the significance of what both had seen.

'Catherine was both noble and brave for at the age of eighteen she presented herself to the Emperor Maximius who was violently persecuting the Christians, and castigated him for his cruelty.'

Bernardino looked up from his paints. 'Maximius again?'

'Even he. Catherine emerged from the debate victorious. Several of her adversaries, conquered by her eloquence, declared themselves Christians and were at once put to death. Furious at being beaten, Maximius had Catherine scourged and then imprisoned. Yet Catherine effected so many conversions even from her cell, including that of the Emperor's wife, that she was condemned to die on the wheel, but, at her touch, this instrument of torture was miraculously destroyed.'

Bernardino continued to sketch furiously. But today his mind did not paint idealized scenes of sanctity on the wall for him to copy. Today he saw only the Countess, and her end. He drew the wheels on which she was to be metaphorically and physically broken, and blasted them with the might of angels, till their gears and cogs spilled forth. Here he gave a nod to the mechanical drawing of Master Leonardo, not God in the machine but the machine in God, and he wondered afresh at the tortures that mankind prepared for its own. He heard his friend's voice crack behind him as she ended the story. 'The Emperor, enraged beyond control, then had her beheaded and angels carried her body to Mount Sinai where later a church and monastery were built in her honour.'

The Abbess sank into a pew and covered her eyes in prayer, or weeping, or he knew not what. Bernardino watched, not moving, as she grieved for what she had lost – far, far more than a childhood friend. Her innocence had gone too. When she raised her head her cheeks ran with tears.

Suddenly martyrdom had a human face as both had witnessed for the first time in a pair of sheltered lives, one human being killed by another. 'It is well that we saw what we saw,' said Sister Bianca at last. 'I have told you many tales now, of Saints and sinners, martyrs and the best of men. Here I sit, preaching to you these glib homilies of the canonized and the horrors that they bore. That *I* should presume to make *you* a better person, to bring *you* into the faith. It was arrogance and pride.' She rose and began to pace before Bernardino, agitated. 'But until today I did not know of what I spoke. I did not know of true courage in the face of death. My ministry here is sheltered, my life is one of quiet contemplation. I have been raised in wealth and comfort and never given succour to the sick or been among the dying. Here we give alms to the poor, but they are an orderly poor; the respectable and able-bodied are brought here and we throw coins at their feet. The ones with the pox, or the limbless ones that have been devoured by leprosy wait outside the Hall of the Believers for their comrades. They all believe fervently, but they are not admitted lest we sisters catch their contagion. I have never put myself in the way of sickness or danger or death. Here we hide; we call ourselves brides of Christ but yet we are virgins; we have never known the heat of a bed or what it may drive the human heart to do. We know nothing of love or what it is to give birth, or any of the trials of mortal women. Henceforth my ministry will change,' the Abbess asserted, driving her fist into the palm of her other hand. 'My faith shall assume a more practical nature. I and my sisters must go out into the world, take our ministry out to the people of this city, make life bearable for the unfortunates of this place.'

Bernardino was touched by the change in the Abbess. In return he acknowledged something of the change in him. He left his perch and took the hand that bore the ring of office. 'I too,' he said. 'I had never seen such a thing. I have never been a soldier, and have been mocked for the fact.' He echoed Gregorio's words that he could not forget. 'While young men die, I *paint* men dying. While they bleed on the battlefield, I try to find the right carmine to paint their blood. Every face I depict at its end has a calm acceptance of a horrible fate, but this is merely a trope, my notion of what I thought the moment of death can be. The Countess can teach me much about the human face of sacrifice.'

'Then if you paint her here, you do her justice. God makes us all differently. Your gift is not in swordplay or battle – you would likely die in the first skirmish,' Bernardino smiled ruefully, 'but you paint like an angel. Perhaps this day may change us both. We have both crossed the Rubicon,' acknowledged the Abbess, 'and can never go back. It is passing strange that is the death of a sinner and not a Saint that has thus altered us. And if you can paint what is real, what is human, as well as what is divine, you will have no equal, and my friend will not have died in vain.'

And so he did. And another man who had been changed by that fateful day, also kept his word and wrote a novella on the life of the Countess of Challant. And at the close of his story Matteo Bandello wrote:

'And so the poor woman was beheaded; such was the end of her unbridled desires; and he who would fain see her painted to the life, let him go to the Church of the Monastero Maggiore, and there will he behold her portrait.'

CHAPTER 36

The Dovecot

Selvaggio had finished. He had planed and lathed and sand-
ed, and now the dovecot was perfect, standing proud and
bone-white with the wick wood gleaming in the weak sunlight. The sturdy pole was driven hard into the ground, the
housing round with a conical white cap of a roof and two
arched doorways for the residents. The little tower nudged
his memory as he fashioned it, to remind him of an image
of the cloud-capped crenellations of Camelot, but the scene
was gone as soon as it had come to him. He stood back, and
surveyed his work proudly. It was a palace of dovecots. He
had worked tirelessly on this bird house as it was to be a gift
for the one he held most dear on her name day.

For it was now nearly a year since he had fought the
Swiss mercenaries in Amaria's defence. Amaria and Nonna
were both at the market, for the lessons of last year's Saint's
day were still fresh and Amaria now went nowhere alone.
Grandmother and granddaughter had gone to buy victuals
for the feast; they were to have *Zuppa alla Pavese*, the meat

broth with eggs, bread and butter which had been invented as a supper for the Royal prisoner Francis I. At Amaria's insistence they had also gone to seek the lady in red who sold the famous amber liquor known as Amaretto, to see if a few meagre centimes might buy a small draught to toast Sant'Ambrogio. Mention of the Saint had led Selvaggio's thoughts back to that fateful day, one year ago, when he had killed three Swiss but could only recall that he had Amaria in his arms for the first time.

There had been other times since then, stolen moments before the dying fire when Nonna had retired to bed. They had remained chaste but Selvaggio knew he could not hold his passions in check for long. He wanted Amaria for his own, but did he have a right to take a wife when his past remained a blank to him?

A fluttering at his feet pulled at his attention and he smiled down on the remainder of his gift. In a netted basket on the frozen ground were two turtle doves, snow white and hopping against their prison bars. He lifted them out with the hands of experience and set them in the little arched doors of the cot. He should clip their wings against flight but they seemed contented to stay, so he desisted for now, not wishing to blot their happiness. As they billed and preened he considered names for his gift and his memory surprised him once again as he began to recall tales of antiquity, as perfectly as if he read them before his eyes. Hercules and Megara? Tristan and Isolde? Triolus and Cressida?

Or the story he had loved the best, the doomed love of Lancelot and Guinevere, whose guilty embrace was witnessed by a cuckolded Arthur? No; for all these lovers had made sad ends; he wanted these doves to be named after a couple who had enjoyed a happy conclusion to their tale. Ah, he had it. He smiled as the ideal pair of names came to him from he knew not where.

Perfect.

CHAPTER 37

The Cardinal Receives a Gift

Gabriel Solis de Gonzales, Cardinal of Milan, was used to
such little tributes as his flock liked to give him. A life of
indigence and self-denial was not for him. He was quite
happy to preach in the Duomo about camels and needle-
eyes but he saw no need to impoverish himself in order to
enter Heaven. He felt his place in Paradise was assured by
his purgation of the Jewish menace. So he was not wholly surprised when an interesting-looking bottle of liquor
was delivered to him. It was the colour of burnt sugar, and
when he lifted the stopper – Venetian glass, he noticed ap-
preciably – there was the sweet smell of almonds. He was
not surprised by the gift, but the servant who brought it
in was not his usual groom of the chamber. This man was
small and ugly. 'Where is Niccolò?' asked the Cardinal im-
periously, after the small pause necessary to recollect his
groom's name.

'He took sick, Your Eminence. The water fever.'

The Cardinal sniffed fastidiously. Better to replace Niccolò then, for he did not wish to contract the gripes too. Best to find a replacement. This was how the Cardinal rewarded many years of devoted service. 'What is your name?' asked the Cardinal.

'Ambrogio, Your Grace.'

'Hmmm.' A good Milanese name. But this man would not do – he had too much in his face which called the Hebrew to mind. He would be dismissed too – but tomorrow would be soon enough. The liquor tempted the Cardinal. 'Who brought this? It has no direction.'

The man shuffled. 'I know not, your Eminence. I think it came from his Excellency the Duke, as the Sforza's man was just lately here.'

The Cardinal tisked faintly at this man's incompetence. He dismissed him with a wave, confident that he would never have to see this feckless servant again. In this he was quite right.

In the absence of Niccolò or an apt replacement the Cardinal extinguished the candles himself, and climbed into his velveted four-poster in his cap and gown. He took a goblet from his night table and drank the draught down while reading a book of homilies on the excrescences of the Jew in the Spanish language. He enjoyed the sentiments and the liquor together and drank on till the little bottle was empty. Really, the flavour of almonds was quite delightful. At length the book fell from his hand and he slept.

He did not sleep, of course. He was dead. For what the Cardinal did not know is that another liquid that has the scent of almonds is the lethal compound Prussic acid. This powder, extracted from the leaves of the cherry laurel, is so deadly that even the poisoner that sold it, in the small streets behind Mantua's cathedral, felt moved to warn the lady who bought it from him of its effects. She had nodded quickly and taken the vial in her white hand, a hand, he noted, with the three middle fingers all one length.

The Cardinal's newest and last servant ran rapidly down the steps of his dead master's palace. He paused only to throw a cloak over his livery, and conceal the empty bottle he had taken from his master's bedside. He ran to his horse where it stood silently behind a hedge of yew. He rode hard till he came to the open country. The river was a broad silver ribbon threading through the night. He flung the bottle far from him, and above the hoofbeats heard a splash as the river accepted the crystal bottle and made it its own. He reached the Villa Castello at daybreak and saw his mistress watching from her window as the sky paled. She came down at once to meet him, and he was too exhausted to do more than throw his reins over the dovecot and leave his horse to crop grass as he almost fell to the ground. She did not trouble him with long interrogation. 'Did you see him?'

'Yes.'

'Is it done?'

'Yes.'

She breathed relief. 'I excuse you from your tutelage of the boys today. Go and get some sleep.' As he entered her door she called him back. 'Isaac?'

'Yes, my lady?'

She searched for the words. 'Your God would be proud of you.'

He smiled the smile that was his only beauty, and sketched a *shalom* with his hand. 'Yours would too, my Lady.'

CHAPTER 38

A Baptism

'I cannot stay. Saint Catherine was the last of them.' Once more, Bernadino paced, wolflike, in the nave of a Holy place. 'I must go. If yesterday taught me anything it is that there is nothing more important than living the life you are given, even if it is in sin. I have made a friend of God while I lived here. I know now that he is real, when once I thought he was not. I think he loves me too, despite my many flaws. But life is short. I know, at last, how to paint. I learned yesterday. And now I have to go, and live the life that I must, even if I am damned for it.'

'Who is she?' The Abbess's eyes were open and candid. Bernardino was caught off guard. 'Who?'

'The lady.'

'Which lady?' Bernardino's mind ran over the speech he had given, at a loss to know where Simonetta's name appeared. Bianca moved from him and pointed to Saint Ursula. 'This one,' she said, then she strode to the panel of Saint Maurice and her finger picked out the lady in the foreground in a red dress. 'And this.' Her black skirts swept the floor as she turned to point: 'Saint Agatha, and Saint Lucy, and Saint Apollonia. Even,' she indicated the last of all, 'Saint Catherine. Here in her own chapel she has the look of the Countess of Challant indeed. But here on this panel, where she stands next to Saint Agatha, she is that secret lady once again. The lady who appears everywhere in this place yet you have never once spoken of her. Even in my mother.' She pointed to the spectre in white who knelt on the lunette above Saint Catherine and Saint Agatha. 'She was indeed a beauty, but you have flattered her with a superior countenance. Even I, one that loved her well, must admit that.'

Bernardino smiled ruefully and placed his head in his hands. He laughed. 'You do not flatter my painting skill.'

The Abbess sat on the pew next to him. 'Bernardino. You know how highly I prize your work. But look again. There are subtle differences, but all these ladies are the same woman.'

He rubbed his eyes fit to dislodge them from their sockets and when he opened them he looked afresh at his work. Sister Bianca was right. He had painted Simonetta over and over again since he had come here. He had painted her as Saint Ursula looking down at the red-winged angel that was Elijah. He had painted her, in great detail, in a red dress that he had never seen her wear attending the dedication of Saint Maurice's church. There she stood, resplendent in her finery, the scarlet of her dress crossed with gold, with her hair caught in a jewelled fillet studded with seed pearls. Great were the happenings in that painting, as Saint Maurice founded his church among the dead; but it was the lady in red with her strange hands folded in prayer who drew the eye and pulled the viewer into the painting. I am one of you, she seemed to say. I am a witness to this day. And – he almost laughed – he had painted Simonetta standing outside her own house, that very villa with the rosy plaster walls and the elegant portico that he had seen but once, as he bade her farewell. He had even painted the window at which she had stood that day when he took his leave, and placed in it a figure with shoulder length red–gold hair wearing a man's russet hunting tunic.

And there was more. He turned around as his greatest work revolved around him. Every woman that he had painted since he came here had something of her in it, in form or figure, face or hands. Most of the women had her colouring, and even when they didn't they had her eyes, or her gestures. He didn't know whether the feeling that bubbled in his chest would end in laughter or tears. That he had thought her forgotten! That he had lain awake in his cell desperate to remember her face! She was here before him, a hundred times over, more real in his depictions than when he had painted her from life in Saronno. Then, captivated by her person, he had not been able to see her as she truly was. Here, separated by more than just distance, his denied heart had remembered her in every particular, and his faithful hands had drawn her countenance every day. There were but two dames that were not Simonetta in that place: Saint Scholastica and a grieving acolyte at the Entombment of Christ. Both wore the black habit of a nun, and the plain kindly face of Sister Bianca.

'Well?' smiled Sister Bianca.

'You are right. There is…a Lady. You are a clever woman to have seen so much when no word of it was spoken.'

'These dames told me much, of course. But there was another clue, and it is this.' She went again to the delimiting wall and found a small symbol in the frescoed panel, so small it would have fitted on a missive that could be crushed in a white hand; a piece of vellum that took leave of a lover. It was a heart that held a fleur-de-lys of leaves within. 'Like the lady,' said Sister Bianca, 'this symbol is everywhere. Here on the shawl of Saint Catherine. On the bodice of Saint Ursula. And most often on the cloak of the Magdalene, as she witnesses the death of her lover-Lord, and when he reaches out to her from beyond the grave.' In the Hall of the Nuns the Abbess pointed to the blood-red cape, covered in the leaf-filled hearts, wreathing around the stricken, love-lorn woman that Christ loved above all. 'When I saw that I knew that you were captive,' she turned back and smiled, 'and then you painted your fair jailer again and again.' The Abbess sat beside him again, with a look of intent inquiry. 'Who is this lady with red hair and white skin, and eyes oval as almonds? Who is she that moves with such grace, that inclines her head like a Saint and carries her body like a queen? She must be a rare beauty indeed.'

'She is a rare beauty,' replied Bernardino, exhaling a breath of defeat. 'But she is no Saint. Her name is Simonetta di Saronno. She is human; just a woman, like other women. And because of her sin and mine I am here. But now I know that I cannot be without her, and yesterday's events showed me that our sin was perhaps not so great.'

'Might you tell me?' the question was gentle, as if to an errant child.

'We loved too soon after her husband's death, and in the wrong place. She was my model for the Holy Virgin in Saronno, and we embraced in the church. We were seen and denounced. She is Godfearing, and sent me from her. I went for her sake more than my own, but now I know that I cannot stay away. Life is not life without her. She is all that matters now.'

Sister Bianca shook her head as she looked at the frescoes. 'I think you will be painting her for the rest of your life.'

Bernardino shrugged, as if it was easy to cast off his gift. 'I think history has enough of my paintings. The best of my work is here. My Master was right.'

'Your Master?'

'Master Leonardo. He said that I would not be able to paint until I first learned to *feel*. And he was right. What I painted in the white church of Saronno was mere confection. I tickled the white walls with decoration as if I embellished a cake. Here I walked into a black cell and I have turned it into a jewel box. I know I will never do better, and that history will judge me on *this* place.' His sweeping gesture took in the entire of the hall, and the many chapels, now peopled with numerous figures. Now he could see that the frescoes held none of the staged classical attitudes of his work in Saronno, nor the nerveless antique tropes of his former work. They were no longer refined, aristocratic and courtly. Here the figures lived with a vibrant naturalism; the fuzzy *chiaroscuro* with which he had aped Leonardo was now pulled into sharp focus which was real, definite and alive. Bernardino was no longer constrained by form or moderation. His passions had set him free: the brush was made flesh.

Now, too, he could see that his work had kept step with his growing faith; now the light of devotion shone from *within* the figures, not without. Bernardino felt that he addressed a learned colloquy of Holy figures that had gathered to hear him. The long-dead and the living convened together: Alessandro Bentivoglio, Sister Bianca's father, knelt in his splendid robe of white and grey, black and gold, and behind him, Saint Stephen stood with the rocks that had killed him scattered at his feet. The Abbess's dead mother Ippolita knelt over Saints Agatha and Lucy, all three wearing the face and form of Simonetta di Saronno. And there too,

were Bianca and her brother Anselmo, portrayed as Saint
Scholastica and her twin Saint Benedict, smiling beatitude
from the pilasters. In their raiments of glorious colour, precious pigments of lapis lazuli, periwinkle and malachite, the
past and the present shone down from the arches and span-
drels, the oculi and lunettes. The colours and drapery of
the fabrics were spectacular; the *sottinsù* or perspective of
the figures was so marvellous that it seemed that they bent
down to bestow their grace on the world below. Bernardino had created reality from illusion – the fictive marble
and niches he had painted looked as real as if they had been
carved by a mason, rendered with shadows and forms that
were not their own. He knew this was his master work. 'But
it is no longer admiration that I crave,' he said, almost to
himself, as if answering a question that had not been asked.
'I want only her, and we will live in sin, if sin it is, if she will
have me. I will live on her doorstep and plague her every
day if I must.'

The Abbess thought for a moment before she spoke. 'My
dear Bernardino. Had you never thought that such a pass
may not be necessary? You have become God's friend, so
you say. He does indeed love you, despite your faults, as he
loves all his children. Might it not be possible to proceed in
His path?'

'What can you mean?'

'I mean marriage. It is one of the sacraments, a state most
beloved of God.'

'Marriage?' Bernardino said the word as if for the first time.

'Of course.' The Abbess smiled her half-smile. 'Had you not thought of it before?'

'Never…how is it possible?'

Sister Bianca laughed. 'I know little of the world, it is true, but I think it is usual to ask the lady and wait for her to say yes.' She mocked him gently.

'But…'

'You have been here for close on two years. Her husband died when?'

'At Pavia. A year before I came here.'

'Then the poor soul has been gone three years, God rest him. She has had time enough to mourn. Respect is due to the dead but the young should live their lives, not spend them in bereavement. The Church and Canon law allow a widow to remarry after a certain time, and that time is now past. She is yours if she will have you.'

Bernardino's heart began to beat strong, and his eyes burned. Marriage. He had never thought that Simonetta and he could be together legitimately in the eyes of God. But if her scruples would allow it, if he had done penance enough, it was possible. There was no impediment in Church or law, only the scandal that had plagued them at the start, and all scandals must die at last.

'But I know nothing of her life since I left. I had given her up for lost. I do not even know if she still resides in

Castello. Or even if she has met another.'

'Do either of these events seem likely? Did she seem attached to her home?'

'Very much so. In fact she came to work for me to preserve her home for the honour of her dead husband.'

The Abbess nodded with approval. 'And did she seem fickle? One that would form another attachment?'

'No. I am sure she loved me, and it tortured her because she felt the same disrespect to her first love.'

'Then go and seek her. Why not? You can but try.' The Abbess stood before Bernardino could protest. 'There is but one more thing needful before you may marry. And it can be achieved this evening at Vespers.'

As the Vespers bells tolled on Bernardino's last night in the monastery of San Maurizio, he stood, bareheaded at the font. He wore a white shirt and held a candle. The chapel was filled with the sisters that had favoured him with friendship these past years in the cloister, herbarium or library. He knew but a handful of names, yet they were all his friends. And before him, one among their number that he had come to love as a blood sister. She poured the Holy water over his head and he gasped at the shock, the purity of the cold. As he drunk from his first communion cup, and looked into the dark carnelian red depths of the chalice, he looked up to the panel he had painted of the Man of Sorrows. Jesus lay prone, spurting lifeblood into the Grail cup, the very blood that Bernardino now drank, and he found it passing strange that in all his growing knowledge of the lives of the Saints he had never till now thought of the ultimate suffering of the lonely and sorrowing Christ. *'Noli me Tangere'* indeed, 'Touch me Not' – Bernardino had painted him thus too, here in this hall. He raised his eyes to the painted lunette, and then a great revelation, a realisation, burst in upon him. There on the panel a hand reached out between loved ones, one to touch the other, but Bernardino had painted the opposite of the traditional tableau of the *Noli me Tangere*. Here, now, the Risen Christ reached his hand out to the Magdalene in welcome, just as Simonetta had once reached out to Bernardino in pity and been spurned. Bernardino was ready to touch and be touched, and he knew why; the Son of God's body was supported by those who loved him; the Magdalene, Mary his mother and Saint John bent close at his end – he was not *alone* in his awful fate. At that moment Bernardino resolved he would not die alone. He wanted a wife and the children of his body to be with him. Unshed tears stood in his eyes at the notion, but they spilled soon enough as the sisters sang *'Gloria, Gloria!'* in a crescendo of exultation. He looked up as the angels – *his* angels soared above his head, wheeling and revolving in their heavenly measure. For that moment they were not the seraphim that he had painted but were real. They had come to bear witness to his Baptism, to his communion, to his acceptance of God at last, here in the

Hall of the Believers where this lost sheep at last belonged, before they returned to their niches in the dark blue sky with the golden stars.

As he took his leave from the circus gate Bernardino bent and kissed the Abbess's hands. He did not look at the jewels of her ring as he had when they met but closed his eyes and kissed the rough skin with real affection. She, too, noticed the difference and said, 'You have given me a great compliment. For when we close our eyes when we kiss, be it the head of a child, the feet of a Saint or the lips of a loved one, that kiss means everything. For only then do we shut out the world and remember to *feel*.'

As Bernardino raised his face to the eyes that were so like Anselmo's he had a sudden moment of resolve. Yesterday they had both been changed, they had both lost their innocence, and she had professed a wish to know more of the world. They had both professed a desire to seize each day of their lives in different ways. He did not wish her to leave the world without knowing that her brother lived in it.

'I must go,' he said. 'But you should come with me. There is a man, a good man...the best friend that the world holds. He would be glad to know you, for though he is not yet your brother, he is your father's son.'

CHAPTER 39

A Wedding

Selvaggio and Amaria were married in Pavia in the church of Saint Peter of the Golden Sky. The gilded ceiling arched overhead and the priest's solemn Latin rolled around the golden firmament and back to its children on earth. Never were two happier than those joined here, and the icon of Sant'Ambrogio witnessed the scene, and was glad.

Nonna sat at the front of the church, black lace on white hair. She leaned her forehead on her clasped hands as she prayed. She had known that Father Matteo would oblige with this ceremony, for he knew Amaria well as he had come to know Selvaggio. The priest had no hesitation to join two of the same name – Selvaggio was married under the name Sant'Ambrogio too – for it was not the first time the priest had joined two of the Saint's orphans. He knew the groom's story and was comfortable that there could be no consanguinity in the case.

As the kind old man intoned the lesson that groom and bride had chosen for their own special reasons, Nonna found the words imbued with new meaning as she saw her two dear children lock eyes and clasp hands.

'Blessed is everyone who fears the Lord, who walks in his ways. For you will eat the labour of your hands. You will be happy, and it will be well with you. Your wife will be as a fruitful vine, in the innermost parts of your house; your children like olive plants, around your table. Behold, thus is the man blessed who fears the Lord. May the Lord bless you out of Zion, and may you see the good of Jerusalem all the days of your life. May you see your children's children. Peace be upon Israel.'

The words seemed to be written for them, and the family they had become, the family they might one day have. During the prayers Nonna shut her ears to the words and thanked God in her own way, sincerely and reverently. She had ever been devout, even through the dark days of Filippo's death. But today Nonna had been moved to cut a measure in the square where Filippo had burned. For God had given her Amaria, and now Selvaggio, and their children would grow like olive plants around her table. Her heart was full.

The bride and groom looked as shining as the Saints that observed from the walls. Amaria was in the new green of spring leaves, her dark hair twisted with seed pearls that Nonna had prised from the mouths of their suppertime oysters. Amaria's erstwhile friend, Silvana, stood by as a handmaid, with an expression as sour as the bride's was joyful. Who would have thought that an orphan of the woods would have preceded her to the altar?

Selvaggio was in the dark red feast-day doublet of Filippo himself, and though it was a mite tight, no-one would notice, so handsome did he look with his beard trimmed and his hair slick. Yes, Amaria looked like the queen of May and Selvaggio was her king. Nothing, not the handfasting of the two with silver ribbons, nor the laying of hands on the Holy Book, nor even the Latin cadences of the lesson that the priest read regularly at marriage services, penetrated the groom's memory; to prompt him, gently, that he had done all this before.

CHAPTER 40

Phyllis and Demophon

It was a peerless summer day when the Abbess and the artist reached Castello. Sister Bianca recognised the place from the fresco of the dedication of Saint Maurice, for Bernardino had painted this very house in San Maurizio down to the last window and gateway, the last tile and stone. The rose honey of the brick, the shady arches of the loggia, all were there before her eyes; just as they appeared on the great panel in the Hall of the Believers, providing an exquisite background for the story of Saint Maurice. Square, elegant and intensely separate; the house was at once welcoming and forbidding.

Bernardino, who had been in a jitter along the road these past few hours, stood at the gates almost exactly two years since he had been there last, the day Simonetta had turned away from him with his drawing in her hand. He found the place much changed.

The winter rose hedge from whence he had taken his leave of Simonetta was now green with glossy leaves and bursting with coral buds. The almond groves were pollarded and ordered in their neat lines, the fruit trees now espaliered neatly on the garden walls. The pleasure gardens of old were restored, new trout ponds reflected the sky and even the little conical dovecot had been washed and whitened. The house itself had been improved, the arches of the loggia were repaired, the old ivy stripped and the faded lilac of wisteria twisted up the frontage. There were new gates on the new columns, and glass quarrels in the casements. Bernardino noted this new prosperity and his heart sank. Was it a new husband who brought new life to this place? Sister Bianca laid a hand on his arm to quiet him but he shook it off and strode up the path, unable to bear the suspense for a moment longer. He must see her, even if it were for the last time.

Sister Bianca followed and saw her at the same time that Bernardino did. Miracle of miracles; she wore the red dress of his picture, crossed with golden thread and fretted with seed pearls. Her hair was bound with a pearl cincture and glowed the red of carnelians. But she was so alive, so animate! She was no painting. Her white face was flushed with laughter, and her red curls escaped from their binding to wind about her neck and ears. Her skirts were kirtled to her waist as she ran round the largest tree in the grove in a scene of domestic felicity. But there was no husband in the case; just a pair of golden children, laughing, and tumbling, both holding a switch of green and white almond blossom, chasing the lady. Cutting and thrusting with their harmless swords. At length she would catch one or other of them and kiss their little cheeks or necks in a picture of maternal love.

Bernardino was deeply moved – she could have been their mother, were it not for two things; their ages made the thing impossible, and the older one he recognised. Could it be true? It was Elijah, the Jewish boy for whom he had painted the dove, and bought the marble. Evangelista, the candle angel with the red wings that lived forever on the walls of San Maurizio.

Bernardino marvelled at this new Simonetta, the laughing, smiling *living* woman, not racked by the pains of love or bereavement, of disloyalty and disgrace. Not penurious, or proud, as she came to him for help in her husband's clothes. Not chilly and remote as she sat for him posing as the Queen of Heaven, as far above mortal passions as the cold moon itself. She too had changed, and he had never wanted her more. Sister Bianca saw too – her good heart thrilled at the scene and she recognised Saint Ursula playing with the candle angel, but she feared for Bernardino – how could he forget a woman like this? This was not the distant, proud lady she had envisaged; the cold chatelaine who tortured her lover. Here was a warm lovely creature who could make a man's life an earthly paradise. What would her friend do if she would not have him?

At last Simonetta tired of the game and fell in the groin of the roots of Rebecca's tree, on the green grass above Manodorata's grave. She leaned back, exhausted, on the trunk where her friend had breathed his last as his sons fell in her lap. She had seen to it that they played here, she had banished superstition and made it their playground, and she spoke openly of their father and mother until they did too.

She held the boys tight with one head on each shoulder and closed her eyes. The sun was so bright she could still see the almond leaves shifting above her like dark fishes that switch back and forth with the tide. When she opened them again she thought she had the sunblindness, for there stood Bernardino Luini.

Sister Bianca's doubts vanished as Simonetta stood wonderingly and took him in her arms, both laughing and crying. Both said the other's name over and over, and both thanked the God that they had each separately come to know in the dark days of their separation. Their mouths met in a long hard kiss, their eyes closed as they drank each other in; thankful, profoundly thankful, that all that had been wrong was now right. The Abbess, only human after all, strained to hear what they said, but could not understand what came next. For between kisses, Bernardino called Simonetta '*Phyllis*', and she laughing, as if completing a password, replied, '*Demophon*'. The Abbess might have been shocked to learn that the two invoked a pagan myth from ancient Greece, where a woman who thought she had lost her love was turned into an almond tree, but was saved by his return, and blossomed in his arms as he brought her back to life and to love again. But the Abbess did not understand the reference, nor was she in the mood for censure. Instead she took a little boy's hand in each of hers, and drew them to her. 'Could you show me the game you were playing just now?' she said. 'I would very much like to learn it.'

So as Bernardino and Simonetta plighted their troth under the almond trees as the blossom drifted across their lips and lashes, the Abbess of San Maurizio hoisted her habit above her knees, exposing her pale hairy legs to the sun for the first time in years, and ran round an almond tree chased by two little Jewish boys, laughing like a parrot and whirling like a dervish.

Simonetta di Saronno and Bernardino Luini married in the Sanctuary of Santa Maria dei Miracoli in Saronno, the church of the Miracles. Simonetta decided that she must look the past in the face and be churched publicly in order to begin her new life in the open. In a change to her first marriage though, they married not at the main altar but in the Lady Chapel where the bride watched herself from the walls – peering down from the frescoes painted by the groom. They were attended by a brother and sister in Christ, and a brother and sister in blood, for Alessandra and Anselmo Bentivoglio met and forged a friendship at once; the bond of the same character and the same father more than outweighed the division of a different mother and upbringing.

Even the townsfolk blessed the match – the Amaretto liquor had brought great prosperity to the area, and the mistress of Castello was a wealthy patroness of the vintner, the butcher and every other victualler in the town. Not the baker though – he had died mysteriously some weeks past; and only Father Anselmo, administering the last rites, had noticed a wicked dagger in the shape of a Maltese cross buried deep in the man's chestspoon. The priest kept his peace though, and so did Simonetta; and if she knew that a large part of her popularity stemmed from her being a known anti-semite who had personally dispatched the vile Jew Manodorata, she did not question it. Better to be reputed as such and keep her little family safe.

For it was at home, with her family, that the real wedding took place. Under Rebecca's tree, they said their vows again as the boys held an arch of blossom over their heads. Bernardino and Simonetta exchanged an almond, and this time she crushed it with her teeth, chewed it well and swallowed it down, tasting at once the full sweet flavour of the nut. Another difference: they toasted this wedding with Amaretto, the drink Simonetta had made for Bernardino. They drank from two sides of the same silver cup and Bernardino marvelled at this surpassingly fine liquor that his new wife had made. 'What do you think?' she asked, a small wrinkle of anxiety sitting atop her brow.

He smiled. 'I think that true art is not only found on the walls of churches,' he said.

They feasted there under the trees till the boys golden heads drooped. A strange feast indeed – attended by a nun and a priest who sat like bookends, for all the world a modern day Benedict and Scholastica. Also in attendance, drinking from the same flagon, were a Jewish tutor and his lady – a mute convert from Taormina – who nonetheless laughed and sang as readily as the rest. For their feast there were a mixture of Christian and Jewish dishes, and the songs that they sang as the Amaretto flowed came from the four points of the compass: folk songs of Lombardy, wedding hymns from Milan, Hebrew chants from the east and peasant airs from Taormina and the hot south.

At length Veronica put the boys to bed and Anselmo and the Abbess took their leave, to return to the priest's house in the town. Bianca had taken a sabbatical of a sevennight from the monastery, leaving the business of the place in the hands of her trusted sub-Prioress. She intended to spend the week as the guest of her brother, in prayer and contemplation and joyous conversations to fill in their missing sibling years. Then she would return willingly to her home, refreshed and ready to implement the changes in her ministry that she had resolved upon on the day of the death of the Countess of Challant. She privily hoped that she could persuade Anselmo to come with her, for a short sojourn in

Milan, to be re-united with his father.

The newlyweds sat on as the stars came and the luna moths began to glow and flutter above them. Night was another country, and their discourse changed with the territory. The frivolity of the day was gone. Their joy remained, bone-deep, but with a new sobriety they talked of all that had passed in the last two years. Simonetta told Bernardino of her distillery, and the terrible story of Manodorata and Rebecca.

Bernardino recounted the tales of the Saints to whom he had given his wife's face, and the awful and important death of the Countess of Challant; an event that had changed him forever. At last they fell silent and sat, just holding each other, glad that they had found the way home from where they had both been.

'Did it need to happen?' asked Bernardino at length. 'Did we waste those two years? Might we not have begun our journey then?'

Simonetta's head was on his chest, listening to his heartbeat as he spoke. He felt her shake her head. 'No. Those years were not a waste. And our journey did begin then, it began the day we met. We just needed to travel our roads alone for a while.'

'For what reason? I who am older than you, have less time left. Should we not have remained together?'

Simonetta was frightened by his heartbeats now; she knew they were finite in number and shifted her head so that she may no longer hear them counting down. Yet she stood by her position. 'I could not accept you then. There was too much to do – to atone for. Now enough time has past – we both did penance for what we did, and we have both come to Faith at last. I, who was brought up in religion, turned my back on it for a while, when I thought God had forsaken me. But he was there all the time, watching. He gave me back myself and my house, he saved the boys, and I returned to Him again.'

'And I,' said Bernardino, 'a faithless heathen, with no stomach for religion, found the true path in San Maurizio. You have returned to it, and I have found it anew.'

'And how strange,' went on Simonetta, 'that my contact with those of another faith has brought me *closer* to God, not further from him. I have learned, at last, that God is God; he is the same for all of us, it is only our worship of him that differs.'

Bernardino closed his hands over hers, imprisoning them. Her long fingers steepled within his; a prayer within a prayer. 'Might we not have learned this together?'

Simonetta shook her bright head. 'I think not. We needed to heal, to be whole before we united. And from our sorrowful separation has come good things – you have done the best work of your life which will be admired for generations.'

'And you have invented Amaretto, which will be enjoyed for just as long!'

Bernardino's voice was teasing, and Simonetta smiled; but her face was soon serious again. 'And yet these things were not the best of it. The best of it was the friends that we made and lost.' Simonetta thought of Manodorata, and Bernardino of the Countess who Bianca mourned.

'And the friends we have made and kept. The Abbess, Anselmo.'

'And the boys,' Bernardino smiled fondly.

Simonetta warmed at the thought of her sons, and how they had taken readily and unquestioningly to Bernardino's presence. Elijah, already aquainted with the man who had once painted his hand, had noted, with his beady intelligence, how happy his mother had become since Bernardino had come to them. The boys missed their father enough to yearn for a replacement, but there was much here that was new. Bernardino had a lively humour, and a quick, teasing wit that Manodorata – an excellent father in so many ways had lacked. Bernardino's accessibility and playful sense of the ridiculous, the very characteristics in which he differed so wildly from their dead father, only served to endear the children to him. Bernardino, in turn, set out with determination to make a friend of the boys. As Simonetta watched the three of them play – for all the world as if there were no difference in their ages – she pondered on the stories that Bernardino had told her of his lonely childhood. She sensed, now, that he was so *ready* to love them; he was ripe for it. The sluicegates had opened and his affection flooded forth. She knew he intended to love them as he was never loved as a boy, and was heartily glad of it. Simonetta noted that already, in the short time Bernardino had been at Castello, he had kissed and held the children more than she had ever seen Manodorata do in a brace of years. She saw him looking at the boys with an air of revelation; and his next words echoed her thoughts.

'The boys best of all.' He took his arm from round her shoulders and rubbed the back of his neck, as if perplexed. 'It is passing strange for me. I never longed for children, always thought myself too selfish to take joy in them. I thought I could never be happier than if I possessed you at last,' he clasped her tight once more. 'And yet here I am with not only the woman of my heart, but a ready-made family whom I adore.'

'And now they will be happy,' she rejoined. 'The townsfolk will leave us be. We will be celebrated; you for your art, me for Amaretto, and the boys will be safe.'

They were silent for a time, lost in the past and the future. The sky darkened or the stars brightened, and the wind murmured through the almond leaves, prompting their fair owner of something she had forgot. Remembering, Simonetta pulled a small piece of vellum from her bodice. She handed it to her husband, battered for she had carried it every day since he had gone, warm for it had lived next to her heart. 'Do you remember this?' she asked, with half a smile.

Bernardino took the parchment. 'Of course I do. I painted it on the unhappiest day of my life, the day I thought
I had lost you forever. And I painted it again, tens, scores,
hundreds of times on the walls of San Maurizio. Every single Magdalene, and most of your Saints wear that emblem
somewhere on their raiments. 'Twas the secret code of my
love for you – at once hopeless and hopeful – and only Bianca found the key.' He traced the symbol, so well known
to him, with his fingertips. 'And now, my dear heart, do
you know the meaning of the rune, you for whom it was
designed?'

Simonetta rested her head between his neck and shoulder, and breathed in his skin. 'I think I do. I did not know
for ever so long, but I have learned much in your absence.'

'Go on.'

She pointed at the cognizance, her hands pale in the
moonlight. 'There is a heart, of course, and within it, a trinity of leaves, like a fleur-de-lys.'

She felt him nod. 'What leaves are they?'

'The leaves of the almond tree.'

'And is there more?' he prompted her, gently.

'No. No nut or fruit is depicted there. Just the leaves
inside the heart.'

'Why?'

She heard the urgency in his voice; it was too dark, now,
to see his dear face, but it suddenly seemed terribly important that she knew the answer to the riddle. 'Because we

were not together; and without our union there could be no fruit. The tree would be barren. No flowers or harvest; just artifice and ornament. Beauty without fecundity. Phyllis did not blossom until her Demephon came home and freed her from desolation.'

Bernardino exhaled relief, and pulled her close for a long kiss, the catechism over. They stayed thus till they felt warm raindrops fall on their faces. 'Come,' he said. 'I have a new wife. And by this moon I think it is already my wedding night.' He pulled her to her feet, softly laughing with delicious anticipation, but as they walked through the scented dusky groves, he began, again, to speak. 'Strange,' he said, 'that in Saronno where we met I saw you as the Virgin and painted you as the Madonna again and again. Yet in San Maurizio I did not paint you as the Queen of Heaven but as Saints and martyrs, mortal women; and that other Mary, the Magdalene.'

Simonetta took his arm, and her voice when she spoke was teasing. 'Perhaps you saw me then as a fallen woman, as Gregorio the squire called me; a woman who wantonly kissed you on the steps of the church.' She was amazed how easy it was now to speak lightly of that shattering event.

He did not smile. 'Perhaps. Perhaps I idealised you, made you my icon of womanly perfection, the Madonna personified. Mother, wife and all things loving and good.' His voice was earnest and halting as he felt his way through the maze, in an effort to unravel the truth. 'Then I taught myself to despise you once I had possessed you, despite the fact that I myself brought you low. Perhaps it had more to do with my own mother, and the way she denied me love, in the way that you denied me yourself too. For she was a Magdalene indeed – they even shared a profession.' Now he smiled, but even in the dusk she could see that the hurt had not yet gone. She longed to take it all away, to love him as he deserved for the rest of his life.

Now they left the leafy alleys behind and walked the steps to the loggia, and it was she that spoke next. 'And if you paint me again, my husband, what shall I be then?'

He turned her to him and took her face in his hands. She was bathed in the amber light from the house, the alchemy of candlelight turning her to gold. Yet she was not an icon or a statue, she was *real*, and his wife. He felt his heart fail. 'I will paint you as you are,' he said. 'A mortal woman. But it may yet be that I will paint you as the Virgin once again. For in San Maurizio, in all the tales that were told to me, I have learned that all women, be they never so Holy, are all human; and all men likewise.' He kissed her, to demonstrate the point, and they went inside.

They crept up the stair to her solar, following the trail of almond blossom which Veronica had scattered to guide their way. Bernardino was silent, thinking, and Simonetta waited.

'One thing more before our discourse is done,' he said, at last. 'Do you remember once, in Saronno's church, you held out your hand to me, and I turned away?'

She turned back on the stair and looked down on him. *Noli me Tangere.* His face was so raw and vulnerable. She loved him so much at that moment that she could not speak. She nodded.

'I will not do so again,' he said, in a voice so soft that it was almost a whisper.

She held out her hand to him, he took it, and together they climbed the stair.

His hard body lay atop her soft one, and they kissed a hundred, a thousand times until her lips and cheeks were raw with the scrape of his stubble. His hands were everywhere, charting the landscape of her body; on her breasts, between her legs, in all the places she knew she had longed for. Sometimes gripping so hard that there was almost pain, sometimes grazing her flesh so softly and unbearably that she became shameless, guiding his hands and forcing his touch. And then he entered her and the yearning stopped. He lay still for many moments, within her, above her; wolf-grey eyes locked into lake-blue ones, staring deep, deep into the depths. This moment of joining, that Simonetta now knew she had imagined for three long years, flooded her with such pleasure that she had to bite her lip to keep her from crying out. She marvelled at how different it was, this animal act, how different he felt; this new husband, from the old. He fitted, he filled her up. With Lorenzo she had been a girl; young and untried, half a woman who needed half a man –

a boy playing at soldiers – to make her whole. With Bernardino she felt as if two people, who had suffered and learned survival apart, had at last come together to make a couple. A pair; equal in love and life and their separate endeavours. This was not the love of youth, it was the love of age and maturity; of adult passions so much more real and fulfilling than the courtly posturings of her adolescent union. It was so good, and so *right*, that she could hardly bear it. Bernardino began, at last, to move. And she forgot Lorenzo.

Hours later, Bernardino rose to close the casement against a sudden chill breeze. He saw dark storm clouds rolling in across the bottle-green plain from the direction of Pavia. There would be thunder and lightning this night but he cared not. He could not waste another moment on the vista when there was a view more beautiful awaiting him within the solar. His new wife: more lovely than ever, all tumbled and golden and abandoned on the bed. Their union had been more, so much more than even he had ever dreamed. How thankful he was now that she had not given herself to him cheaply, all those years ago; that they could now live honestly in the light, as man and wife, without the torture of conscience on the rack of scandal. His heart was full – he was at once completely happy and could ask for nothing, long for nothing. And as he slid beneath the coverlet and felt her arms close around him, he felt that nothing could ever divide them again.

CHAPTER 41

Selvaggio Wakes

Another storm, in another season, rolled over the same Lombard hills to disturb the nuptial slumbers of another groom. It woke Selvaggio in the middle of his wedding night, and his heart was too full of happiness to let him sleep again. He turned on his side to his dear Amaria, and her dark fan of hair under his hand was soaked from the rain misting through the open casement. He smiled – he had opened it after they had coupled for the first time, a sweet hot, short consummation for God and the Law, before they spent the next hours exploring each other. Their love had brought the sweat to their skin, so he had opened the window and the cold air rushed in with a shock. Now he rose on silent feet and trod quietly so as not to disturb his new wife, and his Nonna where she slept on the truckle downstairs. He closed the casement against the rain and the threat of thunder. He looked about for something to dry Amaria's hair, but was unaccustomed to this room. The fireside bed, where tonight Nonna rested, was usually his.

So as he sought a balmcloth or garment to swipe the rain
from the coverlet he thought the chest at the foot of the
bed seemed a likely place. And so it proved, at once he
found a folded cloth, blue in the moonlight. It was somewhat besmottered but he unfolded it anyway. The lightning
cracked and lit the cloth day-bright for just a heartbeat, but
it was enough. His finger traced the three silver ovals, that
his ancestors meant for almonds, and he fell to his knees. A
casement opened in his mind and cold memory rushed in.

He knew everything, all of it, in that instant.

CHAPTER 42

The Church of Miracles

I am Lorenzo Giovanni Battista Castello di Saronno.

Now, I remember it all. And remembrance brings his unwelcome brother, realization. I know that I must leave.

I kiss her once before I go. Amaria; the one that I love but must no longer call wife. I swear that she smiles as she sleeps, and my heart cracks. I weaken and move to wake her, but steel myself not to. How can I explain that I am married already, and thus have dishonoured her with the double-headed sin of adultery and fornication? Better that she thinks the worst of me – better to be a feckless, faithless husband, a deserter rather than a bigamist. Better that she forget me, and when the church releases her, she can love again. Why does this thought hurt most of all?

And Simonetta, the love of my youth, what will I say to you, at our joyless reunion? Your name was once poetry to me, but now I can hardly utter it. You are no more real to me now than a dream, or a painting on a wall with two dimensions but no capacity to live in this new world of mine. Poor, guiltless lady, how can I return your love now this new love has come to me? And yet I must. We are married, and I will be your husband till I die in truth, as I so nearly did.

I take nothing but the blue banner and my cloak. I creep downstairs like the adulterer I am, past Nonna who snores slightly. More than a mother to me, I wish I could kiss her too, and tell her to look after my Amaria. But of this instruction, there is no need.

It takes me more than a sevennight to walk to Saronno, begging like a pilgrim and taking my rest where I can find it under the stars. I go to the Sanctuary church of Santa Maria dei Miracoli, where that first, dreamlike marriage took place. I think to find the good Father Anselmo within; I know now it was his preaching that I once heard, echoing through my memory. His voice it was, guiding my own as I read the scriptures aloud to my Amaria; recalling the thousand masses that I once heard, here in this church. Perhaps the padre knows how my lady Simonetta does, and how the shock of my coming will affect her. I do not go to Castello directly, lest the appearance of Lorenzo-Lazarus should overcome her.

The place is greatly changed – what was once a plain white church is now an Ethiop's cave, a treasure chest, a rainbow. There are paintings everywhere – frescoes crawl over every inch, and my eyes have entered paradise, even though my heart burns in hell. Despite the sight, my flesh heats with the agony of loss, like my name – Saint Lorenzo. Save for the crowd of Saints no one is within, except a single fellow hanging high at the rafters and scratching at an image with a paintbrush. The face he paints holds me at once, for it is Simonetta di Saronno, as surely as she is standing in front of me. She is just as I recall her; as beautiful as the day, but now insubstantial. Her fairness can no longer touch me. To me, true beauty wears a more dusky countenance – it has the olive warm skin and raven hair of Amaria.

I find my voice at last. 'Did you do this?'

The fellow spins round on his ropes, as if he expected someone else.

'Yes,' he replies. 'It has been a long road, but at last it is done. This face is the last of it, and the best of it, long overdue.' He smiles, as if at a private jest.

'It is wondrous indeed,' I say, speaking the truth. 'If miracles truly happen here, then this is surely the greatest.'

He descends, pleased by the compliment. 'I thank you,' he says as he finds his feet. He is shorter than I by a hand, and, on closer scrutiny, a good bit older. But he is slim and handsome enough.

'She is very fair, your subject,' say I.

He smiles, and is suddenly my own age. He looks like a man who owns the world and is perfectly happy in it. I envy him. 'I'm glad you think so,' he says. 'She is my wife.'

A hammer strikes in my chest, and I think my ears have

deceived me. 'Your…wife?'

'Indeed. I am Bernardino Luini, the artist,' and indeed I do think I have heard the name, 'and this is Simonetta, formerly Simonetta di Saronno, now Simonetta Luini.' He said the name with pride. 'She sat as my model for the Holy Virgin, as you see. The frescoes are to be dedicated tomorrow, in fact, on the day of Saint Ambrose.'

I nod, dazed. I knew the Saint's day well. We had come to the parade every year of our marriage, Simonetta and I. But what I remember now is that this time last year I had taken Amaria in my arms for the first time, and carried her away from the Swiss mercenaries.

My new friend and rival looks at me closely, so heaven knows what he sees written in my face. I make an attempt at pleasantry. 'Is there still a feast, and a parade of the reliquaries?'

'There is. Attended by the new Cardinal, whom we like much better than the old one, God rot his bones.' The artist's eyes narrow. 'Do you know these parts?'

'I used to.'

The fellow claps my shoulder. 'Then you must attend,' he said, clearly in a mood to be friends with the entire world, even with a pilgrim he had never met before. 'I will present you to my wife.' He is plainly eager to show off his prize.

I choke on the remembrance that just a short week past, I had been the same happy, proud groom, wanting to show my Amaria to all the world.

'Till tomorrow then. You must meet her,' he says.

Tomorrow. I would see Simonetta tomorrow. She that had been my wife, and was my wife still, till death parted us. We had been married here, in the sight of God, and the law of God bound us still. I take the artist's proffered hand. Poor fellow. He does not know that I am here to take his world away from him, that I am Arthur to his Lancelot and I am about to claim back my Guinevere. I am sorry that he is soon to feel as I feel now.

'Right gladly I will,' I say.

CHAPTER 43

The Banner

At first Amaria could not believe Selvaggio had gone. She searched everywhere – went to all the places they had been together in Pavia. The wells where they had met, and he had asked her to be his. San Pietro where he had saved her life, and then saved it again by marrying her. All the woods and walks, bridges and falls where they had spent the happiest of times, she went back again, lest he had once again lost his memory, and was somewhere, dazed, waiting for her to take him in her arms and make all things right again. She asked everyone she met if they had seen her husband. Most folk knew of him, for they had been a familiar sight, going everywhere together two by two like the creatures of the Ark. But no one had seen him since the wedding day.

As the days passed Amaria grew thin and silent. She could not eat. She was worn to a shadow. Nonna, stricken too, did not know how to help her granddaughter. The two women revolved around each other, unable to look at the other's face, so great was the pain that was writ there.

As the days became a week, Amaria began to spend long hours at the dovecot Selvaggio had made for her. The pair of white doves which he had bought her as a gift, she began to tend obsessively; as if they were children he had left. She coddled them in her hands, cooing in their own voices and stroking their snowy feathers. He had named them Phyllis and Demophon, but said that he did not know why. She called them by these names, names that seemed strange to her, but ones that must be kept because he had so christened them. When Selvaggio had been gone a week, she discovered that Demophon, the male dove, had flown from the dovecot in the night. She took Phyllis in her hands and kissed her head. She felt no sympathy for the bewildered bird, who cocked her head from right to left, looking for her errant mate. Instead Amaria took her rabbit knife and did what she had been too enamoured of the birds to do on her wedding day – she spread Phyllis's right wing like a fan and cut out the two long prime feathers. The blood ran dark over her hands. The bird flapped in protest but Amaria did not flinch. She remembered, suddenly, the day she had killed the red hen for Selvaggio without a moment's hesitation. That day she felt she had grown, and become a woman, for there was now someone to look after, someone to love. The pain of loss was suddenly so bad she could hardly stand. She put Phyllis back in the dovecot, alone. 'There' she said, with triumph. 'Now you cannot fly away. You must stay here, with Nonna and me. Three old maids together.' From nowhere, laughter shivered her ribs and she rocked, crowing with mirth like a mad woman, till the shiver became a retch and she vomited, violently, onto the straw. The chickens came to peck at her leavings, and she was suddenly frightened. I cannot live without him, she thought. This will kill me.

Meantime, Nonna sat rocking in the chair Selvaggio had made for her, as she had taken to doing. For the second time in her life she gave way to tears. How much greater was this second loss of her life, than when she had seen Filippo dead? For this time Amaria, her dear child, suffered too.

And there was more joy and pain to come, for Nonna had lived in the world and knew why Amaria was vomiting. She grieved that the girl was doomed to repeat her own life, pouring all her love into the child Selvaggio had left. This child would grow like an olive plant around their table, not, now, as part of a happy family but as a crutch to two lonely abandoned women. A child that reminded them daily of him who had gone.

Gone. A dark thought stopped her rocking and led her upstairs to the dorter. The blue banner, folded and put away, had Selvaggio found it? Nonna opened the chest at the bed's foot. The banner was missing.

He had not lost his memory again. He had found it.

Nonna blamed herself bitterly. She had hidden the banner, folded it and kept it away, telling herself that she would show him one day, but that day had never come. She should have burned it so that they would be safe, or else shown him at once, the day that he woke from his wounds, so that he could begin to remember straight away before this great love had grown between him and Amaria. But she had hidden the thing, and said nothing, because she had wanted him to stay. And now she had brought immeasurable, killing grief on the girl she loved the most in the world.

She sat heavily on the bed, her hand on one of the four heavy posts he had made for it. A chill grey hand clasped her heart and she gasped at the pain. Most unusually for such an active soul, she felt that she had to lie down on the bed. Just for a while. The cold hand squeezed her heart again and she allowed her eyes to shut. She had endured one great loss in her life and survived it. She knew she could not do so again.

CHAPTER 44

The Feast of Sant'Ambrogio

I walk the well-known streets of Saronno and marvel that
I could have forgotten so much. How could my mind have
lost the years I lived here, and loved here, and wived here?
And now, as I mingle with the feast-day crowds in my pil-
grim's garb, my heart is in my mouth with the thought that
I will see my wife again, the wife I no longer want or love,
and divide her from her new life. But it is the law of God.
Forgive me, Simonetta!

I line the streets with the many, and wait for the procession of the reliquary of the Saint. Many of the good people
of Saronno are jug-bitten already, for all that, it is only Sext.
My eyes search the crowd for her, and the husband that
I have already met, but they are not in the street. I soon
know why. A cheer goes up and I turn with the crowd; she
is there, seated in a bower of flowers, on the balcony of the
mayor's house. My heart falters – she is beautiful indeed,
and smiling in a way I never saw. Simonetta. Were we really
wed once? It seems an age ago, another life indeed. There

is something new about her. Her hair is a little shorter, her features more rounded. But above all, she looks as if a torch lights her from within. Could the man beside her, the dark-haired artist who also waves at the crowd, be the reason for this transformation? He holds her close, possessively, as the crowd salute their Queen of Heaven, the model for the frescoes shortly to be dedicated.

Another mystery. Simonetta was unknown to the town when I was her husband – we were private people. How has she gained such adulation? From being an artist's model? I suppose that *may* bring honour on the *Comune* of Saronno. Or has she done the town some service in my absence? As the procession begins and the costumed servers pass, I strain to keep the couple in sight through the passing motley of the town's livery. I duck under one of the passing horses to gain their side of the street, earning a curse from one of the local Signori. I know him. I sold him the very mare that now dances over my head.

I draw closer now. The two heads – one red, one dark, are close together. Kissing? No. Whispering and bubbling with laughter. My stomach shrivels. So I was once with Amaria, until my trickster memory brought me back to my duty. I look closer through the fancy open carving of the balcony, to see if their hands are clasped. But I see something else.

Two golden haired children – boys – sit low behind the carving and watch the spectacle. One, the elder, shares sweetmeats and toys with his brother with an affection and propriety that is affecting to see. And now I see that the couples' hands are indeed clasped like lovers. But each rests their other hand on the golden head of a child, fondling the locks with love.

Like parents.

My head spins. How can this be? I have not been gone so long! My eyes fix on the town's fairest maids as they march by holding arches of almond blossom – *my* almond blossom – and I try to resolve my thoughts. Of course. The children must be his. He has some years on Simonetta – perhaps his wife is dead and his children now call my wife mother. I look on the familial scene and I grieve that I will divide them all. But it must be done. I approach, for the time has come to reveal myself; when I am carried away from this domestic scene by the press of numbers. The maids with the almond branches are passing something into the crowd. I jostle closer and see that they are filling small wooden cups from the flasks they carry – like naiads distilling their own sap the amber liquid gushes forth and the crowd sups so heartily that barely have they finished pouring but the cups are proffered for more. A cup is thrust into my hand and I drink. The draught is sweet and yet bitter, with the taste of the almonds of my home. It tastes wonderful. It warms my chest and gives me courage. It is time. But another cheer pre-empts me; this bounty has something to do with Simonetta, for with difficulty she rises to her feet, and I nearly fall from mine. For here is something to give me pause indeed.

She is with child.

Now I must sit on the pavings, among the horse dung and the almond blossom, as the liquor and the sight swirl my senses. Simonetta and the artist are having a child. How can I divide them now? I make an adulterer of both, a bastard of the child, and orphans of the two golden children I have seen that they love so well. I press my hands into the balls of my eyes, and when I take them away, the answer is in front of me. For Saint Ambrose passes by, in the glorious gold litter of his reliquary, and through the crystal panes of his casket I see his little bleached bones. My heart freezes for a heartbeat as I look on his mummified head and see the dead orbs of his eyes gazing straight at me. Amaria's Saint, my Saint, Sant'Ambrogio, is trying to tell me something. I pray to him for guidance, pushing through the crowd to keep the contact of his eyes, willing him to speak. But the Saint remains silent, and passes through the crowd, away from me. He says naught to guide me, and suddenly I understand. He is silent; I must be too. It *cannot* be God's will that I divide two families and cause pain when all have already suffered much. The Saint has given me his sanction. I am resolved, absolved. I will break the sacrament of one marriage to preserve two more.

Lorenzo Giovanni Battista Castello di Saronno is dead. Let him rest.

I pull my hood closer over my head, and take one last look at Simonetta before I turn away. Beautiful and abundant, I see the reason for the change in her swelling beneath her gown. I bless her before I turn away. I bless them all, all of her new family, with the Saint looking on.

Now I must be quick. I am bearded, and hooded, and greatly changed, but here live people who watched me grow. I leave the crowd, and slip down a narrow street. I am safe. A fellow bumps my shoulder hard, sees my pilgrim's cloak and mutters an apology. His breath smells of *grappa*, not almonds. I fatally raise my eyes to his, and both pairs widen. It is Gregorio.

He falls to his knees and kisses my hand, and says the name I have almost forgot.

'Signor Lorenzo! It is a miracle! The Saint has brought you home!'

I curse with all the words in my lexicon over his matted head. He is bloated, and bearded too, but still my squire whom I loved once as a brother. I free my hand and change my voice as much as I can, affecting the drawl of the Lombard. 'May I help, you, my son?'

He looks up, puzzled. He is drunk, a tendency of his youth has clearly taken hold in his age. 'Are you not?… Surely…'

I see he is no longer sure, and press home my advantage. I feel like the Blessed Peter, denying knowledge of his Lord. 'Son, I am a stranger to this town.'

His heavy brows join as his joy drains away. 'Forgive

me… I took you for… Are you not Signor Lorenzo di Saronno?'

I shake my head, and decide, now and for ever. Thrice denied, the cock crows. 'No. My name is Selvaggio Sant'Ambrogio.' I turn and walk away, sorry at once that I have crushed him. I know what I owe him, and what we once were to each other. I know too that if he tells the tale around the town he will be dismissed as a drunk, and that his gossip will not damage the golden family that I have left. He calls after me and my blood chills.

'Pilgrim! At least bide a while and have a drink, for the love of Christ! For you have the look of my old Master that I loved well!' I keep walking, knowing now that I am safe, and they are safe. He calls again, now so faint I can hardly hear.

'Pilgrim! Where are you going?'

I do not turn, but call out to him the word that warms my heart. 'Home,' I say, and at last I permit myself to smile.

CHAPTER 45

Selvaggio Goes Home

It takes me less time to go from Saronno to Pavia than it did to get from Pavia to Saronno. Then my steps were dogged by reluctance, and a heavy heart. Now my heart is light, my step is quick. I do not rest until my legs give way, and then my sleep is only a few hours before I wake, thinking of her. *Amaria.* If only you will forgive me, then all will be well!

I know where she will be. I find my way through the woods outside the city, till I come to the *pozzo dei mariti*. As I see the wells and hear the splashing of the falls I look for her. She is there, sitting, gazing into the pool where we pledged our troth. She looks so thin, and so pale and sad that my heart wrenches. Her rounded form is now wasted to nothing; the green dress of our betrothal now hangs from her. Her hair hangs in lank swags and her eyes are dull and dead. What have I done to her? Then I understand. I have taken her life from her. It is time to give it back.

I slowly walk up behind her, my footfalls soft in the dew-ed grass. In the water my face appears beside hers, and her eyes look into mine, wide with shock and instantly awash with tears. I want to take her in my arms at once, but have to ask the question. My hands are on her shoulders. 'Do you know what they say of this place?'

'They say that…if you look into the pool, you can see the face of…your husband,' she says wonderingly, as if in a dream.

'And is it true?'

She looks at me then as the tears spill, and I know what she has suffered in the last week. 'You tell me.'

'I think it is.' I turn her round to face me. 'I love you, Amaria Sant'Ambrogio.' I say the words she had first taught me. '*Mano*,' I say as I take her hand. '*Cuore*,' as I place her hand on my heart. '*Bocca*,' I say as I kiss her, tenderly on the mouth. She kisses me harder than last time, and holds me tighter, and I kiss her again and again, whispering through both our tears that I will never leave her again, my love, my wife. Her colour and beauty return and she laughs with pure joy. I know what she will say next.

'Come home,' she says. 'We must tell Nonna.' But this time she adds more words – words that toll in my chest like a death knell. 'She is taken very ill.'

We hurry home, my wife explaining what had come to pass, and my steps quicken still faster, spurred by the fear that we would be too late.

CHAPTER 46

Simonetta Closes a Door

Simonetta stood alone on the battlefield.

Veronica of Taormina, at Bernardino's insistence, had brought Simonetta to Pavia in the carriage – one of the profits of a thriving business – for Simonetta could no longer ride. Veronica stayed behind at the nearby stream, with the carriage, gentling the horses and waiting patiently for her mistress. Veronica stroked the velvet noses and hummed her southern songs into the twitching ears to quiet them. The horses would not have crossed the brook onto the scarred plain even if she had bid them. They knew what had happened here. They could smell the dead, hear the ghostly battlecries, and shied and started at every breeze. Veronica narrowed her eyes against the whip of the wind and kept her far-seeing gaze on her mistress. Simonetta had walked a long way out.

Veronica of all people knew what her mistress had to do, for she had lost a husband too. Like Simonetta she had found a second, greater love, in Isaac; but knew that sometimes memory prompted respects to be paid to that first attachment. Veronica knew, too, that such rites must be carried out alone. But her gaze never wavered as she watched Simonetta, even when her mistress walked further, to the very centre of the great expanse. She was an easy mark, for as well as the massive bear furs she wore, her body was full and abundant: she was with child, and very near her time.

Simonetta huddled into the bear pelt against the cruel wind that riffled the fur. The gust snatched at her hair and pulled the burnished tendrils from under the hood, the shifting sunlight turning the strands to a brief bright copper. The cloak smelled faintly of sweet sandalwood; the scent of Manodorata, its former owner. She was suddenly gutted with loss. As she blinked back tears she almost laughed at herself. She had come to mourn one man and wept for another. She had never mourned her own father when the plague had taken him, but now acknowledged that Manodorata had been as a father to her, one that she had never knew she wanted, never knew she missed. He had been her guide and her friend when she had needed him most, and she missed him every single day. She was glad that he lived on in Elijah and Jovaphet; his sons, her sons, and now Bernardino's sons.

This was the first time she had left them alone, her three boys. Bernardino had encouraged her to go: happy beyond measure, he could deny her nothing, not even this. Since the feast of Sant'Ambrogio, when she had sat with her family and been fêted by the crowds she had felt an increasing restlessness – she was not unhappy, never that, never again. Bernardino had teased her, saying she was a mother bird building her nest, and such feelings were common for a woman nearing her confinement. But she knew it was not so – something had changed in her that day; something had prodded her conscience, prompting her of a task unfinished, work undone. Gradually it had dawned in her consciousness what was missing, what was needful and she had come here with Bernardino's blessing. His only concern had been the toll the length of the journey would take upon her and their babe, but he had been mollified by her agreement to take Veronica and ride in their fleece-lined carriage. She had left them in the great kitchens, which, despite the family's new-found wealth, had remained the heart of the Villa Castello. Her own heart gladdened as she remembered the scene she had left – Bernardino had spread the great board with all his precious charcoals and pigments, and laid down vellum for the boys to decorate. 'I shall teach them to paint,' he declared with his customary confidence, 'for that is what they shall do when they are grown.'

She smiled fondly. '*Both* of them are to be painters?'

He pointed to her stomach. 'All three.'

She kissed them all, expecting tears from the little ones, but realizing with a gladdened jolt that they were happy with their new father. Elijah was already Bernardino's slave because of the episode with the dove, but even little Jo-vaphet settled happily down to the day's activities. By the time she had gone the three were more decorated than the vellum, Bernardino more than the children. She had smiled, not censured. She cared not if she returned to find the villa frescoed like the church in Saronno. A process had begun, and it was pleasing to her.

She now felt many leagues away from that glowing hap-py place. Here it was cold not warm, she was utterly alone instead of in company, and she walked among the dead, not the gloriously alive. She took a breath of the chill air and turned around in a full circle. The plain was dappled in darkness and light as pregnant clouds scudded across the sky interrupting the sun. It lay flat, quiet and innocent, giv-ing nothing away. To the north, the city of Pavia lay like a crouching scarlet dragon, the houses huddled like scales, the towers the spines of its back. For long moments she walked the battlefield. She would never find the right spot – she would never know where Lorenzo had fallen. She only knew that it was now four long years to the day since the field had accepted his body and the libations of his blood. Four years. And what lessons had been learned? Just a few short months ago Simonetta had heard tell in Saronno of how a French army at Landriano under Maréchal Saint-Pol had been decisively defeated by the Spanish forces of Antonio di Leyva, Governor of Milan. The cycle had begun again. And if that cycle, like the wheels of the great siege engines that broke the body of Saint Catherine, turned inexorably to bring battle again to this land, the cycle of ignorance and the prayer-wheels of prejudice revolved too. For news had reached Saronno too of how thirty Jews had been burned alive in Bazin in Hungary, in this very year of 1529, for the ritual murder of a child who was later found alive. Simonetta shook her head. This was the very crime that she had first heard laid at the starred door of Manodorata.

Yet here at Pavia the scarred soil had long since healed, and hardy grasses pushed through the guilty ground; even flowers now dotted the sward. If the world lived in circles, nature circled too and pushed forth shoots of hope and health, however tainted the soil. At one such spot, where the wildflowers grew and the grass was bright with a patch of sunlight, Simonetta knelt at last and placed her hand flat on the ground. She knew now why she had come. It was not the irrational whim of a pregnant woman. She had needed to close the door. She had come to say goodbye.

All those years ago, when the news was fresh and the grief was new, the *Comune* of Pavia had forbidden 'searchers' from coming to seek their dead, through risk of pestilence and the utter confusion of thousands of maimed bodies. Simonetta had never been able to bring Lorenzo home, to see him closed in a casket, to sing masses for his soul. No grave was there that she could visit yearly, mitigating her grief as the seasons wheeled around. Now such things would be put right.

Simonetta beckoned across the great space to Veronica, who tethered the horses and came to her, bearing the twin burdens that were too heavy now for her mistress. She carried a shovel slung over her back, and in her arms she carried two long parcels, wrapped in the silver and blue di Saronno banners, swaddled like babes against the four winds. Veronica set down her load and dug a shallow pit in the hard ground while her mistress rested. Simonetta could read in her maid's solemn face the recollection of her own husband's burial, and regretted any pain the girl might feel – hoped that she might too benefit from this day. For what had seemed the end for Veronica then had been a beginning too, as Isaac had come to her.

At last, Simonetta laid the two long bundles in the soil. She could barely distinguish between them through the swaddle – both long, cold, steel but it did not matter. Both were culpable, both were bringers of death.

The sword and the gun.

Veronica scattered the soil over the weapons till they were gone from sight.

Simonetta's mind was as blank as the black soil; she could think of no last words, no prayers or songs of leavetaking, just an overwhelming sense of rightness. She did not want to keep Lorenzo's ancestral sword for maudlin recollections on winter evenings, nor hand it on to a son who was not his own.

It ended here.

The di Saronno name would now be one of trade, not warfare, and she would be as proud of it today as her ancestors had been in the past. The world turned, and the battles continued, but she would have no part in them. She was in the business of *creating* life. Bernardino, too, did not kill nor maim; he used his gift to make the earth more beautiful, and he would leave the world a better place than the one he entered.

His passion for his work had returned with their marriage and he had begun one last painting of her as the Virgin, fascinated by the changes that her pregnancy had brought to her body and face; another manifestation of his mortal Madonna. This panel painting, half complete and leaning by the fireplace as its glaze dried, showed her rounded and serene, every part of her plumper and glowing save her pale hands. She was cradling Elijah, with Sister Bianca looking on benevolently. 'I shall call it *The Virgin and Child with Nun in Adoration*,' announced Bernardino, in a tribute to his friend who had returned to her ministry in San Maurizio. Simonetta had finished her sittings and noted the lack of any background or context to the painting. She and Elijah and Bianca seemed to float in space, with nothing beyond them save the flat sheen of the glaze. Elijah had teased his new father: 'Perhaps we are spirits, mother; bogles and goblins that float over the plains of Lombardy.' And he had run round the house shrieking 'whooooooooo', making ghostly faces to fright his little brother. Bernardino had smiled but kept his peace. When Simonetta questioned her husband, Bernardino refused to let her see what else he had planned for the painting's background. ''Tis a surprise,' he said. 'You shall see it on your name day, in one short month, when you are twenty-one.'

She had asked no more, happy in her pregnancy and content in their two children. It gladdened her that their sons would be raised to live by the brush not the sword. She smiled a little at the saccharine motto that had come to her; a fitting blazon for the Luini arms. She suddenly had a longing to be back home, but her business was not yet done. She dismissed Veronica again: 'I'll not be long.'

She laid her hand down once more, on the soil that Veronica had levelled, where the sword and the arquebus and Lorenzo's blood lay beneath. 'You were the love of my youth,' she said, 'but now I am grown. The world changed and took you away from me, and I changed too.' Then, from beneath the lacings of her bodice she took out a milk white almond, warm from her bosom, and pushed it into the cold ground. Just like the one he had given her on their wedding day. She covered the nut completely, gave it back to the earth like the offerings the Romans made to the ground, to nourish their crops and appease the gods. Her own God sat in his Heaven again, the years of doubt behind her. She was happy. It was time to take her leave of Lorenzo. 'Goodbye,' she said.

Simonetta rose with difficulty, her hands under her belly,

round as a gourd. The child kicked inside her with a strength and urgency she had not known before. She gasped with pain and pleasure, unable to move for a moment. She saw Veronica start towards her with concern on her face, but she shook her head at her maid and smiled. The movement subsided and all was well. All was more than well. The clouds split suddenly and the sun burned down as she walked to the carriage without looking back. She resolved to remember Lorenzo with gladness, and every year on this day have a requiem mass sung in Santa Maria dei Miracoli in Saronno for his soul. The rites that she had been too numb with grief to afford him would be his at last.

Saronno. Her heart was thirled with joy as she knew she would be back with her family in a few short hours. Simonetta lifted her hand to her face to smooth her wayward curls and the ring on her knuckle caught the sun with a glitter. She splayed her strange, pale fingers at arms length to admire the design, proud as any new-wed girl of her betrothal ring.

Bernardino had had it made for her; he had taken the commission all the way to Florence, returning at last to the city of his youth. There along Ponte Vecchio where the finest goldsmiths in the world wrought their alchemy, the greatest craftsmen among the best – the first among equals worked in a humble shop with a six-pointed star over the door. Simonetta had sent Bernardino there – she knew that the Hebrew artisans within were those who had made the golden hand of her dearest, lost friend. Bernardino had only to cross the threshold and utter the dead man's name, to be given the very best of attention. It was just as well. For the design of Simonetta's ring, conceived and sketched by her betrothed, was a difficult one – not to be entrusted to the amateur. It was a delicate wreathed heart wrought in curlicues of gold. Inside the heart fanned a fleur-de-lys of three gilded almond leaves. But sitting atop the leaves were three oval almonds of the di Saronno arms, represented by a glowing trinity of freshwater pearls. Fortune's wheel had turned too; full circle, and the tree had borne fruit.

Veronica approached and took the outstretched hand with one of her rare smiles. As she helped her mistress into the carriage it began to snow; small, delicate blossoms that would not threaten their way.

Without knowing why, Simonetta di Saronno tipped back her head, and opened her mouth to let the flakes in.

CHAPTER 47

Epilogue

Lorenzo Giovanni Battista Castello di Saronno died in Pavia on the twenty-fourth day of February in the year of Our Lord 1525. But Selvaggio Sant'Ambrogio lives. I know because I am he. I am settled happily in Naples; I thought my secret safer if my family and I removed from Lombardy. Family? Yes, let me tell you of the people that are dearer to me than any I have ever known.

Nonna still lives – she lived again the day that she opened her eyes and beheld me stooping over her sickbed, the day that I found Amaria again at the *pozzo dei mariti*, the day I came back from Saronno. The sickness she had was in her heart, and the only physick she needed was my return. I am humbled, and do not deserve such a grandmother, such a friend. The warm winds of the south agree with her heartily, and now I do not think she will ever leave us.

My son was born in the summer and we named him

Gregorio, the name of a distant memory, of one that deserves the honour. He is the delight of my eyes, and as he grows he plays on the floor of his father's workshop, with the wood shavings. For I must tell you that now I am quite a prosperous man, and a well-respected citizen of Naples. The furniture that I make sells very well, and I was able to buy a large Neopolitan house. How strange it is that I, the last of the noble line of di Saronno, have become a carpenter and a tradesman! Yet I enjoy the work, and love the wood; it has meaning, a reality and immediacy a world away from the veneer of courtly pursuits. One keepsake alone came with us from Pavia, and it is something that I made and am proud of; the dovecot stands in the centre of our fine new courtyard, and our dove has new friends to delight her, something which in turn delights my wife.

Ah, my wife. Her heart is full of happiness and prosperity suits her well, yet for all her fine silks she still has the kindest heart of any creature that lives. Now she will tend our own children, as she once tended her husband; and as she will one day care for our children's children too.

Sometimes I hear news from Saronno. I heard it said that Simonetta and Bernardino also had a son, whom they named Aurelio. I set to work and carved an entire Noah's Ark of tiny pairs of animals, each no bigger than a thumbnail, complete with a wooden boat to keep them in. I sent a runner all the way to the Villa Castello, with the gift wrapped in a red silk parcel, and strict instructions not to

name me as benefactor. I hope that he had joy in it. (I did
not know just how much at this time – for many years later
Aurelio Luini followed his father's footsteps to the monastery of San Maurizio in Milan and painted a miraculous
fresco of Noah's Ark, a worthy inheritor of his father's talent. You may still see it there today.) I know that Evangelista learned to call father the man that had once painted a
dove in the palm of his hand, and that little Giovan Pietro
followed his brother's example.

And Simonetta? I know she found true happiness as
Luini's wife, and the mother of his sons. I never saw her
again – but I saw her likeness. Bernardino once said that
Lombardy is covered in blood and paint; the blood drains
away, but the paint stays for ever. You may see Simonetta
yourself if you go, as Amaria and I did, to the Museo Civico
Gaetano Filangieri, in Naples. Look for a painting called
The Virgin and Child with Nun in Adoration by Bernardino Luini. There you will see a Madonna and Child sitting in an almond grove while a nun with a kind face reads
to them from the scriptures. In the background, among the
trees, walks a man. A man that displays only one hand of
flesh, for the other golden hand is hidden in his cloak. A
man that was killed by the Madonna's arrow in that very
place, in the name of friendship. The child in her arms is
his eldest son, an orphan of the war between one God
and another. The Virgin has white hands, and the third and
fourth fingers are all the same length. They are the hands

of the artist's wife and the mother of his children.

They are the hands of Simonetta di Saronno... the Madonna of the Almonds.

THE END

The Unicorns in the Ark

The idea for The Madonna of the Almonds came from the legend of the well-loved liqueur Amaretto di Saronno, now known as Disaronno Originale™. The story tells of a love affair between a beautiful widow (an innkeeper in the legend) and the artist Bernardino Luini of the da Vinci school. Luini supposedly painted the widow as the Virgin in the Sanctuary church of Saronno in 1525, and she invented Amaretto for him as a gift of love. Though this tale forms the skeleton of the book, it should be made clear that the Amaretto drink mentioned in these pages bears no other relation to Disaronno Originale™, either in ingredients or method of production. The secrets of Disaronno Originale™ remain in the keeping of the Reina family of Saronno, as they should.

It would be futile, however, to deny the existence of Bernardino Luini, who is now revered as the greatest artist of Renaissance Lombardy, comparable even to his Master, Leonardo da Vinci. In fact, Bernardino's presence in the Monastery of Saint Maurice in Milan was so secret, and the work there was so accomplished, that for many years the frescoes were attributed to Leonardo himself.

Little is known of Bernardino's biography, so I have taken certain liberties with the story of his life, in particular the parentage of his two oldest sons Evangelista and Giovan Pietro. His work, however, speaks for itself. Visit by all means the beautiful sanctuary church of Santa Maria dei Miracoli in Saronno, (now called the Santuario Beata Vergine dei Miracoli) but if you would see Bernardino's true genius, cross the threshold of Monastero San Maurizio (Ex Monastero Maggiore) in Milan, the decoration of which was Luini's greatest achievement.

All three of Bernardino's sons followed him in his profession, and all of them, at different times, added to their father's work in San Maurizio.

Evangelista (Elijah) Luini became a painter of note and settled in Genoa, where he is known to have painted the civic arms on the lighthouse there in 1544.

Giovan Pietro (Jovaphet) painted the celebrated Last Supper in the Hall of the Nuns in San Maurizio. The apostle John (who leans his head tenderly on the shoulder of his Lord) is clearly portrayed as a woman, and, in fact, appears in another of Giovan Pietro's frescoes as the Magdalene.

Aurelio Luini was the youngest and most talented of Bernardino's sons, and as such he inherited the fabled *Libricciolo*, Leonardo's scrapbook of human facial anomalies. Perhaps because of this, he became a talented painter of grotesques. His contribution to San Maurizio's decoration was a beautiful panel fresco detailing the Flood. Careful observers will note that among the couples of existent animals entering the Ark is a pair of Unicorns.

And Simonetta di Saronno? She exists on the walls of San Maurizio in the face of every female Saint and every Magdalene, and in Saronno where every Madonna is the same woman. Many of these Holy ladies wear the symbol of the heart of almond leaves somewhere about their person. To me it is suggestive that this beauty with the red hair and the white hands, and the hooded Lombard eyes, lived in Bernardino's lifetime and heart. Or perhaps she never existed at all. There are Unicorns in the Ark, and like Aurelio Luini's fresco, some of this book is real, and some is not.

ACKNOWLEDGEMENTS

The kernel of the story of the Madonna of the Almonds came from enjoying a glass (or two) of Amaretto one Christmas with my husband. He was reading the back of the box that the bottle came in, which tells of the legend of Disaronno's origins. He turned to me and said '*that's your next book*'. So thank you, Sacha for the idea and for being there all the way through the 'distillation' process!

Thank you to my history teacher Jennifer Gill for first fostering my interest in the Italian Wars, and for her information on the Battle of Pavia. Thanks to my sister Veronica Fiorato and also Elizabeth Glover for their assistance on early ballistics, and to my father Adelin Fiorato who was invaluable on the work of Bernardino Luini.

Many thanks once again to my fantastic agent Teresa Chris and the wonderful team at Beautiful Books, especially Simon Petherick, Tamsin Griffiths and Katherine Josselyn.

This book deals partly with the Jewish experience in Renaissance Italy so I am particularly grateful to Linal Haft for reading the book from a Jewish perspective.

The portraits of the boys in this book were painted in the style of my own children, so thank you, Conrad and Ruby, for letting me borrow your characteristics.

Thanks to the makers of Disaronno both then and now, and to the long-dead Bernardino Luini – may you emerge, at last, from Leonardo's shadow.

Coming soon

The Venetian Contract

MARINA FIORATO

1576. A Turkish ship steals into Venice bearing a young and beautiful stowaway. Feyra, a gifted harem doctor, has risked her life to bring a vital message for the Doge. But time is short and she has many enemies.

Feyra is not the only stranger in Venice. The ship carried a deadly cargo: a man more dead than alive, a 'gift' from the Turkish sultan. Within days the city is infected with bubonic plague.

In despair the Doge commissions the great architect Andrea Palladio to build a church so magnificent that God will save Venice, and commands the city's finest plague doctor to keep him alive to fulfil his work. But Dr Annibale Cason has not counted on meeting Feyra. Now in hiding, she can not only match his medical skills, she can also teach him how to care.

Now read on . . .

www.marinafiorato.com

PROLOGUE

Venice

Christian Year 1576

Sebastiano Venier, Doge of Venice, gazed from the stone quatrefoil window, with eyes that were as troubled as the ocean.

His weather-eye, sharpened by many years at sea, had seen the storm approaching for three days, clotting and clouding on the horizon and rolling in across the sickly amethyst waves. Now the maelstrom was here, and it had brought with it something more malign than ill weather.

With his flowing white beard and noble countenance, the Doge had been immortalized by Tintoretto and been compared to Neptune who also ruled a seabound kingdom. He had even, in hushed tones, been compared to the Almighty. A profoundly devout man, the Doge would have been deeply troubled, for different reasons, by each comparison; but today he would have given anything to have the omnipotence to save Venice from her darkest hour.

He watched as six figures, huddled together against the elements, hurried along a dock already glazed with water at every flow of the tide, the ebb tugging at the hems of their black robes. The cloaks and cowls gave them a monastic look, but these six men were men of science, not religion. They dealt in life and death. They were doctors.

As they drew closer he could see their masks clearly;

bone-white beaks curving in a predatory hook from the dark cowls. The masks were frightening enough, but the reason for them even more ominous.

They were his *Medico delle Peste*. Plague doctors.

They were six scholars, men of letters from good families, all schooled at the best medical academies, one for each of the six *sestieri* of Venice. To see the Doctors together was an ill omen. Doge Sebastiano Venier doubted that they had ever even met together before; and they seemed to him to swoop like a murder of crows at a graveside. Perhaps his own. His shoulders dropped for an instant; he felt very old.

He watched the doctors wade along the peerless Riva degli Schiavoni, one of the most wondrous streets in the world, and knew that any minute now they would enter his great white palace. The Doge's skin chilled as if sea-spray had doused him. He leaned his head against the cool quarrels of glass, and shut his eyes for one blessed instant. If he hadn't done so, he might have seen a Venetian galleass sailing swiftly away on the dark and swelling waters; but he did close his eyes for a couple of heartbeats, just to be still and breathe in the salt ether.

The smell of Venice.

Sebastiano Venier straightened up, reminding himself who he was, where he was. He looked at the delicate stonework of his windows, the finest Venetian glazing keeping the thunder of the sea from his ears. He looked up, tilting his noble head to the ceiling and the peerless frescoes of red and gold painted over hundreds of years by the finest Venetian artists, covering the cavernous, glorious space above. And yet, all the riches and the glory could not keep the Pestilence from his door.

The Doge settled in his great chair and waited for the

doctors to be announced. They filed in, dripping, and semi-circled him like vultures, the red crystal eyepieces set into their masks glittering hungrily, as if ready to peck the very flesh of him. But the moment they began to speak, the Doge ceased to be afraid of them.

'We had expected it, my lord,' said one. 'In the botanical gardens of the *Jesuiti*, there have been of late unusual numbers of butterflies – hundreds upon thousands of them.'

The Doge raised a single, winter-white brow. 'Butterflies?'

The doctor, failing to register the steel in the Doge's tone, prattled on. 'Why, Doge, butterflies are well known to be harbingers of pestilence.'

'It is true,' chimed in another. 'There have been other signs too. There is a bakery in the Arsenale, and when you tear the loaves in twain, the bread itself begins to bleed.'

The Doge rapped his fingertips on the arm of his chair. 'The fact that the pestilence has arrived in Venice is not a matter for debate. The *question* is, how to best treat the Plague.'

It was no use. One physician wanted to combat the pestilence by advising his patients to wear a dead toad around the neck. The next advised backing a live pigeon into the patients' swollen buboes in the groin and armpit, so that the tail feathers could draw out the poison. They began to talk over one another, their beaks almost clashing, the masks now ridiculous; the doctors' learned, mellow voices raised in pitch until they were quacking like so many ducks.

The Doge, irritated, found his attention wandering. These physicians were charlatans, buffoons, each one more self-important than the next. His eyes drifted to the shadow of an arras, where a man, an old man like himself, stood listening; waiting for the moment when the Doge would call him forth, and tell him why he had been summoned.

The old man in the shadows – who happened to be an architect – was not really listening either. Always more interested in buildings than people, he was admiring how the stone cross ribs above his head described the curve of the ceiling, and how the proportions of the pilasters complemented the great panels of the frescoes.

Like the Doge, he had felt an initial jag of fear when he had seen the doctors enter the room. Everyone, from the Doge to the meanest beggar, knew what the masks meant. The Plague was in the city. But the architect was not overly concerned. There had been a minor outbreak of Plague two years ago, and he would do now what he'd done then. He would leave the city and go into the Veneto; perhaps back to his old home, Vicenza. There, in the hills, he would wait and plan and draw. He would sip wine while he waited for the Plague to slake its own thirst. With a fast boat to Mestre and a faster horse to Treviso, he could be at Maser by sunset, at the house of his good friends the Barbaro brothers. There would be room at their house, he knew it; after all, he had built it. As soon as he had found out what the Doge willed he would be gone.

The Doge had heard enough. These doctors could not help Venice. They would dispense their potions and remedies, make gold along the way, and some citizens would live and some would die. He grasped his chair until his knuckles whitened and as he looked down in despair. His own hands depressed him – gnarled and veined and liverspotted. How could an old man hold back the Plague?

He cleared his throat. He must act. He could not let his legacy be to allow this jewel of a city to be blasted by pestilence. The Doge's old heart quickened. He got to his feet, his blood rushing to his head. 'You are dismissed,' he said to the doctors, slightly too loudly. 'Get out.' He flapped his arms as if to scare them away like the crows they were. He waited till the doors had closed behind them. 'Andrea Palladio,' the Doge said, his tones ringing out in the great chamber, 'come forth.'

Palladio stepped from the shadows, and walked to stand before the Doge's great chair. The wind rattled at the casements, bidding to be let in, bringing its passenger the pestilence with it. Palladio fidgeted, anxious, now, to be gone; but the Doge, his anger spent, had taken his seat again, and seemed in a reflective mood.

'Have you heard of the miracle of Saint Sebastian of Giudecca?'

Palladio frowned slightly. Although he had never met the Doge before, he knew of him by repute; a sea lord of forty years standing, deeply devout, respected, and intelligent enough to have avoided the Republic's dreadful prisons through many successive councils of The Ten. Had Sebastiano Venier come to the greatest office too late? Was his mind now addled? Through the windows he could see the island of Giudecca, battered by rain, but still one of the most beautiful *sestieri* of Venice, curving round the back of the old city like a spine. 'Yes, of course.' He answered slowly, wondering where the question tended. The Doge began to speak again, as if telling a tale or preaching a parable.

'In the grip of the last great Plague in 1464, a young soldier came to the gates of the monastery of Santa Croce on Giudecca and called out for water. The sisters were all within, the Lady Abbess herself suffering from the pestilence. The *portonera*, one Sister Scholastica, came to the gate. When she cast her eyes on the young man she saw he had armour of shining silver, hair of golden fire and eyes of sapphire blue. Awed, she passed him a cup of water on the convent's wheel, and he drank. The vision thanked Scholastica and instructed her and all her sisters to pray to Saint Sebastian day and night, and drink of the water of the well. If they did this, the convent would be spared of the Plague. Then he struck his sword to the ground and departed from her, as if no more than a wisp.'

Palladio, who had been wondering how fast he could get to Mestre once the Doge was done, felt prompted by the sudden silence. 'What happened?' he asked.

'The Lady Abbess recovered that night, as did every other nun who was ill. None of the other sisters was touched by the Plague, and all those who drank of the well were saved.' The Doge rose and stepped off his dais. He walked to Palladio and faced him, looking down from his greater height. 'The monastery was a place of pilgrimage for many years, and the people took the waters from the well for the Plague, and later, other ailments. When I was born, four doors away from Santa Croce in the Venier Palace, I was named Sebastiano after this miracle. But now the convent is a ruin.' He fell quiet.

The wind whistled into the silence. Palladio thought he knew, now, what was required of him, and his heart sank. For years he'd wanted to build on Giudecca, an island with good ground of solid rock and some of the best vistas on to the lagoon. For years he'd petitioned the Council of Ten for a site there, to no avail. But now, when all he wanted to do was quit the city, the very thing he wanted most was to be presented to him. Palladio's thin mouth twisted in half a smile. Sometimes he thought that the Almighty had a rich sense of irony. 'And you want me to rebuild the monastery of Santa Croce?'

'No, not precisely that.' The Doge crossed to the window once again. 'Look at them, Andrea.' With a sweep of his gnarled hand he invited Palladio to look down on to the wondrous expanse of Saint Mark's Square. Two prostitutes strolled below the window in their traditional yellow and red, and despite the lashing rain, their breasts were bare and swinging freely as they walked.

Palladio, too old to be moved by such sights, spotted one who was not; a man watched them from the arches of the Procuratie Vecchie, his hand revoltingly busy in his crotch. The watcher beckoned the women into the arch with him, and, as soon as a coin had changed hands he pushed one against one of the noble pillars of the loggia, rutting and thrusting below her bunched skirts. The other woman pushed her hand down the back of his breeches to assist her client's pleasure. 'In the *street*, Andrea,' said the Doge, turning away. 'In the very *street*. That magnificent pillar, constructed by your brother-architect Sansovino to make this square the most beautiful in the world, is now a polly-pole.' He sighed in counterpoint with the wind. 'The licentiousness, the decadence, it is getting worse. Such behaviour used only to manifest itself at Carnevale, for two short weeks of the year. Now such sights are commonplace. We are known for it abroad. Derided. They do not speak of Sansovino's pillars, nor your own villas and churches. They speak of the whores that ply their trade in the streets.' The Doge placed his hand on the window catch, trying it, as if to make sure the miasma was kept out. 'And once word spreads about the city that the Plague is with us, it will be worse. The shadow of death does strange things to a man – he becomes lawless, and he feels he must rut and steal and lie and make coin while he may.'

Palladio was trying to connect the fractured tracks of the Doge's discourse, the miracles and the harlots.

'Only one man can save these wanton, wonderful people from the Plague, and from themselves, and it is not I.'

Palladio thought of the six doctors of the *sestieri*, none of whom seemed to be worthy of the mantle of saviour. Then he realized that the Doge was speaking of Christ, and he arranged his features into an expression of piety. The Doge turned his watery blue eyes upon him. Pale and rheumy, the orbs looked old and defeated. '*You* are that man.'

Palladio's expression of reverence dropped with his jaw.

'Don't you see? God is punishing Venice. We need an offering, a gift so great that we will turn the edge of the divine anger and stay His hand from smiting our city. If medicine cannot help us, then we must turn to prayer. You, Andrea, you will build a church, on the ruins of the convent of Santa Croce. You will work in the footsteps of Saint Sebastian and build a church so wonderful, so pleasing to the glory of God, that it rivals His creation. And when you are done, the people will come, in their hundreds and thousands, and turn to God; they will praise Him with their voices and thank Him upon their knees. The power of prayer will redeem us all.'

Palladio blustered his reluctance. 'But . . . I'd thought,

of course I'd be honoured, but perhaps I could direct operations from Vicenza or maybe Treviso . . .'

The sentence died under the Doge's eye, and the wind whistled in mockery. The Doge let a moment pass before speaking. 'Andrea. We are old men. The time left to us is short. You will stay in Venice, as will I. There is no greater service you can render your city than this. Don't you see?' He took Palladio's shoulders in his hands, with a surprisingly strong grip. 'You are entering into a contract with God himself.'

Palladio remembered that as a young mason he always used to find fossils in the stone that he worked. No day would pass without him finding at least one nautilus, fossilized in its perfect Vitruvian spiral, compressed and entombed for thousands of years in the Carrera marble. And now he was equally trapped: his appointment held him; he was imprisoned, literally, in stone.

He recognized the devotion in the Doge's eyes and knew that Sebastiano Venier would not be gainsaid. How could he ever have thought the Doge's eyes were those of an old man? They blazed now with the blue fire of the zealot, the fire of Saint Sebastian. Even if he'd had the courage to refuse, the proximity of the prisons settled the matter. Palladio bowed his head in silent acquiescence.

The Doge, who had not been anticipating a refusal, called for his chamberlain. '*Camerlengo*, take Signor Palladio to his house – he is to have everything he needs. And, *Camerlengo*,' he called as the chamberlain was about to follow Palladio through the great doors, 'now find me a *real* Doctor.'

Chapter 1

Constantinople, Ottoman Year 983
One Month Earlier

Feyra Adalet bint Timurhan Murad took extra care with her appearance that morning.

Her father had already left the house, so she could not – as she often did – put on *his* clothes. It was common in Constantinople, among the poorer families, for women and men to wear the same; male and female clothing was so similar anyway, and there was often only enough money for one good suit of clothes; for one good pair of shoes. Feyra and her father were not badly off, as Timurhan bin Yunus Murad was a sea captain of good rank and standing, but Feyra still approved of the tradition: it helped her to hide.

Today, her father must have had an appointment of some consequence, and an early one at that; for when Feyra opened the carved lattice shutters of her window she could see that the sun had barely risen over the city. The domes and the minarets that she loved were still only silhouettes, describing a perfect negative contour of darkness bitten out of the coral sky. Feyra breathed in the salt of the ether.

The smell of Constantinople.

She looked out to sea, barely yet a silver line in the dawn light, wondering what lay beyond it. For an instant she felt a yearning for another land, for those places that lived for her only in the stories of a seafaring father.

But Feyra's reverie had cost her time. Turning away from the view, she faced, instead, the rectangle of silver that hung on the wall, edged in enamel and polished to almost perfect reflection, distorted only slightly by the dents of the metal. It had been brought back for her by her father from some Eastern land over some Eastern sea and had hung in her room since she was a baby. As a child the mirror had been a curiosity; it had shown her what colour her eyes were, what her face looked like as she pulled it into odd shapes, how far her tongue could reach when she stuck it out. Now that Feyra was a woman, the mirror was her best friend.

Feyra looked carefully at her reflected self, trying to see what the men saw. When she'd first noticed men staring at her in the street, she had begun to cover her hair. Then they stared at her mouth, so she took to wearing the half-face veil, the *yashmak*. She had even chosen one with sequins at the hem, so that the gold would draw their eyes away from hers. But still they stared, so she switched to the *ormisi*, a thin veil about a hand span in width that was worn over the eyes. When this didn't work she surmised that her body must be attracting the male gaze. She began to bind her budding breasts so tightly that they hurt, and yet still they stared. *Why* did they stare?

Feyra had read enough sonnets and odes of the lovesick to know that she did not confirm to the ideals of the Ottoman poets. Nor did she even resemble the maidens who featured in the bawdy macaroons her father's sailor friends sang; she overheard them, sometimes, when she was in bed and they were downstairs at dinner and had had too much to drink.

Feyra did not consider her amber eyes, large but slightly slanted like a cat's, round and dark enough to be praised in song. Her small, neat nose was too upturned for beauty. Her skin was the colour of coffee, not dusky enough for men to write poems about. Her hair, falling in thick swags and ringlets to her shoulder blades, was not silken and straight enough for the poets, and the colour was wrong too: every shade of tawny brown, not one of them dark enough to be compared to a raven's wing. And her wide, ruddy mouth, strangest of all, with the top lip bigger than the bottom, was a generous shape that could not, in even the most heroic couplet, be compared to a rosebud.

To her, her features – taken separately, taken as a whole – were unremarkable, even odd. But they seemed to have some strange power that she didn't understand, and certainly didn't welcome. Even her disguises had limited efficacy. If she covered her eyes, men looked at her mouth. If she covered her mouth, they stared at her eyes. If she covered her hair, they looked at her figure. But she still had to try, for the inconveniences of her daily disguise were nothing to the consequences of revealing herself.

The Feyra in the looking-glass raised her chin a fraction and the reflection encouraged her. Today she must wear feminine garb; very well, she would make the best of it. She began her ritual.

Wearing only her wide billowing breeches made of transparent silk, Feyra took a long, cream bandage and tucked one end into her armpit. She pulled the material tight to her flesh, round and round her ample chest. When her breasts pained her and her breath felt short, she was grimly happy.

Now it was time for the gown. Feyra's father had brought her gowns of gold and silver satin, brocade, bales of samite and Damascene silk from the four corners of the world. But they lay untouched in a sea chest below the window. Instead she had bought a plain shift dress, a *barami,* in the Bedestan market. The dress fell without folds to the ground, disguising her shape. Next she added the upper gown, the *ferace,* bodice buttoned to the waist after which it was left open.

Then she combed and plaited her hair, coiling it around the top of her head like a crown. She struggled with the curls that crept from her veil by the day's end however hard she tucked them back. Every day she tried to tame them. She placed and tied a veil of thin taminy over her hair, and tied it around the forehead with a braided thread. Then she damped the tendrils around her face with rosewater and pushed them viciously back until not a single strand could be seen.

Over it all she crammed a four-cornered *hotoz* cap, which buttoned under the chin, and a square *yemine* veil to cover her whole face. Then she took a length of plain tulle and wound it around her neck several times. She looked in the mirror again. Effectively swaddled, she was unrecognizable. Her clothes were the hue of sand and cinnamon, designed to blend in to the city and offer her camouflage. The only flare of colour were the yellow slippers of her faith – leather slippers with upturned toes that were fastened over the instep, practical and proof to water and the other more noxious fluids she was wont to encounter in her job.

Dressed at last, she added no ornaments to her apparel. Feyra had gold enough – she had as many trinkets as an indulgent father could provide, but bangles and baubles would draw attention to her – and what was more, interfere with her work.

Feyra's finishing touch was born of utility, not fashion

nor status: a belt, bulky and ugly, an invention of her own. It held a series of little glass bottles and vials, each in an individual leather capsa, all strung together on a broad leather band with a large brass buckle. She strapped the thing beneath her *ferace*, so it was completely hidden at her waist while at the same time making her dumpy in the middle and giving her the silhouette of a woman twice her age.

By the time she was finished, the sun was fully up and the sky had bleached to a birds-egg blue. She allowed herself one more glance at the city she loved, now described in every daylit detail. The heartbreaking curve of the glittering bay, the houses and temples lying like a jewelled collar upon this matchless curve of coastline. Crouching like a sentinel of the Bosphorus was the great temple of the Hagia Sophia, where the Sultan's hawks rose on the thermals from the sunbeaten golden dome. Feyra forgot her moment of yearning; she no longer wanted to know where the sea went. She vowed, instead, that she would never leave this city.

The wailing song of the *muezzin-basi* floated in a sweet, mournful thread from the towers of the Sophia to her ear. *Sabah*, sunrise prayer. Feyra turned and ran, clattering down the stairs.

She was very, very, late.

If you have enjoyed this, you will want to try Marina Fiorato's other historical novels set in Italy:

The Glassblower of Murano

Venice, 1681 . . . Venetian mirrors are more precious than gold, a secret jealously guarded by the Republic's sinister Council of Ten. When the greatest glassblower of them all, Corradino Manin, sells his method to the Sun King, Louis XIV of France, a chain of events is set in motion that will echo down to the present day. For as Manin's descendant Nora comes to Venice in search of new hope, the treacherous secrets of the past will threaten her happiness – and even her life.

∞

The Botticelli Secret

When the spirited Luciana Vetra, part-time model and full-time whore, models for Botticelli's painting *La Primavera* and goes unpaid, she steals an unfinished version of it in revenge – only to find out that someone is ready to kill her to get it back. As friends and associates are murdered around her, Luciana turns to the one man who has never exploited her beauty – Brother Guido della Torre. But will whore and monk prove to be each other's downfall?

∞

Daughter of Siena

The Palio is Siena's famously dangerous and hard-fought horse race. But two women watching have far more than the coveted prize at stake. For beautiful Pia of the Tolomei, it is her last hope of escaping a violent marriage. For Violante de Medici, isolated in her palace, it marks what her enemies intend to be her last month as Siena's ruler.

The trumpets sound. And into the piazza rides an unknown horseman. What he does during the race will not only change the lives of Pia and Violante, but alter the course of the Medici dynasty itself . . .

From Byron, Austen and Darwin
to some of the most acclaimed and original
contemporary writing, John Murray takes pride in
bringing you powerful, prizewinning, absorbing
and provocative books that will entertain you
today and become the classics of tomorrow.

We put a lot of time and passion into what we
publish and how we publish it, and we'd like to
hear what you think.

Be part of John Murray – share your views with us at:

www.johnmurray.co.uk

 johnmurraybooks

@johnmurrays

johnmurraybooks